TRUTH OR DARE

CAMPUS GAMES BOOK #4

STEPHANIE ALVES

Editing: Wonder and Wander Editing Co.
Cover designer: Stephanie Alves

ISBN: 978-1-917180-08-5

This book contains detailed sexual content, graphic language
and some other heavy topics such as self-harm and domestic
violence.
You can see the full list of content warnings on my website
here: stephaniealvesauthor.com

Happy Reading!

Also by Stephanie Alves

Standalone

Love Me or Hate Me

Campus Games Series

Never Have I Ever (Book #1)
Spin The Bottle (Book #2)
Would You Rather (Book #3)
Truth Or Dare (Book #4)

For all the people who think they're hard to love:
There will be someone that will find it as easy as breathing.

TRUTH OR DARE - Stephanie Alves

Never Be The Same - Camila Cabello ♥

You Belong With Me - Taylor Swift ♥

We Can't Be Friends - Ariana Grande ♥

Cry Baby - The Neighbourhood ♥

That Way - Tate McRae ♥

Invisible String - Taylor Swift ♥

Six Thirty - Ariana Grande ♥

So High School - Taylor Swift ♥

Consume - Chase Atlantic ♥

Everything I Wanted - Billie Eilish ♥

Block me out - Gracie Abrams ♥

I Don't Like Darkness - Chase Atlantic ♥

I Think I'm Lost Again - Chase Atlantic ♥

Nervous - The Neighbourhood ♥

Guilty As Sin - Taylor Swift ♥

Nobody Gets Me - SZA ♥

Say Don't Go - Taylor Swift ♥

1

Gabriella

Love fucking sucks.

Granted, I've only ever been in love once, but it still sucks.

Having to watch my best friends happily in love, cuddling, laughing, and smiling with their boyfriends?

Gag.

I'm happy for them. Of course I am. But it's hard to witness when I have absolutely no one. Sometimes I wonder if there's something wrong with me. Am I so unlovable that it's impossible for someone to look at me like I'm their everything and love me like they need me more than anything in the world?

Probably.

I take another sip of the shitty punch they serve at these parties, trying to wash away all the thoughts plaguing my mind.

"You're late," my roommate since freshman year says, sliding beside me.

I tut, shaking my head. "You can't rush perfection, Madi." I shoot her a wink, flipping my hair over my shoulder.

"You're still hovering over the drink table?" she asks, eyeing me.

"I'm still deciding," I say, squinting at the alcohol in front of me.

"On?" Madeline asks, raising her eyebrow at me.

"Which one will get me the drunkest and make me forget the orgy going on over there," I tell her, gesturing with a nod of my head at our little group of couples—ugh—and flashing her a teasing grin.

"You're so dramatic," she replies with an eye roll.

"I know." I wink. "I should take your job." Madeline is an actress, and a good one at that. She just landed a small role in a TV series, and while it's not Hollywood yet, I have no doubt in my mind that she'll get there.

Madeline and her boyfriend, Lucas, make a beautiful couple and will have a beautiful family, and a beautiful life.

And I'll probably still be alone.

"So, you're just going to stay here and get drunk alone?" she asks.

I lift my shoulders in a shrug. "Wouldn't be the first time."

My best friend lets out a sigh, shaking her head. "Come hang out with us once you're done," she says, nudging me on the arm.

My nose scrunches as the alcohol burns my throat. "Hard pass."

Madi heads back toward the group, and I grab a cold beer from the cooler, cracking it open. I quickly swallow it down, wincing at the taste. It's not the best, but it'll do the job.

The first time I ever got drunk, I was fifteen. I still remember the night so vividly, even if the next few hours are a complete blur.

Chris snuck into my bedroom through the window, like he always did, holding a bottle of whiskey he swiped from his dad's stash. He plopped down on the floor next to me, we cranked up the music, and knocked back the whole bottle.

It was fucking awesome. It was the first time my mind just… shut off.

I didn't hear a thing. Didn't feel a thing.

And I've been chasing that feeling ever since.

As I reach for my fifth drink of the night, I feel a body slide beside me. Shifting my gaze away from the drinks, I glance over at the brunette who's clearly checking me out. She pretends to grab a drink, but I catch the way her eyes keep flicking back to me. Running my tongue over my teeth, I give her a once-over. She's cute. Long legs, tatted skin, and that septum piercing looks badass on her.

She flashes me a smile, turning her body to face me. "Hey."

I focus on her dark brown eyes when I return her smile. I've always had a thing for brown eyes. There's something about them, like warm chocolate swimming in a pool of caramel.

They remind me of—

"Hi," I interject, wanting to give myself a night off from thinking about him. It rarely ever works. At some point, he always pops up in my mind. It's inevitable.

"So… do I have to buy you a drink to get your name?"

I tilt my head, a playful grin spreading across my face. "Seeing as the drinks are free, I don't think that would work. I'm Gabriella, but call me Gabi or I might not reply."

"Gabi, got it. I'm Jess," she says with a smirk. "I haven't seen you before," she says, arching a pierced brow at me. "You new?"

I let out a scoff, turning to face her. "Do I look like a freshman?" I joke. I mean, I might look young, but seriously? I'm about to start my senior year.

Her smile widens as her eyes drop to check me out. "No, you do not," she says, slowly mapping my body with her eyes. "That was just my lame way of throwing you a compliment."

I scrunch my nose as I take another sip of my drink. "Don't know that being compared to a baby freshman is a compliment."

"Fair enough." She leans in closer, and I catch a whiff of her flowery perfume. "Then how about I just tell you that I couldn't keep my eyes off you all night?"

I fake gag, tilting my head with a playful smirk. "That's just cheesy," I tease, the corner of my lips curling up.

Jess laughs. "So you're not a fan?"

"Depends."

"On?" She leans in, her eyes sparkling with mischief.

I lift my shoulder in a casual shrug, meeting her gaze. "Whether or not you can come up with something better in ten seconds."

"Are you putting me under pressure?" she teases, her voice laced with humor.

"Nine," I respond, playing along, my eyes twinkling with mischief.

Her eyes widen. "Fuck. Ok."

"Eight," I say with a smile.

She blows out a breath. "You really know how to stress a girl out."

I nod, sipping the last of my drink. "I'm not easy."

"I see that," she replies with a grin. "But I'm still interested."

I blink, surprised. She is? Why do I kind of wish she wasn't? "I didn't scare you away?"

She shakes her head, her hand lingering on my waist. "Definitely not." I meet her gaze, feeling a flutter of anticipation in my chest. "You want to get out of here?" Her breath tickles my ear as she whispers, sending a shiver down my spine.

I think about it, really think about it. Here's this girl, right in front of me, wanting me—even if it's just for tonight. Jess is attractive, funny, and would undoubtedly be a hell of a good time, but…

"That's a no, isn't it?" she asks, removing her hand from my waist.

My throat feels dry as I swallow hard, meeting her eyes. "I'm really sorry." I shake my head, his face flashing in my mind, as it always does. "You seem really cool, I'm just—"

"Not available?" she interrupts with a tilt of her head, her expression understanding.

I let out a strained chuckle, feeling a pang of guilt in my stomach. "Something like that."

She nods, a hint of disappointment flickering across her features. "I get it," she says with a smile, though I can tell it doesn't quite reach her eyes. "Whoever they are, they're lucky."

She grabs a drink out of the cooler, shooting me a quick smile before she melts into the party crowd. I'm left standing here, all alone again.

Then my phone buzzes, and I snatch it up eagerly. His name lights up the screen, stirring up a whole mess of conflicting emotions.

This whole situation is so confusing.

I'm hung up on someone who doesn't even want me, not like I want him, stuck pining for him while he's off living his life thousands of miles away. And here I am, sitting alone, trying to drown out all these thoughts with whatever cheap booze I can find.

Forgetting about Chris feels impossible, and honestly, I don't want to. He was always the best part of my life. Still is.

Leaning back against the table, I tap on his latest text. My heart starts racing, and I close my eyes, letting out a frustrated groan.

Damn it. Why did it have to be him? After everything we've been through, after all this time, he's still the only one I want.

I glance around the crowded room, filled with people dancing and having a great time. There are plenty of options here, plenty of pretty faces that will without a doubt offer me a distraction for the night.

But the thought of waking up tomorrow with someone else… Guilt gnaws at my insides, and my stomach churns. It's not worth it. I can't even entertain the thought. Especially when one simple text from Chris can make me feel more than any fleeting hookup ever could.

Christopher:

> You home?

Gabi:

> Nope, at a party

Three little dots dance on the screen, and I watch them eagerly, wondering what he has to say. I wait until his message finally appears.

Chris:

> Just wanted to send you something

Gabi:

> A million dollars?

Chris:

> If I had it, it would be yours

A warm feeling spreads through my chest as I smile at my phone, noticing he's typing again. His next message pops up, along with a link that makes my grin widen. I already know what it is.

I sigh, leaning off the table, my phone firmly in hand as I make my way through the party. It's kind of boring in there, and the alcohol hasn't hit me yet.

Pushing through the doors, the brisk wind slaps me as I step outside, closing the door behind me. I settle onto the steps, clicking on the link Chris sent me, which leads me to a new song.

He sends me songs sometimes. Songs that remind him of me, that he enjoys, that he thinks I'll enjoy too. Whatever the reason, I always look forward to these texts. Pressing play on those songs makes me feel connected to him in a way.

Chris:

Reminded me of you

I smile, leaning back until my head gently meets the door. He knows me so well. Sometimes I wonder if he's the only person in the world who really understands me, maybe even more than I understand myself.

I click on the song and press play, closing my eyes as the music begins to fill the air. It wraps around me, sending shivers down my spine—or maybe it's just the alcohol finally kicking in. Whatever it is, I lean into the moment, letting myself be carried away by the melody.

Every lyric feels like it was written just for me, and I squeeze my eyes tighter as my throat starts to burn and my nose tingles with the threat of tears, frustration bubbling up inside me. Fuck.

Why does he know me this well?

Why is he the person I had to fall in love with?

"It's not the right time."

My eyes snap open at the sound of my roommate Madi's voice. I quickly sit up, pausing the song and blink away the wetness building in my eyes.

"The sooner you tell her, the sooner you can get it over with," I hear her boyfriend, Lucas, reply.

"I know," Madi replies. "But… she's my best friend, Lucas. I can't just drop this on her."

My body tenses as I hear those words. Unless Madi has suddenly found a new best friend, she must be talking about me. At least, I hope so. Because if I find out someone else has taken my place, I'm gonna—

"I want to live with you, princesa." My eyes widen at Lucas's words. "I've spent my whole life waiting for you, and I didn't even know it," he tells her. "And now that I have you, I want every second, every minute, every day with you."

Wait a minute.

"I know," Madi replies with a sigh, her voice tinged with uncertainty. "I want that too, but…"

"We can wait," he says. "You're graduating next year. We can hold off until then?"

I push myself off the steps, rounding the corner where those two are tangled up in each other like they're two seconds away from making front-page news.

I would have thought after what happened last year, Lucas would have learned by now not to get caught, but apparently not.

I clear my throat, and watch as they jump apart, Madi gasping at the sight of me standing behind her.

"How much did you hear?" she asks, her frown deepening as she glances back at her boyfriend.

I shrug. "Enough to know you're leaving me," I say, gesturing to her boyfriend with a disgusted expression on my face. "And that you two seriously need to get a room."

Lucas chuckles, but Madi sighs, taking a step closer toward me. "I wanted to tell you," she says with a frown. "I just didn't know how."

I nod in understanding. If Lucas isn't over at our apartment, then Madeline is over at his. Those two can't seem to spend a night away from each other, so it's only logical that they'd want to move in together.

"You know men are messy, right?" I tease.

My best friend smiles, recognizing that I'm giving her my blessing of sorts. "Can't be messier than you."

I click my tongue, shaking my head in mock indignation. "That's low."

She chuckles, the sound filling the air with warmth. "So, you're not mad?"

I shake my head, a hint of sadness creeping in, but I press my lips together in a smile. "No, of course not. I am going to miss you, though," I tell her, already dreading going back to an empty apartment. Madeline and I have lived together since we were paired together in the same dorm freshman year. It's going to be tough not having her around anymore. "But I get it," I say with a shrug. "You want to live with your boyfriend. I just give you a week before you're begging to move back in."

"No way," Lucas says, wrapping an arm around Madi's waist. "I can't wait to live with her." He gently turns her face until their lips meet, and they start making out in front of me.

I mean... *come on.*

"Ugh." I shove them playfully. "I'm leaving before I have to witness you guys fuck again."

Madi pulls her lips away from Lucas, her eyebrows furrowing as she looks at me warily. "Wait. What do you mean, *again*?"

I grin mischievously, blowing them a kiss. "Bye."

"She saw us have sex?" I hear Madi ask her boyfriend, who just laughs in response.

Yeah, I witnessed it, and I almost wished I could pour bleach on my eyes to erase the image. I mean, her room was *right there*. Two steps and I could have avoided another trauma.

The music pulses through my chest as I step back inside, making my way toward the front room where our other friends are hanging out.

I sink onto the couch beside Leila, flashing her a smile. "I like you."

Her lips twitch with amusement. "You're drunk."

Huh. Didn't even realize it, but maybe I am. "Doesn't change the fact that I like you." I playfully boop her on the nose. "You know why?"

"Never do that again," she says, wiping her nose with a playful scowl. "But why?"

I sigh, leaning my head against her shoulder. "Because you still have your own place."

"That's it?" she asks with a chuckle. "You have low standards," she teases.

"Yeah," I admit with a nod. "Rosie moved in with Grayson. Madi's moving in with Lucas—"

"Wait. She is?" Leila's eyes widen with surprise.

"Yep," I confirm with a sigh. "But I like that you didn't move in with Aiden."

"I'd move in with her in a heartbeat," Aiden chimes in.

"I like having my own place," Leila tells him, lifting a brow.

"Liar," he replies with a grin. "You hate it when I have to go back home to get more clothes."

Leila rolls her eyes. "Only because Tiger whines whenever you're gone," she says, narrowing her eyes at him. "That's the only reason."

11

It's true. Their cat is head over heels for Aiden. I mean, it's practically obsessed with him. It hates me though, which, same, because it's a cat, and cats are evil.

Aiden just chuckles, wrapping his arms around his girlfriend. "I love it when you lie to me. Tell me you hate me, baby."

Leila narrows her eyes at Aiden. "I hate you."

He grins, leaning down to press his lips against hers.

Grayson groans. "You two need help."

I let out a scoff. It's not often I agree with Grayson, but he's right. They do.

Aiden and Leila love to tease each other, and as much as I want to hate their little foreplay love fest going on, it's nice seeing them so happy.

"You're just grumpy Rosie's in New York," Aiden tells his best friend.

"I'm not," Grayson lies, downing the rest of his drink.

He is.

Rosalie is an amazing fashion designer, and works with Grayson's mom in New York sometimes, so whenever she's gone, he turns into a grumpy asshole. Not too different from how he normally is.

"Fuck," he groans, running a hand through his hair in frustration. "This party sucks."

Aiden chuckles. "It's okay to admit you miss her, dude."

Grayson meets Aiden's gaze and swallows hard, his expression softening. "Fine. I miss her. Happy?"

I swallow. I know how he feels. Except Rosie will be back in a few days, whereas I don't know when the next time I'll see Chris is.

My phone buzzes, and I pull it out, seeing his name light up the screen. A familiar ache grips my stomach, reminding me of the distance between us.

As I said.

Love fucking sucks.

2

Christopher

"Dude." The pounding on my door snaps me out of a half-asleep daze. I groan, rubbing my eyes as I struggle to wake up fully. "Turn down the music."

My eyes snap open, the brightness of the sun coming through the window, momentarily blinding me. I glance toward the radio playing music on the bedside table and curse under my breath. Forgot to turn it down again.

Bang. Bang. Bang.

"Ok. Jeez. I'm going." I roll out of bed, cursing at the chill of the floor beneath my bare feet as I stumble toward the door, my head throbbing with each step, and lower the music.

I rub my eyes, trying to shake off the fog of sleep as I groan. It's way too damn early to be awake, especially since I crashed at six in the morning after a late-night gaming session with Gabi.

I catch sight of myself in the mirror and quickly run my hand through my hair, trying to tame the bedhead before I open the door and step out into the hallway. The delicious smell of bacon wafts into my nostrils, and I follow my nose into the kitchen, where I find Liam, my roommate, busy at the stove.

"Look who's finally up. You know it's half-past-one, right?" Liam teases, glancing over his shoulder at me.

"Slept late," I mumble, plopping down at the kitchen island and eyeing up his cooking. "Looks good."

"Seriously," he says, sliding a few strips of bacon onto my plate. "How can you sleep with the music blasting like that?"

I shrug, popping a strip of bacon into my mouth. "Always have done," I tell him between chews. "It doesn't bother me."

"Well, it bothers me," he says with a shake of his head. "Not all of us stay awake the whole night."

"Jetlag?" I say with a smirk, teasing him.

"You've been here four years," he says with a scoff. "Doubt that jetlag is still an issue, dickhead."

I raise my eyebrows, scarfing down the bacon. Can't believe it's been that long. Four years.

"You staying around for the summer?" Liam asks as he flips another piece of bacon in the pan. "Or you going back to the states this year?"

The mention of going back to America makes me freeze. Can't go back there. At least not home. "I don't know yet," I admit, my voice a little strained.

He nods, turning off the stove and plating up his breakfast. "Well, you can always stay here," he says. "But I'm moving out at the end of the month so…"

"Already?" My eyebrows shoot up in surprise.

"Yeah, man. I got a job up north, so I need to move soon. You'll be good paying rent?" Liam asks, arching a brow.

"Yeah, it'll be fine," I assure him. At least I have one thing going for me. This job I snagged a few months back as a game developer is pretty awesome. I practically get paid to game all day.

15

"Great." He finishes off his breakfast, tossing the plate in the sink. "I'm going to work late tonight. You want to come to the pub with the guys once I'm done?"

My phone buzzes, and I glance down at it, seeing my favorite name in the world.

Gabi:

Guess what?

"Think I'm staying in," I say, pushing myself off the stool.

"Alright. Suit yourself. Later."

"Later," I mutter, nodding toward him before heading back into my room, closing the door behind me. The music still plays softly in the background, and I crank it up, letting the beats thump through the room as I sink into my chair and pull out my phone.

Chris:

What?

I see her typing and a grin spreads across my face. I can't help but run my fingers through my hair, a nervous habit I've had since forever. It should be illegal for those three dots to make me smile this much, but they always do. It's been like this ever since I was twelve years old, just a little prepubescent kid head over heels for my best friend.

Gabi:

> Oh my god. You're awake.
> How?

I chuckle, my fingers tapping over the keys as I reply.

Chris:

> My roommate woke me up

Gabi:

> We should kill him

I scoff lightly, shaking my head at her exaggerated response. She really is one for the dramatics, isn't she?

Chris:

> Jesus, woman. I know I like
> my sleep, but that's excessive

Gabi:

> I'm just looking out for you

> Can I call you?

My eyes narrow at the screen, a furrow forming on my brow as I read her text. She never used to ask. She would just call me whenever, like it was second nature, and start talking about everything and anything. But she doesn't do that now.

I don't even bother replying before calling her, because, honestly, if I did, she'd know what a stupid question that was. There isn't a moment in my life where I don't want to hear Gabi's voice.

I hear her little breaths of excitement when she answers the phone, and it brings a grin to my face. "You sound like a dog."

"Wow," she scoffs. "You really know how to compliment a girl, Chris."

I chuckle, the sound rumbling in my chest. "Did you listen to the song I sent last night?"

"I did."

"And?" I ask, sinking back in my chair, my fingers tapping against the desk as I put the phone on speaker.

"It's beautiful."

A warmth spreads through me, and I can't help but smile. *Just like you.* "As soon as I heard it, it reminded me of you."

Everything always does. I don't think I can live my life without being reminded of her. Wherever I go, whatever I do, there's always something that will be a reminder of the girl I love.

"It must be early over there, right?"

I chuckle, rubbing my eyes. "Depends on what you consider early. It's almost two p.m."

"You stayed up late last night though. I hope I didn't ruin your sleep."

I scoff, feeling a smile tug at my lips. "Don't worry about that. You'll always be my favorite reason to lose sleep."

She lets out a soft laugh, that sounds like the gates of heaven opening. God, I miss that laugh. Miss hearing it in person. Miss *her*. "Don't get soft on me, Hudson."

I chuckle, settling into my gaming chair and grab my controller, ready to dive into the game I've been working on recently. "Why are you calling me this early anyway? Don't you have class today?"

"Nope. My dance teacher's sick. I've got the day free. What about you?"

"Nothing much," I reply, glancing down at the phone. "My life is boring, Gabi." *Especially without her.*

She really doesn't know how much I miss being around her. She's my home, and an adventure all at once.

"Well… you always know where to go if you're bored of living in London."

"Yeah?" I smirk. "Where's that?"

"Barcelona," she replies, her voice laced with a hint of excitement.

I chuckle, leaning back in my chair. "You want to go to Barcelona?"

"Are you kidding?" she says with a chuckle. "Spending all day eating tapas and getting a tan?"

"Sounds amazing."

"Yeah," she agrees. "And you'd be there with me."

"Yeah?" I love that she's adding me to her imaginary plans. Love that she thinks of me, because I think of that girl nonstop. Every single day.

"Of course." She scoffs. "No trip is complete without you."

No trip is complete without you. Why do I love the sound of that so much?

19

"That's good, because I'd hate to be anywhere without you," I reply, a teasing expression in my voice.

She doesn't laugh. Doesn't reply. The weight of her silence hits me hard. I moved to London without her. And ever since then, the night I left has hovered over us like a dark cloud, a topic we've both tiptoed around.

I run a hand down my face, trying to shake off the tension. "So, are you excited about the summer?" I throw out the question, hoping to shift the conversation away from the awkward silence that just hung between us.

"Yeah," she replies with a sigh. "I'm excited about Jane's wedding. You know it's the first ever wedding I'm attending?"

"Shit. I forgot about that."

I tear my eyes away from the screen and glance down at the phone as Gabi's words sink in. Gabi's sister is getting married, and I won't be there. She invited me a few months ago, and I never replied. I stared at that invitation for days, wondering what would happen if I went. Gabi would be there. I'd finally be able to see her again. But the wedding is in our home town, and I haven't been in South Carolina since I left, four years ago.

Gabi's voice cuts through the game's soundtrack, drawing my attention back to the screen. "I'm not looking forward to going to this thing alone though," she admits, and I can almost picture the expression on her face, the way her brow furrows when she's deep in thought. "I wish you were here. We could have gone together."

"You do?" I ask her, my brows raising. I really want to be there, too. I want to see her again. Face to face.

"Of course," she replies. "I always want you with me."

My heart thumps at her words, and I lean forward, as if somehow I could bridge the distance between us.

I think about what it would be like to see her again, to see her face and hold her in my arms and be able to look into her eyes in person. My body warms at the thought. My lips twitch as I load up my laptop, and start searching for flights.

He's in prison.

And Gabi *wants* me there.

There's nothing stopping me from hopping on a plane and going to visit her.

Just for the summer.

3

Gabriella

Age fifteen

I don't even flinch when I hear my window slide open in the middle of the night. A grin spreads across my face as I roll onto my side, and turn on my lamp. My eyes drift down to the black sneakers just visible beneath my curtains before they're pulled aside. My smile grows when I see Chris quietly drop down from the windowsill onto my bedroom floor.

His hair, soaked from the rain, falls onto his face, and he meets my eyes. "Were you sleeping?"

I shake my head and scoot over, making room for him in my bed. You'd think I'd be worried about my parents finding a boy in my room, let alone in my bed, but I'm not. Not with Chris. He's my best friend, has been since middle school. We've always been inseparable, and these sleepovers have become a part of our routine.

They've been happening for so long that I expect him to climb through my window every night. Sometimes he doesn't come, though. On those nights, I lie awake, my heart pounding in the silence, straining to hear his footsteps or the familiar sound of the window sliding open. Eventually, I fall asleep and wake up the next morning, the bed cold and empty.

He hasn't visited in weeks, and I've tried to hide my disappointment, but it's been hard. I miss him. I miss our late nights, playing video games, listening to music, and talking until we fall asleep. So, seeing him now for the first time in over three weeks makes my heart race. I've really missed my best friend.

Chris rakes a hand through his wet hair, glancing at the empty space in my bed. "I don't..." He looks away, closing his eyes and letting out a deep sigh. "I don't think that's a good idea, Gabi."

I furrow my brows, feeling a sharp ache in my chest. He hasn't been here in so long, and now that he's finally here, he doesn't want to sleep over? What's going on with him?

"What do you mean?" I ask, lifting my head. "You always sleep over. I thought—"

I bite my tongue, the words catching in my throat. Not always. Not for weeks now.

Chris's eyebrows knit together in a pained expression. "Do you..." He blows out a breath, struggling to find the right words. "We're growing up, Gabi." When he looks at me again, his face is serious, almost stern. "I don't think it's a good idea for us to sleep in the same bed anymore."

"What?" I chuckle, finding the idea ridiculous. "Are you serious?" That's what he's worried about? Sure, we're not kids anymore, and we're growing up, but that shouldn't change anything between us. "Chris, it's not like something's going to happen with us," I say, scrunching my nose at the thought. "We're just friends."

Chris's jaw tightens as he looks at me. I watch the muscle in his jaw twitch as he grinds his teeth. His features are more defined than I remember. He's grown too, I guess. Bigger, taller, more muscular.

"Are you sure?" he asks, his voice strained, as he glances at the empty space beside me on the bed.

"Yes," I assure him, rolling my eyes. He's being ridiculous. Nothing's going to change just because we're getting older. He's my best friend. He'll always be my best friend. "Now come in, please," I say with a groan, lying back down on my pillow. "I need your cuddles."

Chris lets out a sigh, tugging at the strands of hair at his nape. He closes his eyes for a moment, and I frown, realizing how much this is bothering him. But when he opens his eyes again, he lets out a breath and kicks off his shoes. "Fine," he says, pulling off his light gray hoodie, which is covered in wet patches from the rain.

My eyes drift to the sliver of his stomach that peeks out when he pulls his hoodie off, and my body warms unexpectedly.

"Move over," he mutters.

I snap out of it, glancing up at Chris, now in a black long-sleeve t-shirt, his jeans still on. I open my mouth to ask if he's going to take his jeans off but decide against it after our earlier conversation.

I move back, giving him space to climb into the bed. Once he settles in, I snuggle up against him, laying my head on his chest. My ear presses against his heart, which is racing out of control, and I snuggle closer.

His hand reaches over and begins to rub my back. *God*, I really missed this. I really missed him. A soft sigh escapes my lips as he continues to stroke up and down my back, his touch calming.

24

"Are you…" His voice catches, so he clears his throat, trying again. "Are you sure it's fine?" he asks.

"Yes," I assure him. "More than fine." I snuggle closer, feeling the warmth of his body. "You're so warm and comfortable," I mumble into his chest, the beat of his heart under my ear as I hold onto him tightly. "I feel safe here, with you."

Chris lets out a breath, his body relaxing a little more against mine. His hand continues its soothing motion on my back, and I can feel the tension gradually leaving his muscles as the rain continues to patter softly against the window.

"I feel safe with you, too," he murmurs, his voice barely above a whisper.

My chest warms, and I can't help but smile against him. I like that. I like that he feels safe with me because he's the only person I feel truly safe with. And that's why I want to tell him.

He hasn't been over in so long, and when we're at school, there's never a right moment to say it. So, I've just kept it bottled up inside of me, and it's been eating me alive. But now, with him here, I feel like maybe I can finally tell him.

"I did it," I blurt out, and squeeze my eyes closed, bracing for his reaction.

"Did what?" Chris asks, his hand on my back stilling. "You mean you watched the new Channing Tatum movie without me? Because I'm kinda glad. I *really* don't get what you see in him."

I let out a laugh, because first of all, he's *so* wrong. "No. Not that," I say, lifting my head to meet his eyes, and swallow down the nerves, shaking my head. "I… I lost my virginity."

Chris freezes, his eyes widening in surprise, and for a moment, neither of us moves. "You…" He swallows hard. "You did?"

"Yeah," I confirm quietly.

"When?" Chris asks, his voice slightly strained.

"A few weeks ago."

"A few…" He closes his eyes briefly, a heavy sigh escaping him. "With who?"

I twist out of his hold, sitting up in bed, suddenly feeling defensive. "Why are you acting so weird?"

"I'm not," he insists, sitting up beside me. "I just…" He runs a hand through his hair, tugging at the strands, clearly struggling for words. "Why didn't you say anything?"

"Why have you been avoiding me?"

His eyes widen a little in surprise. "What?"

"You haven't been over in weeks, Chris," I point out, my eyes dropping to my lap when he swallows harshly. "When could I have told you?"

"I don't know," he replies with a shrug. "At school."

"This isn't the sort of thing I blurt out between classes. I wanted to talk to you," I admit quietly.

His eyes meet mine, and I can't figure out his expression. I hate not knowing what he's thinking. "Who was it with?" he asks.

"Andrew."

Chris lets out a scoff, arching a brow at me. "Seriously?"

"Hey," I chuckle, tossing a pillow at him.

He laughs when it hits his chest. "I mean… you could have done better."

"Yeah," I say with a sigh, lying back on Chris's chest and look up at the ceiling.

"How was it? Was it everything you wanted it to be?" he asks.

I twist my head to look at him, raising an eyebrow. "You really want to know?" Chris is acting weird about this whole situation, and I can't figure out why.

"Sure," he says with a sigh. "Why not?"

"It was…" I trail off, wrinkling my nose as I think back on it. "Weird."

"Weird?" Chris quirks an eyebrow, an amused look in his eyes.

I nod against him, feeling a flush of embarrassment creeping up my cheeks. "Yeah. He was just so stiff, and smelled like cheese."

Chris's chest shakes with laughter. "Sounds like a night to remember," he says, the laughter slowly dying down as a thoughtful silence settles between us. "Do you regret it?" he finally asks after a few minutes.

"I guess it's too early to tell," I admit, a shrug lifting my shoulder. Andrew wasn't exactly the best, but we were both pretty nervous. I wonder if anyone actually enjoys their first time. Maybe if I waited for someone I really cared about, it would've been different. But right now, I can't think of anyone I really like. Not like—

Interrupting my thoughts, I turn my head to meet Chris' gaze. "What about you?"

"What about me?" he replies.

"Any girls?" I ask him, a little unsure why I'm bringing this up. Chris has never really talked about that part of his life, and I can't shake the curiosity about whether he's ever been with someone or if he even likes anyone.

27

"No, Gabi," Chris says, his eyes locked on mine. "There are no girls."

"None?" I furrow my brows, surprised. "Any boys then?"

He holds my eyes, and I suck in a breath. I recently came out to him, and told him I think I'm bisexual. I'm still figuring it out. I know I find girls attractive, but I've never been with one. I haven't really been with anyone except for Andrew. It's all so confusing, and I kept it a secret for so long. When I finally told Chris, it felt like a huge weight was lifted off my shoulders. He was so supportive, just like I knew he would be.

But maybe he's been holding out on me too. I find my answer when he shakes his head.

"Girls," he reaffirms with a smirk. "And there's no one."

"Not even Taylor?" I tease, wagging my eyebrows at him. "You know, I think she's into you." I've noticed her looking at him all the time, smiling in his direction. Sometimes, it hurts a little in my chest when I see them together. I don't even know why. I mean, I know he'll always be my best friend no matter who he dates, but… I don't really like seeing him with anyone but me.

"Yeah, well," he sighs, "I'm not into her."

My shoulders drop in relief. I don't know why I like hearing him say that. My stomach settles, and I drop my head onto his chest again, wrapping my arms around him.

"You know you can tell me, though, right?" I mumble against his chest. "If you like anyone. I won't judge you."

His chest moves as he blows air from his nose. "I know, Gabi."

A smile spreads across my face, and I let myself close my eyes, appreciating that Chris is here now, even if he hasn't been in a while. I always sleep better when he's here.

He feels safe, warm, kind. Everything I need.

But that sense of safety vanishes at the sound of a plate shattering, a gasp catching in my throat. I tense, clutching onto Chris as his grip tightens around me.

The door swings open, and my stomach twists. I hold onto Chris desperately, but when I see my sister's face peering through the doorway, I relax my hold on him.

She narrows her eyes at us. "He needs to leave."

"No."

"He shouldn't even be in your room. Or in your bed." Her eyes narrow further. "If dad found out—"

"Don't be weird. He's my best friend," I interrupt. "Nothing like that will ever happen between us," I tell my sister. "Girls can be friends with guys, you know."

I haven't told my sister about my sexuality, but I know she'd have my back. She trusted me enough to tell me she's gay a few years ago, and she made me swear not to tell anyone else, especially Dad. I've never seen her that scared, which makes me freak out about how Dad would react if he knew about me.

She rolls her eyes, but her shoulders tense when another cry comes from downstairs. "Gabi. He needs to leave," she repeats.

"No," I say, firmly, clinging to Chris like a lifeline. "He's heard them before. I don't keep anything from him." Tears prickle at the corners of my eyes, but I hold my sister's gaze. "I need him here with me. He's not going anywhere."

She lets out a sigh. "Then stay in your room," she instructs. "And don't let dad find him."

When she closes the door, I sit up in bed, wiping my eyes with my sleeve. "I hate him," I mutter through clenched teeth

29

as the sound of my mom crying echoes through the house. "I wish she would just leave him."

"I know," Chris murmurs, reaching out for me. He cups my face with both of his hands. "Trust me. I know."

Another loud noise pierces the air, followed by more crying, and I rip off the covers, jumping out of bed. "I can't just sit here and let him—"

"Gabi, stop," Chris whisper-yells before I reach the door. "Your sister told you to stay here. You know it'll just make him worse."

I shake my head, my eyes fixed on the door. "I can't keep letting him get away with this."

"And I can't let him hurt you," he says, his voice closer now. I feel him standing right behind me, his hand grabbing mine and twisting me around. My tear-filled eyes meet his. "Either you stay here, or I'll go out there. Your choice."

I inhale sharply, my heart pounding in my chest. "You're not going out there."

He nods. "Then come here," he says, pulling me into him. I don't resist. I can't. I just let him pull me toward him, and I cry my heart out, drenching his t-shirt with my tears.

I hate sitting here and hearing their endless fights. I hate that he hurts her. I hate that I can't do anything about it.

My teeth graze against my lip where I still feel the scar from my attempt to stop him. I was too small, too weak. I couldn't do anything.

And I hated that feeling.

Chris's hands cup my face, his touch calming me. He's the only one who truly understands, who knows every part of me.

"It's going to be ok," he lies. "Come here. I have a new song for you. Reminded me of you as soon as I heard it."

I sniffle, meeting his eyes as he slips my headphones over my ears. The music starts up, and the melody wraps around me, drowning out the world's noise. All I can focus on is the song in my ears and the sight of my favorite person in the world.

A soft smile tugs at his lips as he guides me back to bed. I nestle my head against his chest, feeling the rhythm of his heartbeat. He starts rubbing my back the way he knows will always calms me down. He pulls the duvet over us and I settle against him, closing my eyes, feeling his heartbeat underneath me until I fall asleep.

4

Christopher

As the cab pulls over, my heart races uncontrollably. I haven't seen her in four years. Not since that night. I still remember every painstaking detail of it. And yet, here I am, without a plan, without a clue as to how this will go. All I know is that I'm desperate to see her.

The sun hits my eyes when I open the door and step out of the cab.

"Need any help with your bags?" the driver asks, his voice gruff as he glances at me through the rearview mirror.

"Nah, I'm good," I reply, squinting against the glare before reaching for my suitcase.

The driver gives a curt nod, and as I shut the door, he takes off, disappearing into the traffic. I tighten my grip on the handle of my suitcase, scanning the unfamiliar surroundings.

Reaching into my pocket, I pull out my phone, the screen lighting up as I bring up her location. We've always shared our locations with each other, even when we were living thousands of miles apart. It was our way of staying connected, of feeling close despite the distance.

I glance at the map, confirming she's close by, and my lips twitch into a half-smile as my heart beats faster. After all this time, I'm finally going to see her. My thumb hovers over her contact, then finally lands, pressing the call button.

Here goes nothing.

"Hello?"

Her wary tone makes me smirk, as I try to find her in the crowd. "You sound scared."

"You never call me at this time," she replies, suspicion lacing her voice. "What time is it over there?"

She's right, but what she doesn't know is that I'm not in London. I grin as I reply, "Twelve-thirty."

"What?" Her voice rises in disbelief. "That's not possible. It's twelve-thirty here."

I chuckle. "I know."

My eyes sweep through the crowd, and then...

There she is.

My heart lurches in my chest at the sight of her. I suck in a breath, feeling a rush of emotions as I take her in. It's surreal to see her in the flesh again, and for a moment, I forget to breathe.

Fuck.

She's so fucking beautiful.

How is it possible that she's somehow even more beautiful than I remember?

A smile curves my lips as my eyes drop to her outfit. From the gym bag thrown across her body, I assume she just came from dance class, which explains the black sports bra, baggy white sweats, and my old blue baseball cap she stole from me way back when.

"You know..." I say, a grin spreading across my face as I gaze at my best friend. "I'm going to want that baseball cap back."

I watch as her hand instinctively reaches up, touching the fraying edge of the cap, and her eyes widen in disbelief. "What? How did you—" Her eyes darts around, then lock onto mine, and for a moment, time stands still, and the air is wiped clean out of my lungs. It's been so damn long since I've had her eyes on me. "Am I dreaming?"

I shake my head, laughter bubbling up inside me as I meet her gaze head-on. "It's way too early for that."

"I can't believe this," she murmurs, shaking her head in disbelief. "Are you really here right now?"

"Come here, and find out," I reply, unable to suppress the grin spreading across my face. If I have to spend one more moment without her in my arms, I'll go insane.

Without a second thought, she drops her gym bag and races toward me, a huge, gorgeous smile lighting up her face. A laugh escapes me as I quickly pocket my phone, barely having time to prepare before she jumps into my arms, wrapping her legs around my waist.

I pull her close, wrapping my arms around her. Tears prick my eyes as I finally feel her against me. God, I've missed her. It feels like my soul is whole again when she's in my arms.

"You're here," she murmurs against my chest. I tighten my hold on her, savoring the feel of her in my arms. Her head fits perfectly against my neck, and I let out a shaky breath, feeling her cling to me.

"How are you here?" she asks again.

I chuckle, blinking away the tears threatening to spill. "There are these things called planes," I joke, trying to lighten the moment. "Not sure if you've ever heard of them before."

Gabi pulls back a little, playfully slapping at my chest before lifting her head to meet my gaze. Our eyes lock for the first time in forever, and it almost knocks the wind out of me. I love her eyes. The striking blue contrasts beautifully with her dark brown hair, and it leaves me breathless. She looks like a goddess.

Her breath hitches as we stare at each other for what feels like an eternity. Don't want to look away, though. I don't want to let her go, I don't want her out of my arms. But I know I have to.

"You should probably get down," I mutter, even though it's the last thing I want.

"Yeah." Gabi releases a heavy breath, and we linger in the same position for a few more seconds, neither of us wanting to break this moment. Eventually, she chuckles, unwinding her legs from my waist to slide down my body.

"God, I forgot how short you were," I tease.

Gabi doesn't reply immediately, her gaze fixed on me, clearly surprised. "I can't believe you're here," she says again.

"I decided to surprise you," I tell her, though that's not quite the whole truth. As soon as I heard Gabi tell me she wanted me here, I couldn't resist. I never could resist when it comes to her.

"Well, that was a hell of a surprise," she scoffs, a hint of amusement in her tone. "But why are you here?"

I shrug, meeting her gaze with a smile. "I decided to come spend the summer with you."

Her eyes widen. "Wait. Really?"

"Yeah," I reply, nodding, my lips twitching.

"The whole summer?" she asks. "Two full months?"

"Two full months," I confirm, a grin spreading across my face. "I have to go back to school in September."

"I can't believe this." Her grin is so infectious, I can't help the smile widening on my face. *Missed seeing that.* "Where are you staying?"

My smile fades, and I curse under my breath. "Shit. I didn't think about that." The only thing on my mind was seeing her again. After that, it's like my brain shut down.

Booking those plane tickets was a spur-of-the-moment decision. I didn't consider what I'd do here or where I'd stay. All I heard was Gabi saying she wished I was here, and the next thing I knew, I was on my way.

I think I'd do anything she asked, without hesitation. And that's always been the case.

"You didn't think about where you'd be staying?" she asks, amusement dancing in her eyes. "Come on, Chris. You're the organized one."

I let out a scoff. "Looks like you've become a bad influence, again."

She smiles, her gaze meeting mine with a hint of mischief. "Just how I like it." Glancing behind her, she adds, "There's a café over there, and I'm starving. Want to grab a bite before we figure out all the boring adult things?"

"Lead the way."

5

Best idea ever

Gabriella

Secretly pinching myself under the table, I confirm—when the sharp pain radiates through my arm—that this is, in fact, not a dream. Chris is really here, in the same country as me, sitting just inches away.

I'm still in shock, trying to process it. When we talked on the phone a few days ago, and I half-jokingly said I wished he'd come here, I never thought he'd actually show up. I'd said something similar countless times since he moved to London, but he never came. His usual responses were, 'I wish I could be there too' or 'I miss you too,' but he never visited.

But now here he is, staring down at the menu, with the same wavy hair I've always loved, the same soft brown eyes I can't stop thinking about, and the same beautiful face I remember.

But he's different too. His jaw is sharper, his muscles more defined. He's older, taller, and even more handsome than the last time I saw him.

"I'm starving," he says, and his voice sends a shiver through me. We talk practically every day, so I'm used to hearing his voice on the phone, but hearing it in person floods my mind with memories of late nights spent talking about everything and anything.

I blink, watching as his eyes scan the menu. "Me too," I say, sighing as I open my own menu. "I haven't eaten since two hours ago."

Chris lifts his head, a smirk tugging at his lips. "I just spent fourteen hours on a plane with terrible food," he says with a soft laugh. That laugh warms something deep inside me. It feels like every one of my best memories. It feels like late nights, pancakes, music, and video games. It feels like *home.*

"You haven't eaten since you got off the plane?" I ask, furrowing my brows.

He lowers his menu, his lips lifting into a smile. "I got off the plane an hour ago," he says. "I came straight to you, Gabi."

My stomach flutters, and I glance down at the menu again. "So, catch me up," I say, trying to focus on the words on the page instead of how my pulse races at six simple words. "What have you been doing since you left?"

He chuckles. "You know what I've been doing."

I shake my head when I look up at him. "I heard it through the phone," I correct him. "That's not the same thing." Lowering the menu onto the table, I shoot him a grin. "I want to hear it from you."

He smiles, holding my gaze, then shrugs, breathing out a sigh. "I applied to college when I moved there, got accepted, and studied computer science…" He tilts his head, lifting a brow at me. "You've heard all of this before. Are you sure you're not getting bored?"

"I could never get bored of you," I say with a tilt of my head.

His smile returns, and he rakes a hand through his hair, tugging on the strands at the back. A habit he's had since forever. "I got into game design, and even found a job that pays well and lets me work from home," he says with a shrug. "And now I'm here."

I blink, waiting for more. "That's it?" I finally ask, disbelief evident in my voice.

He shrugs again. "Yeah," he says. "Pretty much."

I shake my head, tutting at him. "Four years, and that's all you have to tell me? Where are all the crazy stories you're not telling me?"

He lets out a soft laugh that warms my insides. "All of my best stories are with you."

My lips tug into a smirk, loving the sound of that. "Is that right?"

"Yeah." He sighs, leaning back in his chair. "You're the bad influence in my life."

"Wow." I scoff, playfully rolling my eyes. "I see why you didn't visit, then."

His face drops, and he shakes his head. "Gabi—"

"I'm kidding," I say, waving him off. "I know you were busy with classes and stuff." I lift my head, blinking up at him. "Were you... also busy with something else?"

"Like what?" he asks, furrowing his brows.

"I don't know," I lie, lifting my shoulder in a shrug. I know exactly what I'm asking him. "Friends, parties." I glance up at him, swallowing before I say, "A girlfriend, maybe."

He closes his menu, sliding it to the side with a sigh. "No."

"No?" I echo, eyebrows raised in curiosity.

"I mean, I had friends," he says, running a hand through his hair. "They were cool, I guess. Fun to hang out with, and good people, but… they weren't you."

My heart skips a beat at his words, a warmth spreading through me. It's a relief to hear that he didn't replace me during his time in London.

"And the... other things?" I coax, my heart pounding with anticipation.

He hesitates, his gaze flickering away for a moment before meeting mine again. "We went out sometimes," he admits, a faint smile playing on his lips. "We hit up pubs, and Liam, my roommate, threw parties at the apartment sometimes, but again..." He smiles, his gaze locking with mine. "Nothing compares to when I'm with you."

But there's still one question lingering, unspoken between us, and I can't help but wonder why he's avoiding it.

"And the last thing?" I ask, tapping nervously on the table. His eyes drift to my fingers, and I stop abruptly, taking a sip of my drink to mask my nerves.

Inside, though, I'm freaking the fuck out. A million thoughts race through my mind, each one louder than the last.

"No."

I freeze, setting my cup down carefully. "No?" I repeat, my voice betraying my surprise.

"No girlfriends," he confirms.

"None?" I press. Why the hell am I goading him? He already said no. I should be happy with his answer and drop it.

"None," he affirms.

"In four years?" I blurt out before I can help myself. *Dear god, someone stop me.*

"Yeah," he replies with a sigh, a hint of amusement in his tone. "What about you?"

"Me?" I ask, trying to keep my tone light despite the sudden rush of nerves.

"Yeah," Chris nods, fidgeting with his hair and tapping his foot nervously. "Any... Dated anyone?"

I let out a nervous laugh. "Wouldn't really call it dating," I admit, feeling a flush creeping into my cheeks.

"Right."

The silence that follows is suffocating, and I hate silence with a passion.

"Where the hell is the damn waitress?" I mutter under my breath, scanning the café for any sign of the server. Spotting a girl with brown hair in the café's dark red uniform, I flag her down eagerly. But when she turns to face me, I freeze.

Recognition flashes in her eyes as she approaches. "You again," Jess says. I can't help but notice that she's not wearing the septum piercing she had at the party.

Of all the places to run into her. Is the universe against me or something?

"Hi," I say, forcing a smile. I glance subtly at Chris, whose brows are furrowed as he watches us.

"Gabi, right?" she asks, her gaze flickering between me and Chris.

"Yeah," I confirm, my nerves pricking.

She nods, her eyes drifting to Chris. "So, is this..." she trails off, leaving the question hanging in the air.

"No," I interject quickly, cutting her off before she can say anything else. I can sense her curiosity, probably wondering if he's the person I mentioned being unavailable for. And Jess wouldn't be wrong, but the thing is... I'm not unavailable. I'm single, and technically, I can date whoever I want. But the truth is, I don't want to. The only person I want is... him.

I swallow hard, tearing my gaze away from the waitress and back to Chris, who is now looking at me with curiosity.

"Huh," Jess says, a smirk playing on her lips.

I turn back to her, trying to ignore the knowing look in her eyes. "We'd like to order," I say, gesturing towards the menu.

"Sure," she replies as she flips open her notebook. "What would you like to order?"

I point to the burger on the menu, waiting for Chris to choose his order. It feels like she's been here for an eternity and a flash all at the same time. And by the time she finally leaves, Chris glances at me, a hint of curiosity in his eyes.

"You know her?" he asks, his tone laced with intrigue.

I shrug, a sigh escaping my lips. "Sort of. I met her at a party."

"Oh," he chuckles, but it lacks the usual warmth. "The thing you don't call dating, right?"

"I didn't sleep with her," I blurt out, my words rushing out before I can stop them. Why did I say that? Clearly, I've hit my head somewhere because what the fuck am I doing right now.

He arches a brow, his expression unreadable. "Okay?"

"Just... wanted to clear that up," I mumble, feeling my cheeks heat up.

Chris smiles, shaking his head. "You don't need to tell me, Gabi. That's your business."

"I know. I just... I tell you everything," I admit, though it's not entirely true. *Not everything.* I glance up, catching his smile.

"I know. You never shut up," he teases, his chuckle easing some of the tension between us.

"Hey," I protest with a smirk.

He chuckles, shaking his head. "I really missed you, Gabi."

I sigh, feeling my heart clench at his words. "I really missed you too, Chris."

"Coming in hot." I twist my head to see Jess placing the food down in front of us, flashing me a smile before she leaves.

"Fuck, I'm starving," Chris says, digging into his BLT.

"Me too. I just came from dance class," I tell him before taking a big ass bite out of my burger.

"I figured," he replies between bites, washing it down with a sip of his drink. "Nice hat, by the way," he adds, smirking as he gestures to my cap—his cap—that I stole from him, and wore for years.

His smirk makes me narrow my eyes at him. "I'm not giving it back."

He shrugs casually. "We'll see about that."

"Never, Hudson," I repeat my words from years ago before taking another bite. I love this hat. I love wearing something that's his. "Where are you going after this?" I ask him. "Have you figured out where you're staying yet?"

"In the last ten minutes?" He shakes his head. "No, not yet. Didn't really think much through besides coming here," he admits with a nervous laugh.

"You could go back home?" I suggest, though the thought of him being so far away from me brings an ache to my chest. I've just got him back. I don't want him to leave me just yet.

Chris shakes his head again, his eyes meeting mine. "No," he says firmly, swallowing down his food. "No, that's not an option. Besides, I came here to see you."

His eyes soften when they land on me, and I can't help but smile, loving the familiarity of his words. He used to say that a lot back in high school. I remember the nights he'd sneak into my bedroom, out of breath as if he had been running. I'd ask him what's wrong, and he'd always say the same thing. *I just came here to see you.* Those were the nights we'd stay up playing video games, listening to music, and sneaking downstairs for snacks until we passed out in each other's arms.

I miss that.

I miss how effortless everything felt between us back then. And how much I want it to be like that again.

A light bulb flashes in my mind, and I can't help but grin.

Chris eyes me suspiciously. "Why are you smiling like that?" he asks. "Nothing good ever follows that kind of smile."

"I just had an amazing idea," I tell him, unable to stop smiling like an idiot.

He pauses mid-chew, clearly intrigued. "Which is…?"

"Why don't you stay here?"

He furrows his brow, clearly confused. "What do you mean?"

"I mean... Why don't you stay with me," I say. "In my apartment."

He stops chewing, his eyes widening in surprise. "You mean... move in with you?"

"Why not?" I ask with a shrug. "We practically slept in the same bed every night." Chris shifts uncomfortably, and I'm quick to add, "Of course we won't be doing that anymore." I let out a little laugh. "But, Madi moved in with her boyfriend and left me all alone," I say with an eye roll. "And you know I hate being alone." He smiles a little, maybe remembering all the times he stayed with me. "And you don't have a place to stay." I shrug again. "It sounds like a perfect solution to me."

Chris sighs. "I don't know, Gabi."

"Are you scared, Chris?" I ask, wagging my brows.

He smirks, his eyes twinkling with amusement. "Of what, exactly?"

I lift my shoulder in a playful shrug. "That I'll turn all your clothes pink."

He chuckles, flashing me a smile. "I wouldn't even be surprised if you did."

Hope builds in my chest and I grin. "So, is that a yes?"

He exhales slowly, his expression thoughtful. "You're really sure about this?"

"I am," I affirm, nodding. "You came here for me, so why not live with me until you need to go back?"

He seems to mull it over, and a smile slowly spreads across his face, shaking his head in disbelief. "We're really going to live together?"

"We're living together," I confirm with a grin. "This is going to be so much fun. I'm a genius. Best idea ever."

6

Late night pancakes

Gabriella

This is the worst idea I've ever had.

What the hell was I thinking, asking Chris to move in?

Sure, he's my best friend, and I'd love to spend more time with him, but did I really think it would be *easy*? It was hard enough dealing with my feelings for Chris when he was miles away in London. Now that he's here, it's going to be a million times harder.

I can't sleep. And that's a huge issue. Usually, I'm the first to fall asleep. I love sleep. I don't even have to try; I just close my eyes and drift off. But tonight is different.

I can't stop thinking about Chris being just a room away from me. Right. Next. Door.

It's driving me crazy. I haven't been this close to him since high school, and the old feelings are flooding back, stronger than ever. I roll over, staring at the ceiling, willing myself to relax, but my mind keeps replaying every smile, every touch, every moment we've shared.

I let out a breath, my mind wandering back to those nights when I'd lie like this, my head resting on his chest. It feels like a lifetime ago.

Everything has changed between us, even if I never wanted it to. I never expected him to be back, and now he is.

Just for the summer.

And then he'll go back to London in a few months, and then I'll have to face another year—or however long—without seeing him again.

And what if I never see him again? What if he prefers his life there, decides to stay in London, meets someone, and—

"Ugh." The thought makes me groan.

I kick the covers off, swinging my feet over the edge of the bed. I can't do this. I can't sit here all night, thinking about what-ifs.

"I need some food," I murmur to myself, slipping out of bed and into the darkness. Without bothering to turn on the light, I head for the door, cracking it open.

The bright light from the kitchen floods my face, making me squint. Blinking to adjust, I see Chris, rummaging through the cabinets.

Chris twists his head at the sound of my door opening. "Oh shit," he says, quickly closing the cabinet. "Did I wake you? I'm so—" His words trail off, his mouth falling open as his eyes widen, scanning down my body. "Fuck. I, uh…"

I glance down, suddenly aware that I'm only wearing a t-shirt and panties. "Shit." I turn, and head back into my room, grabbing a pair of sweatpants and pulling them on. "Sorry for the strip show," I joke, trying to lighten the mood.

"No, it's… uh, fine. It's your apartment," he stutters, still looking flustered.

"It's yours too," I point out, stepping out of my bedroom, now more decent. "At least for the next two months."

"Right." The muscle in his jaw ticks. "I hope I didn't wake you up."

I shake my head, leaning against the kitchen island. "I couldn't sleep."

"Me either," he says, a smile curling his lips. Chris's smile is my favorite thing in the world. "Jet lag."

I tilt my head. "Why is that funny?"

He shakes his head. "I used to make that excuse all the time in London. Now it's actually true."

My smile fades a little. He has a whole life away from me, with people who aren't me.

"I was just looking for some cereal," he says, gesturing with his thumb behind him. "Do you have any?"

My lips twitch. At least that hasn't changed. "You still eat cereal as a midnight snack?"

He nods, raking a hand through his curly hair. "Nothing better, in my opinion."

"I can think of something better," I tell him, flicking my hair behind my shoulder, a playful glint in my eyes.

"Yeah?" he asks, his gaze tracking my movements before his lips turn up in a smirk. "What?"

"Pancakes."

He lets out a soft laugh, and it eases my heart to hear it. I haven't heard that in person for such a long time. "Now?"

I flutter my eyelashes innocently at him, a playful smile dancing on my lips. "You always made the best ones," I tease, my tone lighthearted. "And I'm craving them so bad."

He flashes me a smile, his eyes twinkling with amusement, and opens the cabinets again. "Where are your mixing bowls?"

"Wait. Seriously?" I chuckle.

"You want pancakes, right?" he asks, arching a brow.

I was only joking about him making me pancakes. I wanted to remind him of all the amazing times we had together, but if I'm honest, I don't think I've had pancakes since senior year of high school, when Chris made them for me last. "Well, yeah, but—"

"Then we're making pancakes." He grabs a bowl from my cabinets and opens another. "Do you even have the ingredients?"

I tut, shaking my head. "Wrong thing to ask, Chris. Always assume I don't know where anything is."

He turns to face me, blinking. "How did you survive without me?"

"Madi did everything around here," I say with a shrug. "But she had to move in with her boyfriend, and leave me to fend for myself." I exaggerate a sigh. "I'm not built to be alone, Chris."

He laughs as he turns around to face me, and pulls me into his embrace. "No, you're really not."

I was half kidding when I said I wasn't built to be alone, but in this moment, pressed against him, it feels like I'm breathing again. Truth is, I despise being alone. The silence, the empty space—it suffocates me. I crave noise, music, and the presence of others.

A shaky breath escapes my lips as I squeeze him close, my chest aching. "I really did miss you," I whisper against his hoodie, my voice barely audible over the thumping of my heart. I don't think I'll be able to bear it when he eventually has to leave again.

"Me too," he murmurs, pressing a light kiss to my hair. "Most people in London like to go to sleep early."

I blink away the tears that threaten to spill, a laugh bubbling out of me. I pull back to look up at him. "You mean, they're normal and don't like to stay awake until five in the morning?"

Chris scoffs, a smile playing on his lips as he wipes his thumb over my cheek. "I'd much rather be weird with you than normal with anyone else."

God, my heart feels like it's being torn. I love him so much. More than words can express. More than I can understand. More than he'll ever understand.

"Fair warning," I say, reluctantly pulling away from him. "I don't know if you remember, but I'm not exactly the best when it comes to baking, or cooking, or anything involving a stove." The urge to return to his arms is overwhelming, but it's a dangerous place to be. It stirs up emotions I shouldn't entertain, clouding my thoughts. I rarely think clearly, but with Chris, it's crucial.

"I remember," he chuckles, running a hand through his hair. "So, that hasn't changed in four years?"

Four years. It always catches me off guard how long it's been. It feels like it was just yesterday that we were in my parents kitchen. "I think I've regressed," I admit, scrunching my nose.

He chuckles. "How is that even possible? You almost burned down your house at one point."

Yeah. That was a fun night. We were high, and wanted to make brownies, which wasn't the best combination mixing weed and ovens, especially when it comes to me. But the point is, no one died, so… I consider that a win in my books.

"Madi cooked when she lived here, and when she didn't, we had takeout." I hold my hands up. "I don't attempt things I know I suck at."

He shoots me a look. "You could never suck at anything."

"Well…" I tease with a smirk.

Chris scoffs, shaking his head as he turns around to grab some more ingredients. Watching him move around my kitchen feels surreal. It's like we've stepped back in time, and for a moment, everything feels right again. He pulls out the flour and eggs, placing them on the counter.

"Found them," he announces, casting a quick glance in my direction. "Can I trust you to crack eggs?"

I push off the island, sidling up beside Chris. "Sure," I say with a shrug. "When has a little shell ever hurt anyone?" I tease, flashing him a playful grin.

His brow raises, and he chuckles. "I'll tell you what." He cracks two eggs into the bowl, shooting me a sideways glance. "Why don't you just sit down, and I'll take care of this."

I shoot him a grateful grin. "That's why I love you."

I watch Chris expertly add ingredients to the bowl, memories flooding my mind. I've said those three words to him before. So many times I can't even count. I think of all the times I didn't mean it like I do now. How those three little words held a completely different meaning back then.

He lets out a soft laugh, his eyes meeting mine. "Yeah."

And how he'll never know how different those three little words mean to me now.

7

Nothing has changed

Christopher

Gabi flops onto the couch with a sigh, wearing the biggest smile I've ever seen. "Those were, without a doubt, the best pancakes you've ever made." Her smile is even brighter than when I surprised her yesterday.

Seeing her smile has always been my favorite sight in the world, and that hasn't changed. I've witnessed so many versions of her. Laughing, crying, bawling in my arms with blood trickling down her. Every time she smiles, my heart blips a little at seeing her happiness. But then again, it might just be *her* that has this effect on me. Even a half-second glance from her can make my heart flip over in my chest.

"You've said that every single time I made pancakes," I chuckle, joining her on the couch.

She looks up at me with the prettiest smile I've ever seen. "Because they're always the best."

My cheeks heat up, loving that she likes something I made for her. "You know…" I glance over at her, struck by her beauty. Her dark, straight hair spills over her shoulders, her face free of makeup, and those intoxicating blue eyes stare up at me. I swallow, clear my throat, and blink, trying to get back on track. "I actually haven't made them in a while," I admit.

"What?" she asks, her eyes widening, making the blue stand out even more. "Chris, that's a criminal offence. Why not?"

My head tips back, a laugh bubbling out of me. I love how dramatic she is. I don't think I've ever met anyone like Gabi, and I don't think I ever will.

"Because I only like making them for you," I tell her, flashing a smile.

I love doing anything for her. The only reason I ever got into baking was to satisfy her munchies when we'd get high. She used to devour anything she found in the house. One day, I made her some crappy boxed brownies, and she ate them like they were gold. I remember how my stomach flipped every time she let out a little moan or told me how good they were. Making her happy became my favorite thing, so I learned how to make decent, homemade ones, and it kind of stuck.

Anything I ever did was for her.

Gabi pushes at my shoulder. "Chris, you big softie."

I fake wince, laughing at how she's so right. She can't even fathom the lengths I'd go for her.

I blow out a breath as Gabi lays her chest on me, her touch overwhelming me to the point where I can't even breathe properly. "I'm so stuffed," I say, adjusting my position so she can lay her head on my chest. "There's no way I can sleep now."

"Really?" Gabi mumbles against my chest. "I feel like I could pass out."

I chuckle, gently moving her chocolate brown hair out of the way so I can see her beautiful face. "I know you could." She always had a talent for falling asleep within minutes. "Do you want to go to bed?" I ask, trailing the tips of my fingers across the skin of her back. Memories of us from five, six, seven years ago come flooding back to me. Her head on my chest, my hands rubbing up and down her back until she fell asleep in my arms.

It's been so long that I was scared things would be different between us. But they're not. She's still my best friend, we're still comfortable with each other, and I'm still in love with her.

Nothing has changed.

I feel her head move against me as she shakes her head. "Hell no. I'm not ruining our first sleepover together because of *sleep*."

Her words, slightly slurred from tiredness, make me chuckle. "I'm staying for a while, Gabi," I assure her, slowly stroking her back. "We'll have plenty of other nights."

She shakes her head again. "It's not enough," she mumbles, making me freeze. She's right. It's not enough. Two months isn't nearly enough after spending four years away from her. But it *has* to be enough. Because when summer is over, I have to go back. "Stop trying to get rid of me," she says, twisting out of my hold so she can sit upright. "Here. Grab the controller. Let's play a game. That'll keep me awake."

I smile. We haven't played together, in a while, at least not in person. "I can't wait to kick your ass," I joke, grabbing the remote from her hand.

"Pfttt." Gabi shoots me a playful glare. "I've gotten better than you remember."

I arch an eyebrow. "Really? Did you forget I practically do this for a living?"

She waves me off, rolling those gorgeous eyes of hers that I love so much. "Sure, but there's this guy who plays like a pro. We've played together a few times, and I might have picked up some new tricks."

The end of her sentence drowns out as my heart bangs against my chest. "Guy?"

"Yeah." Gabi shrugs, starting up a game. "He's great. Dude's an amazing basketball player, too. He's huge. Like so tall it hurts my neck to look at him."

I can hardly hear her over the pounding of my heart, shaking my head slightly as I blink at the side of her face. "Oh, I... I thought you said you weren't dating anyone?"

I doubt she'd hang out and play video games with just any random guy she hooked up with, right?

"What?" Gabi's head snaps to the right, facing me with a twisted expression. "Ew. Gross. No. He's dating Leila."

"Leila?"

"Yeah. One of my best friends. I think I've mentioned him before. Aiden Pierce. Captain of the basketball team?"

The name rings a bell, and I nod, feeling heat creeping up my face. "Right. Yeah. Sorry."

Gabi shivers, her face twisting. "I can't believe you thought I was dating him. He's kind of like the brother I never had," she explains. "And Grayson is like the brother I didn't want."

I let out a laugh, feeling a sense of relief wash over me. She didn't refer to me as a brother, and I hope to God she never does.

"He uh…" She smiles a little. "He actually wants to meet you."

55

"He knows about me?" Honestly, I don't even remember the guy. Every time Gabi calls me, I get a little distracted by the sound of her voice, and by the fact I'm talking to my best friend.

"Yeah. I talk about you a lot." I like that. Fuck, I *really* like that. My friends are sick and tired of hearing me talk about Gabi, so I'm really fucking happy that she talks about me too. "Last year, Madi was busy with her career and everything going on with Lucas. I didn't want to bother her with my stupid problems, so I guess Aiden and I kind of got close."

I blink, my brows dipping. "Bother her with what?" I ask.

She shrugs, not meeting my gaze. "Just things."

The worst possible scenarios flood my mind, and I drop the controller, sucking in a breath. "Gabi—"

She lowers her controller, and meets my gaze. Swallowing hard, she shakes her head. "I didn't, okay? It wasn't *that*. I just needed to talk."

My heart breaks a little. "And you couldn't do that with me?" I was the one person she would always tell everything to, and the fact that she didn't, feels like a punch to my gut. Actually, it feels like a knife digging inside my skin.

"I tell you everything, Chris," Gabi says, with a sigh.

I feel a lump form in my throat, a sinking feeling settling in the pit of my stomach. There's something she isn't telling me. Something she went to some other guy for.

"But?" I coax, afraid of what her answer might be.

My eyes drift to her slender neck, noticing the subtle movement as she swallows. "It was just a small issue. Not important at all."

Not important my fucking ass. It's obviously important if she felt like she couldn't come to me. I drop my eyes, trying to see if I can see any—

"Stop that!" Gabi's voice cuts through my thoughts, and I lift my gaze until our eyes meet. I see the tears welling up, her eyes turning glassy.

Fuck. My heart pounds against my chest as I run a hand through my hair, tugging at the strands in frustration. "If you didn't tell me—"

"It's not that," she repeats, shaking her head. "I promise."

I promise. Her promise settles the turmoil in my stomach, and I blow out a breath, not wasting another second before I pull her into me. She's never lied to me. And she's never broken a promise. Her shaky breath makes me close my eyes as I clutch onto her tightly.

"I just… I felt alone, Chris," she mumbles. I snap my eyes open, guilt churning inside of me. "You were in London, and I needed to talk to someone."

I pull back, clutching her face in my hands, staring into her glassy eyes. "You can talk to me, Gabi. Doesn't matter where I am. If you need me, then you call me, text me, hell, just send me a plane emoji and I'll get on the next flight and be there for you," I tell her, my heart pounding in my chest as I hold my whole world in my hands. "No matter what."

She shakes her head. "I can't disrupt your life like that, Chris."

I want to shake her, to tell her that she couldn't disrupt my life if she tried. I pull her into me again, pressing my lips on the top of her head. "There's no life if you're in it, Gabi," I mumble against her. "You are my life." She lets out another shaky breath as she wraps her arms around me. "I'm here now, Gabi. You're not alone. You have me."

"For two months," she mumbles, tightening her hold on me.

I close my eyes, the weight of her words sinking in. "Always," I correct. She's always had me, more than she realizes. Pressing another kiss to her head, I pull back and hand her the controller. "Come on. Let's play a game so you can get some sleep."

Gabi wipes her eyes and shoots me a glare that looks adorable as hell. "Three games."

Her eyes are heavy with exhaustion, and I doubt we'll get through three games, but I nod as I grab my controller. "Fine."

She smiles and lays her head on my chest, turning on her side to face the TV as I press play. "There's a party on Friday," she says, her gaze fixed on the screen. "I could introduce you to my friends." Her head lifts, and her eyes meet mine. "Maybe you could come?" The way she asks, unsure and a little nervous makes me smile.

The idea of going to a party doesn't really excite me, but doesn't she know by now that I'd do anything she wanted? If Gabi wants me there, and wants me to meet her friends, there's no way in hell I'm saying no to that.

"I'd love to," I assure her.

"Yeah?" she asks, her eyes lighting up.

I chuckle, nodding, and her smile widens before turns her attention back to the TV as we play a game. She doesn't even make it through one game before I hear her soft snores, the controller slipping from her hand and rolling to the floor.

I press my lips together in amusement as I lean down to press a kiss to her forehead, closing my eyes as we both drift off to sleep.

I dare you

Gabriella

"Are you sure you don't want to ditch this and go back home?" I ask, searching his face for any sign of discomfort. I know Chris isn't into parties or being around people in general. While I thought it was a good idea for him to meet my friends, I should have suggested somewhere less… crowded.

Chris exhales, his lips curling into a reassuring smile. "You don't have to keep checking on me," he says. "I'm fine, Gabi. I'm always fine when you're here."

My chest eases at his words. "Really? I know these parties can be a lot."

He takes my hand, giving it a reassuring squeeze. "I promise I'm fine," he says, flashing a warm smile. "I want to meet your friends."

"You can always meet them another time," I say, holding onto his hand a little tighter. The warmth of his touch calms me. It always has done. Every one of his touches settles something in me. The way he gives me gentle forehead kisses, how he wraps his arms around me, comforting me, and how he cradles my face in his hands. "You don't have to force yourself to do something you don't want to do."

His face lights up with a grin. "Who are you, and what have you done with my best friend?" he says with a laugh. "You never used to say that. You loved to corrupt me."

I roll my eyes dramatically. "I wouldn't say I *corrupted* you."

"We almost got arrested," he says, his eyebrow raising in amusement.

My lips twitch with the memory of that night, but I can't help but shoot him a playful glare. "You're making me out to be the bad guy."

He laughs, a sound that tugs at my heart, and pulls me into him, wrapping his arms around me in a tight embrace. I don't think I realized how much I've truly missed him until now. Sure, we talked every day, texted, called, played games together, and I convinced myself it was the same as having him beside me.

But I was so wrong.

There's nothing like this. There's nothing like feeling his warmth, hearing the steady rhythm of his heartbeat against my ear. There's nothing like the familiar scent of his cologne that hasn't changed since I last saw him. There's nothing like *him*.

"You're definitely the bad one in our friendship, Gabi. Always have been." He pulls back, and I already miss him.

"And you're just so *good*," I say with a smile, reaching up to pinch his cheeks. "It's adorable."

He returns my smile, and I realize my hands are still on his face. The warmth of his skin beneath my fingertips sends a shiver down my spine. I can't help but get lost in his eyes as my touch trails across his cheek.

Chris's smile slips slightly, and I suck in a breath when his hand covers mine, halting its movement.

He clears his throat, dropping both of our hands. "Come on," he says, pressing his lips together in a smile. "Let's go meet your friends."

My smile disappears as we make our way through the crowd. Why the hell did I make things awkward and touch his face like that. I sneak a quick glance up at Chris, wondering what he's thinking.

"Oh hey." I turn to my right and spotting Aiden among the crowd. His familiar grin greets me as he nods in acknowledgment. "You finally made it. I was starting to think you wouldn't show."

"I don't miss a good party," I tell him, reaching over to grab a beer. "You know that."

He nods, letting out a laugh, and his gaze shifts to Chris beside me, his eyebrows lifting as he shoots me a knowing grin. I narrow my eyes at him.

He knows too much.

"Hey man," Aiden says, turning his attention to Chris. "You must be Chris. I've heard a lot about you."

"Yeah," Chris responds, awkwardly reciprocating Aiden's hug. I can't help but watch with amusement dancing in my eyes. "I, uh, I've heard about you too," Chris says with a smile, brushing his hair back.

Aiden scoffs. "If it was from Gabi, then I assume it was all bad things."

My eyes roll as I flip him off, but Chris laughs, shaking his head. "No, not at all. She actually seems to think you're the best gamer around." He grins, his eyes sparkling with mischief as he meets my gaze. "I've got to say, I can't wait to prove her wrong."

Aiden laughs, giving Chris a friendly tap on the shoulder before turning back to me. "I like him."

"Yeah," I reply, my gaze lingering on Chris as a soft smile plays on my lips. "I do too."

"Come on," Aiden says, flashing a grin as he grabs a couple of sodas from the ice bucket. "We're all hanging out over there. Grayson has his tongue halfway down Rosie's throat, but I'm sure he'll come up for air long enough to say hi."

"I doubt that," I mutter to Chris with a smirk. "That guy only cares about two things. Cars and Rosie."

Chris smiles as we join the others, but when we arrive, it's clear that Aiden wasn't exaggerating. Grayson and Rosie are making out, completely absorbed in each other, oblivious to the world around them.

"I think I'm gonna barf," I tease, pretending to gag.

"Grayson, come up for air, brother, please," Aiden says, plopping down on the couch beside his girlfriend, Leila.

Grayson pulls away from Rosie, groaning as he flips Aiden off. "I'll be sure to remind you of that when you sneak Leila in at night," he says, running his hand through his hair.

Aiden arches a brow. "I do no such thing."

Grayson lets out a scoff, shaking his head. "Who are you trying to kid?"

He grins, lifting his shoulder in a shrug as he hands her the soda. "We've got company," he says, nodding towards Chris and me. "I'm trying to behave."

"You've never behaved a day in your life," Leila says.

He shrugs, swinging an arm around her shoulder. "You love me anyway."

63

I nudge Chris on the arm. "Careful, Chris. They're about ten seconds away from fucking."

Aiden chuckles against Leila's lips, and Grayson glances at us, his gaze lingering on Chris for a moment before turning back to me with a subtle nod. "Who's this?" Grayson asks me, his tone teasing. "Your new toy for the night?"

I freeze, feeling a flush creep up my neck as I glance back at Chris, whose cheeks are turning redder by the second.

"Dude," Aiden groans, smacking Grayson on the back of his head.

"Ow," Grayson says, rubbing his head. "What was that for, asshole?"

"That's Gabi's best friend," Aiden explains, shooting Grayson a pointed look.

"Wait. What?" Madi twists her head, her gaze bouncing between me and Chris. She frowns, wiggling her fingers between us. "He's your what?"

"Are you jealous, Madi?" I tease, fluttering my eyelashes playfully. "Are you two going to fight for me?"

Madi smiles, shaking her head. "Do you want me to fight for you?"

"I mean…" I let out a scoff. "It would be nice to feel like I'm loved now and again," I say with a shrug.

"I'm not treating you like a chew toy," Chris says, arching a brow with a hint of amusement.

Madi sighs, rolling her eyes. "Fine. I guess I'll share."

I grin. "That's fine by me."

"How come you never told me about your secret best friend?" Madi asks me, her tone curious. "You talk about *everything*."

"I guess I've replaced you," Aiden interjects with a grin, crossing his feet on the table in front of him. "I was the *only* one who knew." He shoots Madi a playful wink, but Leila clears her throat pointedly. "Okay, fine, Leila knew too. I told her."

"Of course you did," Grayson says with a scoff. "There isn't a single thing you don't tell her."

Madi's still waiting for my response, so I gesture to her boyfriend, who's gazing up at her with hearts in his eyes. "Need I remind you, you were busy last year? 'I hate Lucas, I love Lucas,'" I sigh, shaking my head. "There was a lot to process."

She glares at me. "I definitely didn't say that, and you could have always told me. You know that."

Chris glances at me, and I shrug, not wanting to get into it. "Well, now you know. This is Chris. Say hi, Chris."

"Hi."

"And he's staying with me for the summer, okay, bye." I reach to grab his hand, eager to escape from the sudden interrogation, but Aiden's voice stops me.

"Wait a minute." I freeze, feeling their gazes boring into me as I turn slowly to face them. "He moved in with you?"

I shrug, pretending like it's not a big deal. "Yeah. Madi moved out. I needed a roommate, and Chris is only staying for two months. So…"

"Two months?" Aiden asks, his eyebrows lifting as he glances at Chris.

"Yeah. I, uh… I go back to school in September," Chris explains.

"I'm so glad I graduated," Grayson says with a shake of his head.

I watch as Aiden glances down at Leila, who shifts uncomfortably, and lets out a sigh, looking away. Aiden frowns, clutching her chin to make her look up at him. She shakes her head, and lifts off the couch. "I need some air." Aiden's eyes follow her as she leaves the room, and he sighs, drinking his soda.

"Have you been drafted by a team, too?" Chris asks Grayson.

Grayson nearly spits his drink out, shaking his head. "Nah. Aiden's the basketball player, not me. I'm working at this garage nearby," he explains, glancing down at Rosie. "I wanted to leave for so long, but now… I have a reason to stay." Rosalie smiles up at him, her eyes twinkling with the love I know she has for him. They're so pure, those two. "And then when this one graduates, I guess I'll go wherever she goes."

"Rosie's a fashion designer," I chime in, nodding towards her. "And Grayson's a simp."

"I heard that," Grayson grumbles, shooting me a scowl.

I gasp dramatically. "Great. Your ears are working."

Grayson flips me off, and I laugh, nudging Chris on the arm. "What do you think?" I ask him, feeling a twinge of nerves about what he thinks of my friends. "You can be honest. Grayson's annoying, right?"

Chris chuckles, shaking his head. "No, he's great," he says. "They all are. You've found amazing friends here."

Yeah, I really have. I'm lucky to have found these guys. They've made the last four years better than I thought possible. "It doesn't compare to us, though," I admit, my gaze softening as I look at him.

Chris's face lights up into a smile as he reaches out, his hand covering my thigh. I glance down, feeling the warmth of his touch seeping through the fabric of my jeans.

His hand moves as he lifts his palm off my leg, his finger tracing a path across my leg. My heart quickens in my throat as I watch his movements, realizing what he's doing.

He remembers.

His fingers continue to trail across my leg, forming patterns as I try to decipher our secret language, only for us.

Ditto

I smile, glancing up at him when he pulls his hand back. We came up with this silent code, our secret language, a way to speak when we surrounded by people. My heart beats out of my chest at the reminder, loving how everything is still the same between us despite the time and distance apart.

"Yeah?"

His nod is slow, almost hesitant as he smiles. "Every time I went out with the guys in London, I always pulled out my phone wanting to text you." He pauses, his eyes searching mine, as he swallows. "Wanting you there."

My heart flutters at the knowledge he felt the same way I did. I've lost track of the amount of times I'd zone out, wondering where Chris was, and what he was thinking. And he was thinking of *me.*

"And now you're here," I say, smiling at the fact that he came all this way because I told him I wanted him here.

He grins, dipping his head in a nod. "I am."

I blink, feeling my smile disappear when I remember he won't be here for long. "For two months," I say, swallowing.

His smile wavers, a hint of tension flickering across his face. "Yeah."

67

"It's fine," I say with a shrug, though I feel the complete opposite. "I know the deal."

"I still hate thinking about it though," he admits quietly.

"Me too."

Chris exhales, running a hand through his hair. "Is it just the girls that are graduating next year?"

"No. Lucas still has quite a bit left," I reply, gesturing to Lucas.

"I only applied to Redfield last year," Lucas tells him. "So I guess I'm stuck here for a bit longer."

"And James," Grayson adds. "He still has another year left."

Chris turns to me, furrowing his brows. "James?"

I grin, letting out a sigh. "Ah. James. I miss him."

"Me too," Lucas says with a sad nod. "He's my best friend," he tells Chris. "He doesn't go here, though. He goes to college in the city."

"Do you go to school around here?" Grayson asks Chris as he takes a sip of his beer.

"Nah," Chris replies, shaking his head. "I actually study in London."

Grayson freezes, eyes drifting to me. "Fuck. That's... far."

"Three-thousand, six-hundred and twenty miles," I say, noting everyone's eyes on me. "But who's counting?" I say with a scoff, taking a sip of my drink.

Aiden clears his throat, lifting his brows. "That's cool, though. I've always wanted to go to London," he says. "What do you study?"

"Computer tech," he says, joining me on the couch. Our shoulders press together, and I lean into him without a second thought. "I actually got a job as a game developer."

68

Aiden's eyes light up with excitement. "Oh shit, that's cool," he says, his eyebrows shooting up in surprise. "We should play sometime. I'd love some real competition."

I shoot him a glare. "Hey, you said I was improving."

Aiden chuckles. "I was just being nice."

"Dick," I mutter, crossing my arms.

Aiden laughs, pulling out his phone. "Here, let's exchange numbers and set up a gaming session."

"Yeah, okay," Chris replies.

I turn my attention to the girls. "Should I be worried that Aiden's trying to steal my best friend right now?"

As Rosie and Madi exchange smirks, their expressions falter, and I follow their gaze to Tiffany standing beside Chris. My stomach churns at the sight of her.

"If you're handing out numbers, then I'm interested," she says, her gaze lingering on Chris as she flashes him a smile. "I don't think I've seen you around here before. Hi, I'm Tiffany." Her short black bob sways as she steps closer to him.

"Hi. I, uh… I don't go here," Chris explains with a swallow. "I'm just visiting for the summer."

Tiffany's smile widens. "That's perfect," she replies. "I'm starting to get bored of the guys around here."

"More like they're getting bored of you," Grayson says, with a scoff.

Tiffany ignores Grayson's comment, her attention fully on Chris as she checks him out, running her tongue over her teeth.

I'm going to be sick.

"Did your boyfriend break up with you again, and you want to make him jealous?" I say, narrowing my eyes at her. "Is that why you're acting so desperate?"

She gives me a sly look, reaching for her phone. "You seem like you could use some new friends," she says, a smirk on her lips as she glances at Chris. "How about I give you my number, and we can hang out sometime?"

I hate this. I hate it so damn much. When he was in London, I could pretend he wasn't with anyone, that he wasn't kissing or touching anyone. But now he's here, and there's a girl right in front of him who's clearly very interested in him. And I can't do anything about it.

He's my best friend.

That's all.

Even if I'm in love with him, all we are is best friends, and I can't do anything to change that. If he wants to date this vulture, then who am I to stop him?

He turns around, meeting my eyes, and I try to tell him my feelings through my eyes.

Please, don't date her.

Don't give her your number.

Please.

Don't break my heart.

Even though Chris knows me inside out, he can't read my mind. I swallow hard, feeling my heart sink as I watch him turn around and focus on Tiffany.

I can't do this. I can't watch him flirt and date and—

"I'm good," Chris says, making my head snap up.

"What?" Tiffany's voice breaks the silence, confusion evident in her tone.

"I don't want your number," Chris replies firmly.

70

My shoulders drop with relief, and I smile as I keep my eyes on the back of his head.

"Are you kidding?" Tiffany says with a scowl. "You don't want my number?"

"Are you deaf?" Aiden snaps, scowling at her. "He said he's not interested. So why don't you get the hell out of here and leave us alone?"

Tiffany glares at Aiden, jutting out her hip as she places her hand on it. "Where's your girlfriend?" she asks. "Off with another guy again?" She lets out a mocking laugh. "Wouldn't surprise me. I always knew she was a slut."

"Call my girlfriend a slut one more time," Aiden challenges, stepping right in front of her. "I dare you."

"Or what?" she retorts, arching a brow. "What are you going to do about it?"

"I can't do anything," Aiden says, his jaw clenched as he looks down at her. "But she can." He gestures to me with a lift of his chin.

Hell yes. Let me beat this bitch up.

I grin, rising from the couch to stand beside Aiden.

"I only said the truth," she sneers, shooting me a smug look as she sizes me up. "You know what they say. The company you keep..."

My blood boils. God, I want to punch her so badly. I press my lips together, lifting a hand to wipe my eyes with my middle finger. "I'm shaking with tears," I say, my voice dripping in sarcasm. "Now get out of here before you lose a tooth today."

"Bitch," she mutters, flipping her bob over her shoulder as she walks away.

Leila walks back inside, freezing when she sees Tiffany walk past her. "Did I miss something?" she asks, her brow furrowing.

Aiden walks toward her, grabs her by the waist, and lifts her up, which makes Leila yelp, before he carries her out in his arms.

"What the hell was that about?" Grayson asks, gesturing to the door where our friends just left.

I shake my head. "I have no idea."

I relax as Chris cups my face with his hands, his eyes searching mine. "Are you okay? That girl was—"

"Evil," I finish simply, my voice tinged with bitterness from years of dealing with Tiffany.

His brows furrow, worry evident in his expression as he tucks a strand of hair behind my ear. "Did she call you a—"

He pauses, unable to bring himself to even say the word. He's so pure, and good, and *I love him.*

"Yeah," I confirm, feeling a knot tighten in my stomach after Tiffany's outburst in front of him. Chris knows I'm not a saint, and he's never judged me for it, but it still stings to hear that kind of insult when he's here. "Are you okay?"

His brows shoot up, a flicker of surprise crossing his face. "I was kind of shocked by how forward she was," he admits. "But yeah, still good, Gabi."

I nod, meeting his gaze. "And you didn't want to give her your number?"

"Are you kidding?" he responds with a slight frown. "She was awful."

I let out a chuckle. "Yeah, she was," I agree. "But, you didn't think she was pretty?"

A small smile plays on his lips as he rubs his thumb over his cheek. "I thought you'd already know," he says, arching a brow. "She's not my type."

My heart skips a beat, Chris' words from so long ago echoing in my mind.

9

She's not my type

Gabriella

Age Sixteen

It's fucking freezing, and I'm desperately in need of a drink.
Whose brilliant idea was it to hang out at the beach in
September, anyway? This bonfire isn't keeping me warm at
all. My skin shivers as I lift my head, scanning the beach for a
head of dark curls. I squint, struggling to see in the darkness,
and let out a harsh breath when I don't see him.

Where the hell is he?

I pull out my phone to check the time, flinching when I
feel a hand wrap around my leg. As soon as I turn, I break out
into a smile when I see Chris looking down at me. His fingers
start to move slowly across my bare skin, just above my knee,
leaving a trail of goosebumps. I keep my eyes on his fingers,
trying to figure what he's spelling out.

You ok?

I nod, smiling up at him. "I am now that you're here," I
say, loving how his smile widens at my response.

"Are you sure?" he asks with a smirk. "You're shivering."

"Just a little cold," I admit. Kinda wish I'd thought to bring
a sweatshirt or something.

His eyes travel down to my bare legs, and he shakes his head in mild exasperation. "You're wearing shorts," he points out, arching an eyebrow. "Of course you're cold. You need more layers."

I roll my eyes playfully, reaching over to snatch the navy baseball blue cap off his head and place it on mine. "There. Layers," I say with a smirk. "I'm keeping this, by the way."

He lets out a chuckle. "Fine by me."

"Where were you?" I ask him. "I've been looking for you for hours."

"Debating whether or not to come," he replies with a sigh, brushing his hair back. "Almost stayed home."

When Nate invited me to the bonfire tonight, it was a no-brainer to invite Chris, so the thought of him almost staying home makes my heart sink. My lips pull into a frown. "Why?"

He shrugs, and my eyes drift to his throat, watching it bob as he swallows. "This kind of thing isn't really my scene," he says. "Besides, the only person I talk to is you."

"You know that's not true," I say, arching an eyebrow. "You know other people here besides me."

He sighs, a smirk playing on his lips. "Fine. Let me amend that. The only person I *want* to talk to is you."

My cheeks heat up, feeling a warmth spread through me that has nothing to do with the bonfire, and I let out a laugh, nudging his shoulder with mine. I take his hand and place it on my lap, tracing my fingers across his palm.

Me too.

I shoot him a grin when I'm done, and he presses his lips together, pulling his hand back. "Don't think that's true."

"No?" I ask, furrowing my brows.

His expression falters for a moment before he smirks, shaking his head. "I think you forgot someone," he says, glancing behind me.

I turn around and see my boyfriend walking toward us. "Oh," I mutter. "Right."

"Fuck, it's cold," Nate says, dropping down on the sand beside me. "You want a drink, babe?"

The wind blows my hair across my lips, and I brush it away, glancing up at him. I hate when he calls me 'babe.' I don't know why. I should like it. He's my boyfriend, after all. "Sure. Thanks," I reply, forcing a smile.

I reach out, grabbing the beer can, and crack it open. I have no time to take a sip before his lips land on my neck. I make a noise, trying to move away, but his hand wraps around my waist, keeping me in place as he kisses my neck and jaw. "You look so hot today," he murmurs.

I let out an awkward laugh, painfully aware of Chris sitting right beside me. I attempt to break it off, pulling away from Nate. "You say that every day," I say, trying to keep the discomfort out of my voice.

"Well, you do." I freeze as Nate leans in again, his lips leaving open-mouthed kisses on my neck. His hand begins to wander towards my inner thigh, and I shift uncomfortably.

"I need a drink," Chris announces, rising from the sand and making his way towards the cooler deeper into the beach. He settles into a beach chair and cracks open a can.

I spot a girl walking towards Chris, her blonde hair catching my eye. *Taylor*. She gestures something to him, and he nods before she takes a seat beside him. I squint, observing their interaction. Chris runs a hand through his hair as they talk, and she laughs, reaching out to touch his arm, and I force my eyes away.

"I'm cold."

Nate moans, his lips trailing to my jaw. "What?" he murmurs, clearly distracted.

"I'm cold," I repeat, my skin shivering.

He groans, annoyed. "Who the fuck cares?" he says. "You smell good," he grunts against my skin, grabbing a handful of my thigh as he resumes kissing my neck.

My skin prickles with discomfort, and I pull back, swatting his hand away from my thigh. "Can you stop?" I snap, furrowing my brows in frustration. "We're in public."

"So?" Nate scoffs. "Half the people here are making out."

He moves in again, but I pull away again. "Well, I'm not in the mood."

Nate lies back on the sand, letting out a groan as he buries his head in his hands. "You're never in the fucking mood," he mutters bitterly.

It's obvious he's pissed that I haven't put out since we slept together over a month ago. But honestly, the idea of going there with him again makes me tense up.

My first time wasn't the best, and I hoped it would be different with someone else. When Nate and I started dating a few months back, I held off on sleeping with him, even though he made it clear he didn't want to wait. I just didn't want to rush things or end up regretting it, again. But when I finally caved and gave him what he wanted, it was... bad. I don't know if it's me or him, but ever since then, I've been finding excuses to avoid sleeping with him again.

My eyebrows shoot up, taken aback, and he shakes his head. "Come on, Gabi. You can't expect me to wait forever. What's the point in having a girlfriend?"

Dick. "And what's the point in having a boyfriend when you don't even care about me other than getting in my pants?" I fire back, feeling my blood boil. "I said I was cold, and you said 'who the fuck cares.' You didn't even offer me your jacket."

"Oh my god, you're so dramatic," he grunts, rolling his eyes in frustration. "What good would it do if I gave you my jacket?" he snaps back. "Then we'd both be cold." His eyes dart behind me, and he gestures with a nod of his head. "There's a jacket right there. Put that one on."

I turn my head, spotting Chris's black zip-up hoodie lying on the sand beside me. With a shake of my head, I push myself up from the ground, brushing the sand off my legs. "I need a drink."

He lifts his arms in frustration. "I literally just brought you a drink."

I toss the can of beer onto the sand. "Oops. Slipped," I say with a shrug. "Guess I need another one."

"What the fuck?" Nate murmurs, irritated as he wipes the spilled alcohol off his jeans.

I turn around, grabbing the jacket Chris left behind and throw it on before zipping it up, and fix the cap on my head.

Stepping over the chairs and blankets scattered on the sand, I make my way into the beach, heading towards the cooler sat right behind Chris and Taylor.

Bending down to grab a beer from the cooler, I lift my head at the sound of Taylor's giggles and see Chris smiling back at her.

He's smiling at her.

I've never seen him smile like that, at least not with anyone else.

I thought he only smiled like that with me.

Apparently not.

Taylor leans in closer, whispering something in Chris' ear, and a strange sensation settles in my stomach. I furrow my brows, watching them intently, feeling my heart pound in my chest. He said he wasn't interested in her last year. So, what changed?

I glance back at them, my gaze fixed on Taylor. Her figure has definitely changed since last year. Her boobs are bigger, her waist is thinner, and her blonde hair frames her tanned skin perfectly.

Is that what Chris likes? Girls who wear short skirts, with blonde hair and big boobs?

The can clanks against the others, and I curse silently as Chris and Taylor turn around, noticing me.

"Hey," Chris says, furrowing his brows. "Did you get lost?"

"No, I came to get a drink," I reply, holding up the can my eyes shifting between them. "Am I interrupting something?"

"Actually—"

"No, of course not," Chris interrupts, flashing me a smile as he runs his hand through his brown curls. "We were just talking."

"I... I think I'm going to go find my friends," Taylor says, her gaze lingering on Chris. "See you later?"

"Yeah, sure," Chris nods in response.

She lifts off the chair, making her way towards the bonfire to meet up with her friends, and I turn to face Chris, sitting on the beach chair beside him. "I stole your jacket," I tell him with a smirk. "It's mine now."

He chuckles, shaking his head. "You didn't steal it. I left it for you."

My brows dip. "Why?"

Chris smirks, his eyes fixated on his jacket draped over my body. "You were cold."

My stomach flutters. Chris didn't even hesitate to take off his jacket for me without me asking, unlike Nate, who's supposed to be my boyfriend, who acted like it was the end of the world.

"So... Taylor, huh?" I ask, raising my drink to him.

Chris turns to face me, taking the can out of my hand and takes a sip without hesitation. We share everything. Always have. "Yeah," he replies with a nod, handing me back the can. "She kind of ambushed me when she saw me sitting here."

"And here I thought the only person you wanted to talk to was me," I joke, my lips twitching into a smirk, though my stomach sours at the thought. "Taylor seems nice, though."

"I guess," Chris replies with a shrug.

I take a sip of my drink, feeling the alcohol burn my throat. "She also seemed interested in you," I add.

He blinks in surprise. "You think?"

"Yeah," I tell him, swallowing the knot forming in my throat. "Are *you*?"

My heart thuds loudly in my chest, and I can't explain why. Taylor *is* nice. She's always been nice to me, and she really is beautiful. So why does the thought of them dating make me feel sick?

I watch as the muscle in his jaw ticks, and he blows out a breath, lifting his shoulder in a shrug. "I don't know."

My stomach churns again, and I figure I must be coming down with the flu or something. "Really?" I say, handing him my drink again.

"You sound surprised," he says, taking another sip.

That you're interested in her all of a sudden? Yeah, I'm surprised. "She just... really isn't your type, is all," I say instead.

Chris chuckles, raising an eyebrow at me. "And what's my type?"

I blink up at him, furrowing my brows in thought. "I don't know," I admit. "You don't really talk to me about that kind of stuff."

A fleeting thought crosses my mind. *Am I his type?* I quickly dismiss it. What am I even thinking? Chris is my best friend.

Chris shrugs. "It's just not something I usually talk about."

I look up at him, a hint of uncertainty gnawing at me. Chris has been my whole world for years, the person I've always relied on and thought I knew inside out. But now, looking at him, it feels like there's a side of him I've never seen.

"So she *is* your type?"

He swallows, his gaze locking with mine, and then he blows out an agitated breath, running a hand through his hair. "You were making out with your boyfriend the whole time, Gabi," he says, his brows furrowed in frustration. "You can't blame me for hanging out with her."

"Well, I'm here now," I reply with a shrug. "You can hang out with me."

He blinks at me, a hint of concern in his eyes. "What about your boyfriend?" he asks.

I shrug, taking a sip of beer. *He won't be my boyfriend for long.* "Don't worry about him," I say, waving a hand. The truth is, I don't think I even like Nate that much, and it seems like the only thing he wants from me is the one thing I don't want to give him. "I'd rather spend time with you."

The corner of his lips curl into a soft smile as his eyes meet mine. "Yeah, I'd rather spend time with you, too."

My heart does a somersault at his words, and I return his smile, feeling a rush of warmth as he lays a blanket over both of our legs. I lean my head on his shoulder, loving the comfort I feel whenever I'm with him. "So, you don't want to hang out with Taylor anymore?" I ask.

"Nah," he replies, glancing at me. "She's not my type."

10

You're not a love guru

Christopher

I was named after my father.

I remember my mom telling me one night as she tucked me into bed. I was about seven years old, and even then, I knew it wasn't a good thing. She spoke softly, probably trying to make it sound okay, but it just made me feel worse. From that moment, I hated my name. I didn't want any connection to him, even if it was just our shared name.

I always wondered if she ever looked at me and thought about him. If she ever saw a part of him in me. If she thought we were the same.

My phone rings in my hand, and I stare at the contact name, a shiver crawling up my spine. I can't escape him. Even after moving to the other side of the world, I still can't escape him. Hearing my own name is a constant reminder, because it's his name too.

I hit decline and fling my phone onto the couch. Leaning forward, I bury my head in my hands, thoughts racing. I hope that he doesn't find out I'm back in America.

"Hey, you there?" The voice breaks through my thoughts.

Peeling my hands away, I glance down at my headset resting on the couch, and I slide it back onto my head. "Yeah. I'm here."

"Where did you go?" Liam asks.

"I just... had a call," I reply, my voice trailing off.

The game kicks off when we hit play, and I get lost in it. It's been a while since I've played with the guys, and I kinda miss it. But I've missed Gabi even more. We've been catching up for the past week, and it feels like time has flown by in a blur.

"So, how's life back in America?" Liam asks.

I chuckle, feeling a weight lift off my shoulders. "Better than London."

"Fuck off," he scoffs. "London will always be better."

I shake my head, grinning. London is cool, but wherever Gabi is, is where I'd rather be.

"Seriously though," he says. "How's it been?"

"It's been good," I reply with a smile, thinking of Gabi. "Nice to catch up with everyone again."

"You went to see her, didn't you?" Liam's voice is teasing.

"Dude," I reply, rolling my eyes.

"What?" he says with a laugh. "Can't blame me for asking about the girl you can't stop talking about."

Yeah, okay, maybe I've rambled on a bit too much about Gabi. It was really hard being away from her, especially for as long as I was. But... the longer I stayed away, the easier it was to keep my distance, even though every fiber of my being missed her like crazy. "Actually, we're, uh… living together."

"Fucking hell, you move fast."

"It's not like that," I confirm, with a shake of my head. "Just shut up and play the damn game."

84

He laughs. "Fine, I won't pry. But you're happy, yeah?"

The door swings open, and I glance over to see Gabi entering the apartment, her headphones in place as usual, and her gym bag slung over her shoulder.

"Yeah," I reply to Liam, a smile spreading across my face at the sight of her. Living with my best friend again means I get to see her every day, and we can have gaming marathons until two in the morning, falling asleep together. Sure, I'm still hopelessly in love with her and can't do anything about it, but other than that... "I couldn't be happier."

"Oh, hey," she says, catching me staring at her. "You're up."

I chuckle. "Dance class went well?" I ask, sliding my headset around my neck.

"Yeah," she replies, pulling her bag off her body with a sigh. "It was tiring, but I feel all bendy now." Her smirk widens, and she wiggles her eyebrows.

Fuck, I love her. There's no one else in the world that gets me like she does. No one else that can make me laugh, or smile like she does. No one else that has every inch of my heart and soul like she does. There's only her, and I think it's only ever going to be her.

Even if I can't have her.

"We can play a game together if you want," I offer with a shrug. "I was just finishing up with the guys."

"Sure," she says, leaning down to pull off her sneakers. "I'll just get changed, and I'll be right out."

"I'll wait," I reply, watching as she disappears into her bedroom and closes the door behind her.

"Who was that?" Liam's voice breaks through the headset, and I freeze, realizing I had forgotten the guys were listening in. Whenever Gabi walks into the room, the whole world stops for me. It's been like that for as long as I can remember. Sliding the headset back on, I quickly adjust my mic and resume the game. "No one."

"Oh shit," Liam says with a laugh. "That was her, wasn't it?"

"Who?" Tom asks. "Someone fill me in here."

"The girl Chris never stops talking about. I swear the dickhead has her name tattooed somewhere on his body."

"I definitely don't."

"Wait a minute," Tom says, sounding surprised. "Why the hell didn't I know you had a girlfriend? Is it new?"

Tom and I aren't as close, so he doesn't know about Gabi, or how I feel about her. And while I wasn't planning on sharing the details of my non-existent love life, it turns out these guys are even bigger gossips than Gabi.

"She's not my girlfriend," I reply with a sigh. "She's…" Everything. My whole world. The reason my heart beats. "She's just… my girl."

"Your girl?" Liam snorts. "Bro, you're in deep."

"I'm gonna hop off."

"Avoiding the question, I see," Liam replies, amusement lacing his words.

"Bye," I say, exiting the game.

"You didn't have to leave just for me," Gabi's voice breaks through, and I tear off my headset, freezing in place. How long has she been standing there? Did she hear me call her my girl? I hope to hell she didn't.

"No, it's fine," I reply. "They were being annoying. I'd much rather play with you."

She smiles, and as always, my eyes drink her in, savoring every detail of her beautiful face, her stunning blue eyes, and her dark hair that always smells like the sweetest coconut.

Gabi drops down onto the couch beside me, her legs folding into a criss-cross position as she reaches for the other controller.

"Were you working on Real Unleashed?" I can't help but smirk, hearing the project I've poured countless hours into being mentioned by her. "I'm dying to see it."

"No, not today," I answer, firing up our favorite racing game. "It still needs a lot of work before it ever reaches your eyes," I admit with a smile. Balancing creating my own videogame with my role at Horizon Creations is a challenge. I hardly get the chance to explore all the features I want to add.

"I could always help you," she says, tearing her gaze from the screen to flash me a smile that makes my heart race. How does she still have this effect on me after all these years? "You know I'm great inspiration."

I chuckle before admitting, "Actually, I, uh..." I clear my throat, feeling a flush creep up my cheeks. "I designed a character inspired by you."

She freezes, turning her head to face me with wide eyes. "You did?"

"Yeah," I admit with a shrug, feeling my heart pound in my chest. "You helped me come up with the idea in the first place," I tell her. "Of course I would."

Gabi was crazy about Jumanji when she was younger. I swear, she must've seen that movie a million times. She was obsessed with the idea of getting sucked into a real-life game. So, when I was brainstorming my own little game a while back, I came up with the concept of four characters waking up

87

on a beach, and then suddenly the whole island turns into this giant game, and they have to find a secret passage to get back home.

Gabi was the very first character I crafted.

Georgina is a badass dark haired and piercing-blue eyed character who takes on the role of the group's leader.

And the second character I designed was *Connor*. He's Georgina's best friend, and completely obsessed with her.

I might have made their inspirations a little too obvious, but considering Gabi won't lay eyes on the final game for a while, I won't sweat about it just yet.

But thoughts swirl in my mind about when she'll realize that the character based on me is head over heels for the character based on her, and how soon she'll connect the dots to real life.

"Fuck yeah." I snap out of my thoughts, redirecting my attention to the TV where Gabi effortlessly crosses the checkpoint, leaving me miles behind.

"How the hell?" I mutter, narrowing my eyes at the screen, determined to catch up with her.

"Not my fault you were distracted," she says with a smirk, her focus unwavering on the screen as she races toward the finish line. "You shouldn't have been daydreaming."

What would she say if she knew she was the one I was thinking about?

Who I'm always thinking about.

"Looks like I'm about to lap you," she says with a grin.

"No way am I letting that happen," I mutter, crossing all of the shortcuts as I close in on her.

"What?" she huffs, stealing a quick glance at me. "You're such a cheater."

"Are you kidding?" I retort with a laugh. "You took advantage of the fact that I wasn't even playing."

She tuts, trying to move away from me in the game. "That's being a genius, not cheating."

I laugh, maneuvering closer toward her car until I'm right beside it. She nudges my elbow, making my car drift off course, and I narrow my eyes at her. "Look who's cheating now."

"Shut up. You win all the time."

"And I'm about to win, again," I tell her, hitting the back of her car, causing it to spin out of control.

"You little—" She turns her attention toward me, her hand reaching for my controller. "Gimme."

"No fucking way," I reply with a laugh, a grin spreading across my face as she tries to grab the controller from my hands. "Stop trying to tackle me. It's not going to work."

Somehow she maneuvers herself to straddle me, determined to grab the controller which makes us both to topple to the ground. "Jesus," I grunt when I roll to the floor. "You really hate losing, huh?" I tease with a smirk, lifting the controller out of her reach.

"I wasn't losing," she pants, trying to reach for my controller. "You were cheating."

"You're literally tackling me to the floor," I point out, arching a brow.

"Then do something about it," she says, a mischievous grin creeping on her face. "Unless you're too weak."

I grin, dropping the controller to the floor above my head as I grip her waist in my hands. With a swift movement, I flip us over so now I'm on top of her, pinning her arms above her head with one hand.

"How the hell?" she mutters, eyebrows furrowed in surprise.

"You underestimate me, pretty girl. Just because I let you take control, doesn't mean I'm weak," I say with a smirk.

Her eyes widen at the nickname I haven't used in forever, and the smile slips off my face when I realize I'm lying on top of her, pinning her hands underneath mine. My gaze drifts down to Gabi's chest, rising and falling with each deep breath. My eyes squint when I notice two small metal bars under the white tank top she's wearing, and the air gets sucked out of my lungs.

Holy fuck.

I look into her eyes, the bright blue staring right back at me, widening as her breaths grow deeper and faster. My hand around her waist tightens, and my eyes drift down to her lips. What the hell am I doing? I can't think straight right now. I've wanted her for so damn long. I can't even remember a time when I didn't want this girl.

"Chris," Gabi whispers, her tongue darting out to lick her lips.

"Surprise!" Our eyes widen when the front door opens, and voices fills the room. "We're all... Wait. Where the hell are they?" a deep voice says.

Gabi and I exchange wide-eyed glances as we hear them enter the apartment. Quickly, I lift myself off her and try to compose myself, the moment between us completely shattered.

Gabi jumps up, letting out a breath as she narrows her eyes at them. "You guys could have knocked."

"You told us it was supposed to be a surprise," Madi says, holding up a wine bottle in her hand, her brows furrowed as she looks between us.

"Yeah, well, I changed my mind," Gabi says with a sigh. "Knock next time."

Their eyes turn to me, and I run a hand through my disheveled hair, feeling my heart start to race. I really hate being the center of attention.

Aiden smirks, glancing between us. "Did we interrupt something?"

Fuck. Fuck. Fuck.

"You interrupted me beating Chris's ass at a game," Gabi replies with a smirk I don't know what to make of.

What just happened back there has never happened before, and I'm freaking out about it while she's laughing it off.

"Really?" Aiden asks with a laugh, arching a brow. "I thought you were a pro or something."

I huff out a laugh, shaking my head. "She cheated."

Grayson makes a noise of agreement, sitting down on the arm of the couch, his arm wrapped around Rosie's waist. "Don't I know it. It's the only way she wins."

"He was distracted," Gabi replies with a shrug. "I just took that as my advantage."

And it was all fun and games until we ended up on the floor, my body pinned to hers, mere inches away from her lips, and I nearly did something we'd both regret.

Jesus.

"What are you guys doing here anyway?" I ask, shooting a glance at Gabi. "Did I forget they were coming by?"

Gabi glances at me. First time she's looked at me since whatever the hell happened between us. "I know you hate crowds, and parties so I thought it would be nice if we all hung out together in a more quiet place."

My heart picks up pace, pumping with all the love I have for her. Meeting her friends was fun as hell, but being surrounded by that many people was a lot for me. I tried to act like I was okay, focusing on breathing and concentrating on Gabi, but she could sense it. Of course she could. That girl knows me better than anyone else.

"I should have probably asked you first," she says with a laugh as she takes a step closer. "I just thought it would be fun for us all to hang out again."

I smile down at her. "It was a great idea."

"You sure?" she says, taking another step closer to me. I can't breathe when I'm around her. Or think at all, clearly, because I pull her into me and wrap my arms around her.

"Yeah, Gabi," I say. "Thank you."

"Uh… I hate to interrupt whatever's going on," Madi says, breaking up the moment between Gabi and I as she pulls away from me. Fuck. I forgot they were in the room. "But I can't find my wine glasses anywhere."

"*Your* wine glasses?" Gabi asks, lifting her brow. "If I remember correctly, you moved out. They're not yours anymore."

Madi rolls her eyes. "I bought them."

"And left them here," Gabi says with a grin. "They're mine now."

Madi narrows her eyes at Gabi. "Did you move them?"

Gabi shrugs. "Might have."

"Why the hell did you move them?"

Gabi sighs, dramatically. "I wanted to get back at you."

Madi shoots her a dry look. "By moving my wine glasses?"

Gabi just grins back. "It's annoying you though, isn't it?"

Madeline lets out a groan. "Just… show me where they are so we can drink some wine."

With a chuckle, Gabi walks toward the kitchen, motioning for Madi to follow as she shows her where she hid the glasses.

"You okay?" Aiden's voice pulls me from my thoughts, and I turn to find him standing beside me, concern etched on his face.

"Of course," I reply, running a hand through my hair.

"Yeah?" He gestures toward Gabi with a nod of his head, a knowing look in his eyes. "When we walked in, it looked like you guys were—"

"We weren't," I finish for him. "She just tackled me to the ground to try and rip the controller out of my hands." My lips twitch, a chuckle escaping me. "I assume that was something you taught her?"

He shakes his head, holding up his hands. "That's all her. I don't need to play dirty." He grins. "I know we don't really know each other, but I feel like I do with how much Gabi talks about you."

I'm reminded of the fact that Gabi confided in Aiden with something she felt like she couldn't tell me. But the fact that she also talked about me, to the point where Aiden feels like he knows me, makes me smile.

"She does?" I ask him.

He smirks, nodding. "Yeah, man. She doesn't really talk about much else."

Grayson groans, sitting on the couch. "I find that hard to believe," he says with a dry look. "Gabi loves to talk."

I let out a laugh, knowing that's true. Nights of us talking until the sun rose come to mind. Gabi somehow always had something to say, something to tell me, to talk about. And I just loved hearing her voice until we both drifted to sleep.

"How's it been?" Aiden asks. "Living with her?"

"Great," I tell him, glancing back at Gabi who's now fighting Madi for the corkscrew. Madeline's boyfriend, Lucas watches with an amused look on her face. "She's my best friend, I missed the hell out of her."

He hums, nodding thoughtfully. "Is that all?"

I turn my attention to Aiden, furrowing my brows at his question. "What do you mean?"

"Is she only your best friend?" Aiden clarifies.

My pulse quickens as I lick my dry lips. "I don't—"

"You don't have to tell me," he interrupts, raising his shoulder. "You can if you want, but I think I already know."

"You…" I furrow my brows. "You know?"

"Yeah," he replies with a smirk. "I can tell."

I frown. "How?"

He grins, and I don't even mind that I've basically confessed my feelings for Gabi to a guy I hardly know. "I'm good at this stuff. I could tell with him," he says, gesturing toward Grayson. "It was as clear as day how he felt for Rosie, even if he was an idiot about it."

"Fuck off," Grayson replies with a scowl.

"And I could tell with Lucas and Madi," Aiden continues. "Those two were about as subtle as fire." He chuckles. "And I can tell with you."

I swallow, feeling a knot form in my stomach. "She's my best friend," I tell him. "That's all there is between us." It's not a lie, not technically. But it's definitely not how I feel about her.

"If you say so," he grins, clearly not buying my attempt to hide all the feelings I've kept buried all these years. "But if you want some help, I'm your guy."

"Stop trying to meddle in their relationship," Grayson interjects. "You're not a love guru."

"I could be," Aiden counters. "I got my girl like that," he says, snapping his fingers.

Grayson scoffs. "Such bullshit. She didn't even like you at first."

Aiden sighs. "Okay, fine. That's true. But after a few months and a *lot* of convincing, it was as easy as that." He snaps his fingers again, and I let out a laugh. "Trust me. I can help you get her."

"Oh great." I snap my head at Gabi's voice. "Aiden's found a twin."

Leila snorts. "He's about five inches taller than Chris. Wouldn't exactly call him a twin." She lowers herself down on his lap and Aiden grins, snaking an arm around her waist to pull her back into him. It's a little shocking to believe she didn't like him when they're attached at the hip.

Gabi finds her place beside me, holding a glass of wine. "I thought they'd bring food, or beer, not this," she says, taking a sip.

I let out a laugh. "Not much of a wine drinker?"

She shrugs. "As long as it can get me drunk, it'll do." I catch the uncertainty flickering in her eyes as she lifts her wine glass, holding it up to me. It's a moment just between us, a reminder of the memories we share. Without a second thought, I reach down, taking her glass, and bring it to my lips, taking a sip, reassuring her that nothing has changed between us.

"Are you telling me I'm going to have to deal with drunk Gabi?" I tease, letting out a soft chuckle.

She grins back. "Get drunk with me, and you won't have to worry about that," she suggests. "Besides, I tend to come up with my best ideas when I'm drunk."

Another laugh escapes me. Some things never change with her. "I'm scared," I joke.

"I'm serious," she insists with an eye roll.

"Me too," I say, arching a brow "Did you forget the night we almost ended up in jail?" I remind her, the memory still vivid in my mind.

She tuts, shaking her head. "That, Hudson, is what I like to call… *inspiration*."

11

A little high, very pissed

Christopher

Age Sixteen

"Here."

Gabi holds the joint toward me, and I grab it, taking a drag. The smoke enters my throat and I hold it before taking another drag.

The sound of a can cracking grabs my attention, and I turn my head, seeing the beers in Gabi's hands before she hands one to me.

We sit in silence as we watch over the city, just the noise of the cars and people surrounding us. It's quieter than normal seeing as it's later in the evening, and I kind of like it. It's not the usual quiet that's deafening and consumes my brain, but the kind that feels almost peaceful.

Gabi loves this spot. We usually come here on nights when her dad is drunk, and loud, and hates the sight of me, which is more often than not these days.

At this point, sneaking around with her is all I'm used to. Whether it's sneaking into her bed in the middle of the night, or sneaking out of her house. My house is off-fucking-limits, so here it is.

Pouring the can back, I gulp down the alcohol, seeing Gabi shiver from the side. I glance at her. "Are you cold?" She's wearing denim shorts, and a baggy sweatshirt, and her skin is covered in little bumps. She has to be cold.

Gabi blinks, pulling her knees up. "Would you give me your jacket if I was?"

"You know I would," I say without an ounce of hesitation. I'd take the clothes off my body and give them to her, if she needed.

Gabi's lips twitch into a smile, but it disappears when she sighs, and looks out below us. "Nate wouldn't."

My jaw ticks. I hate the sound of his name, especially coming from her. "No?" I ask, although I wish we could stop talking about him for good.

"No," she admits, wrapping her arms around her legs. "I told him I was cold when we were at the bonfire, and he looked at me like I was crazy. Didn't even offer his jacket." She looks at me, and swallows. "But you did."

My teeth grind together. Fucking hate that guy. Hate when she talks about him. Hate seeing them together. Hate how he makes her feel. "Of course I did. He's an idiot for not jumping at the opportunity to see you in his clothes," I admit, because seeing her in my hoodie last week made my heart thump so loudly in my chest I almost called the ambulance.

"Really?" she glances at me with those bright blue eyes that feel like a stab to my throat. The wind blows in her hair, and she looks so beautiful I can't stand it.

I swallow, breathing out a laugh. "You're my best friend. I have to be nice you," I say instead, nudging her on the arm.

She laughs along with me. "Like you wouldn't be lost without me."

That's definitely true.

Without a second thought, I pull off my jacket, and wrap it around her shoulders. The cold air hits my skin, but I couldn't give a fuck right now. Seeing her smile up at me, grateful, like she can't believe anyone would ever do something like that for her makes it all worth it.

I get lost in her eyes, the shape of her lips, the way her dimples pop when she smiles, but Gabi turns her head at the sound of a car pulling up below us. Her face contorts into a frown, and I follow her gaze.

The black Honda Civic I'm used to seeing Gabi in makes me narrow my eyes. "Isn't that—"

"Nate's car," she affirms. "Yeah."

We watch in silence as he puts the car in park, right outside the movie theatre, and steps out of the driver's seat. Yeah, that's him. Same douchey haircut, same ugly ass clothes. Who the fuck wears a button down to the movies?

"I thought you said he was out of town with his parents this weekend?"

She frowns, looking down as Nate rounds the car. "That's what he told me."

He reaches for the door handle, and out walks Taylor in a mini skirt and sneakers, reaching for his hand.

"You've got to be fucking kidding me," Gabi spits out. I turn my attention to her, seeing her scowl down at them. "She was flirting with you last week, and now she's throwing herself at my boyfriend?"

I should be focused on the last word that makes my skin crawl, but I couldn't care less about hearing her refer to him as her boyfriend. I'm a little too focused on the fact that Gabi noticed Taylor was flirting with me last week.

I shouldn't be thinking about it. It's stupid, and probably means nothing, but… it has to mean something if she noticed it, right?

I shake the thought away when I see Nate lean down, and press his lips to Taylor's.

Fuck.

I look at Gabi seeing her eyes narrowed. She doesn't even look sad, just… angry, and I can't help that a part of me is glad to see it. I shouldn't be happy that her boyfriend just cheated on her, but I can't help it.

Truth is, I've witnessed Gabi date assholes like him for years, and every time, it breaks me a little inside. It's hard seeing them with her. Kissing her, touching her, holding her when I can't.

Sure, we sleep in the same bed practically every night, and I know a ton more about her than any of those assholes ever bothered to learn, but it's still like a knife directly through my heart.

So, yeah, I'm kind of happy Gabi can see how much Nate doesn't deserve her. He never deserved the luxury to kiss her, or to even lay a finger on her.

And in asshole fashion, Nate grabs a handful of Taylor's ass as he pushes her against the car, and kisses her, right here, in the open.

"Wow," Gabi says with a scoff, slightly shaking her head.

The buzz from the blunt is completely gone and I reach out to pull Gabi into me. "Are you okay?"

She nods, eyebrows tugged together as she looks down at the both of them. "I mean… I was kind of holding out on him for a while," she admits. "It's to be expected, right?"

"No," I reply, clutching her face in my hand. "You should be with someone who respects you no matter if you sleep with them or not, Gabi," I tell her, my heart racing as those bright blue eyes makes my chest pound. "You deserve so much fucking better, and I hate that you don't realize that."

Her lips part slightly as she keeps her eyes on me, and my heart beats even harder. She's pressed against me, so she can probably feel the pounding in my chest, but there's nothing I can do to calm it down, not when she looks at me. I'm so fucking in love with her while she's focused on some other asshole.

She'll never see me like I see her.

"Chris," she says, keeping her eyes on mine.

"Yeah?" I breathe out, feeling her soft hair under my palm.

She smirks a little. "Truth or dare?"

I blow out a breath. "Gabi," I say, shaking my head. "I don't think now is the time."

"C'mon," she pleads. "I really need this." I turn my head, seeing her brows knitted together. "Please."

I don't even know what she wants to do right now, but for her, I'd jump head-first into the deepest, murkiest waters.

"Dare."

"This is fucking insane," I tell her, watching as she shakes the can in her hand.

"Come on, live a little," she says, a small smirk on her lips.

"I'll make you eat those words when I get arrested tonight."

She laughs, shaking her head as we climb down the hill. "You won't," she assures me, though I have very little faith in her right now. "I won't let anything happen to you, Chris."

I groan, glancing at Nate's car. "I don't think you can promise me that." When she shakes the spray can in her hand again, I blow out a breath. "How the hell did you get a hold of that, anyway?"

"My sister," she says with a smile. "I kind of threw it in her shopping cart when I was at Redfield with her last month, and she didn't even question it."

I breathe out a laugh. "Of course she didn't."

"Will you keep a look out?" she asks me.

She turns her head, trying to see if anyone is around, and when the coast is clear, she takes a step forward, but I reach for her wrist, halting her. "Gabi." She turns her head to me, eyebrows furrowed. "I know he hurt you, and you deserve to be upset, but—"

"I'm not, hurt, Chris."

I frown. "You're not?"

She sighs, shaking her head. "I was going to break up with him."

My frown deepens. "You were?" It's the first I'm hearing of this, and while my heart does a little flip in my chest, I try to keep my cool.

She nods, dropping her hand. "I was going to tell him it was over when he came back from his trip. Truth is, I didn't even like him that much," she admits with a shrug. "I just…"

She doesn't finish her sentence, but I already know.

"Yeah," I reply.

She hates being alone. She dates these stupid guys because she hates being alone, but… Damn it. She's not alone. She sleeps in my arms every goddamn night.

"You're drunk," I tell her with a sigh. "You're not thinking right."

"I'm a little drunk," she admits with a sigh. "A little high, but I'm very fucking pissed," she tells me, making me press my lips together. "He begged and begged and *begged* until I finally gave in and fucking slept with him, and he doesn't even have the common decency to break up with me before he mauls another girl?" Her nose flares, and she shakes her head. "I'm not just going to sit around and let him off the hook."

Fuck.

I didn't know that.

My chest boils at the thought of that prick with her, touching her, kissing her and before I know what I'm doing I hold out my hand. "Give it."

"What?" she asks, furrowing her brows.

"Give me the can, Gabi."

She slowly hands me the can, watching me warily. "Are you sure?"

I sigh, grabbing it from her before I pull up my hood. "I already know I'm going to regret this, but yes."

Gabi smiles—fully breaks out into a smile—and shakes her head. "I really love you right now, Chris."

I blow out a breath, my heart breaking at her words. "Yeah."

I turn around and head towards his stupid car, Gabi's words ringing on repeat inside my head. There's no point in giving them a second thought, though. Because I know she doesn't mean it the way I want her to.

103

I blow out a breath and shake the can once I've reached his car, looking around to make sure no one sees me. The car park is pretty empty and I start to spray the car.

"Fuck." Some of the paint sprays back onto my hoodie, and I step back, spraying a C on the side.

"Hurry," Gabi calls out as I move onto the next letter.

Once I spray the final letter, I step back and feel Gabi slide beside me, staring at his car, the word 'CHEATER' sprayed in white. It's a little sloppy since I've never done this before but it'll do the job.

"You think he'll get the message?" I joke.

Gabi lets out a laugh. "Loud and fucking clear." Her hand brushes against mine, and I look down to see her grab the can from my hands.

"What are you doing?" I ask her, furrowing my brows. "We need to get out of here before anyone sees us."

She shakes the can and heads toward the back of his car. "I just need to add some final touches."

I watch as she starts to draw a dick on the back of his car. I let out a scoff, crossing my arms as I watch her finish off the other ball.

"Hey!"

I snap my head to the left, seeing Nate running towards us, Taylor standing at the door with wide eyes.

"Oh shit." I quickly grab hold of Gabi's hand and pull her as we race out of there. She lets go of my hand to pull her hoodie over her head, and her steps slow down. "Run," I call out, reaching my hand out. She takes it and I intertwine our fingers together as we book it down the street.

"What the fuck!" Nate yells behind us, slowly coming to a stop as we run away from him.

"Why the hell are they out here already?" I ask, my breath in huffs as we keep running. "They just went in less than an hour ago."

Gabi laughs, out of breath. "Maybe they got bored and wanted to fuck."

I let out a scoff, remembering what we did to his car. "Well, they won't be, now." My guess is, Nate will be too worried about his car to even entertain anything else tonight.

My head turns back when I hear the distant sound of sirens, and I widen my eyes. "Shit."

"He called the cops?" Gabi asks, shocked. "What a fucking pussy."

I want to laugh, I really do, but I currently have the cops on my ass, and I'm shitting it. I quickly turn the corner, heading into an alley that takes us back into our neighborhood, and come to a stop when I hear the sirens blast past us.

"Fuck," I groan, clutching onto my side. "I think my spleen is about to burst." I lift my head, sweat dripping down my face as I look at Gabi. "The things I fucking do for you."

She lets out a laugh, pulling down her hood. "Well, I didn't think he'd call the cops," she says.

"We graffitied the guy's car, Gabi. That's a criminal offense."

She laughs at the reminder of what we did. "Do you think he knew it was us?" she asks.

I groan, slowly lifting up until I no longer feel like I'm about to pass out, and let out a deep breath. "No, I don't think so," I tell her, brushing my hair back. "Though the message we left might give him a clue," I admit with a smirk.

Gabi doesn't seem to find it funny though. Her eyes widen, and she shakes her head. "No. I told you I wouldn't let anything happen to you and—"

I quickly clutch her face. "Hey. Calm down. He doesn't have any proof," I assure her, seeing her shoulders relax. "And if he tries to blame you, I'll just tell the cops you were at home with me."

She sucks in a breath, her eyes locking in on mine. "You'd do that for me?"

My lips curl into a smile as I look down at my best friend and the girl that makes my heart beat. "I'd do anything for you, Gabi."

12

Reminder: Knock on the
bathroom door

Gabriella

I suck at school. Always have.

In high school, I was always falling behind, trying to catch up with everyone else and failing miserably. Homework felt impossible, tests were a nightmare, and no matter how hard I tried, I just couldn't get it right. But there's one thing I'm really good at.

Dancing.

It's the one thing that makes me feel like I don't totally suck. When I'm dancing, it's like everything else fades away, and I can just be myself. I feel confident and free, moving to the music, and for once, I actually feel like I belong somewhere.

I live and breathe dance. I always have, ever since I was a little girl. It's the one thing that's always felt right, like it's a part of me. I can still picture those old videos my mom would play for me, showing baby Gabi bouncing around in her diapers. It's like dancing has been in my blood from the very beginning.

I was terrible at first, of course, but even back then, I knew this was my calling. It's the only thing I've ever felt truly skilled at, and the one thing I've worked my ass off for.

Which is why I'm rushing to get to class, ten minutes late. It's not entirely my fault, but Cassie won't care about excuses. She's relentless when it comes to being on time. My hand reaches out, grabbing the door handle, and I slip inside just as I hear a frustrated sigh.

"Gabriella, what did I say?" Cassie sighs, shaking her head in disappointment.

"I know." My chest pounds as I catch a moment to breathe. "But it wasn't my fault this time. There was a massive traffic jam from an accident, and I was stuck in traffic forever."

"She always has excuses."

My eyes narrow at Tiffany who whispers loudly at the girls around her. I don't hate people often. There's only a few people on that list, but Tiffany is definitely one of them.

She was Leila's roommate back in freshman year, and when we became friends, we tried to befriend Tiffany too, but there's no befriending a witch.

"Not that it's any of your business, but it's not an excuse. It's the truth," I shoot back, feeling my blood boil.

She scoffs, screwing up her face at me. "Are you sure you weren't late because you were with a guy?" She blinks, tilting her head. "Or was it a girl this time?"

Tiffany's the kind of person who thinks she's better than everyone else. She's been a jerk since day one. She shamed Leila for having casual sex, like it was a crime to be single. I wouldn't be surprised if Tiffany was just jealous, since her boyfriend was all over every girl but her. But since they've broken up, she's still the same vile, awful girl I can't stand to be around.

But it doesn't end there. When she found out I was bi, she made it her mission to let me know how much it bothered her. I never understood why. It's not like it has anything to do with her. Unless...

"Do you want to fuck me?" I ask her, closing the distance between us. "Is that the problem?"

She widens her eyes, blinking a few times. "What?"

I shrug, stepping closer once more. "You love talking about my sex life, and calling me every name under the sun." The memories of her calling me a slut and hitting on Chris in the same breath come flooding back. I curl my fists beside me, narrowing my eyes at her. "Do you *want* me, Tiffany?"

"Ew." She steps back, her shoulders hitting the mirror. "Get away from me. I have zero interest in you."

I shake my head, a bitter laugh escaping me. Am I seriously still dealing with people like this? I thought I'd left this crap behind in high school. Apparently not. "Then stay away from me and my friends, and we won't have a problem," I grit out, closing the gap between us.

"Alright," Cassie calls out, her voice tinged with frustration. "Let's all cool down. This isn't a boxing ring." I can't help but chuckle under my breath, the image of putting Tiffany in her place in an actual boxing ring bringing a fleeting sense of satisfaction. But deep down, I know it's wishful thinking. People like her don't change.

I've been hiding my whole life. I knew I liked both girls and guys from a very young age, but I kept pushing it away, convincing myself it was wrong. But it was undeniable. The same attraction I felt for guys, I felt for girls too. It wasn't

109

until I opened up to Chris and confided in him that it finally clicked for me. Still, I never dared to act on it, not while I was in high school, not while anyone could have told my father.

When I came to college, I thought I would finally be able to stop hiding. Being with a girl for the first time was nerve-wracking as hell. It was scary, new, and amazing. I was so excited to finally be myself and not have to deal with people's unnecessary opinions. But what I didn't realize then was that there are always going to be people like Tiffany and my dad who hate me for just existing.

"Alright, everyone, work on your stretches, and we'll start soon," Cassie announces to the class. Then she turns her head toward me, curling a finger, signaling for me to come over to her.

"I didn't touch her," I say, holding my hands up. "I wanted to. God, I want to punch her so bad, but I didn't."

Cassie smirks for a second, but then her expression softens, her authoritative demeanor slipping back into place as she sighs. "You can't let her get to you, Gabriella."

No one calls me Gabriella. At least not anymore. So hearing it, makes me stiffen a little, my dad yelling my name in the back of my head.

"Easier said than done," I reply with a scoff. Leaning in closer, I continue, "If you'd just let me hit her. Just once…" I trail off, letting out a deep breath. Probably wouldn't change anything, but I'm sure it'd make me feel a whole lot better.

"I can't condone violence," she says, her tone serious, but then the corner of her lips lift slightly. "At least not in this room. If it was anywhere else…" Her shoulder lifts in a shrug.

My expression relaxes, and I chuckle. "I'm going to miss you when I graduate."

"Yeah. Yeah." She sighs. "I know. I'm the best." Another laugh bubbles out of me. "And so are you."

"I know," I say with a nod.

She smiles warmly. "Good. I just wanted to make sure you knew. You're amazingly talented, Gabriella."

"Yeah, I know," I repeat, a smirk playing on my lips. "Tiffany can say whatever she wants about me, but we both know she'll never be better than me when it comes to dancing."

Cassie scoffs, a playful glint in her eye. "Honey, she's hardly better than you at anything."

I smile up at her, admiring her. "I honestly think you're my mom in another universe."

She gasps dramatically, placing her hand on her chest. "I'm way too young to be your mother."

I chuckle. She's only eight years older than me, but when I joined her class as a fresh-faced freshman, having just lost my mom two years before, I kind of clung to her.

"A cool auntie, then," I suggest.

She smiles back warmly. "I'll always be here for you, okay? Even when you leave Redfield and become a famous dancer, swimming in millions, and forget about me."

I scoff, shaking my head. "I'll never forget about you. And we don't even know if I got in yet."

"Right. Of course," she says, winking at me before scrolling through music on her phone.

I blink. "You know something?"

She shrugs, a playful smile lingering on her lips as she gazes at her phone. "Maybe."

"What?" I press, leaning in eagerly. She sets her phone aside, and bends down with a smirk, ignoring me as she starts to stretch. "What do you know?" I ask, desperate for answers.

She straightens her back, and flashes me a grin. "Let's get started people," she calls out.

I narrow my eyes at her. "I hate you."

"I know, honey," she says with a wink. "Now get into position. Have you been stretching?"

I blow out a breath. "I've mastered the splits like you told me to. What more do you want from me, woman?"

With a laugh, Cassie reaches for her phone to press play. Stepping back, I adjust my position, smoothing down my shirt in the mirror and tucking it into my sports bra.

The room fills with the loud bass of the music, and Cassie launches into the new choreography. I focus intently on her movements, soaking in every detail and marking the steps as I watch her. The music fills the room, and I break out into a grin as I watch her move, her long braids swaying with each fluid motion. She's so incredibly talented, and it pains me to think she might be wasting her gifts on a bunch of idiots.

Except for me, *obviously*.

The music fades out as she finishes demonstrating the new choreography, turning to us with a sigh of relief. "So, what did you guys think?" The girls clap and cheer, showing their support, and Cassie laughs, taking a bow. "Alright, ready to learn the choreo?"

An hour later, I'm on the verge of dying.

Okay, maybe not quite, but *really* close. Cassie always works my butt off. I like to think it's because I'm her favorite, but honestly, she's just all about perfection, pushing us until we've got it down.

"You killed me," I mutter, sprawling out on the cool wooden floor. "I'm officially deceased. Call the undertaker."

"Quit lying on the floor," she retorts, a hint of amusement in her voice.

I groan and shake my head. "Legs. Don't. Work."

"It's because you didn't stretch," she replies, prompting me to narrow my eyes as I sit up to face her. "Next time, don't be late, so you can properly warm up."

"I demand a refund," I say, shooting her a glare.

"The class is already finished," she replies, raising an eyebrow and resting a hand on her hip.

"I'm talking about the last four years. This is emotional torture. Scratch that, physical torture."

She shakes her head. "Cut the drama and head on home. Aren't you getting hungry by now?"

At the mention of food, my stomach rumbles, and I shoot her a surprised look. "How did you guess?"

She gives me a dry look. "You're always hungry."

I chuckle, admitting defeat. "Guilty as charged. So," I say, crossing my feet on the ground as I smirk at her. "Got any snacks?"

"Does this look like a restaurant to you?"

I shrug. "I feel like you owe me compensation for putting me through torture."

"I'm closing up in five," she says. "Are you sure you want to risk being stuck here all night?"

I laugh. "Alright, alright," I relent, pushing myself up from the floor and waving her goodbye.

By the time I pull into my driveway, I'm desperate for a shower. Sweat soaks my clothes, and I can't wait to peel them off. I slip my headphones over my ears as I step out of the car and hit play, letting the music fill my ears.

"Chris?" I call out as I step through the front door, pulling the headphones off and wrapping them around my neck.

No answer.

My gaze shifts to his closed bedroom door, and I figure he must still be asleep. He's been here for over a week now, but his sleep schedule is still all over the place.

I kick off my sneakers and head into my bedroom, swiftly pulling off my t-shirt, leaving only my sports bra on. I grab a fresh pair of sweats and a tank top, ready to take a steaming hot shower.

As I disconnect my headphones, the music starts playing from my phone's speaker. Humming along to the song, I leave my bedroom, and push open the bathroom door.

"Ughh. Fuck."

My head shoots up in confusion, and my phone slips from my grasp and clatter to the ground at the sight in front of me.

Chris' eyes widen in shock as he turns to face me, and I meet his gaze, taking in the sight of him standing in the shower, completely naked, with his fist wrapped around his cock.

13

This is not fucking happening

Christopher

My eyes squint open as light sneaks through the curtains. I groan and reach for my phone on the nightstand. Shit. It's almost noon, and I'm only just waking up. I thought a week back home would be enough to adjust to the time change, but I guess I'm still not there yet.

I was always one to stay up late anyway, especially when I'd sneak through Gabi's window to spend the night in her room. She never wanted to go to sleep when I was there. She used to get so excited to see me, as if her bed was just a second option for me. Little did she know, staying in her room was the only way I could fall asleep.

It took me a long time to get used to sleeping without her when I first moved to London, and even now it's still really hard. The night I moved in here, and we spent the night playing video games, was the best night's sleep I've had in years.

I glance at my phone, checking Gabi's location and seeing she's still at her dance class. With a groan, I lift myself out of bed and head out of the room.

The counters are cluttered with wine glasses from the guys coming over yesterday. They stayed late, and neither Gabi nor

I had the energy to deal with the mess. I groan at the sight, knowing I'll have to deal with it sooner or later.

Later.

Gabi probably won't be home for a while, so I have time to clean up before she's back.

But right now, I need some food. The place is too quiet without Gabi here, so I play some music on my phone, filling the room with noise. Then, I grab a bowl from the cabinet and fill it with some cereal.

I manage to take a couple of spoonfuls before the music on my phone abruptly cuts off, replaced by an incoming call. Glancing at the screen, I wonder if Gabi is calling me.

But it's not her.

My body tenses at the sight of the familiar name flashing on the caller ID, a knot forming in the pit of my stomach. Even miles away, he still manages to loom over me. He still has a hold on my life. On me.

Fuck him.

Will this ever stop. Will he continue to call me, and make my life a living hell every single fucking day? I thought I'd get rid of him when I moved to London, but here I am, four years later and he's still here, even when he's behind prison bars.

I press decline, and the music resumes. Staring down at the bowl, I drop my spoon inside, my appetite vanishing from the sickening feeling in my stomach.

With a sigh, I drop the bowl into the sink, along with the rest of the dishes left from yesterday, and make my way toward the bathroom, needing a shower to clear my head.

I close the bathroom door behind me, and hastily peel off my t-shirt, tossing it into the laundry basket along with my sweats and boxers.

As the warm water covers me, my body relaxes, and I brush my hair back, letting the water fall over my head. Glancing down, my eyes lock on Gabi's coconut shampoo, and I reach for the body wash beside it, lathering it over my skin.

I had forgotten what she smelled like when I left, but when I came back, it hit me like a wave, invading my senses every damn day.

Images of Gabi flood my mind constantly. No matter what I'm doing, she's always there, lingering in my thoughts. But this time, it's different. This time, it's images of her pinned beneath me that consume my thoughts, and I groan as I remember her full lips, parted, looking up at me with desire, her body pressed against mine.

"Fuck." I let out a groan, dropping my hand to my hardening cock, soaping it up before I give it a firm stroke. A moan escapes my lips as I picture the small metal bars poking through her sheer, white tank top.

She didn't have nipple piercings in high school. When did she get them? Why did she get them? I wonder what her tits looks like with them.

"God damn it." Before I can stop myself, I'm jerking off to thoughts of her. A montage of Gabi fills my mind, and groan after groan leaves my lips at the sight.

God, she's so fucking beautiful. I've always thought so. Ever since I met her. But it was a few years later that I realized how *hot* she was. How my body reacted to hers whenever she was close, how just one smile from her could make my heart pound out of my chest. I knew then I didn't just like her as a friend.

I felt so guilty—still do—thinking about her like that. She's my best friend. I'm not supposed to think of her this way, but fuck. I can't help it.

I remember Gabi asking me if Taylor was my type all those years ago. I don't know how to tell her that I don't have a type. *Gabi's* my type. Long, dark, gorgeous hair. Bright blue eyes I can't get enough of. A gorgeous body that felt so good underneath me. Full pink lips that I love whenever she smiles.

And now I'm thinking of her parting her pretty pink lips, and taking my cock between them.

"Ughh. Fuck," I groan as I stroke my cock, tighter this time, my balls drawing up so tight, they feel like they're about to explode.

But before I can finish, a loud crash makes me freeze. My eyes shoot open, and I turn my head to see Gabi standing outside the bathroom door. Her mouth is slightly parted, and her eyes are wide.

My hand drops, and my eyes widen in horror, mirroring hers.

This is not fucking happening.

Please, for the love of god, tell me this is just a dream and isn't actually happening.

"Fuck. I'm sorry," Gabi says, turning around, before hastily closing the bathroom door behind her.

Shit. Shit. Shit.

I quickly wash the soap off my body and turn the shower off before hopping out and drying myself off as best as I can. I catch my reflection in the mirror, and I stare back at it, wondering what the hell I'm going to do.

"Fuck," I grunt, closing my eyes.

Once I've pulled my clothes on, I hesitate for a second before opening the door, finding Gabi leaning against the back of the couch. Her attention shifts to me as she hears the door open, and our eyes lock together.

I see her throat move as she swallows, and I hold eye contact, neither of us knowing what to say. I want to know what she's thinking. Is she freaking out?

"I'm sorry," she finally blurts out. "I should have knocked, or—"

I shake my head, water dripping from my hair. "You don't need to be sorry, Gabi," I tell her. "I should have locked the door." I run a hand through my wet hair. I thought she'd be gone for a while, and I just didn't… think.

"I thought you were asleep," she says, lifting herself off the back of the couch. "I was playing music and didn't hear the shower, and—"

"It's fine," I interrupt her. She's definitely freaking out. I don't want this to change anything between us. She's clearly horrified by seeing me naked, and while the thought feels like a knife to the chest, I get it. We're best friends. Nothing more. Have been since we were twelve.

"Are you sure?" she asks, her eyebrows pulled together.

"Yeah," I reply, a smile tugging at her lips. I almost reach out and pull her into me, but after what happened, I think it's best if I don't.

She nods slightly, her eyelashes fluttering as she blinks. Her tongue darts out to wet her lips, and she lets out a deep breath. "You were…"

"Yeah." A muscle in my jaw ticks as we look at each other, and my heart beats faster.

119

A smirk tugs at her lips as she tilts her head. "You do that a lot?"

Fuck. Gabi thinking about me jacking off isn't helping the situation. "Can we not?" I ask with a groan, needing to adjust my cock that's hardening each second her eyes are on me.

Her smile widens a little and she tugs her bottom lip between her teeth. "What were you thinking about?" she asks, her eyebrows wagging at me.

Jesus. "Gabi," I warn her.

"What?" She blinks, innocently. "I can't ask?"

You. I want to tell her. *I was thinking about you.* I doubt she'd take it well, though.

"Did you…" Her eyes drift down to my cock, and in response it twitches in my pants.

"No," I reply, already knowing what she's asking. It's hard to come when my best friend of ten years walks in on me jerking off over her, and freaks out. I quickly turn around so she can't see the outline pressed against my pants, and start soaping up the dishes, hoping to distract myself from the awkward tension between us.

"Oh," I hear her voice behind me. I almost groan as a zing of pleasure curls up my spine. *Christ.* I'm not even looking at her, and she still affects me.

"Just drop it," I plead, though *I* won't stop thinking about this for a while.

"Dropped," she says, and I look over my shoulder at her. "Already forgotten," she repeats, holding her hands up.

I narrow my eyes at her, a smile playing at the corners of my lips at the expression on her face. "You're thinking about it, aren't you?"

She groans, burying her head in her hands. "It's impossible not to. You were *naked*."

"I know," I reply with a chuckle, drying off my hands before I turn to face her.

"It's just…" She lifts her head from her hands, peering up at me. "We've never seen each other like that before."

I blink, thinking back to yesterday. How I couldn't take my eyes off her tits pressed against the tank top, and the metal bars on them. "Yeah," I reply, my throat feeling dry. "It would be weird for us to." I lift my eyes to hers.

"Weird." She nods. "Right."

My eyes drop to the pile of clothes beside her. "You can go shower now," I tell her. "It's free now."

"Right," she says, blinking down at her clothes before she grabs them. "I'll just be—"

"Yep."

"And I'll lock the door."

I drop my brows. "I won't walk in, Gabi."

"Right. Of course not." She laughs, turns around, and walks toward the bathroom.

My head drops in a sigh, and my eyes catch on a piece of fabric lying on the back of the couch. My eyes narrow as I pick it up.

A lacy, white thong.

Fuck me.

"I just—"

I turn around, seeing Gabi standing outside the bathroom, eyes locked on the lacy fabric wrapped around my finger. "Forgot this?" I ask her, swallowing hard at the image of her wearing this.

Christ.

Someone fucking call an ambulance because I feel like I'm about to die of a hard-on.

"Sorry," she says with a chuckle before reaching over to grab it from my finger.

"It's fine," I manage to say, though my voice feels raspy.

Gabi nods silently, pressing her lips together, before turning around and closing the bathroom door behind her.

I groan when I feel my dick twitch in my pants.

It's not fucking fine.

14

Girls' night, plus James

Gabriella

I saw Chris's dick.

The image is burned into my mind. I keep replaying the moment I opened the bathroom door and found him standing there, head bowed, water dripping from his hair, his hand pressed against the shower tile, and his fist wrapped around his cock.

I can't stop thinking about the soft moan he let out as he jacked off. Or the way his eyes were screwed closed from pleasure.

I just can't *stop* thinking about it.

Which is why I need a drink now more than ever.

"I can't stay long," Madi says, tugging on my arm as we walk into the party.

"Me neither," Leila adds. "I have a photoshoot tomorrow and need to wake up early."

"Booo," I say, blowing a raspberry. "Come on, it's been so long since we had a girls' night." James clears his throat, making me chuckle. "Girls' night, plus James," I amend, and he shoots me a grin. "It's the first time in forever that you guys don't have your bodyguards with you."

"I'm with her," James says, nudging his shoulder against mine. "You guys need to learn how to live without your boyfriends," he adds with a scoff.

"And isn't that your boyfriend right over there?" Leila points out with a smirk, gesturing towards Carter Ruthers, a few feet away.

James rolls his eyes. "I live far away. Sue me for wanting to see my boyfriend every once in a while."

I let out a gasp, feigning hurt. "You're ditching me for a piece of ass?"

He nods unapologetically. "The hottest," he says with a wink. "I love you, but I gotta go." He blows me a kiss before turning around and heading off to his boyfriend.

"Traitor," I call out, watching him wrap his arms around Carter before they share a kiss. My lips lift in a smile seeing them so in love.

It's all I do these days. Watch people be in love, happy, and in relationships, while I hide the way I feel.

And drink.

Speaking of…

"We're getting drunk tonight," I announce to the girls, handing Madi and Rosie each a beer. Rosie wrinkles her nose at it but cracks it open anyway. I glance at Leila. "You want one?"

"Did you forget I stopped drinking?"

No, I haven't. Leila used to be my drinking buddy since the other two could never keep up with me, but she stopped when she started dating Aiden.

"You don't miss it?"

She shakes her head. "As long as I get to kiss Aiden without reminding him of every bad memory he's ever had with alcohol, then I'm good."

I smile at one of my best friends, seeing how in love she is and what she's willing to do for him. "Wow. That's so… sweet," I say, my brows rising. "Could never be me," I add before tipping back the can and gulping it down.

She chuckles. "You say that now, but I've seen how you are with Chris."

I blink, feeling my heart quicken at her words. "I don't know what you mean," I say, though I know she's fully aware of my feelings for Chris.

"Speaking of… Where's *your* bodyguard tonight?" Madeline asks.

I shrug, taking another sip. "He's at home." They exchange knowing smiles, and I narrow my eyes. "And he's not my bodyguard or anything else," I'm quick to clarify. "He's just my best friend."

"That's not all he is," Rosalie says. "We've all seen how you two are together."

My throat tightens as I shake my head. "There's nothing else going on," I insist, though the image of Chris in the shower yesterday flashes back into my mind. "He's my best friend. Has been since we were twelve, and I just so happened to see his dick yesterday. Vodka?"

"What?" Madeline asks, widening her eyes.

"Do you guys want vodka?" I repeat. "I feel like beer isn't doing the job."

"No," she says, giving me a dry look. "Say that again."

I let out a sigh. "I might have... caught a glimpse of his dick yesterday."

125

"Might have?" Leila asks, arching a brow. "What exactly happened?"

"I got back home," I start, my fingers fidgeting with the cap of the vodka bottle. "Went to take a shower, and there he was, standing under the water. And..." I pause, swallowing at the reminder. "He was jerking off."

"Oh my god."

"Yeah." I tip back the bottle and take a swig.

"What happened?" Leila asks, her curiosity piqued.

"I freaked out."

"You freaked out?" Madeline asks, furrowing.

"At first, yeah," I admit. "I just... We've never seen each other like that before, and it shocked the hell out of me."

"And then?" Madi asks.

I shrug. "I closed the door, and waited for him to come out, apologized for barging in, and made some jokes about it."

"Of course you did," Leila says, an amused smile playing on her lips. "And nothing else happened?"

"No," I confirm. "We're good. Best friends like always."

Madeline shoots me a skeptical look. "You guys have been best friends forever, and you saw him naked for the first time yesterday, and that's just it? You guys are back to normal?"

"I don't know what to tell you," I say, feeling my heart racing.

"Gabi, we're not idiots," Rosie says. "We can see you're into him."

I glance at Leila, seeing her smile back at me knowingly. She knows just how true that statement is. Last year, Aiden and I got close seeing as he's the only one who loves playing video games just as much as I do, and during that time, I confided in him about Chris. About everything that happened

126

between us, and how I felt about him. He told Leila—
obviously—and eventually I turned to her for advice and
support.

"She's not just into him," she says, lifting a brow at me.

Madi furrows her brows, turning her attention to Leila.
"What? What do you mean?"

Their gazes all settle on me, and I let out a deep exhale.
"I'm kind of in love with him?"

"Wait, love?" Madi asks, her eyes widening with surprise.

"For how long?" Rosalie chimes in, her eyes brimming
with curiosity.

"Sometimes it feels like I've been in love with him
forever," I admit, slumping back against the wall. "But I think
I realized it senior year of high school."

"That long?" Madi asks, her eyebrows raised.

I nod, a frown forming on my lips. "He left, and I felt so
lonely, and so sad," I say, squeezing my eyes shut. "I tried to
convince myself I just needed to move on, and be with other
people. But…" I pause, opening my eyes and looking down at
the drink in my hand. "There's just no moving on. Not from
him."

It's always going to be Chris.

"How do you know he doesn't feel the same?" Madi asks.
"If you just talked to him—"

"No," I interrupt, shaking my head. "I'm not doing that.
I'm not ruining everything between us for a stupid crush."

"Gabi." Her eyes soften, and she reaches out, tugging on
my hand. "It's not just a crush."

"Doesn't matter," I tell her, ripping my hand away. "I'm
not ruining our friendship. Chris means everything to me, and
if this is the only way I can have him, then so be it."

Madi sighs, nodding, but then she tilts her head. "And you're okay with that?"

Am I okay with pretending like my heart doesn't beat every second of the day for him? Am I okay with eventually watching him date someone, make a life with them while I silently harbor these feelings? *No*. "There's nothing more I can do," I say instead. "Besides, he's leaving again soon. There's no point."

"What about what happened yesterday?" Leila asks. "There's no way you guys can just go back to normal after that."

I feel a knot form in my stomach. I sure can't. Every second of what happened yesterday still lingers in my mind, and I don't think I'll forget it anytime soon. But this morning, when Chris woke me up, he acted like it never even happened. We talked, we joked, we played games like we always do.

I pour back the contents of my cup, and hold out the bottle. "Drink."

"Gabi."

"Please," I gulp. "I need to forget for a bit."

Rosie snatches the bottle from my hand, pouring its contents into a cup before downing it in one gulp. Her face contorts with disgust at the taste, but she manages a smile. "I haven't been drunk in a long time," she says, chuckling.

I returning her smile, and before I know it, Madi grabs the bottle and follows suit. "I'm only having this one drink," she insists with narrowed eyes.

15

Drunken confessions

Christopher

"Honey! I'm home." Gabi's slurred voice echoes through the dark room.

Blinking, I tear my eyes away from the TV as Gabi walks inside.

Maybe 'walks' is the wrong word.

She sways against the door, managing to close it before tripping and dropping to the ground.

"Gabi?"

"Obviously," she replies, with a scoff. "Were you expecting anyone else?"

When she mentioned going to a party with her friends tonight, I stayed home, just waiting for her. I paced the apartment all night, wishing time would speed up so I could see her again.

And the later it got, the more I was worried sick about her possibly hooking up with someone tonight. The thought made my stomach churn, and I did even more pacing, checking my phone to confirm that—yep—she was still at the party. I know eventually I'll have to face the reality of her dating someone, but I'm just not ready for it yet.

The memories of seeing her with other guys in high school still haunt me. I don't think I could handle witnessing it again.

So, I just waited. Hoping and praying she would be back home soon… alone. What I didn't expect was for her to be *this* drunk, though.

"What are you doing here?" I ask, rising from the couch to approach her.

"I live here," she says, frowning at me.

"I mean, why are you on the floor?" I clarify, leaning down to look at her. "It's three in the morning."

"Oh. I lost track of time," she says, chuckling as she tilts her head back against the door. "I just came back from the party," she explains, her words slurred.

"I know." Against my better judgment, I brush her hair behind her ear, meeting her gaze as I do. God, she's so fucking *pretty*. Even in this state, drunk and stumbling to the ground, she's the most stunning girl I've ever seen. "I stayed up, waiting for you."

She blinks, her lips curving up into the cutest smile. "You did?"

"Of course." It feels like all I ever do is wait for her. "You obviously need my help," I say, smiling down at her. "How much did you drink tonight?"

She shrugs. "I don't know. Not a lot." I shoot her a skeptical look, and she sighs. "Okay, fine. A lot."

I let out a laugh and wrap my arms around her waist. "Come on," I tell her, lifting her up into my arms.

"You're taking me to bed?" she asks, wiggling her brows at me. "Buy a girl dinner first."

"Jesus," I breathe out a laugh. "You're wasted."

"And you're so cute," she says, running her fingers through my hair. My face drops, and she looks down at me with her brows tugged together. "Why are you frowning?" she asks, gently smoothing two of her fingers over my eyebrows. "You don't like when I compliment you?"

I shake my head, carrying her to her bedroom. "I love when you compliment me."

"Then what's the problem?" she asks, wrapping her arms around my neck.

I look up, our eyes locking, and I sigh. "I just wish you were sober when you did."

"Why?" Her eyebrows furrow, and for a moment, I'm tempted to lean in and press my lips to hers. I want to kiss her *so* bad. She's so pretty, and smells so good, and is saying all the right things but...

"You won't remember it in the morning," I murmur, pushing her door open before I place her down on her bed.

I pull off her shoes, setting them neatly by her nightstand. When I glance up, her top is halfway across her chest before she pulls it off and flings it across the room.

I lift off my knee, feeling a rush of breathlessness, and quickly turn around.

"Why aren't you looking at me?" she asks.

I hesitate, feeling the heat rise in my cheeks. "You're... getting changed."

She sighs. "I saw you naked yesterday." *Christ*. I squeeze my eyes closed, trying to regain my composure. "Shouldn't we make it even?"

I glance behind my shoulder for a split second, catching a glimpse of Gabi's brown hair spilling over her chest, clad only in a lacy black bra. Fuck. Quickly, I snap my head back into place and grab one of her t-shirts, handing it to her. "Here," I tell her. "Put this on."

I feel her hand take the t-shirt from me, and I focus intently on a spot on the wall, trying to ignore the tension in the air, until I hear rustling from her sheets.

"Are you…" I turn around, slowly. "Are you decent?"

"Yeah."

I turn to her, finding her lying on her side, wearing a black t-shirt, her gaze locked on me. "Are you okay?" Gabi frowns, shaking her head. "What do you need?" I ask her, wondering if she wants water, food, or something else.

Her tongue darts out, moistening her lips. "You."

I blink. "What?"

She scoots back, pulling back the covers. "I want you here with me."

I run a hand through my hair, my head shaking, heart pounding. "Gabi, I don't think—"

"Please?" she interrupts, her big blue eyes pleading. "I feel safe with you."

I can't deny her. I never could. "Fine." She scoots back even more, and I hastily remove my hoodie before climbing into bed beside her. All night, I waited for her, my mind consumed by worst-case scenarios, but now, with her cuddled up against me, it feels like I can finally breathe again.

"You're so warm," she murmurs, trailing her hand over my chest. My heart pounds harder, faster, beating only for her. "And cozy." She nuzzles into my neck. "I missed this."

I wrap my arm around her, as I rub along her back, feeling the soft fabric of her t-shirt beneath my fingers. "I missed this too, pretty girl."

She inhales sharply, lifting her head to meet my gaze. "I love when you call me that."

Her eyes hold mine, and my heart pounds as they flicker down to my mouth.

I stop breathing.

Fuck.

Pressing a kiss to the top of her head, I murmur, "You need to sleep," closing my eyes before she can act on the impulse she'll undoubtedly regret in the morning.

Gabi is the most beautiful girl I've ever laid eyes on.

Even with her makeup smudged on her face, hair tousled against her pillow, and soft snores escaping her parted lips, I can't tear my gaze away from her.

I hardly slept last night, my eyes glued to her as she slept, making sure was okay and didn't puke.

But looking at her now, I feel more awake than ever.

It's really hard for me not to believe there's a God when something as beautiful as her exists.

A smile curves my lips as I reach out and brush her hair back, tucking it behind her ear. She lets out a groan as she stirs, starting to blink awake.

"Chris?" she murmurs, her voice thick with sleep.

I chuckle at the sight of her with one eye open and the other squeezed shut. "Expecting anyone else?"

"Oh, god," she groans, closing her eyes. "Please stop screaming."

"How much did you drink last night?" I ask, a little worried. She would get drunk in high school, but never like this.

"I don't even know," she says. "I lost count."

My brows dip. "Why the hell did you drink so much?"

She sighs, shaking her head. "I need a shower," she says, ignoring my question. "And food. And sleep."

"How about one thing at a time?" I offer.

"Food first."

"Good," I say with a smile. "Because I made pancakes."

She shoots up, sitting upright in bed. "You did?" The hangover seems to hit her all at once as she drops her head in her hands and groans. "Oh, fuck."

"You're such an idiot," I tease, sitting up alongside her.

She lifts her head and narrows her eyes at me. "Don't insult me when I'm dying."

"You're not dying, you drama queen."

She sighs. "Everyone calls me that. I'm starting to think I'm in the wrong profession."

"No way," I say, shaking my head. "You were born to dance."

A confused look crosses through her face. "You've seen me dance?"

I let out a snort. "You're kidding, right? Did you forget when you made me dance with you to Dancing Queen after we ate those brownies?"

She blinks. "You remember that?"

I breathe out a laugh, running my hand through my hair. "There isn't much I don't remember about you, Gabi." My jaw ticks. Even prom. I remember every painstaking detail of that night. "Come on," I say, lifting off her bed. "Let's get you fed before you fall asleep again."

She sighs. "I'm too tired to walk."

"Is that an excuse for me to carry you?" I ask her, arching a brow.

She lets out a dramatic gasp. "I would never do that," she says, but then she flashes me a grin. "But yes."

I chuckle, turning around. "Hop on."

I feel her legs wrap around my waist as she leans against me. I tighten my hold around her legs and stand up, carrying Gabi out of the bedroom with her draped over my back.

"Don't let me fall," she says, her lips brushing against my ear as she wraps her arms around my neck.

"I never will," I reassure her.

"Really?" she asks, and I glance up to see the mischievous look on her face, her brown hair spilling over her face. "What if I do this?" Her hands slide up my neck, and she starts to tickle me.

Little shit. "Then I'll just do this." I retaliate by moving my fingers up her bare legs, tickling her mercilessly, before I swing her around to my front.

"Oh my god," she laughs between breaths as I continue to tickle her. "Stop. Stop. Okay, fine. You win."

I stop tickling and chuckle, gazing up at her. "You gave up way too easily."

Her smile fades as our eyes meet, and it's just now that I realize I'm holding her in my arms, her bare legs wrapped around my waist, wearing nothing but underwear and a t-shirt, with her lips only a few inches from mine.

Her chest rises, her breathing quickening, and I can't rip my gaze away from her.

Fuck. I can't think. Not when she's right here in front of me, looking at me like she might want me as much as I want her.

Her nose scrunches up, and she sniffs the air. "Do you smell burning?"

My eyes widen as I remember the pancakes cooking on the stove. "Shit." I quickly set Gabi down and sprint toward the smoke filling the apartment.

"Jesus," she coughs, waving the smoke away from her face. "I thought you were good at cooking."

"I am," I try to defend myself as I turn off the stove and toss the pitch-black pancakes into the trash can.

"I beg to differ," she says, a hint of teasing in her tone. "I'm starting to regret asking you to move in." She sighs. "There are no benefits except burnt pancakes."

My eyes narrow, a playful smirk tugging at my lips. I can't help but think of other benefits I could offer her.

"I'll remember that the next time you want to cuddle," I joke.

"I was only kidding," she says with a laugh, wrapping her arms around my midsection. Her head tips up, gazing up at me. "You know I love living with you."

Yeah, so do I. Even if it is hard seeing her every day, and hiding my feelings constantly, I wouldn't give it up for anything in the world.

I'll miss this when I have to leave in September.

"Why don't you get in the shower while I finish up the pancakes," I tell her.

She groans. "I don't want to."

I chuckle at her lips pulled into a frown. "By the time you shower, the pancakes will be done."

136

She sighs, dropping her arms. "Fine. But you better hurry up."

I grin as she heads into her bedroom, grabbing a stack of clothes before disappearing into the bathroom.

With some batter still in the bowl, I begin scooping it onto the pan when my phone suddenly pings with a text. I quickly grab my phone from my pocket and check the screen.

Grayson:

> What the fuck did Gabi do to my girl?

I furrow my brows when I see he's typing again.

Grayson:

> Rosie is wasted. Granted, it's the cutest shit I've ever seen, but I don't think she's ever been this drunk in her life

> She's puked like three times, and counting

Lucas:

> I've never seen Madi that drunk either. I don't think she's even been drunk before

> What the hell happened last night?

> Chris, I know you see this

137

I glance at the pancakes sizzling in the pan, flipping them over with a spatula before quickly typing out a reply.

Chris:

I didn't go out last night

Grayson:

No shit. It was girls night or whatever

Lucas:

Plus James. He came home, arms linked with Madi, wasted as hell. He gets clingy when drunk, so he ended up cuddling me until he fell asleep.

Grayson:

That's adorable. Pics?

Lucas:

Fuck you. How is it dealing with puke?

Aiden:

HA. My girl doesn't drink bitches

Grayson:

> Where's the block button?
> You can't block me. I live with you

Aiden:

Grayson:

> Not if you keep being cocky

Aiden:

> Hey. I didn't make Rosie get drunk.
> Chris, man. Back me up here

Chris:

> Once again. Wasn't my fault

Aiden:

> No. But it was your girl

My lips twitch, reading it over. *My girl.*

Fuck. I run a hand through my hair. I really like the sound of that.

"I'm showered." I quickly tuck my phone into my pants at the sound of Gabi's voice, and when I lift my head, my heart stops.

Holy shit.

"Is that..." My voice trails off as I drink in the sight of her. "Is that my hoodie?" My mouth goes dry as I take in the sight of her wearing my clothes. My heart thuds loudly in my chest, and I struggle to compose myself.

Fuck that. There's no way I can calm myself down when she looks like *that*, fresh from the shower, with her wet hair draped over her shoulders, and my hoodie on her body.

"Yeah," she replies with a shrug, her voice soft. "It looked comfortable. Is that okay? I can take it off if you want?"

My heart races as I struggle to reply. "No!" *Fuck*. I clear my throat, shaking my head. "No," I say again like a normal human being this time. "Of course it's okay."

"Great," she says, plopping down onto the stool. "Now gimme the pancakes." I chuckle, placing the pancakes onto a plate before handing it over to her.

Gabi drowns them in syrup, and dives in. "God, these are so good," she says, going back for another bite. "I think I'll keep you around a little longer."

I smile, glad to see her happy, especially considering there was a time when she wasn't. I still remember that night vividly, the memory of it like a knife to my chest. It lives in my mind like a nightmare. I still remember her clinging to me, and pleading me not to leave. And now, I find myself saying the same words I uttered to her back then.

"I'll stay for however long you want me to."

16

A nightmare coming to life

Christopher

Age Seventeen

Peeking over the edge of the bushes, I see him open the door and call out my name. My heart hammers in my chest as I hold my breath, praying he doesn't find me. My lip throbs, and I swipe my thumb over it, flinching at the sight of blood smeared on my skin.

I lift my head when I hear the door close, sucking in a breath before stepping out of the bushes, but I stay hidden, ready to dive back in if he comes out again.

My bones are shaking, and I blow out a deep breath, desperately trying to calm down. My heart is racing, pounding against my chest.

Fuck.

I slap a hand on my chest, feeling like I can't breathe. My throat's tight, pulse is going nuts. My eyes burn as tears threaten to spill, and my stomach's doing somersaults. I squeeze my eyes shut, hoping it'll all just *stop*.

I'm so fucking sick of feeling like this.

I just want it to stop.

I lift my head, looking up at the window I sneak into way too often. The soft light of her lamp is on. *She's still awake.*

I take a deep breath, feeling my pulse start to calm itself down.

I shouldn't go there. I shouldn't bother her with all my problems. Even if she makes them all go away.

She just lost her *mom* for fucks sake.

A little over a week ago, her mom passed, and Gabi's been off since then. Quiet, sad, like the light went out in her eyes. Her dad's been worse than ever before. Considering the asshole abused his wife until the day she died, you would have thought he'd be happy she's no longer around. But he's not. I'm terrified one day he'll start taking his anger out on Gabi instead. She promised me he hasn't laid a hand on her, but the fear still lives in my mind.

Since Gabi's sister is away at college, she's all alone in that house, and even though going up there won't help her, I feel a need in my bones to just *be* with her.

I reach for the flask tucked in my pocket, taking a swig, craving the familiar burn that scorches my throat. My head's a jumble, voices shouting like a crowded room, and there's *no way out*. I screw my eyes shut, wishing it'd just shut up.

My hand throbs where the cut stings, and I wince as I pour some alcohol over it, feeling the pain intensify. "Fuck," I groan, biting down on my bottom lip as the fiery sting shoots through my body. I focus on the burn, wanting the pain, *needing* it, and I shake off the excess liquid pouring onto the cut as all the noise just leaves my brain.

I make my way to Gabi's front lawn, hands tucked tight in my pockets, eyes fixed on her window above. I run a hand through my hair, then close my eyes briefly.

I should probably go.

She doesn't need me.

But I need her. And my heart pounds against my chest at the thought of leaving. I don't want to. I want to be with her. Being near her makes everything else fade away, all the noise in my head just stops.

I glance to the side, spotting her dad's car parked nearby. He's probably inside. If he catches me here, he'll be pissed. He can't stand the sight of me, and the feeling's definitely mutual. He doesn't want me hanging out with Gabi, thinks I'm some kind of bad influence or whatever.

I almost laugh.

More like the other way around.

I take another sip, my gaze fixed on her window.

Tick. Tick. Tick.

The seconds pass by, each one dragging on like an eternity. I blow out a breath, slipping the flask back into my pocket.

Fuck it.

I can't stay away from her, no matter how much I probably should.

I grab onto the drain pipe, jumping up, trying not to make too much noise. If her dad ever catches me sneaking into his house... I don't even want to imagine it.

Pulling myself up, I wince as my hand grazes the pipe, biting down on my lip to stifle any sounds of pain. I manage to haul myself up and grab onto her window latch with one hand.

With a quiet creak, I lift the window, and slip inside. My hand reaches out to open her curtains, before I hop down to the ground, relieved to be inside her room.

I quickly scan the room, my eyes darting around, searching for any sign of Gabi. Shadows flicker across the walls in the dim light.

"Gabi," I whisper, trying to keep my voice low. "You in here?"

I take a hesitant step forward, the floorboards creaking beneath me. I spot her bed unmade, pillows scattered on the floor, and her record player left open, silent.

"Hey, you here?" I call out.

I hear sniffles, and my eyes widen. "Gabi?" I whisper, my heart clenching in my chest.

I round her bed, spotting Gabi sitting on the floor, her back hunched over. Her shoulders shake with quiet sobs, and my stomach twists with worry.

"Gabi? What's—"

And that's when I see it.

The blood.

My eyes widen as I take in the sight of thick, red liquid dripping down her arm. My gaze flicks to the razor blade lying beside her, and my stomach drops like a stone.

"What the fuck?"

I drop to the ground, grasping her face in my hands. Her glassy eyes meet mine, tears streaming down her cheeks. Her lips tremble, red and blotchy, as she shakes her head, repeating the same words over and over.

"I'm sorry. I'm sorry. I'm sorry."

"What the fuck, Gabi?" My voice cracks as I speak, my eyes blurry with tears. I glance down at her arm, covered in blood, and my heart lurches in my chest, nausea crawling up my throat.

"Chris," she cries out, tugging at my sweatshirt.

Fuck.

I cradle her face, pulling her close as she cries out, and I join her, tears streaming down my own cheeks. My heart feels like it's been ripped apart at the sight. What the hell did she fucking do?

I was so worried about some cuts and bruises when she was here, almost...

I blink away the tears, gripping Gabi's face in my hands, my biggest nightmare coming to life. "Why?" I choke out, my voice breaking. "Why the hell would you do this?" I ask her, feeling my heart lodged in my throat.

"I can't take it anymore," she cries out, her voice trembling with pain. "Living in this house with *him*, having to live without my mom, hating myself for being someone he despises, the thoughts in my head. They're so damn loud. I can't, Chris. *I can't.* I need it to stop. I need it all to just *stop.*"

My lips part on a shaky breath as I look down at her repeating the same words running through my mind. I curse under my breath, pulling her onto my lap, her blood staining my clothes, and I just hold her tight.

She cries out into my chest, and I squeeze my arms around her, just holding her close, trying to drown out her pain with my presence.

I feel so helpless, holding onto my lifeline while she's drowning, not even wanting to fight anymore.

"Why..." She shakes her head, her sobs breaking my heart as she pulls back to look at me. "Why are you still here, Chris?" she asks, her words coming out choked, trembling. "I'm a fucking mess," she spits out. "Why do you bother?"

"Because I'm not giving up on you," I grit out, holding her face firmly in my hands. "You're worth fighting for, even in

145

your darkest moments." I brush her hair back, and wipe away her tears. "You're not alone in this, Gabi. I'm here. I'll *always* be here for you."

Her lips part, shock written all over her face as she cries into my chest. I hold her tighter, lifting her off the ground and gently setting her on her bed.

I glance at her arm, the blood dried on her wrist, and swallow hard, fighting back the anger boiling inside me. I want to storm out there and kick his teeth for making Gabi feel like this. I want to kick myself for hesitating before I came up here. I should've been here sooner, before she...

I take a deep breath, grabbing some wipes and slowly clean her up. Each wince she makes feels like a punch to my gut, and my heart fucking *aches*.

When she's clean enough, I swallow hard, my hand trembling as I hover over her wrist. With a shaky breath, I lean down, pressing my lips against the cuts.

Her soft sobs and sniffles make my stomach drop, and I lift myself up, laying her back down against her pillow. I reach for her messy sheets, trying to straighten them out as best I can.

Gabi scoots over, and I focus on cleaning up the blood on the floor, clutching the razor blade tightly in my hand. I can't believe she...

I swallow down my anger, my jaw clenched tight, and quickly dispose of everything, making sure her dad doesn't find out. From the corner of my eye, I spot her earphones, and her phone lying on the ground, tossed aside like she threw them across the room. My expression tightens as I bend down to pick them up.

Turning back around, I catch Gabi's gaze on me, and her brows knit with worry. "It didn't work," she says, her eyes fixed on the earphones in my hand, her throat bobbing as she swallows. "It doesn't work when you're not here."

Air escapes my nose as my heart clenches in my chest, every part of me hurting for her. "I'm here now," I tell her, sliding into bed beside her.

I place one earbud in her ear, moving her hair out of the way, and then insert the other into my own ear. Fishing my phone out of my pocket, I plug it in, the music playing quietly in our ears.

Gabi's eyes meet mine, and a jumble of emotions knots up in my chest. Her lips drop into a frown, and it feels like a punch to the gut. "I don't want you to look at me differently," she says, her breath trembling.

I furrow my own brows in confusion. "What do you mean?"

She presses her lips together, closing her eyes briefly before meeting my gaze again. "I love the way you look at me," she says. "Like you see something I don't." Her eyebrows knit together, a hint of sadness in her expression. "Like you see something in me that's beautiful."

My heart races, and my stomach twists into knots. I wish she could see herself like I do. She'd never doubt how amazing she is to me, how much she matters, how I *need* her more than anything.

"Are you disgusted by me now?"

My expression tightens, her question catching me off guard. She's everything I've ever wanted. She's the reason I wake up in the morning when everything in my brain tells me not to. And here she is, asking me if she *disgusts* me.

"You could never disgust me," I tell her, feeling my heart lodged in my throat. "This changes nothing, Gabi." I wrap my arm around her, pulling her into me until I press my lips to her forehead. "You're still the strong, badass best friend I've always known."

She chokes out a laugh, and my heart flutters at the sound. She tilts her head back, tugging at her bottom lip. "I'm not feeling very strong right now," she admits, her gaze dropping. "I just... I thought it would make me feel better. I thought it would help, or go away, but it's still there." A heavy breath escapes her lips as she lifts her hand to press two fingers to the side of her head. "It's still *here*. I can't escape it. No matter how hard I try."

My stomach churns because... I know exactly how she feels. I know the thoughts swirling in my head, the feelings coursing through my veins, the pain and weight so heavy it makes me want to just... give up.

But the idea of Gabi ever feeling like that breaks me.

"You can't do that again, Gabi," I choke out, my voice strained. "The thought of you hurting fucking kills me." She lifts her gaze to meet mine, her lip quivering. "If you leave this earth..." I pause, my throat tightening as I swallow hard. The thought alone makes me sick to my stomach. I can't even entertain the idea of that ever happening. "I promise I won't be in it much longer."

"Chris," Gabi's voice trembles, tears brimming in her eyes as she shakes her head. "Please... don't say that."

"It's the truth," I grit out, my grip on her waist tightening. My heart feels like it's about to burst out of my chest, and I'm sure she can hear it. I gaze into her blue eyes, missing their usual sparkle. "Did you ever stop to think that maybe I need you?" I ask, watching her eyes widen in surprise. "I *need* you, Gabi. More than you can ever imagine."

Her lips part, and I'm locked into her eyes, feeling her pain deep in my chest. Footsteps echo outside, and I freeze, my eyes widening. I don't wanna leave her, but... "What if your dad—"

"Please don't leave me," she pleads, burying her head against my chest, letting out a heavy sigh. "I need you here."

I need her too. So fucking much. More than is healthy. "I won't," I promise, my voice firm. "I won't go." I'm not leaving this bed unless the bastard drags me out himself. "I'll stay for however long you want me to."

She snuggles closer, her breath warm against my chest. "It's quiet."

I stroke her back, the soft music playing in the earbud we share. "What is?"

"The noise in my head," she explains. "It quiets down when you're here."

I blow out a breath, closing my eyes as I feel her hand clutching my sweatshirt.

They completely fucking disappear whenever I'm with you.

17

Dancing in the kitchen

Gabriella

If music ever disappeared, I don't think I'd last very long.

Music is a part of my soul. It always has been. It's embedded into every part of me. I love how it fills my head and drowns out the noise and the million thoughts in my brain.

So, it's only natural that I have music playing while I make breakfast.

I'd worry about waking Chris up if I didn't know he can't sleep without music. We're the same that way. We're the same in so many ways. I remember the first time he placed his headphones over my ears and helped me drown out the noise.

My parents were arguing, and he just pulled me into bed and told me he wanted to show me a new song. I climbed into bed with him, tucked against his chest with the song blasting in the headphones, until I fell asleep.

I swallow hard, staring down at my plate as I remember the night I desperately tried to drown out the noise with music. Chris wasn't there, and I needed him so badly, and I needed to not *think* anymore. I wanted some peace. I wanted to take the pain away. And then I finally broke. But it didn't help. Nothing did, until Chris showed up in my room.

He's seen every part of me. Every ugly, stained part of me. But maybe that's why he doesn't feel the same way I do. He's seen too much.

I shake the thoughts away as I take a bite of my sandwich, swaying my hips to the music. But when I turn around, I freeze, seeing Chris leaning against his doorframe, arms crossed over his chest, a lazy smile on his lips.

"How long have you been there?" I ask, setting down my half-eaten sandwich on the plate beside my phone with the song still playing, and lower the volume to a soft hum.

"A while," he says with a shrug, stepping away from the door frame and moving closer to me. God, he looks so hot. His curly hair is all tousled from sleep, and I can't help but want to run my fingers through it. My eyes lingers on his t-shirt, noticing the way it hugs his muscles. I catch myself running my tongue over my bottom lip, wondering what he looks like underneath it all.

Sure, I saw him naked last week, but I was in shock, and focused on his thick cock wrapped in his fist. I didn't really have time to look at *all* of him.

But I *really* want to.

I want to know what he looks like without any clothes on, and how he feels against me.

"Why are you secretly watching me like a creep?" I tease, feeling the heat rise in my cheeks as I resist the urge to sneak another look at him.

He chuckles, and I can't help but smile at the sound. "I love watching you dance. You always look so free."

"Yeah," I say, letting out a breath. "I feel it too."

He nods, giving me a warm smile. "You're amazing, Gabs. I can't believe how fucking amazing my best friend is."

I scoff. "Stop feeding my ego," I joke, finishing off my sandwich.

"I'm serious. You're so talented."

Hearing Chris compliment me is everything I never knew I needed. I could survive on his compliments alone. "You really think so?"

He smiles, nodding as he crosses his arms, leaning against the fridge. "Of course I do. And it means more coming from me, since I was forced to be your dance partner," he says with a teasing smirk.

I let out a laugh, shaking my head. "I made you dance with me *once*," I say with an eye roll. "I was high, and you agreed." Chris chuckles, pressing his lips together. "Will you please let it go if I promise I won't ever ask you to do it again?"

He chuckles, a playful glint in his eyes as he wipes a hand down his mouth while watching me. "I didn't say I didn't like it."

"No?" I raise an eyebrow, intrigued.

He smirks, straightening up, and he picks up my phone, skipping songs until he finds a slow one. One my mom used to love. Tears prick my eyes when I hear it as Chris raises the volume, the melody filling the room, and extends his hand towards me.

"You're kidding," I say with a hint of disbelief.

He shakes his head. "I want you to know I'll dance with you whenever you want, Gabi."

"You're such an idiot," I say with a laugh, reaching out to take his hand.

With a swift motion, he shifts so his hand wraps around mine, while his other hand finds its place on my waist. My eyes widen in surprise when he extends his arm, spinning me around before swiftly pulling me back in and dipping me backward.

"You remember," I say, my lips parting at the sight of his smirk. "How the hell do you remember the steps? We were high as hell that day."

My heart immediately quickens, beating back to life, as if I was simply existing until his touch brought me to life. "I could never forget a moment between us," he says, his words sending a shiver down my spine.

His eyes lock with mine, and we stop dancing, just standing there, holding each other, our breaths mingling in the quiet. Time ticks by, but we don't move. I must be dreaming, or hallucinating because I swear his eyes dip to my mouth. And I swear he leans in, ready to—

"Phone," Chris says, pulling back as a ringing noise breaks the moment between us.

I close my eyes for a moment, feeling my heart race before I reach for my phone on the counter. "It's my sister," I say, my breaths a little heavier. "She's probably calling about the wedding."

"Oh right." Chris runs a hand through his hair, almost forgetting that's the whole reason he came to stay with me. "When it is again?"

"Saturday."

"Satu... As in three days from now?" His eyebrows shoot up. "Gabi, are you serious?"

I wince. "I uh... I might have also forgot to ask her if you could come."

"Jesus." He closes his eyes, breathing out a sigh. "You're the most unorganized person I've ever met."

I let out a laugh. "Well you don't love me for my organization skills," I joke.

His throat moves when he swallows. "You're right about that."

I don't even have time to dwell on what he meant by that, because the phone rings like crazy between us. "It won't be a big deal. I'll just tell her now," I reassure him, pressing the accept button.

"Have you packed yet?"

I let out a scoff at the sound of my sister's voice. "Hello to you, too."

My sister sighs. "I'm serious, Gabi. The wedding is in three days. Have you packed?"

"Of course not."

"What?" Her yell makes me pull my phone back, wincing at the noise deafening me. "What do you mean, of course not? It's in *three* days. Why the hell aren't you packed yet?"

"Because it takes an hour tops," I tell her.

"Oh god," my sister says, her voice trembling as if she's dying. "She's going to kill me." I roll my eyes. And everyone says *I'm* the dramatic one.

"Relax," Rachel, my sister's soon-to-be-wife, reassures her. "Everything's going to be fine. Gabi, pack your suitcase."

I scoff. "You can't tell me what to do. You're not my sister."

"I will be your sister-in-law soon," she says. "So you better listen to me, and pack your damn suitcase."

I let out a laugh. "Okay, fine, I'll pack tonight," I promise. "I'm only driving up on Friday, so I've still got time."

"Why on earth are you driving?" my sister asks. "I don't trust you to drive alone."

"I won't be alone," I say, shooting a glance at Chris. "I'm bringing a plus one."

"You're kidding," my sister says. "Please tell me she's kidding."

My eyebrows furrow. "I can't bring a plus one? It's my birth week."

"It's my wedding," she replies with emphasis. "There's no such thing as a birth week."

"Excuse me?" I scoff, shaking my head. "One day isn't enough to celebrate me. I need a whole week."

She groans. "I swear to god, Gabi, when you get married, I'm going to get my revenge."

I chuckle at her empty threat. "It's just one extra person," I try to bargain. "Chris is back for the summer, and I kind of invited him to come to the wedding with me," I explain, glancing at him, noticing him swallow nervously. "I was going to tell you sooner, but I just got caught up in spending time with him and—"

"Wait. Chris?" my sister asks, her voice tinged with surprise. "As in Christopher Hudson?"

"Yeah."

"You're with Chris?" she repeats, emphasizing his name.

"Yeah," I confirm, my smile widening when our eyes meet. "He's kind of living with me."

"Oh my god. I can't believe this. Put him on," my sister says.

I pull the phone away from my ear, leaning in to speak quietly to Chris. "She wants to talk to you," I murmur.

"Why?" Chris whispers back, his brows furrowing in confusion.

I give him a shrug. "I don't know."

He blinks, shaking his head. "What do I say?"

"I can hear you guys," my sister interjects.

Chris takes the phone out of my hand and holds it to his ear. "Hey, Jane," he greets, his lips widening. I hear my sister's excited screech from across the room, and Chris chuckles. "Yes, I'm back," he confirms, licking his lips before continuing, "Yep. I can't wait to see you, too."

My eyes light up with joy as he says goodbye and hangs up. "She said yes?" I guess.

"Yeah," he confirms with a chuckle, handing the phone back to me. "She said she was really excited to see me again after all these years."

"You know what this means, right?" I say, excitement bubbling in my voice.

"What?" he asks, arching a brow.

I shoot him a grin. "Road trip."

18

First to the finish line

Christopher

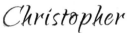

"I can't believe we're going to miss your birthday," Rosalie says with a frown, holding onto her boyfriend's arm.

"I know," Gabi replies with a sigh. "But my sister decided to outshine me and get married on my birth week," she adds, shrugging. "There's nothing I can do about it."

"Which is why we're celebrating today. Now, can we please go?" Madi asks impatiently.

"A summer without Gabi," Aiden muses, adjusting the cap on his head. "I wonder what that will be like."

"Quiet," Grayson retorts with a dry look.

Aiden chuckles, but Gabi shoots him a playful glare. "I heard that," she says. "And lucky for you, it won't be the whole summer. We're only going to be gone for a week or so."

Grayson lets out a scoff. "Still the longest I've gone without hearing your voice."

His girlfriend beside him giggles, covering her mouth with her hand. Gabi, however, just smiles. "Don't worry. I'll be sure to call you guys every day so you don't forget it."

"And you're going with her, I presume?" Aiden asks me.

I nod, sensing everyone's attention on me. "Yeah. It's kind of the whole reason I came here," I say with a nervous laugh, though that's not entirely true. I just came to see the girl standing beside me.

Aiden smirks, knowing that's bullshit, but he doesn't say anything.

"The cab's here," Madeline says, ushering us into the cab. "Everyone get in. We're going to be late."

"Calm down, princesa," her boyfriend says with a laugh, holding onto her arm. "We still have time."

She huffs out a breath. "Well, if someone hadn't taken their sweet ass time getting ready," she says, with a pointed glance at Gabi with narrowed eyes. "Then we would be there already."

Gabi scoffs, flicking her long brown hair behind her shoulder. "You can't rush perfection."

My face breaks out into a grin as I stare at her. She really is perfect. Her black baggy pants hanging low on her hips, and the white crop shows off her tanned stomach, blinging with the belly button piercing she got on her sixteenth birthday.

Madi pulls back the seats. "You two want to go to the back?" she asks, smirking at us. "It's more private there."

"What the hell are you playing at?" Gabi murmurs, furrowing her brows.

Madi glances at me for a second, before turning her attention back to Gabi. "Just trying to make room," she says with a smirk. "Is that a problem?"

Gabi turns to face me and I shrug in response. "That's fine."

"Great," Madi says, stepping aside so we can climb into the back.

Once we're all seated, she shuts the door, and the car drives off.

"Have any of you gone go karting before?" Grayson asks.

"Yeah. A couple of times," Gabi replies.

"I've gone a few times with Leila. I had so much fun beating her," he says, swinging an arm around her shoulder.

Leila scoffs. "Until today. I'm going to win."

"We'll see about that," he replies before leaning down to kiss her.

"I've gone once, with James. It was fun though," Lucas says. "Kinda wish he was here."

"Too bad he'd rather bang his boyfriend all day long," Gabi jokes.

Lucas shakes his head, laughing along.

"I actually haven't gone before," Madi says.

"Me neither," Rosie adds.

Grayson grins down at his girlfriend. "Another first to check off."

"Oh great," Gabi murmurs, glancing at me. "We've got a front row seat to their love making." She fake gags, and I let out a laugh.

"Do you really hate seeing them in love?" I ask her, genuinely curious.

She sighs, shaking her head slightly. "No," she admits. "I love to tease them and kid around, but I'm actually really happy for them. I like seeing them happy."

"But?" I prompt, knowing that's not all.

She sighs again, meeting my eyes just for a second before turning away, gazing out the window as the landscape breezes past us. "But I wish I could have that," she admits quietly. My chest tightens as she continues. "Sometimes I think that I'm

159

completely unlovable." Her voice wavers, and she lets out a soft laugh to cover it. "I think people like versions of myself I constructed for them. They like the jokes and the loud, funny Gabi. But if anyone ever really knew me..." She laughs bitterly. "They'd run the other way."

Her words break me. Does she really think she's unlovable? God, I just want to grab her and look her in the eyes and tell her I'm right here. I'm right here, and I love her so fucking much. I didn't even have a choice. It just *is*. Like the fabric of time itself.

I was destined to love this girl.

"That's not true," I say instead, stuffing all of the words I really want to say deep inside. "I'm right here, Gabi." *And I love you*. "And I'm not running away."

She turns her head, meeting my eyes. "You did once."

My stomach caves in. "Gabi—"

"And you will again," she says as if it's what I want to do. I *didn't* want to leave her when I ran. And I don't want to leave her next month.

I reach out, clutching her face in my hands. "I didn't leave because of you," I tell her, needing her to understand that she was the only reason I stayed as long as I did. "And I'm not running from you." Our eyes lock together, and I try to tell her everything I'm feeling with my eyes. "I'm here to stay for as long as you want me." My heart picks up pace, and I brush my thumb over her cheek. "I've seen every part of you, and..." I pause, closing my eyes. *I still love you.* "And we spoke almost every day for the last four years," I continue, snapping my eyes open. "That won't change just because I go to school somewhere else."

"Not every day."

160

I frown. "What?"

"You said we spoke almost every day whilst you were gone," she clarifies, shaking her head. "But after you left, you didn't speak to me for almost two weeks."

My jaw clenches, and I drop my hand. "That won't happen this time," I promise her.

She swallows. "How do I know that?" she asks. "I don't think I can handle it if I lose you."

Does she not understand that she's attached to every fiber of my being? It doesn't matter how much distance is between us. She's a part of me. Always has been. "You won't lose me," I assure her. "Ever. And the reason I didn't reach out had nothing to do with you. It was all my messed up issues."

Her brows dip. "You really expect me to believe that?"

I search her eyes, hoping to find a flicker of recognition, that she remembers what happened that night, but her gaze remains blank. My shoulders slump with disappointment.

"Of course," I say, trying to keep my voice steady. "It's the truth."

"We're here," Madeline says, breaking the moment as I lift my head to see the indoor go-karting arena through the window.

I glance back at Gabi, breathing out a sigh of relief when she gets out of the car. Following suit, I step out, hoping she believes me.

What happened that night had nothing to do with her. Sure, I was messed up over what went down between us, but I didn't leave because of it.

It was everything that happened after that was the problem.

"Woah," Rosie says, looking around the arena when we walk in.

It's huge, dark, and filled with blue lights all around. My eyes drift to Gabi when she looks behind her shoulder at me. "You want to race me?"

I let out a laugh, loving her competitive side. "I thought that's what we were doing."

She shakes her head. "Only between us," she says. "These guys will probably slow us down anyway."

Grayson twists his head. "Did you forget I basically breathe cars? I've been driving longer than any of you."

Gabi waves him off, turning her attention back to me. "So? What do you say?"

I grin. "You're on."

As we approach the go-karts, Grayson whistles in admiration. "Are you sure you want to do this, angel?" he asks Rosalie, securing a helmet on her head.

She beams, looking up at him. "Absolutely."

"Can she even drive?" Aiden asks.

Grayson places his own helmet on, glancing at his best friend. "I've given her a few lessons in my car," he replies with a shrug. "She's not bad."

Aiden's eyebrows shoot up. "Damn. You must really love her. You don't even let me *look* at your car for too long."

He smiles, his eyes softening as he glances at Rosie. "Yeah. I really do."

Once we're given the rundown and set up in the go-karts, I glance over at Gabi. "First to the finish line when the time runs out…"

"Wins," she finishes for me, her grin widening. "I can't wait to beat you, in real life this time."

I let out a laugh, pulling the front of my helmet down, and turn my attention to the track.

The buzzer goes off, and my foot presses down on the gas, the go-kart behind me zooming past. My eyes lock on the black leather jacket, noticing Grayson is right in front of me. I speed up, tapping the back of his go-kart, making him slow down enough for me to move past him.

"What the fuck?" I hear him mutter behind me.

I let out a laugh as I race beside Gabi, glancing at her for a second before she zooms past me, and turns the corner.

Another go kart races past me, and I make out the blonde hair under the helmet as Rosie hits the side of Gabi's go-kart. I take that as my advantage and catch up to her.

Her head twists and she lifts the front of her helmet. "Two more minutes," she calls out.

I lift my helmet, flashing her a smile. "And I'm right beside you."

"Not for long." She drops her helmet back, and speeds up, zooming past me once again.

I glance back, spotting the rest of the guys way behind, except for Grayson who's on my tail. I press down on the gas to speed up, tapping the breaks slightly when I need to turn the sharp corners.

"Ten."

I glance up, spotting the timer counting down. Shit. Time's running out.

I glance at the go-kart in front of me as Grayson zooms past me. I'm currently fourth on the leaderboard, but he's not who I'm racing with. I grip the steering wheel, and focus on the track, the pedal to the metal as I try to catch up to Gabi.

"Five."

I'm right behind her, and she glances back, noticing me. "Four."

I try to speed up, but Gabi spins to the right, blocking me from moving beside her.

I grin, taking that as my opportunity to spin the steering wheel to the left, driving the opposite way until I'm right beside her.

"Three."

Her go-kart revs as she speeds up, moving slightly in front of me.

"Two."

We're neck and neck, only a second away from the finish line. I see Gabi glance at me, and I smile under the helmet. I love how competitive she is. I love how much she wants to win, no matter what.

"One."

Lifting my foot off the gas, I watch as she zooms past me through the finish line, my own go-kart crossing it a second later.

The buzzer goes off as we slow our go-karts down, and come to a stop.

"I won," Rosie says, lifting out of her go-kart, her pink dress swaying as she rips off her helmet and runs toward Grayson. "I actually won."

He catches her like it's nothing and grins, bringing their lips together. "I'm so fucking proud of you, angel." He grabs her face in his hands looking at her like she's everything. *I know that feeling well.* "Looks like my lessons actually paid off."

I turn my attention to Gabi as she gets off the go-kart, and lifts the front of her helmet, eyes locked on me. "I beat you," she says with a grin.

"You did." I blow out a breath, ripping off my helmet before I approach her. "Congrats."

She blinks up at me, her beautiful face in the helmet. "I actually won. I didn't think I'd win."

I let out a laugh, taking off the helmet from her head, and drop it to the ground. My hands smooth out her hair. "You were talking shit the whole time," I say with a raised brow.

She sighs. "I know. I *wanted* to win, but I didn't think I would."

I smile, unable to stop myself before I lean in, and press my lips to her forehead. "You should always believe in yourself, pretty girl."

She looks up at me when I pull back, and our eyes lock together like a magnet.

"I can't believe you're leaving tomorrow," I hear Rosie say.

I tear my eyes off Gabi, looking at all of the guys, staring back at us. I meet Aiden's eye, and the guy is smirking.

"Actually, we need to leave right now," Gabi says, glancing up at me. "We still have to pack, and the drive there is quite far."

"You're not packed?" Madi asks, her eyes widened in shock. She shakes her head. "Why am I even asking? Of course you're not."

Gabi rolls her eyes. "There's plenty of time," she says. "Besides, Chris already volunteered to help me."

I blink, looking down at her. "I did?"

"Of course," she says with a sweet smile that melts my insides. "You know I'm hopeless without you." She tugs on my hand, pulling us out toward the exit. "Let's go."

I wave the guys goodbye as Gabi walks on ahead of me, and Aiden nudges me when I approach him. "I saw that," he says.

I furrow my brows. "Saw what?"

He gestures toward Gabi. "You slowed down at the finish line." He breaks out into a grin. "Why did you do that?"

I can't even deny it. I just let out a laugh and look at Gabi seeing her smile at her friends. I knew I could have won back there, but… "Look how happy she is."

19

Road trips and dangerous
dares

Christopher

"Look. No hands." Gabi lifts both hands from the steering wheel, grinning at me.

"Jesus," I curse, quickly grabbing the steering wheel. "As much as I'd love to die with you, I'd rather live a few more years first."

She laughs, dropping her hands back onto the wheel. "You're being dramatic. We won't die." But then her smile falters, and she glances at me. "You'd want to die with me?"

I blink, meeting her gaze. *I want to do everything with you.* "I mean, if I *had* to die, then yeah, I'd want you by my side." I pause, swallowing all the other words I want to say to her. "You know how terrified I am of death." I chuckle nervously. "But I think it'd be a little less scary if I was with you," I admit with a shrug.

Gabi smiles, her eyes twinkling in the night sky and she shuffles in her seat, glancing back at the road, as the music fills the car. The silence hangs in the air, and a twinge of worry crosses me. Gabi's never quiet.

"Are you okay?" I ask, glancing at her. "It's getting pretty late. Do you want me to drive for a little while?"

She shakes her head, a smirk playing on her lips. "No. I like having you as my passenger princess," she teases.

I let out a scoff. "Dick."

"Where?" she says, craning her neck to look out of both windows.

I shake my head, chuckling. We've been on the road all day, taking turns driving, and I can tell she's getting a bit delirious. "I don't know why the hell I agreed to spend a whole day in a car with you," I say with a sigh.

"Because you can't say no to me," she replies, her grin mischievous.

No, I really can't. I have a feeling I'd do whatever she asked me to.

I have done in the past.

Raindrops begin to patter against the windshield, one after the other. The sound of the rain grows louder as it picks up speed, coming down hard onto the glass. Gabi reaches out and flicks on the wipers, trying to focus on the blurry road.

"I think we should pull over," I say, raising my voice slightly over the sound of the rain. "It's pouring, and it's getting late. We should rest for a bit, and I can take over driving on the way back."

"What?" She shakes her head adamantly. "No way. It's my turn to drive. Besides, I practically dragged you along with me. The least I can do is get us there."

I scoff. "You did not drag me." She really doesn't seem to understand that I'd do *anything* for her. "I wanted to come, Gabi."

"No, you didn't," she says, stealing a glance at me. "I practically begged you to come with me so I wouldn't have to be alone." She sighs. "You just felt sorry for me."

My lips drop into a frown. Does she really believe that? "That's the last thing I feel for you," I tell her honestly. "I wanted to see you." She turns her attention to me, and my throat tightens with nerves. "I came because I wanted to see you, to be near you. I missed you like crazy, and I wanted to spend time with you."

She holds my gaze, and her lips part. Sometimes, I think she could feel the same as I do. But I've been there before, and I'm not going back. Not when it could shatter my heart, and our friendship into a million tiny pieces.

I clear my throat, tearing my gaze away from her to glance at the road. "Pull over down there," I tell her, gesturing towards the gas station at the side of the road. "We can grab some snacks and rest until the rain lets up."

She groans in agreement and nods. "Yes, please. I'm starving."

I chuckle. "I know. I can tell."

She blinks, tilting her head. "How?"

Gabi gets this drowsy look in her eyes whenever she's hungry. "I just can," I say with a shrug, not wanting to reveal just how well I know her. It surprises me that she thinks I don't know her. She acts like she wasn't the biggest part of my life. I know everything about this girl. More than I should. But that doesn't stop me from thinking about her every damn day.

Every time I see a Ferris wheel it reminds me of her. Every time I see a brownie, it reminds me of her. Of us. And then there are the songs I can't listen to without hearing her. Without thinking of her.

Gabi pulls over into the gas station and brings the car to a stop, then leans her head back against the car seat, letting out a sigh. "How much longer until we're there?" she asks, her voice filled with exhaustion.

I quickly check the map. "About three more hours," I reply.

"Ugh," she groans, closing her eyes. "Why did I think driving was a good idea?"

I laugh, shaking my head. "Because you're too stubborn to go on a plane. Why didn't you, by the way?"

"I'm not stubborn. You didn't have a ticket, and I really wanted you there, and I guess I was…" She sighs, closing her eyes for just a second. "I was scared," she admits.

Scared? Gabi? "Scared of what?"

She glances at me with a glare. "What are people scared of when flying, Chris? Falling, crashing, *dying*."

I know I shouldn't, but my lips lift a little.

Gabi is scared of dying.

Most people wouldn't even bat an eyelash at that. Many people are scared of dying, but I remember a time when she wasn't. When she wished for it.

"Are you…" She narrows her eyes at me, suspicion evident in her tone. "Smiling?"

I quickly wipe my hand across my mouth, trying to hide my smile. "Come on. Let's get you fed before you eat me," I joke.

She flashes me a grin that warms my heart. "I wouldn't eat you," she says, tapping my cheek playfully. "Your face is too pretty for that."

I laugh, knowing she's just joking, but my chest betrays me, fluttering like crazy.

Gabi opens her car door, and I follow suit, immediately feeling the pouring rain drenching me as soon as I step out of the car. I glance at Gabi, seeing the water completely drenching her. "Fuck," I mutter, feeling myself getting soaked with each passing second. "Run." She pulls her hoodie over her head, and sprints toward the gas station. I follow right behind her the rain soaking me to the bone until we finally make it inside.

"Holy shit," she says when we're finally out of the rain. "I'm so wet." She lets out a sweet laugh, and I can't help but look down at her, taking in the sight of the most beautiful girl I have ever been lucky enough to see in my lifetime.

She has her navy blue hoodie pulled over her head, wet strands of hair clinging to her face. Water droplets coat her pale skin, and the cold rain makes her lips look puffy and red.

I realize I'm still staring at her when she licks her lips, and like a moth to a flame, my eyes drift down to them. I swallow down the groan building in my throat, forcing myself to tear my eyes away from her.

Fuck.

Why her?

Why couldn't I fall in love with someone else?

Why the fuck do I want the one person who doesn't want me back?

I run a hand through my sopping wet hair, then step back, and turn around to grab a few snacks. Gabi does the same, grabbing some candy and chips, along with a bottle of vodka.

"Really?" I say with a raised eyebrow.

She shrugs. "If we're not driving, we might as well have a little fun." She winks at me before placing everything onto the counter. "Oh crap." She widens her eyes at me. "I left my purse in the car."

"I've got you," I tell her, pulling out my wallet.

She places her hand on mine, shaking her head. "I can run out and grab it," she says.

I wave her off, placing ten bucks on the counter. "It's fine, Gabi," I assure her. "Besides, what are best friends for?" I flash her a grin.

"You're all set," the cashier says, catching my attention.

"Thanks." I quickly stuff the snacks into a plastic bag and head toward the front door, glancing at Gabi. "Are you ready?" I ask her.

She grins, pulling her hood up. "Let's go."

As soon as we swing open the door, the cold, night air hits my skin, and the rain pours down, soaking us within seconds. We hurry toward the car, laughing as the rain splashes around us, and we quickly slam the doors shut as soon as we're inside.

"Fuck," I mutter, shaking the water from my hair. "The seats are drenched."

Gabi lets out a strained laugh. "I bet you're used to that happening."

I furrow my brows in confusion. "What do you mean?"

"With girls," she says with a smirk, making my frown deepen. "I'm sure you've had a girl in the back of your car, right?" she asks, unscrewing the cap of the bottle of vodka before she takes a gulp.

My jaw tightens, the muscle ticking. I hate when she brings up other girls as if she isn't the only one occupying my every thought.

"Let's play a game," she says, holding out the bottle to me.

I eye the bottle, hesitating for a moment before finally grabbing it from her. Screw it. I take a sip, meeting her gaze. "What do you have in mind?"

"Truth or dare," she says with a grin.

A laugh bubbles out of me. Of course.

"Truth," I tell her with a smirk.

She drums her fingers on her thighs, lost in thought, and then tilts her head. "When was the last time you kissed someone?"

My smile slips, and I let out a sigh, feeling my body tense up. "Can I pass?"

"Nope," she says, taking another sip of vodka. "You need to answer."

The muscle in my jaw ticks as my teeth grind together. I really don't want to talk about this, but I know she won't let it go. "Two years ago," I tell her, locking eyes with her.

She furrows her brows, blinking. "In London?"

"Yeah." I swallow, my throat feeling tighten.

"Oh." She blinks a few times. A moment of silence hangs between us before she tilts her head slightly, her brows furrowing. "I thought you said you didn't date anyone."

Fuck. I hate talking about this. "I didn't."

She sucks in a breath, nodding. "Right." She shakes her head and laughs, but it sounds off. Taking another sip, she gulps down the alcohol before passing me the bottle. "Your turn," she says.

I take a swig and look at her, my eyes tracing her features. "Truth or dare?"

She chuckles and brings her legs up, resting her chin on her knees. "You don't even need to ask."

My head tilts as my lips lift into a smile. "I dare you to let me drive the rest of the way."

Her brows furrow in confusion. "That isn't a punishment."

"I never said it was."

She sighs, tilting her head back against the headrest. "You're too good for this world," she murmurs, almost to herself. Her head turns slightly, blue eyes landing on me. "Too good for me."

"Why do you say that?"

She shrugs, grabbing the bottle from me before taking another gulp. My jaw tightens, and I almost reach out to stop her. I don't want her to get too drunk. "I don't know," she says, licking the alcohol from her lips. "You're so kind, and loving, and…" Her eyes flick to me. "The best person to have around. And I'm—"

"You're what?" I interrupt.

"I'm a mess," she whispers, her bottom lip trembling.

"What?" My heart pounds in my chest. "Why the fuck would you say that, Gabi?"

"Because it's true," she says with a shrug, taking another sip. "My father hates me, I pushed you away. I deserve to be alone."

"No." I grasp her face in my hands, turning it to look directly into her eyes. "You hear me? No. It's not your fault that your piece of shit father can't see how amazing you are. That's on him, not you." My thumb brushes over her pulse point below her ear. "And you did not push me away," I repeat, because it breaks my heart that she still believes that. "I wanted to stay for *you*."

"Then why did you leave?" she asks, her voice rising. "Why did you leave that night?"

I drop my hand away from her face, closing my eyes briefly. "Gabi—"

174

"Tell me," she insists. I run my hand through my hair, gripping the strands tightly in frustration. "You never used to hide anything from me."

"And neither did you," I say, snapping my eyes open.

She furrows her brows. "What are you talking about?"

"What the hell did you talk to Aiden about that you couldn't tell me?" I ask with a bite in my voice, my heart racing. Fuck. The alcohol was not a good idea.

"You really want to know?" she asks, leaning forward.

I let out a bitter laugh. "Gabi, I want to know *everything* about you. I want to know why you felt like you couldn't talk to me."

"I talked about *you*."

I blink in surprise. "What?"

Gabi's eyes lock with mine, and she shakes her head slightly. "I told him all about you. All our stories. How my life starts and ends with you." Her eyes flick away from mine. "I told him you were always there for me, even if you had every reason not to be, and how…" She squeezes her eyes closed, shaking her head. "I missed you like crazy, Chris, and I just needed to talk."

"You could have talked to me," I say, my expression twisted with confusion.

She shakes her head, eyes dropping to the floor. "You had a whole life away from me. I didn't want you to get caught up in my mess."

"Stop it." I lift her chin with my hand, clutching her face. "Stop saying you're a mess and acting like you're a burden in my life."

Her eyes start to well up with tears, and my heart sinks. "Aren't I?" she asks quietly.

175

"No," I say firmly. "You're many things, but you're not a burden. You're the reason I wake up every morning." Her eyes widen in surprise, and I hesitate for a moment but I continue, needing her to understand just how important she is to me. "I need you, Gabi. More than you know," I admit, all the words I want to say caught in the back of my throat. I swallow hard, shaking my head. "You're the reason I want to live."

Her brows dip, concern etched into her features. "You need me that much?"

I tighten my hold on her, brushing her hair back behind her ear as I gaze into her blue eyes. "So much it hurts."

Our eyes lock together, and her lips part. I didn't even realize how close I was to her until I catch the scent of alcohol on her breath. I pull back when I see her eyes glazing over. Fuck, she's drunk.

"Your turn," I say, leaning my head back against the headrest.

"Chris—"

"Your turn, Gabi," I say, my hand running through my hair in frustration, realizing I said too much.

She sniffs, wiping the tears that slipped down her cheek. "Truth or dare?"

She sounds determined, and I know she's going to ask more questions. Questions I'm not prepared to answer just yet.

"Dare."

She raises an eyebrow. "Really?" she asks. She knows I don't back down from a dare, which is why I rarely choose it.

I nod, pressing my lips together. Whatever she tells me to do has to be better than answering her questions about that night.

She unscrews the bottle cap, takes a sip and lets out a deep breath. "I dare you to strip."

"Gabi," I warn. She's drunk, and sad, and this is a recipe for disaster. I start to shake my head, but she stops me.

"You never back down," she reminds me with a smirk. "Strip."

My cock twitches at the command, and I force myself to remain calm. "It's cold."

She replies by turning up the heater, and leans back, eyes raking over my body. "You don't need to get naked. Again." She smirks, her lips curling up at the edges. "You can just take your hoodie off."

This is going to kill me.

I know I shouldn't. She's drunk, and doesn't know what she's doing. This is only going to hurt me in the process. But the look in her eyes is hard to ignore as I pull my hoodie, and t-shirt over the back of my head, tossing them onto the back seat.

Gabi's eyes land on me, and she sucks in a breath, her eyes roaming over my body. Heat rushes through me at the intensity of her eyes on me, and my heart quickens. She's never looked at me like that before.

She's drunk, I remind myself. *It's just a reaction to the alcohol.*

Her eyes drop to my stomach, and I feel her gaze linger on the scar. She reaches out, her fingers tracing along the rough line on my lower abdomen, and I draw in a sharp breath. Her brows furrow in concern.

177

"When did this happen?" she whispers.

"A long time ago," I reply, swallowing the lump in my throat.

"Does it hurt?" she asks, lifting her head to look up at me.

"No," I assure her, meeting her eyes. "Not anymore."

Luckily, she doesn't ask any questions, instead focusing on running her hands over my chest, feeling the ripple of muscles underneath. "I didn't know you had abs," she remarks, her tongue darting out to lick her bottom lip.

My cock twitches in my pants at the sight, and I beg to all the gods out there that she doesn't look down, or this is going to get even more awkward.

I swallow, taking a deep breath as her eyes continue to trace over my chest. "You've never seen me without my clothes," I admit. Her eyes flick up to meet mine, a hint of amusement in them. "Aside from that day," I add.

She chuckles slightly, her eyes dropping to my stomach again. "You've been working out," she observes, her tone almost questioning. Her hand continues to trace the ripples on my stomach, and her eyes lock on mine. "I bet the girls in London were all over you."

She lifts her hand, her fingers tracing lightly over my chest, sending a shiver down my spine. I swallow hard, feeling a rush of warmth at her touch as she moves even closer. "Chris?" she whispers.

"Hmm?"

"Truth or dare?"

Fuck. I can't think. My brain is foggy, it's hot in here, and I want her so bad that I can't remember why this is a bad idea.

Because she'll forget.

I suck in a breath, wrapping my arm around her hand, halting her. "I think it's time we stop."

She frowns, shaking her head. "I don't want to stop."

I rake a hand through my hair. "You're drunk," I remind her.

She shrugs. "Hardly."

My jaw ticks. "You're two sips away from doing something you'll regret tomorrow."

Her eyes narrow slightly. "How do you know I'll regret it?"

Because you have before.

I reach into the back seat, grabbing my hoodie and slip it back on. "Just get some rest," I say quietly, avoiding her eyes. "I'll drive us back in the morning."

Gabi doesn't reply. She kicks off her shoes and turns away from me, staring out of the window until we both fall asleep.

20

Promposal

Gabriella

Age Eighteen

Dripping wet and reeking of chlorine, I sit down next to Chris, grabbing a towel beside him. "You've been sitting here all night," I tell him, arching a brow. "Are you not going to jump in?"

He shakes his head, a small smile playing on his lips as he rakes his eyes down my body, following the stream of water. My heart races, and I feel a blush creeping up my skin as his eyes linger on me. "I'm not big on swimming."

A soft chuckle escapes me as I dry my hair with the towel. "Then why even come to a pool party?"

He shrugs, his gaze locked with mine as he blows out a cloud of smoke. "Because you're here."

I suck in a breath, my heart flipping in my chest. I know he probably doesn't mean anything by that. Stacy invited me to her pool party since her parents would be out of town, and of course, I invited Chris to come along. He goes everywhere with me. We're always together. He's my best friend. But… I can't help the thoughts in my mind, wishing his words and his eyes on me meant something more.

I don't know when these feelings started, but one day I woke up and he went from being my best friend to… *Chris*.

And I don't know what to do about it.

A part of me wants to tell him. A part of me wants to tilt my head up when he's in my bed and we're cuddling, and press my lips to his. I think about it all the time. How it'd feel, if he'd pull away… but nausea creeps up my throat at the thought. He's my best friend. He means more to me than anyone else in this world, and the possibility of him rejecting me and ruining our friendship breaks me.

I can't take that chance. Not unless I know he feels the same.

"So," I say, reaching for the blunt in his hand before I take a drag. "Have you decided who you're going to prom with?"

There's only two weeks until prom, and exactly six weeks until I can finally say goodbye to this town and escape to Redfield.

"Don't know," Chris says with a shrug, taking the blunt from me. "Not really my scene."

"What?" I shake my head. "C'mon. It's a night of dancing and drinking." I wag my eyebrows at him. "What could be more fun than that?"

Chris's smile widens and he lets out a soft laugh. "Maybe," he says, blowing out the smoke.

Maybe.

My hope increases. "Really? Who would you go with?"

Chris turns his eyes to me, holding my gaze. I note his jaw ticking as he stares into my eyes, but then he blows out a breath, and shakes his head. "I don't know."

I swallow down my disappointment, staring out at the pool. My eyes lock on Amy whose eyes are strained on Chris.

181

"Amy might want to go with you," I tell him, turning my head back to Chris who frowns.

"Amy?" he asks, arching a brow. "Where the hell did you hear that from?"

I shrug, glancing down to fix my bikini top, and I can't help but notice Chris' eyes on me when I do. "Earlier," I tell him. "I heard her tell Stacy you were hot."

I remember swinging my head when I heard Chris's name coming from Amy's mouth, and feeling sick to my stomach when I heard her tell her friends she wanted Chris to ask her to prom.

Chris arches a brow. "She did?"

His expression makes me blink. He's never shown interest in her, or any other girls really, but the way he's acting, makes me wonder if part of him is interested. I mean, Amy is beautiful. Short blonde hair, long legs, cute face. They'd look pretty good together. My stomach churns at the thought, but I nod all the same.

"Yeah." I swallow the feelings bubbling in my stomach. "Are you thinking of going with her?"

Chris shakes his head. "I don't even know the girl, Gabi."

"You could get to know her at prom," I say with a shrug.

His brows dip, and he shakes his head. "Why are you pushing this so much?"

I don't know. Even though the thought of Chris being with anyone else makes me feel sick, seeing him with someone else might help me get over him.

The thing is… I don't think getting over Chris will ever happen.

I shrug, glancing back at the pool. "I just don't want you missing out if you're interested in her."

"Well, I'm not."

I snap my attention back to him, my heart fluttering. "No?"

His eyes lock on mine. "No."

The fluttering in my stomach intensifies. "Are you… interested in anyone else?" I ask, my pulse pounding in my throat.

Chris lets out a sigh, putting out his blunt. "You're really inquisitive today."

"It's just a question," I say with a shrug, trying to remain cool. "No big deal."

"Are *you*?" he asks.

I blink. "Am I what?"

"Interested in anyone?"

I shrug. "Not really."

Chris' eyes lock on mine, and he nods, breathing out a sigh. "Yeah," he says, raking a hand through his hair. "Me neither."

"No?" I ask, frowning. "So there's *no one* you want to go to prom with?"

He stares at me, his jaw ticking. "No."

"Oh." *Not even me?* I want to ask. But I don't. It's obvious the thought hasn't crossed his mind. I swallow down, nodding, and blow out a breath. "Luke asked me."

Chris's brows lift. "To prom?"

"Yeah," I reply, with a shrug, glancing back at Luke in the pool. He's splashing water at the girls and laughing, turning his eyes on me. He shoots me a wink, and I turn around, facing Chris whose jaw is tense. "He asked me earlier," I tell him. "In the pool."

His eyes flick to mine, and he shakes his head slightly. "You told me you weren't interested in anyone."

"I'm not."

"But you're going with Luke?" he asks, his eyes hardened.

"Well, it's not like anyone else asked me," I say, my voice raising slightly.

He stares back at me, his lips opening a little before he shuts them again, breathing out a sigh as he closes his eyes.

I want *him* to ask me. I want to go with Chris. There's no one in the whole word I'd rather go to prom with than Chris.

But he doesn't want me.

Not like I want him.

My head lifts when Chris stands up and pulls his hood up. "I think I'm going to leave."

My frown deepens. "Already? But—"

"This isn't really my scene, Gabi. And besides, it looks like you have company now, so…" Chris looks behind me, and I turn back, seeing him look at Luke. "You don't need me anymore."

That's not true. I need him. He's the only person I need so badly I can't breathe when he's not around sometimes. "Chris," I say, standing up, and wrap my hand around his wrist.

"It's fine, Gabi," he says, slowly releasing his wrist from my hold. "It's late, and…" He sighs. "Have fun." He shoots me a smile, and turns around, heading back into Stacy's house.

"Chris," I call out again before he goes in. He turns his head over his shoulder. "Will I see you tonight?" I ask him, not knowing where we stand after tonight. Even if Chris doesn't feel the same, I still love him, and I still feel safe with him, and I want to spend the night in his arms.

Chris lets out a shrug, and glances back at the pool. "Maybe you can stay with Luke tonight."

He walks away, and it breaks my heart.

21

You can always cuddle me

Gabriella

"You're late," my sister says as we walk into the hotel lobby, her eyes narrowing.

"I'm a day early," I reply with a shrug. "That's a win in my book."

She lets out a sigh, shaking her head. "You were supposed to be here hours ago," she mutters, glancing out the window. "The sun is setting for crying out loud."

"Sorry," Chris says, trailing behind me with our suitcases. "That was my fault." He stops beside me, giving me a sheepish glance. "I, uh, told Gabi we should stop for a while since it was raining, and we were pretty tired."

And then I went ahead and nearly fucked everything up. Like always.

My sister grins so wide, I'm almost jealous. "Christopher Hudson," she says warmly.

"Yep," Chris says, letting out a nervous laugh as he brushes his hair back. The rain has left it even messier and curlier, and I'm losing my goddamn mind. "It's me."

"Wow." My sister shakes her head in amazement. "Look at you. You're a man now."

Chris laughs. "I always was."

She shakes her head again, humming thoughtfully. "You were just a little boy when I knew you, but now... I'm so glad you're back." She opens her arms and engulfs Chris in a hug.

"Me too," he murmurs, pulling back. "I haven't been home in a long time."

My brows furrow. He hasn't? What about his mom?

My sister smiles as she glances between me and Chris. "I can't believe you two are finally dating." My eyes widen, but she continues, "I always knew there was something between you two."

My face blanches. "What?" My voice squeaks, so I clear my throat. "No. We're—"

"We're not together," Chris finishes calmly, stepping in to clarify.

"Oh." My sister's brows drop. "I'm sorry. My bad." She looks at me for clarification, and shakes her head. "I just thought... when I called you, you said you were with Chris."

"Yeah. As in he was in the same room," I clarify.

"And you're..." She looks between us, confused. "Living together?"

"Yeah, I uh, I came back for the summer," Chris explains, his jaw tensing slightly. "Gabi wanted me here at the wedding, and I couldn't say no. And I didn't have anywhere to stay so—"

"I invited him to stay with me," I interject. "I had an empty apartment, so it made sense."

My sister nods, pursing her lips. "Well, this makes the situation a little tricky," she says. "Since you RSVP'd with no plus one and decided to bring Chris at the last minute." She glances at Chris, a smile creeping onto her face. "Which I'm

187

so happy about. I assumed you guys were together, and... well, there aren't any rooms available for this weekend."

"Oh." I flick my gaze toward Chris, meeting his brown eyes. We're sharing a room.

A bed.

"I can try to figure something out," my sister says, placing the back of her hand to her forehead. "Maybe you can stay with me and Rachel," my sister suggests.

I screw my face up, shaking my head. "Hell no. I'm not staying in the same room as you guys on the night before your wedding." A shiver runs through my body at the thought. "It's fine," I assure her. "Besides, we've shared a bed many times before, it won't be weird," I say with a shrug, meeting Chris' eyes. "Right?"

His face softens into a small smile as he nods. "Right."

"Great," my sister says with a sigh of relief. "This saves me a whole lot of hassle. I already have so many things going wrong that need fixing, and I—"

"Breathe," I tell her. "Where's Rachel?"

She sighs. "I told her to go to the spa."

"Then go join her," I suggest. "Just relax. This is supposed to be your special day."

My sister scoffs. "That's tomorrow. Today is for stressing." She hands me the key and looks back at Chris. "You're sure you guys will be okay?" she asks again, her brows knitting together.

"Yep," I flash her a smile, turning around to face Chris. "Let's go then, roomie," I say playfully, curling my arm around his as we head toward the stairs.

He looks down at me with a grin. "You do realize I'm already your roommate, right?"

I nod. "But now we're actually sharing a room, and a bed." My brows furrow slightly. "You're okay with this, right?"

Chris nods and flashes me a reassuring smile. "Of course. We've shared a bed before, Gabi. It's nothing new."

He's right. It's nothing new. But I don't know where we stand after last night. He was quiet when we woke up, and has been ever since. I don't know what to make of it. I want to know what he's thinking.

I feel like such an idiot for practically throwing myself at him last night when I know he doesn't want me. No matter what I thought I saw in his eyes last night.

"Don't worry," I assure him. "I'll make a pillow wall so that I don't maul you."

He chuckles. "Maul me?"

"I love to cuddle," I say, smiling up at him. "You know that."

He nods, pressing the elevator button. "Yeah, I know." The doors open, and we step inside. "No pillow wall needed," he says once the doors close, smirking down at me. "You can cuddle me all you want."

My heart pounds in my chest. "Really?" Hope fills my voice, relieved that nothing has changed between us despite how stupid I was last night.

"Yeah," he says with a smile that melts my insides. It should be illegal for someone to be this beautiful. "I love your cuddles."

The elevator door opens with a ding, and I grin as we walk into the hallway. "This is going to be so much fun."

Chris's chest shakes as he lets out a laugh. "I love how you always find a silver lining in everything."

"I'm happy," I admit with a shrug. *He makes me happy.* "I know you have to leave in less than three weeks, but I'm really enjoying spending time with you until then."

I meet his gaze, and he swallows. "Me too, Gabi."

I rip my gaze away from him, open the door, and stride inside. "I get the left side," I tell him, flopping down onto the bed, feeling the softness of the king mattress beneath me as I stretch out my arms above my head.

"Why?" Chris asks, following me into the room, an amused look on his face.

I lift onto my elbows, grinning at him. "Because I called dibs."

He chuckles, running a hand through his hair. "What if I wanted the left side?"

I raise an eyebrow. "Do you?" I'd gladly give it to him.

"No," he confirms with a smile. "It's all yours."

"Great." I jump out of bed, grabbing my suitcase and unzipping it. Packing it was a bitch, so I won't be unpacking everything, but I do need to get my dress out for tomorrow. My eyes lock on the long lilac dress, and I run my hands over the silk fabric.

"Is that what you're wearing tomorrow?" Chris asks from behind me.

"Yeah." I glance at him briefly. "I asked Rosie to design it for me a few months ago. She's got more talent in her left thumb than I do in my whole body, but my sister chose the color, of course."

"It's beautiful," he says.

I nod, agreeing. "It's almost too beautiful for me," I chuckle.

"Nothing's too beautiful for you." His voice is husky, sending a shiver up my spine. I turn to look at him over my shoulder, and our eyes meet.

Thoughts of last night flood into my mind. Seeing his bare chest for the first time, my hand trailing over each muscle as I explored his body. I don't know if it was because he had been drinking that he let me touch him, or if it was because of the dare. But I touched him in a way a best friend shouldn't.

And I want to do it again.

I want to touch him all over, lean into him, and taste his lips. I want to experience everything I've kept buried inside me all these years.

But I can't.

I inhale sharply and draw back, looking up at him. But his eyes aren't on mine, and his cheeks are tinged with a deep shade of red.

"What's wr—" I follow his gaze, confused, until I look down and see my open suitcase, noticing my dark purple vibrator sitting on top. "Oh."

I clear my throat, turning his attention away from the suitcase as he looks at me, his face red with embarrassment. "I'm sorry," he murmurs, running a hand through his hair. "I didn't mean to look… It was just *right there*."

"It's fine," I say with a laugh, quickly burying the vibrator beneath my clothes. "I'm not embarrassed about it."

Chris shakes his head, his face still red. "No. Of course not. You shouldn't be. It's… perfectly normal."

My lips twitch. "Right."

"Were you…" He rakes a hand through his hair, licking his lips nervously. "Were you going to use it? Here?"

191

"Not anymore," I say with a laugh, gesturing to the bed we have to share.

"Right." His eyes dart to the bed, and I watch him swallow hard, muttering a curse under his breath before turning around. "It's fucking hot in here."

"Really?" My brows furrow. "I'm actually quite cold.

He glances at me and nods. "Must just be me then," he says with a nervous laugh as he peels off his hoodie.

My eyes follow his movements, a desire stirring within me to see him remove his t-shirt as well. I want to see all of him again. He's so incredibly handsome. I've always found him attractive, but my feelings didn't evolve into something more until my senior year of high school. Since then, it's undeniable how deeply he affects me.

"You want to go out tonight?" Chris asks, placing his suitcase under the bed.

I glance out the window, noticing the sky is still pretty light, but I shake my head, kicking off my shoes. "I'm kind of tired," I tell him, putting my suitcase away. "Can we stay in tonight?"

"Of course." He flashes me a warm smile. Chris pulls down the covers, and we climb into bed together.

My pulse races as I look up at him. It's definitely not the first time we've slept in the same bed, and it won't be the last. So why the hell am I freaking out?

My throat moves as I gulp and blink up at him. "Are you sure you don't want that pillow wall?" I ask him again.

He chuckles, shakes his head and sighs. "God fucking help me, but no, I don't."

My heart pounds in my chest. "So I can cuddle you?" I fist the sheets beside me, wanting to nestle into him.

"Yeah, Gabi," he says, turning on his side to make room for me. "You can always cuddle me."

I don't waste any time, scooting closer until he wraps his arms around me, pulling me close. I close my eyes and tuck my head against his chest, listening to the steady rhythm of his heartbeat. My stomach somersaults when Chris leans down and presses his lips to my forehead so softly that I nearly melt into him.

I feel so safe with him. I always have. Even when I didn't feel safe in my own head, he was always there to pull me out of the darkness.

I love you.

My throat tightens as I swallow the words, squeezing my eyes shut, trying to drift off to sleep, never wanting to leave his arms.

"Shit," I hear him whisper, prompting me to open my eyes and look up at him. "I forgot to put on music."

I blink. I can't believe I forgot, too. I can't remember the last time I've fallen asleep without music, or some sort of noise, but I was so caught up in how it felt to be in his arms that I didn't even think about anything else but him.

"I don't need it," I assure him, my fingers resting flat against his chest.

He furrows his brows. "You sure?"

I nod, tightening my hold on him. "I have you." I let my words hang in the air, knowing he understands. He quiets the noise within me. All I've ever needed is him.

His face softens into a smile, and he brushes my hair back, tucking my head against his chest once more. "Go to sleep, pretty girl," he murmurs. "I've got you."

22

Gabriella

"I'm finally married," my sister says, beaming with the biggest grin of her life.

I've never seen my sister happier. My heart swells with joy seeing her smile like this. I remember when she wouldn't smile, when she used to hide herself. Just like I used to. "I know," I reply with a laugh. "I was there."

"You almost weren't," she says with a sigh. "Thank you for not being late." Her eyes meet mine, and she winks. "Almost."

Only she would tease me for being 'late' right after getting married.

"You're welcome." I flash her a smile. "So, how's being married?" I ask. "Do you feel any different?"

"After twenty minutes?" Her eyebrows lift, and she laughs. "No. But I doubt I will."

"Why's that?"

She lets out a content sigh, her eyes drifting to the dancefloor where Rachel is dancing with her dad. "Since the day I met her, we've always been connected. Like a tether was tying us together before we even met. I've always felt like she's my soulmate. I doubt getting married will change that."

I watch as Rachel locks eyes with my sister, and they exchange a knowing look that I'm all too familiar with. Glancing around the crowd, I meet Chris' gaze. His lips curve into a smile, and my heart races in my chest.

"She's my best friend," my sister says, drawing my attention back to her. "But you know what that's like, right?"

I swallow nervously. "What are you talking about?"

She smiles knowingly, her eyes fixed on me. "You don't need to lie to me, Gabi. I'm not stupid. I can see you're in love with that boy from a mile away."

Without thinking, I turn to look at Chris again, watching him engrossed in conversation with others. It's been a while since he's been home, so it makes sense everyone wants to catch up with him.

"I saw it back then," my sister continues. "Even though you denied it time and time again, I could see how perfect you guys were for each other." I inhale sharply, meeting her gaze. "And I see it now."

"You do?"

She nods, her white veil fluttering in the wind. "Clear as day." Her expression softens. "Is there a reason you two haven't gotten together yet?"

"It's not like that. Chris is…" I bite my tongue. I can't keep using the excuse that Chris is just my best friend. I can't lie to my sister. I let out a deep sigh. "He doesn't feel the same way," I admit.

"What?" she asks, her brow furrowing.

I shrug, feeling a pang in my chest. "It's just not going to happen for us," I say, the words heavy on my tongue.

Admitting it breaks my heart. I don't think I'll ever get over these feelings I have for him, and I don't want him out of my life. It's all so complicated.

"But you guys…" She shakes her head. "Nothing ever happened between you two in high school?"

"No."

"Really?" she asks, her eyes widening in disbelief. "He slept in your bed almost every night."

I shrug, shaking my head. "He knew I didn't like sleeping alone," I explain. "Especially when dad was drunk." My sister sucks in a breath at the mention of him. "We'd stay up all night, talking, playing video games, and listening to music until we fell asleep." I swallow hard. "Nothing more ever happened."

My sister's jaw drops, and she blinks in surprise. "Ever?"

A hint of a memory, fleeting and indistinct, flickers in my mind, but I shake it away. "No."

She hums thoughtfully, glancing past me. "But you love him, don't you?"

I roll my eyes, trying to deflect. "It's your wedding day. Shouldn't you be a bridezilla or something?"

She smiles warmly. "Today went better than I ever imagined. No bridezilla needed." Her expression turns serious as she fixes her gaze on me. "Now answer my question."

I don't hesitate. My feelings for Chris have been growing since the day we met, evolving into something I know will never go away. "Yes," I admit quietly. "I love him."

My sister's eyes soften and she sighs. "And you're not going to tell him?"

I shake my head. "I can't risk losing him over this. I'd rather keep him as my best friend forever than risk losing him altogether."

My sister shakes her head, her hand resting on my shoulder. "You'll never know unless you try."

My brows furrow as I think about my sister said. What if I tell Chris how I feel and he doesn't feel the same? Being rejected by him scares me more than I ever want to admit. But keeping these feelings buried, and pretending I don't love him might break me.

"Hey," Chris says, catching my attention. I turn to find him standing beside me, his smile lighting up his eyes, and I feel a flutter in my chest.

"I'll leave you guys to it," my sister says with a knowing smile as she walks toward her wife, their hands finding each other's and their lips meeting in a loving kiss.

"They look so happy," Chris says, his eyes lingering on my sister and her wife.

"Yeah," I reply, warmth spreading through me at their happiness. I glance at Chris teasingly. "Did you finally have enough of everyone drooling over you?" I ask with a smirk.

He laughs, running a hand through his hair. "I was dying over there," he admits with a sigh. "I forgot how much I hate talking to people."

I arch an eyebrow. "You talk to me," I point out.

His hand drops to his side, and he smiles warmly at me. "You're different," he says simply.

My stomach flutters like crazy. "I am?"

His eyes meet mine, and I get lost in his deep chocolate eyes, leaning closer without even realizing it. He looks *really* good in his tuxedo, the fit accentuating his figure just right, and his messy curls add to his usual boyish charm that I've always loved.

The distance between us shrinks as Chris licks his lips, as if about to say something. But before he can speak, his eyes lift from mine, a scowl forming on his face as he glances behind me.

I spin around, a frown creasing my face, trying to catch a glimpse of what captured his attention. I freeze, a chill creeping up my spine as my eyes lock on a face I haven't seen in four years.

"Is that—"

"Yeah."

"Why the hell is he here?" Chris grits out.

I have no idea. Why would he be here? I take a step forward, but Chris stops me, his hand wrapping around my wrist.

"Wait. What the hell do you think you're doing?"

I let my wrist slip out of Chris' grasp and turn to face him. "I'm going to talk to him."

"No," he replies sharply, a furrow appearing between his brows as he scowls, moving closer to me. "Absolutely not. You're not going anywhere near him. Let me handle this. I'll talk to him."

"No." My blood grows cold at the mere thought of Chris confronting him. "I have to be the one to talk to him," I tell him, noticing the frown deepen on Chris' face. "He's my father."

Chris' frown deepens, but he releases his grip on me. I swallow hard as I spot my father lurking behind the bushes, scanning the crowd, searching for my sister.

When he notices me approaching, his gaze shifts to me, causing my stomach to plummet. "What are you doing here?" I ask.

He scoffs. "After four years, that's the first thing you say to me?"

"What are you doing here?" I repeat, my voice strained.

He sighs heavily. "It's my daughter's wedding."

A bitter laugh escapes my lips, burning my throat. "You wouldn't know the meaning of that word if it hit you in the head."

He scowls at me, that same old expression I remember from all those times before he lashed out at me, Jane, or Mom. "Spare me the dramatics. You always acted too tough for your own good."

I trace my tongue over the faint scar on my lips, remembering the painful moment I tried to intervene and protect Mom.

It didn't work though. It never worked.

"Get out."

"Don't you dare speak to me like that," he retorts, moving closer. "Have you forgotten I'm your father?"

"You're not my father," I assert, holding my ground. He used to terrify me, enough to make me tremble and cry with anger, unable to stand up to him. But seeing him here now... There's nothing intimidating about him anymore. "You're nothing," I spit out. "I want nothing to do with you, and neither does Jane." His nostrils flare, and I straighten my spine, staring at the man who made our lives a living hell. "She's finally happy and free from you. Leave her alone and get the hell out."

"Look at what the fuck she's done to you," he says, his lips pulled into a disgusted look. "It's her fault you're…"

A bitter laugh escapes me. After all these years, he hasn't changed a bit. He's still the same despicable person he always was. "God, you're pathetic. You can't even say the word."

I spent years living in fear that he would find out I was bisexual. When my sister came out at eighteen, he lost his shit, and threw her out of the house. Thankfully she had finished high school and was off to college. But he forbade me from speaking to her, and I hid myself away, terrified he would scorn me, hit me, *hate me* if he ever found out the truth about me. But the truth is, I couldn't care less about this man's opinion of me now. Not anymore.

"You're acting this way because of her," he spits out. "I saw you and your boyfriend back there. You're not gay."

I don't bother correcting him about the boyfriend part. "You're right," I reply evenly. "I'm not gay. I'm bisexual. I'm attracted to both men and women, and being in love with a guy doesn't change that about me, no matter how much you or anyone else wishes it did."

Disappointed in myself for letting him affect me, I continue, my hands trembling as I clench them into fists to maintain composure. "I hated myself when I lived at home," I admit. "You made me feel like there was something wrong with me, but *you* were the problem." His scowl deepens, but I push on. "I'm proud of who I am," I assert, narrowing my eyes at him. "And I couldn't give a fuck what you think."

"Your mother would be so disappointed," he says, his face contorting with the familiar anger I've witnessed countless times.

"Don't," I warn sharply, feeling my pulse race. "Don't you dare talk about Mom. You have no right after what you did."

He scoffs. "What I did? You mean setting discipline in my own house?"

"You made our lives a living hell!" I shout. "You hurt Mom until the day she died. And now you're alone, miserable, and fucking pathetic."

His eyes widen as he snarls, grabbing my shoulders roughly. "Don't you dare talk to me that way."

Once upon a time, this would have terrified me. But now I just laugh. He really is pathetic.

"Hey!" Chris' voice cuts from behind me, and I feel his presence beside me, a wave of calm washing over me. "Don't you fucking dare put your hands on her." Chris steps between my father and me, pushing at his chest.

"This has nothing to do with you," he asserts, advancing toward Chris. My heart races out of my chest as I swiftly step in front of Chris. I won't let him touch Chris. I'd rather die than let anyone hurt him, especially because of me.

"Don't even think of hurting him," I warn. "You have no control over me," I tell him, squaring my shoulders. "You might have when I was young, and weak and wanted your approval, but I don't want that anymore," I tell him. "I don't want anything from you. I don't want to talk to you, or see you. So get the fuck out of here, and don't come near any of us ever again."

I grip Chris' arm firmly, pulling him away.

"Are you alright?" Chris asks, trailing behind me.

I stop in my tracks, turning to face him. I feel a rush of relief seeing his soft eyes, and without hesitation, I wrap my arms around his neck.

"Dance with me."

Christopher

I've never been one to dance. I don't usually do things that seek public attention, but if Gabi asks, I'll do it. I'll do anything for her.

Even if holding her and being so close makes the part of my brain that thinks shut down. Which is dangerous, especially since we almost crossed a line on our road trip.

"Are you okay?" I ask as she wraps her arms around my neck and gazes into my eyes. My hands instinctively move to her hips as we step to the music.

"Yeah," she says, swallowing hard. "I just want to dance with you. Is that okay?"

"Of course." *More than okay.* I notice the distant look in her eyes as I search them. "What did he want?" I ask, still seething at the thought of him thinking he could put his hands on her.

Gabi shrugs, avoiding my gaze. "Same as always. He wanted to make me feel ashamed of myself," she admits. "I think he came to tell Jane she was making a mistake, or whatever other bullshit he wanted to spew."

I don't hate much, but there are two people on this earth who burn a hate within me. My father and hers. I've seen what her father's opinions did to Gabi. I witnessed firsthand how they infiltrated her mind, affected her, *broke her*.

I almost lost her because of him.

"Good thing Jane didn't see him."

"Yeah." Her eyes dart everywhere, looking anywhere but at me.

We continue slow dancing to the music. "Is that the first time you've seen him since you left home?" I ask.

"Yeah," she replies, her eyes finally meeting mine. "Is this your first time being back home since…?" I nod, feeling a tightness in my chest. Her brows furrow in concern. "You haven't even seen your mom?" she presses.

Guilt churns in my stomach, and I shake my head. "No, I haven't."

She pauses, the intensity in her eyes fixed on mine. "Why not?" she asks. "Why haven't you been back since you left?"

Not now. Not like this. "Gabi—"

"Why did you leave that night, Chris?" she asks, our steps coming to a halt.

"Gabi, please," I plead, my heart pounding.

She shakes her head. "I thought I was your best friend."

"You are," I insist, holding her tighter. "No one else even comes close to what you mean to me."

"Really?" Her brows knit together, a pained frown crossing her lips, and it rips my heart right out of my chest. "Then why won't you tell me why you left me when I needed you the most?"

I inhale sharply. That fucking hurt.

I knew how much she needed me. After her mom died, Gabi was a wreck. She clung to me in her darkest moments, and I let her pull me into that darkness with her. But hearing her say I left her when she needed me breaks me.

I wanted to go back for her.

I really did.

"Everyone thinks we're together."

I stiffen, turning to look at Gabi. I blink a few times, caught off guard. "What?"

Her tongue runs over her bottom lip as she maintains eye contact. "My sister thought we were together, everyone here keeps asking if you're my boyfriend, even my piece of shit father thought we were together." I stop breathing. "And I'm tired of having to explain to everyone that we're not."

What the fuck is she saying right now?

My ears ring as I shake my head, looking up at her. "Gabi, what are you—"

"Why aren't we together, Chris?" she interrupts, her eyes hardened.

My heart pounds in my chest. What the hell is happening?

She had a few drinks earlier, and I scan her features, expecting to see signs that she didn't mean any of that. But her eyes remain steady, her lips sealed, and none of the usual signs of her being drunk are present.

Is she really saying this right now?

"Gabi—"

The music comes to a halt, and we glance toward the stage where Rachel's mom stands with a champagne glass, tapping it lightly.

"Thank you for coming everyone. I'm the mother of the bride…"

Gabi's arms drop from my neck, and I reluctantly release her waist until she steps back. "I need a drink."

I watch her turn away, heading towards the bar. I grit my teeth, wanting the day to end so we can finally be alone and talk about what the hell she meant when she said those words.

24

Truth Or Dare

Gabriella

"Do you think they're fucking?" I whisper, pointing to a random hotel door, flashing him a mischievous smirk.

Chris stares at me like I've grown two heads. "What are you talking about?"

Without answering, I shrug and press my ear to the door, trying to catch any sounds from the other side.

"What the hell are you doing?" he asks, letting out a sound that's a mix between a sigh and a laugh.

"Shhh." I flip my hair over my shoulder and press my ear closer. "I can't hear anything."

"Are you really…" He groans. "Gabi, get away from the door."

I pull back, letting out a sigh of my own. "Maybe I should just ask them?"

He pins me with a glare, wrapping his hand around my wrist. "You're not knocking on some random person's door to ask if they're fucking."

"C'mon, Chris," I plead. "Let me live vicariously through them."

He scoffs, shaking his head as he pulls me away. "You're such an idiot."

A horny idiot.

Abstaining from sex for the past year hasn't been completely terrible. In fact, it was surprisingly easy. I had used sex as a crutch for a long time, craving touch, love, and someone to just take care of me, but I eventually realized I'd never find that with anyone else. The only person who had ever made me feel like that was Chris, and he did it without ever crossing the line of our friendship.

But he wasn't here. He was thousands of miles away with who knows who, and I just wanted... someone.

But sex started to feel meaningless, and nothing ever compared to the feeling of being with Chris. So it became easy to go without it.

Until now.

Every time I look at Chris, my stomach flutters and my core throbs. Add in the fact that I can't use my vibrator because we're sharing a bed, and I'm about to burst. If I can't have an orgasm, then I can at least get drunk. *Or drunker.*

"Maybe they have some alcohol," I point out, ready to knock on their door, but Chris pulls me away once again.

"Trust me. You don't need any more alcohol," he says, right before he pulls me back into him, scoops up my legs, and throws me over his shoulder.

"What the hell?" I mutter, swinging my head back. "Let me go."

He laughs, shaking his head as he carries me down the hallway. "You're a menace. I need to protect everyone from you."

I stop struggling, pausing at his words. "Including yourself?"

He glances back over his shoulder, meeting my gaze. "No, it's too late for me."

I roll my eyes. "How tragic."

"I know," he replies with a chuckle. "It's a real tragedy."

My brows furrow as I twist to look at him. "Does that mean you regret meeting me?"

Chris stops abruptly, swinging me around so I'm facing him. His hands grip my thighs just below my ass, and I instinctively wrap my arms around his neck to steady myself. "No," he says firmly, his eyes locked on mine. "It was the best moment of my life."

My breath hitches, and I stare at him, my fingers itching to run through his curly hair. "Even when I almost got you arrested?"

He laughs. "Especially then. I have zero regrets."

"Zero?"

He nods. "If it wasn't for you, my life would be boring, Gabi."

Our eyes lock together. My life begins and ends with him. Every memory I treasure is with him. Every waking moment, and every time we fell asleep wrapped in each other's arms was with him. Even when my life nearly ended, he was there.

Chris is my *life*.

He's the one.

And I'm sick of telling myself I can't have him.

Earlier, I almost let slip all my thoughts, but I quickly realized it would be a mistake. Now, with alcohol flowing through my system, my head feeling lighter, and his eyes locked on mine, I can't fight it anymore.

"Chris?"

"Yeah?"

"Truth or dare?"

A sigh leaves his lips, and he shakes his head. "Gabi," he warns, lowering me to my feet.

As soon as my feet touch the ground, I look up at him, wanting to be back in his arms. "Come on," I say, tilting my head. "It's still early."

His brows dip. "It's two am."

"Exactly," I point out with a smile. "The morning."

He chuckles, but it fades as he looks at me, running a hand through his hair. "Dare."

I lift an eyebrow. He rarely every picks dare. My eyes drop to his lips, and I think about it. I want it so bad. I want *him* so bad. But what if he doesn't want me? "There's a hot tub on the top floor," I start, licking my lips. "I dare you to jump in with me."

His brows dip. "That's it?"

I nod. "You accept?"

His lips curl into a smirk. "You know I never back down from a dare."

I nod knowingly.

He grabs my hand, and we race through the hallway, up the stairs, until Chris swings open the door to the hot tub.

The place is thankfully empty as I glance around. The room feels cozy and intimate, bathed in soft blue lights that glow in the dimness. The hot tub bubbles, filling the air with a soothing hum.

"I didn't bring a bathing suit," Chris says, glancing at me with a hint of concern.

I shrug with a smirk, reaching around to unzip my dress. "Neither did I."

"Jesus," Chris mutters, his cheeks flushing slightly as he averts his gaze, and I can't help but chuckle.

"Relax," I reassure him. "I'm wearing underwear."

His head turns slightly, glancing at me, and I let the dress pool at my feet. Chris' eyes drop, and they trace my body as if he's mapping it, remembering it.

I've never had his eyes on me before. Not like this.

His jaw tightens, the muscle ticking as his eyes slowly make their way back to my face.

My heart is racing out of my chest. I want to dive in head first. I want to know if there's any chance he feels what I feel, even slightly.

"Your turn," I say, my voice coming out husky.

His jacket is the first thing to go, dropping to the ground. His eyes remain locked on mine as he unbuttons the first button of his white shirt. He maintains eye contact throughout, but I can't help glancing down, mesmerized as each button comes undone until his shirt joins the jacket on the ground.

I suck in a breath, taking in the sight of him standing under the soft, dim lights without a shirt, his muscles defined and highlighted.

God, I want to touch him again.

Then he tugs at the button on his pants, and my breath hitches once again. He pulls the zipper down, and with a smooth motion, discards his pants, throwing them onto the ground.

My heart pounds so hard against my chest, I feel like I'm about to pass out.

Holy shit.

I walk slowly toward him, watching as his chest moves with every breath he takes, until I'm right in front of him.

We're standing in front of each other, in nothing but our underwear, one touch away. One inch, and I can feel his warmth. One inch, and I can press my lips to his.

"Now what?" he asks, his voice strained and husky, unlike anything I've heard from him before.

I take a step to his left and lower myself into the water, sliding into the hot bubbles. I quickly turn around, finding Chris staring at me.

"Jump in," I urge him, leaning against the back of the hot tub.

Chris squats down and slides into the water, his eyes fixed on me. The only sounds are the gentle bubbles and our heavy breaths filling the air.

The water swirls around us as I swim closer to him. "The water feels good."

He swallows, his gaze fixed on mine. "Yeah."

I nod, inching even nearer until our faces are just inches apart. I wrap my arms around his neck with a smile, but Chris freezes, his eyes widening a little.

"Gabi. You're drunk."

"Hardly," I reply, a playful smirk crossing my face. "I had one drink." He gives me a skeptical look, and I relent with a sigh. "Okay, fine. Two. But I'm not drunk, I promise."

His brows furrow as he searches my eyes. He must find what he's looking for because his shoulders relax, and he exhales. His hand grazes my stomach so softly, I doubt he realizes he did it, but my skin warms at the touch. We've never been this close before, not like this. My stomach flutters, and my clit throbs as I press closer to him, my pulse quickening when he firmly grasps my waist under the water.

"Truth or dare," I murmur, our faces mere inches apart.

"Gabi," he sighs.

"You don't want to play with me?" I tease, my eyes hooded with lust.

He releases a heavy breath, his hand tightening on my waist. "Truth."

I blow a raspberry, hoping he'd choose dare. He smirks slightly, and I sigh, meeting his gaze. My eyes drift down to his lips, and I ask the first question that comes to mind.

"Who was your first kiss?"

Chris stiffens, a frown appearing on his lips. "What?"

"Your first kiss," I repeat. "I've always wondered who it was."

He shakes his head, his brows knitting together. "Why?"

I frown, confused by his expression. "I don't know," I say, with a shrug. "I just... You never talk to me about any of that stuff, and I tell you everything," I point out, swallowing nervously. "I guess... I just want to know who it was."

His jaw ticks, and he glances away from me, stepping back until my arms drop from around his neck, and we're no longer chest to chest. "I don't know," he says, avoiding my eyes.

I blink. "You don't know? How could you not know?"

He shrugs, raking a hand through his hair. "I don't remember."

"You... don't remember?" I ask. What the hell is going on?

Chris blows out a breath, shaking his head. "Not really."

I frown, trying to look at him, but he's still looking at everywhere but me. "How?"

He shrugs. "Just don't," he says, glancing at me. "Can me move past this?"

My jaw drops. "Are you... lying to me right now?"

He sighs. "Gabi—"

"Why are you lying to me?" I ask, hurt building in my chest. He's never lied to me before, never hurt me like this. "Who the hell was it?"

He scoffs, his lips curling as he looks at me. "You don't want to know."

"Why?" He shakes his head, turning his head away from me again, but I swim closer to him, and lift my hand, moving his face back to look at me.

"Just drop it," he pleads, his eyebrows furrowing in a pained expression.

But I can't just drop it. There's a reason why he's hiding this from me, and I want to know what it is. I keep my eyes on him. "Tell me who it was," I demand, seeing him shake his head. "Why don't I want to know?"

"Because you don't fucking remember it!" he says, making me freeze, dropping my hand from his face. He squeezes his eyes closed, and sighs. "Fuck. Gabi, I'm sorry I shouldn't have—"

"What?" I interrupt, my mind reeling a million miles per hour. Chris presses his lips together, and my breathing speeds up, struggling to comprehend what he's telling me right now. "What did you just say?"

He swallows roughly, his eyes fluttering closed briefly as he lets out a deep breath, then locks eyes with me. "It was you. You were my first kiss."

25

Gabriella

Age Eighteen

Tonight is all wrong.

This dress is too tight, my hair keeps sticking to my lip gloss, and Chris isn't here.

Am I a horrible person for being more interested in my best friend, rather than my boyfriend, whom I'm currently dancing with?

Maybe.

"Are you not enjoying yourself?" Luke's question catches me off guard, and I turn to face him.

"Huh?"

He furrows his brows. "You keep scanning the room," he says. "Are you bored or something?"

Or something. "I'm just trying to find Chris," I explain. "He said he'd be here, but I haven't seen him yet."

Luke scoffs, shaking his head. "Maybe he went off and hooked up with someone, and he doesn't want you cockblocking him."

My stomach twists at the thought. Is that what I do? Cockblock him? I've never seen Chris with a date or another girl, if I discount that whole thing with Taylor. But is Luke right? Does Chris want a night away from me?

My brows furrow as I glance over my shoulder at the door again. "He said he'd come," I repeat, hoping it's true. "I invited him."

Luke grabs my arm, forcing me to face him, a scowl etched on his face. "You're here with me," he reminds me.

I narrow my eyes. "I know that. But he's still my best friend."

Luke laughs, his tongue poking the inside of his cheek. "Is that all?"

"What?"

We stop dancing and he pulls back, shrugging. "You're acting like you're more interested in hanging out with some random guy than being here with me. I'm your boyfriend, Gabi."

For all of two weeks. Chris has been my best friend for six years.

Luke isn't wrong, though. I am distracted. Being here with Chris would have been so much better.

But... he didn't ask me.

So, I said yes to Luke.

I don't know why I did. I was sad, and lonely and just wanted to feel wanted. And Chris didn't want me.

"I'm going to go find Chris," I tell him firmly.

Luke scoffs. "Of course you are."

"Stop being an asshole."

"Stop acting like a slut."

My eyes widen, and heads turn as Luke's words draw attention. "Excuse me?"

"I've heard rumors about you, you know?" He shakes his head, licking his lips.

"Rumors?" I repeat, my heart banging against my chest at the accusation. "Like what?"

He scoffs. "Like the fact that you jump from one guy's bed to another. Only once. After that…" He trails off, shaking his head. "You become a fucking nun."

I can't find any words. My throat tightens as I swallow, my heart racing.

"Is it him?" Luke demands, narrowing his eyes at me. "You use guys to make him jealous, don't you?"

"You're crazy," I say, rolling my eyes, itching to get out of there.

"Yeah," he laughs sarcastically, giving me a disgusted look. "Crazy for getting mixed up with you when I knew exactly who you were."

My heart pounds as I move closer, poking his chest with my finger. "You don't know a thing about me."

No one does.

The only person who really knows me is…

"I bet Chris does," he sneers, each word hitting a nerve. "I bet he knows all about you." His eyes roam over me, and he shakes his head. "I was waiting for tonight so you'd finally get on your knees for me, but it looks like that's not happening. So I guess we might as well call it quits."

My blood goes cold, and I take a step back. "So you're breaking up with me?" I ask, desperate for this to be over. I should have never said yes to him. I should have just stayed home. Anything would have been better than this.

He shrugs. "I can find another girl to fuck who isn't as much of a mess as you are."

217

I lift my head, take a deep breath, and turn towards the exit. Pushing open the doors, the cold air hits my skin, sending goosebumps across my arms. I wrap my arms around myself, standing alone in the dark parking lot.

Where do I even go?

Jane's in Redfield, Chris isn't here, Mom's gone, and all that's waiting for me at home is just empty, cold darkness. And my father.

I sit down on the sidewalk, stretching out my legs, feeling the chill on my arms. My hand finds my phone in my pocket, and I pull it out to dial Chris.

My fingers hesitate over the button, Luke's words echoing in my mind.

What if he's with someone else right now?

"Leaving already?" Chris' voice startles me, and I turn to see him joining me on the sidewalk, taking a sip from a flask.

My heart quickens, coming alive as soon as I see him. He glances at me, offering his flask with a smirk. His eyes are weighed down, and his crooked smile lets me know he's drunk.

Without thinking, I accept the flask from him and take a sip, feeling the alcohol burn down my throat.

"Where's your boyfriend?" he asks.

"Where were you?" I ask him, handing back his flask.

His fingers brush against mine briefly as he takes it, and drinks. "Around," he replies with a shrug.

"Around," I echo, thoughts of him with other girls swirling in my mind. My heart aches at the idea, but I push forward. "With who?"

Chris shakes his head, his dark, curly hair falling across his face. I have the urge to brush it back, to run my fingers through it and stare into his chocolate-brown eyes.

"I just needed some fresh air," he deflects, completely avoiding my question.

Was he alone?

"Me too," I reply with a sigh, my shoulders slumping. "It was getting stuffy in there."

"Yeah," Chris mutters, his jaw tense. "It definitely was." He takes another sip from his flask and looks at me intently. "Where's your boyfriend?" he asks again. "Does he know you're out here alone?"

I exhale heavily. "I don't think he'd care."

Chris furrows his brows. "Why not?"

I lick my lips nervously. "Because he broke up with me."

"Oh."

I nod, glancing at the flask in his hand. He passes it to me without a word.

"Turns out he just asked me to prom to sleep with me," I say bitterly before taking a large gulp.

"What a piece of shit," Chris says, shaking his head.

I hum, swallowing the alcohol. "Apparently there's a rumor," I continue.

"A rumor?" Chris asks, concerned. "About you?"

I face him with an amused laugh. "And you."

His frown deepens, blinking a few times, and I continue with a laugh. "Apparently I'm a slut who uses guys to make you jealous." I bite my tongue, meeting his gaze. It's not the whole truth, seeing as my I only discovered feelings for Chris recently, but Luke wasn't entirely wrong. I didn't say yes to Luke's prom invitation because I *liked* him. But it was more

219

about my frustration that Chris couldn't see how I felt about him.

Chris swallows, his expression flashing with anger. "He called you a slut?"

I shrug, taking another sip from the flask. "Not just him, apparently." The burn of the alcohol sends a shiver through me. "I don't know, maybe they're right, I—"

"Don't," Chris interrupts firmly. I turn to him as he grasps my wrist, his face twisted. "Don't call yourself that. Don't agree with those assholes. They don't know you."

I swallow hard, feeling a lump in my throat. "But you do."

"I do," he agrees with a nod. "I know everything about you." Memories of him comforting me the week after my mom's funeral come rushing into my mind. I think that's when I started falling for him. When I realized no one makes me feel like he does. "And you're twenty times the person of anyone in there," he adds, his thumb caressing my wrist.

Bang. Bang. Bang.

My heart knocks so loudly I think he'll hear it. I feel my pulse race with each second that passes with his eyes on mine.

His fingers trace the scars marring my wrist, each touch sending a shiver through me. My breath catches when I realize he's spelling out a word.

Truth.

Or.

Dare.

A smirk plays on his lips when he's done, and looks at me, waiting for a response.

My lips lift as a smile tugs at the corners of my mouth. "Dare."

He takes my hand in his, and lifts off the sidewalk. "Come with me."

Ten minutes later, we're standing at the boardwalk, looking out at the ocean and the carnival we love to come to sometimes. My eyes are immediately drawn to the cotton candy, and popcorn stand. I haven't eaten all day, and now with my belly full of whiskey, I'm hungrier than ever.

Chris lets out a soft laugh, pulling out his wallet. My heart jumps. I didn't even *say* anything. I didn't have to tell him, or ask him. He just knows.

"The blue one, right?" Chris asks, his eyes locked on mine.

I nod, a smile spreading across my lips. This terrible night had turned around the moment he sat next to me on that sidewalk. "How did you know?"

Chris shrugs casually. "I have a special place in my mind reserved for all things Gabi."

"Yeah?" I grin. "What's up there?"

A laugh escapes him. "So much."

"Like?"

He hands over the cash to pay for the cotton candy before passing me the stick. "Everything."

"Come on," I say, taking a bite of the cotton candy, letting it melt on my tongue. "Give me an example."

His jaw tenses briefly, but he sighs. "Your favorite foods, favorite drink, favorite movie—anything with Channing Tatum," he says, making me laugh as he stuffs his hands in his pockets. "The way your eyes hood when you're drunk or tired or hungry." I swallow the cotton candy, staring at him intently. Chris swallows too, shrugging slightly. "The color of your eyes, the smell of your hair, the shape of your lips." Our eyes lock, and I inhale sharply. "Your favorite songs, and which ones to play when you're sad. How you like your back tickled…" My eyes start to well up, and his gaze remains steady as he shakes his head. "There's so much, Gabi. So much in here."

Wetness coats my eyes as I try to blink it away, letting out a soft laugh. "You must have a big brain."

He chuckles warmly. "Huge. All filled with information about you."

I blink back tears, laughing along with him. "You're an expert on Gabi?"

His smile soothes my nerves, and he pulls me closer, lifting my chin to meet his gaze. "A+ student, without a doubt."

My smile widens, and I allow myself to glance at his lips, just for a moment. Or two. Or three. I don't know how long I stare, wanting to lean in and press my lips to his.

"Come on," Chris interrupts, his brows furrowed. "We should get home."

"No," I reply, a frown tugging at my lips. "I don't want to. Not yet." This night has been everything I've ever wanted, and more. I'm not ready for it to end.

Chris sighs, running a hand through his hair. "Where do you want to go?"

Anywhere with you. I scan the carnival until my gaze lands on the empty Ferris wheel. "There," I say, pointing at it.

He gives me a searching look. "Are you sure? It's pretty high."

I roll my eyes. "I'm not scared of heights," I assure him. "And besides, what's the worst that could happen?"

"You could die?" he suggests with a raised eyebrow.

I wave him off dismissively. "That doesn't scare me." I see his jaw tighten, his expression hardening as he looks at me, and I swallow my words. He remembers how little it scares me, and I don't want him to look at me the way he did that day.

Like I was weak.

A mess.

Broken.

"Let's go," I insist, tugging at Chris's suit jacket until we're both seated inside the Ferris wheel cabin.

The doors close, and I hold out my hand expectantly. Chris doesn't hesitate, he smirks and pulls out his flask, passing it to me. Unscrewing the lid, I tilt it back and open my mouth, but my eyes widen in surprise when only a few drops trickle out. "What the—" I turn the flask over, shaking it. "There's no more," I complain with a pout.

Chris chuckles. "You drank the whole thing."

I shake my head, wincing as the world starts to blur slightly. "It was your flask," I argue, holding it out toward him.

He laughs, taking it from me. "I had like two sips before you took it away and finished it."

"That's not true," I say, poking his cheek lightly. "You were drunk when you found me."

Chris laughs, but it fades into a sigh. "I needed to be."

Frowning, I watch as the Ferris wheel starts to move again. "Why?"

He shrugs, his gaze distant. "Hurts less."

"What does?"

He sighs again, meeting my eyes. "Everything."

As the Ferris wheel starts to move again, I sway into Chris, feeling the alcohol swirling in my stomach. "Whose idea was it to come on this?" I groan, leaning against his chest.

Chris chuckles, opening up his arm to wrap around my shoulder. "Yours," he reminds me.

"Oh, right." I glance out at the view of the carnival below, a small smile playing on my lips. "It's really nice up here, though."

"Yeah," Chris agrees, his arm tightening around me. I look up at him, our faces just inches apart.

His Adam's apple bobs as he locks eyes with me. "You look really beautiful tonight, Gabi," he murmurs.

It's only us in this little pod, and my heart flutters, a smile curling on my lips in response. "Really?"

He shakes his head slightly, his lips pressed together. "So fucking beautiful."

The compliment sends a warm rush through me. "First time you've said that," I point out.

His brow furrows. "That's definitely not true."

I hold his eyes. "You've never told me I'm beautiful," I counter. I would have remembered if he had.

His frown deepens, and he continues to caress my cheek with his thumb. "I think it though," he admits quietly. "All the time."

My heart races even faster. "You do?"

He nods, a hint of sadness crossing his features. His hand drops from my cheek, running through his hair instead. "Shouldn't have said that," he murmurs to himself.

"Why not? I liked it."

He glances at me, his eyes softening as it drifts down to my lips. They part involuntarily and—

"Ride's over."

I lift my head, realizing our pod is back on the ground as the doors open. Untangling myself from Chris's embrace, I turn towards him. But he's already rising from his seat, and walking out.

"You're going to break a leg," Chris whispers urgently.

"I'm fine," I mutter, though I'm anything but. How does he manage to do this every night? Climbing through my window while I'm completely wasted isn't exactly working out smoothly.

"Put your foot… *Christ*. Just let me help you."

"I've got it," I insist, but Chris grips the pipe outside my window with one hand and hoists me onto the window ledge with the other.

"Are you okay? Jeez, that bear's huge."

"I know," I grumble, struggling to push the oversized white teddy bear that Chris won for me at the carnival inside my window. "Why the hell did I pick this thing?"

"Because with you, it's go big or go home," he replies with a chuckle. "Just get inside."

"I'm trying," I whisper-hiss. "This damn bear won't... Got it," I announce as I finally manage to shove the bear inside.

Swinging my legs over the ledge, I shuffle closer and attempt to smoothly land on my feet. But I end up falling flat on my face.

"Jesus, Gabi," I hear Chris sigh when he swings his legs over my window ledge. "You're wasted."

"I'm not," I protest weakly, but the way my legs refuse to cooperate tells me he's right.

His chuckle warms me from the inside out as he pulls me up from the floor, smoothing my hair back. "You definitely are," he says, his smile so beautiful that I wonder how I ever looked at him before without feeling this flutter inside me.

"I'm not," I repeat. "I'm just... so... tired," I mumble, my eyelids fluttering closed.

He chuckles again, and I feel his lips press against my forehead before he lifts me up into his arms and places me down on the bed.

I crack open one eye, seeing Chris gazing down at me with that soft smile on his lips. "Do you mind if I stay over tonight?" he asks quietly.

I shake my head, settling myself on the edge of the bed. "I love having you here," I admit.

Chris nods, loosening his tie. I take a moment to appreciate how good he looks tonight. The only other time I saw him in a suit was at my mom's funeral, but my mind wasn't really present then.

Tonight, though, I'm soaking in every detail.

I want to ask him for the pictures we took in the photobooth, so I can relive those moments, but I don't want to stop looking at him. I couldn't stop staring at him in the photobooth either. We were squeezed together, me sitting on his lap, both of us drunk out of our minds. I held his face in my hands and just stared into his brown eyes. I wanted so badly to lean in and kiss him. But then the flash went off, snapping us back to reality, and the moment was over.

He chuckles, glancing at the corner of my room at the pile of clothes I have thrown. "You still have my old baseball cap?" he asks.

"Of course," I say with a shrug. "I told you I was keeping it."

He scoffs. "I'm going to want it back at some point," he says, arching a brow as he pulls off his suit jacket.

"Never, Hudson," I say, seeing him smirk as he bends down to untie his shoes. I really love having him here. I love how comfortable he is in my room. How whenever he's here, it feels like home. I tilt my head at him. "Why do we never hang out at your place?"

He snaps his head towards me, frowning. "Why do you ask?"

I shrug. "Just curious."

His brows knit together as he blinks. "I prefer it here," he admits.

"Really?" I say skeptically. "Even with my dad around?"

His jaw clenches slightly. "He's a piece of shit. But you're here."

You're here.

He says that as if he'd follow me anywhere. As if he'd dive headfirst into a fiery lava pit if I was at the bottom.

"I've never seen your room," I point out, a little curious. I've always wondered about it. What color are the walls?

Does he have any art hanging up? Where does he keep his video games?

"It's nothing special," he replies with a shrug, crossing the room to play a record. The vinyl scratches as the song starts, filling the room with music.

I lean back on my hands, watching him. Why is he so secretive about his house? The only time I've been over there was to ask him to come play when I was twelve. His dad answered the door, clearly annoyed, but a few minutes later, Chris came outside, with his hood pulled up, and told me to call him next time, and he'd meet me at my house.

"Have you brought other girls over?"

He glances at me. "No."

"Never?"

"Never."

A sense of relief washes over me at his response. But my mind is still swirling with questions, and before I can stop myself, I blurt out, "Would you ever bring me?"

His jaw tightens as he walks toward me. "No," he answers firmly. "That's the last place I'd take you."

"Why?"

He doesn't answer, instead he pulls back the comforter and sheets on my bed. "You're tired. Get in."

My neck twists as I look up at him. His expression is tense, and I lick my lips nervously. "Aren't you going to help me out of this dress?"

The muscle in his jaw tightens again, and he shakes his head. "You're fucking wasted," he murmurs. "I shouldn't have let you drink that much."

228

"It helps me think less," I tell him with a frown. "I don't feel that hollow feeling in my chest as much when I'm drunk."

He frowns. "Your mom?"

Among other things. But I nod, my nose tingling with the signs of tears building in my eyes. "It's so hard," I say, my voice cracking. "Waking up and not seeing her."

"Fuck." Chris sinks onto the bed beside me, and pulls me into him, wrapping his arms around me. The moment my head hits his chest, I break down, bawling my eyes out. "I'm so sorry, Gabi."

"It's not your fault," I manage to say, shaking my head.

"I'm still sorry." He tightens his hold on me. "I'm sorry I didn't do anything when I knew what was going on." His voice becomes thick.

"I asked you not to."

"It doesn't fucking matter," he replies, pulling back slightly to hold my face in his hands, locking eyes with me intensely. "You're too damn important for me to have let that shit go on." He shakes his head, and my heart pounds harder and harder. "It killed me seeing how much it hurt you. I can't bear to see you hurt again."

"I won't," I say, keeping my eyes on his. "I promise I won't do it again."

"Once is more than enough," he grits out, tears brimming in his eyes as he clutches my face. "You mean too fucking much to me. If you ever..." He trails off, squeezing his eyes shut, unable to finish the thought. "I don't know what I would ever do if you—"

I don't think.

I don't think I even breathe before I lean in and press my lips to his. His hands loosen on my face when I kiss his lips for the first time.

He's frozen at first, maybe in shock or something, but I don't let go. I keep pressing my lips to his, softly kissing me, my shoulders deflating when he doesn't move.

But just as I'm about to pull away, a low groan escapes Chris's throat when he opens up and kisses me back.

He's kissing me back.

Chris is *kissing* me.

His hand tightens on my face, tilting my head back slightly. "Gabi," he murmurs between kisses, his voice laced with pain. "Wait. Fuck. What are you doing?"

I shake my head, pausing to breathe as I grasp the back of his head, pulling him closer and deepening the kiss. "I don't know," I mumble against his lips.

I don't know what I'm doing. I don't know what will happen when this ends, or tomorrow. All I know is that I want this. Right now, right here. I want him.

He hums, pulling back from the kiss. "Gabi. You're drunk."

I shake my head again, my eyes heavy with desire, wanting to kiss him again. "I'm not," I murmur, leaning in again, but Chris stops me, his grip firm as my eyes lift to meet his.

"You are," he says, his lips pressed into a thin line. His brows furrow, and a flicker of sadness passes over his face as he brushes his thumb across my cheek. "You don't know what you're doing," he murmurs. "You don't want to do this."

What if I do?

I don't say that, though.

Being rejected once is enough for me.

My shoulders sag, and I pull away, turning to wipe my eyes. "You're right," I say, trying hard not to make my voice crack. "I'm sorry. I don't know what I was thinking."

"It's fine," Chris murmurs, his breath heavy. He tugs on my arm, turning me back to face him until our eyes meet. "You were sad, and drunk, and... fuck." He squeezes his eyes shut, pulling at his hair. "Let's just go to sleep, okay?"

I nod, sniffling as he pulls me down onto the bed. "You'll stay?" I ask, desperately hoping I haven't ruined everything. I need him now more than ever.

"Yeah," he assures me, lying down beside me and pulling me close, my head resting against his neck, *my safe place.* "I'll stay."

I close my eyes, snuggling closer to him, feeling his fingers begin to trace gentle patterns along my back. My eyelids are heavy with exhaustion, and I must be dreaming when I imagine his fingers spelling out:

I love you.

26

I dare you to kiss me

Christopher

"I kissed you."

A heavy breath leaves my lips. "You did."

I can't stop thinking about that night. I was drunk, and fucked up over spending the whole night watching the girl I love in the arms of some other guy. I wanted her so bad that I didn't even stop her when she leaned in and kissed me. I let her. I kissed her back and got lost in her, starving for a taste of heaven when I'd been denied it for years.

But it wasn't long until the rational part of my brain took over, and I stopped it. I pulled my lips away from hers, realizing she was only kissing me because she was drunk, and sad. Sad about her mom, sad about being dumped the night of the prom.

She didn't want me.

She just wanted *somebody*.

And I really wish I could have been that someone for her, but I couldn't. It would have hurt too fucking much. So I pulled away, tucked her into me, and waited until she fell asleep before crawling out of her bedroom window.

"And you kissed me back," she says, her eyebrows dipping. I can see the memory of that night flooding back to her like a hurricane, and I can't do anything to stop it.

I don't want to.

I've been carrying this part of her, of us for so long knowing she didn't remember what happened, that now that she does, it lifts a weight off my shoulders.

I swallow hard and nod. "Yeah."

Her eyes widen with surprise. "I was your first kiss?" she asks, shaking her head in disbelief. "You hadn't kissed anyone before me?"

Her blue eyes shimmer under the dark blue lights of the hot tub, and I shake my head. "No."

She furrows her brow. "But what about Taylor?" she asks, her hair swirling around in the water as she moves closer.

"Nothing ever happened with her," I tell her. "Or with anyone else."

She sucks in a breath, her gorgeous eyes swimming with uncertainty, and I have a feeling I know what she's going to ask.

The bubbles from the hot tub fill the silence as Gabi takes another step closer, her brows furrowing, and she locks eyes with me. "Why?"

I lift my hand out of the water and run it through my hair. "Why do you think, Gabi?" My heart pounds in my chest as she processes my words, her eyes widening with realization.

"You..." She frowns, shaking her head. "But you left," she says, searching my eyes for answers. "You left that night and didn't come back. You didn't want me back."

"You think I didn't want you?" I ask, narrowing my eyes at her. "You think I don't still want you?"

"You..." Her eyes widen. "You do?"

I'm done pretending that every breath I take isn't for her. That the reason I smile, the reason I feel *anything*, isn't because of her.

"I can't remember a time when I didn't," I say, pouring my heart out as I swim closer to her. "You're all I've ever wanted, Gabi."

Tears well up in her beautiful blue eyes and she shakes her head. "How long?"

"What?"

"How long, Chris?" she repeats. "How long have you had feelings for me?"

I close my eyes, avoiding her gaze. I know what she wants to know. She's wondering if it broke my heart to see her with every boyfriend she'd had along the years.

I open my eyes and meet hers. "Since the day I met you," I confess.

She covers her mouth with her hand, shaking her head in disbelief. "All this time?"

My jaw ticks, and my heart aches. I don't know what she's thinking. Does she hate me for not saying anything? I don't know what I'll do if she walks away from me, and I never see her again.

"I never should have brought it up," I say, reaching out for her. But I hesitate and let my hand drop. "This doesn't have to change anything. We can just—"

"Don't you dare say we can just go back to how it was," she interrupts, anger flickering in her eyes.

My chest heaves with each heavy breath, our eyes locked together. "Isn't that what you want?"

She steps closer. "Is that what *you* want?"

I can't lie to her. Not anymore. "No."

She sucks in a breath, and like a moron, I move in closer until we're inches apart. I can't fight this. I've tried, and failed for years. I'm done trying.

"Prove it," she whispers, pressing her hands flat against my chest, making me suck in a breath as she trails her hands higher, and higher until they lifts out of the water, and wrap around my neck. "Kiss me."

Either my brain short-circuited or I've just heard the love of my life tell me to kiss her. I blink, furrowing my brows. "What?"

She lifts onto her tip-toes until our lips are stacked, but she keeps her eyes on mine. "I dare you to kiss me."

A shaky breath escapes me. "I didn't pick dare."

"I know."

"I don't back down from a dare," I remind her.

"I know that, too."

My hands fly to her hips, and I almost can't believe she's right here, in my arms, telling me what I've always wanted to hear. "If we kiss, it will change everything," I tell her as one last resort to stop her from doing this if she's going to regret it in the morning.

She shakes her head, the breath of her lips landing on mine. "I'm sick of everything being the same."

I frown, squeezing her hips. "That isn't a good enough reason."

"How about because I want you too," she says, pressing the lightest of kisses against my jaw. My body tingles from her touch. "Because I might not have realized my feelings when you did, but because I've wanted you for so long, too."

"You have?"

235

She pulls back, and nods, her eyes hooding slightly. It's not from alcohol, though, or fatigue, but pure lust coating her beautiful blue eyes. "I dare you, Chris. I dare you to—"

I don't even let her finish her sentence.

My lips land on hers, and she moans into my mouth the second I do.

And fuck me, it's the sweetest sound I've ever heard, the best melody, my favorite song. I could listen to it all day.

Her lips part, and I trace my tongue over hers, my hand lowering to the nape of her neck, trailing until I grip her soft hair in my hand.

Gabi tangles her fingers in my hair, and I can't help but let out a groan. "God, Gabi," I pant, wrapping my arms around her legs before I lift her around my waist. Another sweet little sound leaves her lips when she straddles my waist, and it makes me lose my goddamn mind.

"I can't believe I didn't remember," she mumbles against my lips. "How could I not remember we kissed before?"

"I don't blame you," I pant, pausing to take a breather before I kiss her again. "You were so drunk."

She pulls back, with a frown on her beautiful face. "But you remember."

I clutch her face in my hands, running my thumb over her bottom lip, which is puffy and red from my kisses. "I could never forget it," I tell her, my brows furrowing with the memory. "Your taste haunted me for years."

She leans into my touch, breathing heavily. "And now?"

"You taste better than I ever remembered," I murmur, bringing our lips together again.

She wraps her fingers in my hair again and tugs. A groan builds in my throat when I feel her move her hips up and down, grinding against my cock. I let out a low moan, and she eats up my noises as she continues moving her hips, rubbing her pussy over me, only our underwear as a barrier. "Gabi— fuck."

"Chris," she pants, leaving my mouth to kiss my jaw. "Take it off," she begs, making her words clear when she grinds against my cock. "I want to feel you."

Jesus.

I turn around with her still in my arms, place her on the ledge, and hop out of the hot tub. Her eyes, soft and blue, follow me as they drop to my chest, both of us breathing heavily. "I want to lick you all over," she says, running her tongue over her lips.

I let out a laugh, closing the distance to kiss her again. I don't think I'll ever be able to stop now that I've had a taste. "You can do whatever you want to me."

She grins, straddling my waist, and pushes at my chest until I lie back on the ground, gazing up at her. She leans down, brushing her lips against mine, and I get lost in her, grabbing her hips when she begins rocking over me in a figure eight motion.

"Fuck," I breathe out, feeling the heat of her pussy over my cock.

She pulls back with a grin before leaning in again, flicking her tongue over the length of my lips, then trailing down to my jaw and neck.

"Ughhh, fuck." Moans are ripped from my throat as she keeps licking me, flicking her tongue over my chest, moving slowly downward to my stomach.

"I love the noises you make," she murmurs, kissing my stomach.

My hand tangles in her hair. "Good, 'cause I can't fucking stay quiet when you do that."

She lifts her head, smirking down at me. "How about when I do this?" She runs her hand down my stomach, reaching lower until she grabs my cock over my boxers.

My hips fly up at the contact. "Oh, fuck," I groan. Fuck. *Fuck.* She touched me for two seconds, and I'm about to come.

Gabi looks down at her hand over my junk, and she grips it tighter. "I'm holding your dick."

"Yeah." A laugh bubbles out of me.

She rubs me over my boxers. "How do you feel about that?"

I shake my head. How do you explain what heaven on earth feels like? "So fucking good."

"It's not weird?" she asks, tilting her head. "We've been best friends a long time."

I smirk, rubbing my thumb over her cheek. "You forget I've been fantasizing about you for years."

Her eyes widen a little, as if remembering how long I've wanted her, and she licks her lips. "Me too," she admits, sending my heart soaring. "The day I caught you in the shower…"

"I thought I'd traumatized you."

She shakes her head, a grin spreading across her face. "The opposite," she says. "I couldn't stop thinking about how I wished you would have done something," she admits, making my heart pound out of my chest.

"I thought you didn't want me that way," I tell her.

She shakes her head. "I always want you. In every way," she says, punctuating her sentence by reaching into my boxers, and gripping my cock.

"God, Gabi." My head tilts back. "Me too."

I lift my head when I feel her tugging my boxers down, and my pulse races, quickening with each second of her hands on me. I stare down at her face, watching as she keeps her eyes on her hand wrapped around me, until she leans down to tongue the slit.

"Oh fuck." I groan at the feel of her tongue slowly licking me. Her tongue swirls around the head before she wraps her mouth around me, and gives me a long suck. My hips shoot up off the floor, thrusting into her mouth. "Fuuuuck."

She pulls off me, running the tip of her tongue over my whole length. "I want you inside me," she murmurs before taking my cock between her lips again.

"God fucking dammit," I curse, my dick twitching in her hand when she pulls off me again.

"You want that?" she asks, the sight of her making me lightheaded.

"Yes," I pant, my vision going blurry. "God, yes." I tug on her hand, lifting her up until she's straddling me again, and grinds herself over my cock. "Ummfff." My eyes squeeze closed, my dick thrusting along her slit covered by her panties.

"You're so beautiful," Gabi says, tugging on my hair as she leans down to kiss me.

My hands fumble as I try to pull down her lacy black thong. Nerves wrack through me, making my hands shake and my breath erratic.

"Hey, hey." Gabi stops moving, pulling back to cup my face in her hands, her brows furrowed with concern. "What's wrong?"

I shake my head. "Sorry. Fuck." I close my eyes, breathing out a sigh. "I just… I want you so fucking bad."

Her lips curve into a smile, and she leans in, kissing me softly. "I want you, too."

She shuffles off my lap, standing up before she pulls her panties off. I breathe so hard it feels like I'm running out of oxygen. When she sits down again, we both moan at the feeling of her bare pussy rubbing over my dick.

A soft whimper leaves her lips as she moves her hips. "Put your cock in me."

Fuck. Her words make a shiver run up my spine. I don't waste any time, wrapping my fist around my dick, rubbing it between her slit, before lining up at her entrance.

A groan rips from my throat when I thrust the tip inside, and Gabi takes over, slowly dropping down onto my cock until she's buried to the hilt.

"Oh fuck," I grunt, gripping her hips in place. "Fuck, Gabi, you feel…" I heave out a breath when she lifts her hips and drops back down, taking all of me inside of her.

"God," she moans, making my cock twitch inside her. "So, do you."

I lie back, lifting her hips, and help her move up and down on my cock. "You're so wet, and tight, and *fuck*," I moan, pleasure curling my spine every time her tight pussy grips me inside her.

Wrapping an arm around her waist, I flip us both over, and she gasps as she finds herself on her back. I shoot her a grin as I line up, and thrust back inside of her warm heat.

Gabi tips her head back, moaning as my cock tunnels into her. "You feel so fucking good," she pants.

"I've been thinking about this forever," I admit, pinning her hands above her head. Her tits move with every thrust and my eyes drop to them, seeing the metal bars poking through the wet, thin, lace fabric.

I groan at the sight, and lift my hands, trying to pull her bra off her body.

"There's a... hook... Oh god." Her words fall flat when I flick my thumb over her pierced nipples.

Fuck. They're even hotter than I imagined.

"I wanted to see these for so long," I tell her, leaning down to flick my tongue over her pretty pink nipples, with a silver, metal bar through them.

She moans when I suck them into my mouth. "I thought of you when I got them done," she says, making me snap my head to her. I arch a brow. She did? "I wanted to tell you," she admits, tugging her bottom lip between her teeth. "To show you."

My brows furrow as I thrust into her. "I would have died," I tell her. "I haven't stopped thinking about them since I saw them poking through your tank top."

She tilts her head back, her pretty lips parting with a moan. "I'm so close. Please."

I groan at the feel of her walls tightening around me. "Oh shit. I can feel you." I push deeper into her, pleasure surrounding my body. "Fuck, I'm not going to last."

She shakes, gripping my hair to make me look down at her. "Come inside me. I want to see you come."

241

My hips keep moving, but my brows dip. "I want you to come first." She squeezes her pussy around me, making a jolt of pleasure tingle in my balls. "Oh fuck," I groan.

"Come," she orders me. *Fuck, that's so hot.* "Fill me up."

"Jesus, Gabi," I grunt, thrusting a few more times before I spill inside her. I feel her pussy fluttering around me as the orgasm crashes into her, and I keep pushing my cock into her, the pleasure mind numbingly good, until I'm completely spent.

I fall to the ground beside her, my cock still deep inside Gabi. I don't want to pull out, not just yet. I want to feel her a little longer. "That was so much better than I ever imagined."

Gabi lets out a chuckle, and shuffles closer, lying her head on my bare chest, her piercing blue eyes looking up at me. "We just had sex," she says, a smirk tugged at her gorgeous lips.

I glance down at her, trying to regulate my breathing. "Yeah."

"How was it?" she asks, wagging her eyebrows playfully, which makes me laugh.

"So fucking good," I tell her. "Better than I ever thought it could be," I admit, leaning in to kiss her. Her eyes shimmer with happiness as she looks up at me, and my heart swells with emotion.

"I love you," I confess, swallowing my nerves as I watch her smile fade slightly, her eyes widening in surprise. "This might be the wrong time to say it, but… I can't keep pretending I don't. I loved you when we were fifteen. I loved you when we were eighteen, and I love you now." Her breathing quickens, and I keep my gaze locked on her blue eyes, caressing her cheek with my thumb. "I never stopped loving you, Gabi. Not for a single moment."

She stares back at me, her lips slightly parted, her breaths heavy. Shit. Did I rush things too quickly? But when she leans down to kiss me, my heart settles. "I love you too," she murmurs against my lips. "So fucking much."

My smile widens as our lips meet, and I lose myself in her. In her scent, her taste, just her. She's everything I've ever wanted for so long that it feels like I'm dreaming.

She shifts her hips, and my cock twitches inside her. "We didn't use a condom," she points out, making me pull back, my eyes widening.

Fuck. "No." I rake a hand through my hair. "Is that... Are you on—"

"I'm on birth control," she affirms, nodding. "But I forgot to ask you if you were negative."

I stiffen.

Gabi lifts her head, furrowing her brows. "I've never been with a guy without a condom. I'm not usually so reckless but..." She shakes her head. "I didn't think. Not with you. You were right here, and I wanted you more than anything and—"

"It's okay, Gabi," I reassure her, clutching her face in my hands, and place a kiss on her forehead. "We were both at fault. It didn't even cross my mind," I admit.

"I always got checked whenever I slept with someone," she says, glancing at me. "And I haven't been with anyone in over a year."

My brows knit together, and I can't help but think about Gabi with other people. I know she's been with others, as she's told me, including her first time with a girl, but jealousy courses through me nonetheless.

"What about you?" she asks me.

"What about me?"

She shrugs, a hint of uncertainty flickering in her eyes as she shifts her gaze away for a moment before meeting mine again. "I don't really want to hear about any other girls you've been with but we should—"

"I haven't."

Her brows furrow in confusion. "Huh?"

"I haven't been with any other girls. You're my first."

27

Always you

Gabriella

"What?" My eyes widen in surprise as I sit up, peering down at Chris sprawled on the floor. "What are you saying?"

He can't possible mean… *that*. Right?

He looks up at me, his expression softening as he meets my eyes. A faint smile tugs at the corners of his lips. "I've never had sex with anyone else."

"Never?" I ask, my voice rising.

"No," he affirms.

"Not even when you were in London?"

His jaw ticks, and he shakes his head slowly. "No, Gabi."

"But…" I can't make sense of this. This whole time? All these years? "Why?"

He sighs, lifting himself off the ground to cup my face in his hands. "Because you're the only one I've ever wanted."

I don't even realize I'm crying until Chris wipes my tears, his brows furrowing. "Hey, don't cry," he says, pulling me into him. "Please, pretty girl. It breaks my heart."

I shake my head when he places a soft kiss on my forehead. "I love you."

A smile appears on his face, and he swipes his thumb over my cheek. "I love you too."

"I slept with other people."

A sigh escapes him. "I know, Gabi."

He's so calm, and I don't get it. Why isn't he mad? "You don't hate me for that?"

His smile returns as he shakes his head. "I could never hate you."

"I'm serious, Chris," I say, pulling back from him. His frown deepens as his hands drop from my face, but I feel unworthy of his touch now. I don't deserve comfort. "I didn't wait. I didn't even try. When I got to college…" I pause. "I was so messed up over my mom dying, and you leaving, and I thought you didn't want me, and I…" I falter, unable to say the rest.

Chris shuffles closer to me, lifting my chin so I can look at him. "You did nothing wrong. We weren't together."

"But I loved you," I tell him. "I already loved you by then."

He smiles briefly at my confession, but his expression turns serious. "You weren't a virgin in high school, Gabi. I didn't expect you to save yourself for me or whatever bullshit you're coming up with in your head right now. I understand you needed to figure yourself out, especially after your father made you feel like you had to hide who you were." His gaze holds mine firmly. "I don't blame you, and I definitely don't hate you."

God, I love him.

I shake my head, tears welling up in my eyes. "What about you?"

He raises an eyebrow. "What about me?"

His knuckles graze my jaw, and I want to lean into his touch so badly, but I resist. "What if you want to explore?" I ask, my voice trembling. "What if you reach a point where you resent me, where you hate me because you never got to be with anyone else?"

The thought of that happening is like ripping my heart out of my chest. I know I want to be with him. I know it in my bones that he's everything I've ever wanted, but what if, in a few years, Chris gets bored of me?

He lets out a scoff, an amused look crossing his features. "That will never happen."

"Be serious," I insist, frowning.

He tilts his head slightly. "You're never serious."

"I am right now." I need to know he's okay with this, that he won't regret committing to only me. Because if we get together, I can't imagine a future where that changes. He will always be a part of me.

Chris lets out a sigh, moving closer and cupping my face in both of his hands to look deeply into my eyes. "Believe me when I tell you I have never wanted anyone but you. I will never want anyone but you," he says, brushing his thumb over my lip. "I fell in love with you before I even knew the meaning of the word, and I never stopped, Gabi. I'm happy knowing you're the only person I've ever slept with." He closes his eyes briefly. "God, Gabi. I kissed one person. One fucking person, and I wanted to rip my tongue out."

My eyes widen a little. "You did?" I ask, remembering that he had mentioned, during our truth or dare game, that the last person he kissed was two years ago, in London.

He nods, his lips curving into a frown. "Yeah," he says, swallowing hard. "During my first year of Uni, there was this girl who hung out with the guys at the pub, and she made it clear quite a few times she was interested in me." My stomach drops at the thought, though I know I have no right. I can't

248

even imagine how hurt Chris must have felt seeing me with the guys I dated throughout high school. "I was so messed up about everything," he continues. "I've wanted you for years, Gabi. I was starting to lose hope that you'd ever feel the same, so I guess I thought I'd try to move on, and we—"

"Kissed," I finish for him.

He nods. "Yeah."

"And?" I press.

He shakes his head. "I broke it off two seconds later and apologized to her. I told her I was hung up on someone else and just left."

"Me?" I guess, feeling my heart knock against my chest.

He nods, smiling a little sadly. "Always you."

Chris is right in front of me, telling me everything I've dreamed of hearing for years, and I still can't believe it. "What if I ruin this?" I ask, sniffling into his chest. "I can't handle it if I lose you."

He wraps his arms around me, pulling me into the comfort of his arms, and he lets out a sigh. "There's nothing you can do to make me walk away, Gabi," he mumbles against my hair. "I'm not going anywhere. Ever. You've carved your name so deep in my soul I'm afraid if you leave, I'll die."

"Chris."

He pulls back, locking his gaze with mine. "You'll never lose me, Gabi."

"I did once," I point out.

He shakes his head, a gentle smile on his lips. "I was always yours. Always hoping that someday you'd love me back," he says. "And even if that day never came, I'd still be yours."

Memories of the day after prom flood my mind. I woke up with a splitting headache, expecting Chris to be there beside me. Instead, I learned from someone else that he had left the country, a revelation that has since become a sensitive issue between us. Every time I've asked, he's avoided answering, but I'm determined to know the reason he left that day and didn't come back.

"Then why did you leave that night?" I finally ask him, wondering if it was because of our kiss.

He stiffens, releasing his hold on me and rises to his knees. I watch quietly as he pulls on his pants. When he looks back at me, his jaw tightens. "It's late," he murmurs. "We should go to bed."

"Chris," I say, moving closer to him.

He shakes his head, avoiding my eyes. "Someone could walk in."

"Chris," I repeat, louder this time. He meets my eyes, a hint of pain flickering across his face. "Do you love me?"

He exhales heavily, his shirt crumpled in his fist at his side. "You know I do."

I reach out, cupping his face as he often does mine. His eyes futter closed, and I lean in, pressing my lips to his. "Then no more lies," I say. "Only honesty between us from now on."

His eyes reopen, wariness swirling within them. "Gabi—"

"Why did you leave that night?"

28

Prom night: Part II

Christopher

Age Eighteen

I've fantasized about kissing Gabi countless times. I've imagined the taste of her, the sound of her sighs, how her lips would feel against mine.

But when she finally pressed her warm, soft lips to mine, she completely shattered every expectation I had.

It lasted only a few seconds. At first, I was so stunned that I didn't react. But as soon as I realized what was happening, I didn't hesitate. I grabbed her face in my hands and kissed her back, savoring the taste of her for the first time. My chest felt like it was being pried open, the feeling was so intense.

My first ever kiss, and it was with the love of my fucking life.

But it ended as quickly as it started when I realized she was *drunk*.

She had polished off half the flask I had taken from my dad's cabinet. She was so wasted, she couldn't even keep her eyes open properly. She didn't know what she was doing. She was just consumed by sadness, heartbreak, and embarrassment, drowning herself in alcohol.

It meant *nothing* to her.

When it meant *everything* to me.

I don't even think she knew she was kissing me when she was doing it.

It was purely just a reflex.

I love her more than I've ever loved anything, but I also *know* her. I know that Gabi clings to attention and affection like someone would a security blanket. I watched her do it for years.

For years, she dated these guys who didn't deserve her. I don't even think she liked them all that much. She just craved being wanted, being needed.

If only she had looked up whenever she was in my arms, she would have seen that I could give her everything she ever wanted, and more.

It gutted me to climb out of her window and leave her, but I couldn't stay there, acting like nothing happened. Because I knew, when she woke up in the morning, she would either regret it, or not even remember it happened at all.

And I couldn't do it.

I'd gut myself if I knew it would please her. But in doing so, it would leave me dead. Letting her keep kissing me, and touching me when I knew alcohol was clouding her judgement would have destroyed me in the process.

Though it's hard to remember that when I see my house only a few steps away.

I stop in my tracks, my jaw aching from my teeth grinding together. My stomach immediately sours at the sight, and I blow out a breath.

Fucking hate it here.

I hate everything about this place, and I hate who I become once I get inside.

Running a hand through my hair, I glance back behind my shoulder, at Gabi's house, seeing her light off.

She's still asleep.

Thank fuck.

A dip forms between my brows as I stare back at her house, wondering if I can go back there, and just sleep and pretend like nothing happened tonight.

A pang hits my chest. I can't. I can't act like nothing happened when she wakes up in the morning and looks at me riddled with guilt and regret.

"Fuck." I clench my fists, and keep walking to the fucking hell hole that is my house.

My pulse starts to race when I curl my hand over the door handle and twist it open.

Fuck. I feel like I'm going to be sick.

I swallow down the bile crawling up my throat, and take a step inside the dark house. Quietly closing the front door, I try not to make a sound as I walk through the living room.

The minute the lamp turns on, I freeze, my stomach dropping to my fucking ass.

"Where the fuck have you been?"

I turn my head, spotting my father sat on the brown couch my mom loved so much. Now it's just worn-out, tattered, and marked with spilled alcohol stains.

My eyes immediately shift to the coffee table, where I notice an empty glass and a bourbon bottle lying on its side, empty with the cap off.

My jaw tightens as our eyes meet, and I see his bloodshot gaze staring back at me.

"Are you mute?" he spits out. "Where the fuck have you been?"

"I was with Gabi," I reply, calmly. Fuck, I'm tired. I just want to go to bed and crash.

He grunts. "Still hanging around that slut?"

I hate him. I hate him with every fiber of my being. My fists clench beside me, and I force myself to have some self-control. He's drunk, and an asshole, but I can be the better person. I can go to bed, and let him sit here and rot for all I care.

I turn away and head for the stairs, hoping he just lets me go.

But of course, that doesn't happen in this house.

"Where do you think you're going?" he yells, lifting off the couch.

"To sleep."

The house is dark, and moody and so fucking depressing, but his eyes are like fire as they twist into anger. "Get down here right now. I'm not done."

He never is. No matter what I do, he always has a problem with it. It's like he's looking for an argument, and won't let me leave until I give him what he's looking for.

"It's four in the morning. I'm tired."

"You should have thought about that before you crawled back here in the middle of the fucking night." I'm so used to his yelling. I've grown uncomfortably accustomed to it.

When it's quiet, I still hear him shouting. His voice echoes in my head, calling me worthless, saying I've ruined everything.

I hear it constantly.

All the fucking time.

So I drown it out with music, noise, drugs, alcohol, pain—anything to silence him in my mind.

"You think you can steal from me and I'll just let it go?"

I freeze, the weight of his flask heavy in my pocket. "What?"

His hand slams against the stair railing, and I flinch backward. Anger boils through me. I hate that he still scares me. I don't want to be scared of him. I just want to go to bed and sleep. I just want one day in this house when I don't feel *scared*.

"You heard me. You're a fucking little thief."

My heart bangs against my chest, my heart lodged in my throat. "I just want to go to bed."

"I don't give a fuck," he says, his lip curling as he grips me by the elbow. "You weren't too tired to do whatever the fuck it was you were doing with that slut."

I don't think before I shove him off me, swinging around to face him. "Don't you dare call her that again."

I tried. I really fucking tried to be calm, but I can't. I can't handle it when he talks about Gabi like that. When any of them do.

When she told me her date called her a slut tonight, my body went red fucking hot, and I just wanted to storm in there and punch his stupid face.

My father's face lights up, his lips curving as he scoffs out a laugh. He's enjoying this. This is what he wants. He *wants* me to fight back. "Or what?" he says. "What are you going to do?"

"Christopher?" My mother's voice freezes me in place. I look up to see her frail form at the top of the staircase, clutching her robe tightly around her. Her eyes widen in terror as she takes in the sight of my father gripping my collar. "What's going on?"

"Go back to bed," he spits out. "This doesn't concern you."

"It's four in the morning," my mom says, her brows furrowing as she looks between us. "Chris. Where have you been, honey?"

"I—"

"Don't fucking talk to him like he's innocent," my father snaps.

My jaw clenches when I see my mom's face tighten and her arms wrapping around her body even tighter. She's just as scared as I am.

"Come to bed," she says in a calm, quiet voice that breaks my heart. She shouldn't have to be afraid to speak in her own house, to her own son.

But my father's grip tightens, pulling me closer to him. "He's not going anywhere." His hand reaches for my pocket. I don't move as he grabs the flask out, snarling when he clutches it in his grip. "You steal from me, come home in the middle of the night, and you think you can just go to *bed?*"

"Christopher. Just… just let him go," my mother pleads, her voice trembling.

My father's eyes snap up to my mother. "Shut the fuck up or you're next."

My jaw clenches. *He's not fucking touching her.* "Leave her out of this."

"Don't fucking talk back to me," he growls, tightening his grip on my collar. "You think you can do whatever you want, huh?" His head tilts as he stares at me, challenging.

I remain silent, staring back at his face, hate boiling through me. I've never despised anyone as much as I do him. It kills me that I share his DNA. It kills me that I share his name. And it kills me that my mother chooses to stay with him, despite everything.

He jerks my collar again when I don't reply. "Speak!"

I exhale sharply through my nose. "You clearly don't want to hear what I have to say."

No. What he really wants is to start an argument.

He snarls. "What's that?"

I give him what he's after and open my mouth. "I said, you don't—"

I don't even finish my sentence before his fist connects with my jaw, sending my head spinning to the side, and blood spurting from my mouth.

A gasp escapes from above me. "Christopher!"

I glance up to see my mom, hands over her mouth in shock. The pain in her eyes tears at me. "Mom, please, just go to your room," I urge her, wishing she would stay out of it. Whenever she gets involved, it never ends well.

But she doesn't listen. She races down the stairs, gently lifting my face to examine the blood trickling down my lip. Her touch feels like a world apart from my father's, and I almost want to laugh.

How did these two ever end up together?

Why does she stay with him?

These questions have haunted me day after day, year after year, ever since I was seven years old and my father gave me my first busted lip.

"He's fine," my piece of shit father grunts, tugging me away from my mom. "Get the fuck out of here, and let me discipline him."

Discipline. Like beating the shit out of your kid teaches them how to behave. It just makes me fucking hate him and want out of this house.

"Christopher. Please, don't hurt—ahh!"

I barely have time to react before he shoves her into the wall. My eyes widen in horror as I see my mom crumple to the floor, clutching her arm in pain.

"Mom!" I struggle to break free from his grasp to reach her as he tightens his grip on me. "Let go of me!" I shout, pushing against his chest. "Don't you dare touch her."

"And what are you going to do about it?"

My blood boils, anger rising until I can't take it anymore, and I fucking blow. I swing my fist at his face with all the force I have inside of me, watching as his face swings to the side.

His eyes widen in shock as he turns to me, clutching his chin. "You little shit."

My heart pounds in my chest as he advances, landing a punch squarely on my face.

Fuck.

I cough violently as his fist slams into my stomach this time, knocking me to the floor.

"Christopher," my mother yells. I look up at her, and I think I see tears streaming down her face, but I can't tell. My eyes are blurry, and my ears are ringing, and... *fuck*.

I should have stayed at Gabi's.

I should have slept there, and held her against me, and smiled in the morning when she eventually looked at me and said she didn't mean to kiss me, that she was drunk and didn't know what she was doing.

I should have gotten my heart broken.

It would have hurt less than this.

"You think you can punch me?" he sneers, delivering a kick to my lower abdomen, right where the scar from his pocket knife hasn't even healed yet. "You think you're tough now?" Another kick follows.

Blood spurts out of my mouth. My ears ring so loud, I can't even hear him.

I hear my mom, though.

Screaming, yelling, crying.

"Go…" I cough out some more blood. *Go back upstairs. Please.*

"Hello?" I hear her voice tremble. "I need the police right now. My husband is hurting my son."

"What the—" The kicking halts abruptly, leaving me gasping for air, my ears ringing.

"Mom?" I manage to rasp, struggling to open my eyes.

"Hurry. Please. He's ahhh—"

"What do you think you're doing?" my father yells, knocking the phone from her hand as he grips her arm, and she cries out in pain.

"Mom!" I grunt, fighting to lift myself off the ground, pushing through the pain as I try to stand.

"What the fuck did you do, you stupid cunt?"

"Go, Chris!" she screams, tears streaming down her face as she stares at me. "Leave. Get the hell out of here."

My father whirls around, gripping my elbow tightly. "He's not going anywhere."

I watch in shock as my mom picks up her favorite blue vase and swings it at his head.

His grip on my wrist loosens, and he crumples to the ground, knocked out cold.

259

"Go," she repeats, holding the broken pieces of the vase in her hand. "Get out of here."

I shake my head, my heart racing. "I'm not leaving you."

Tears well up in her eyes as she shakes her head again. "I'll be okay, Chris. The police are coming. Just go, honey." The distant wail of sirens fills the air, and her expression softens with relief at the sound. "Go."

I purse my lips, stealing a last glance at her. The sirens grow louder and louder. Finally, I turn and race out of the house.

I run and run and run, pushing myself until I reach the road sign indicating the airport two miles away.

Reaching into my pocket, I pull out my wallet, seeing my passport, card and some cash stuffed inside.

My eyebrows furrow as I see the picture of Gabi and me that we took earlier today in the photobooth at the carnival, tucked away in my wallet.

I run my fingers over the picture. I want to bring her with me. I want to run back, wake her up and take her with me to wherever I decide to go. I can't stay here anymore. I can't take this shit day after day. But I can't do it without her.

My hand falls away from the picture, and I exhale heavily, closing my eyes.

I can't.

She's starting college in a few months. She's already been accepted and found a dance studio nearby. She's pursuing her dreams. She's going to achieve incredible things and be amazing.

I'd only hold her back.

I place my wallet back in my pocket, and wipe my lip, glancing down at the blood on my finger. My chest aches as I look down at the red liquid on my thumb before I wipe it between my fingers.

I grab my phone, seeing it's running out of battery, and I quickly call a cab before it dies.

The next thing I know, I'm at the airport, booking the first flight I see to get the fuck away from here.

London.

29

Gabriella

Some might call me a creep, but I say I'm just in love.

I've been awake for over an hour, just lying here watching Chris sleep.

His arms are spread wide, his head turned to the side. I just watch as his chest rises and falls with each breath he takes, my head resting on my hands against his chest. My eyes trace over his bare, muscular chest. He didn't look like this in high school. He was skinnier, thinner. And now I have a clue as to why.

My brows furrow as I gaze at the scar on his stomach. How many times did something like that happen and I didn't know it?

Why did he never tell me what was going on?

Last night, we made our way back to our room. I was dripping wet from the hot tub, my dress clinging to my skin, but as soon as the hotel door closed behind us, I turned around and begged him to tell me everything.

And it broke my heart.

What happened the night he left was so different from what I had imagined. I woke up drunk and confused, my last memory of us on the Ferris wheel, and I turned to see my bed empty.

It was very strange since Chris usually slept in my room, especially if it was late. So I called him. And called him. And called him again.

But there was no answer.

I started to panic, my mind racing with worry over where he could be and what might have happened. It wasn't until I hurried to his house and I saw his mom standing at the door instead of Chris, that I knew something was wrong.

I'd never really met his mom before. She was really pretty. Looked just like Chris. Brown hair, brown eyes, and the same gentle smile as she told me that Chris had left.

At first, I thought she meant he had just gone out quickly, maybe to pick something up, and would be back at my place later that day. So, I waited in my driveway, sitting on the cold ground, feeling the chill seep into me as I waited for him to return.

But he never did.

Two weeks later, I received a call from an unknown number and answered it, hearing his voice again as he told me he was in London.

My heart aches as I look down at him sleeping with a faint smile on his face.

Last night was so special. It was our first time.

His first time.

I can't stop thinking about it. I haven't stopped thinking about it since he told me.

He waited for me. He didn't want anyone else but me.

And I've slept with... I don't even know how many people.

The thought twists my stomach as I glance at him. I never thought there was a chance for us, or that he wanted me the way I wanted him. But it turns out he's wanted me longer than I could have imagined.

Lifting my head off my hands, I lean over his body and press a kiss to his chest. I've loved Chris for what feels like my entire life. Whether as best friends or something more, he's always been important to me.

I press another kiss right over his heart, unable to find any other way to express my feelings for him. I love his heart. I love his smile. I love how kind, patient, and understanding he is. Even when he was going through much worse than I was without any support, he still comforted me when I needed him.

I hear a grunt as he blinks awake, looking down at me as I kiss all over his chest.

I glance up at him, continuing to kiss down his body until I reach the curls at the base of his pelvis. Pausing, I lift my head. "Is this okay?" I ask him.

A shaky breath escapes his lips. "Holy shit. Fuck yes."

I grin as my hand reaches down, gripping his hardening cock in my hand and swipe my tongue over the tip. "Yeah?"

"Mmmm," he nods. "*God.*"

I suck his tip into my mouth, circling my tongue around him. "No one's ever done this to you?" I ask, already knowing the answer. I suck him deeper, and the moan that comes out of him makes me clench around nothing. I love the noises he makes.

So desperate.

So needy.

So fucking hot.

"Only you," he says letting out a soft noise that drives me insane.

I hum around his dick, bobbing my head up and down as I suck him before I release him with a pop. "I like the sound of that," I say with a grin, stroking his cock.

His eyes soften as he reaches out, running his thumb over my cheek. "You have all my firsts, Gabi," he says. "First kiss. First time. First love."

I lift myself up, crawling closer to him. "I've only ever loved you," I tell him honestly. "You might not have been my first kiss or my first time, but—"

Chris interrupts me with a kiss. He doesn't let me finish my sentence before he grabs my face in his hands and brushes his lips against mine. His tongue swipes across mine. I'm left breathless when he pulls back, pressing his forehead against mine.

"Don't ever feel guilty about that," he says, shaking his head against mine. "I promise I don't hate you for it. I couldn't have expected you to hold off for years when I didn't give you any sign that I loved you."

I know what he's saying is true, but I can't help the curdling feeling in my stomach. "You did," I say, gazing into his soft brown eyes that I love so much. "You didn't know where I stood with you, yet you waited."

"That's different," he says with a sigh.

"How?"

He shrugs. "I've been in love with you for as long as I can remember," he admits.

My heart pounds in my chest. I'll never grow tired of hearing him say that.

"Nate?"

Chris's jaw tightens, but he nods, understanding what I mean. "Yeah. I loved you then."

I still remember asking Chris to help me vandalize Nate's car when I found out he was cheating on me. Chris didn't hesitate. He grabbed the can and joined me, even though he knew it was risky and illegal. He was always there for me, no matter what.

I crawl up his body, wrapping my arms around his neck. "Did it hurt?" I ask quietly. "Seeing him with me?"

Chris looks up, meeting my eyes with a sad nod. "I mean, yeah. I hated seeing you guys cuddled up at parties. I hated when he would kiss you, but..." He trails off.

"But?" I prompt.

His eyes lock with mine, and he smiles. "But I spent every night in your bed. I was the one you told everything to, shared everything with." His thumb traces along my waist, his gaze staying fixed on my face even though my breasts are pressed against his jaw. "I loved that way more than I hated seeing a few kisses and some hand-holding."

My heart aches with the love I have for him, and I shake my head, a frown forming between my brows. "How did I not see it?" I say, frustrated with myself for letting so much time pass without realizing how he felt about me.

"I hid it," he says, curling his hand around my waist. "I didn't want anything to ruin our friendship, Gabi."

"Remember the bonfire?" I ask him, my breath catching as his eyebrows furrow.

"Yeah?"

"I was so jealous of Taylor," I admit, both to him and to myself. "I don't think I realized it at the time, but I was jealous."

"Gabi," he says, shaking his head as if he can't believe it.

"I left Nate alone to come and talk to you because I couldn't stand seeing her with you," I tell him. "When you told me you didn't know if something might happen between you two, my heart fucking broke." My throat feels tight, and I swallow hard. "I hated the thought of you being with her."

"I didn't want her," he tells me. "I was just sick of seeing you and your boyfriend together, and—" His jaw clenches, and he shakes his head. "I didn't want anyone but you, Gabi," he says, tucking a strand of my hair behind my ear. "I can't even remember what she looked like."

"She was pretty."

"Not as pretty as you," Chris says, holding my waist in his hands, as he shakes his head. "No one is." His eyes finally drop to my tits that are practically pressed against his mouth and I watch as he swallows, staring at them. "Fuck," he groans, his voice coming out raspy and sexy as hell. "You're so fucking beautiful." He opens his mouth and takes my nipple inside, sucking the sensitive bud.

I buck against him, feeling his tongue tug on the metal bars, before he sucks on them lightly. "That feels…" I can't even speak. I close my eyes, moans trickling out of my throat as he releases me before moving to the other one, giving it the same attention. "Chris." A pop rings my ears when he pulls off, and I snap my eyes open.

"Can I—" He glances up at me, nervous, warily. "Can I try something?" he says, gripping my waist tighter.

I nod, raking my hand through his hair. "Anything."

His lips part on a shaky breath. "I want…" He closes his mouth again, squeezing his eyes closed.

I can't help but smile. "You can say whatever it is," I encourage him. "It's you and me, Chris."

He open his eyes, staring back at me, and nods. "Yeah." His lips curve in a smile. "It's you and me." Those words from his lips make me exhale heavily as he runs his hands down my back, and grips my ass. "I want to eat you out."

A groan climbs out of my throat when he squeezes my ass in his hands.

"I want to lick your pussy and feel you come on my tongue."

"Fuck," I moan, bucking my hips into him. My pussy throbs, and I have no doubt that if he moved his hands to my front, he'd find me dripping for him. "Are you sure you're a virgin?"

A laugh bubbles out of him. "I'm not anymore."

I click my tongue, grinning down at him. "That's right. I popped your cherry."

"You're such an idiot," he says with a grin, leaning closer to kiss me. "Why did I ever tell you that?"

I laugh against his lips, but it dies down when he kisses me, our mouths moving in sync as his tongue swipes over mine. I begin to shift off his lap, so I can lie down on the bed, but Chris stops me, pulling back to look at me.

I frown. "I thought you wanted—"

He shakes his head. "Not like that," he says.

My frown deepens. "Then how—"

"I want you to sit on my face."

Fuck.

"Yeah?" I ask him, breathless at the thought.

He nods, grunting as he bucks his hips up, making contact with my thigh. "Fuck yes."

268

He lies back on the bed, propped up by two pillows, and his hands grip my hips, pulling me up until I'm straddling his chest, and my pussy is an inch away from his mouth.

"Fuck," Chris grunts, staring down at me as he grips my ass in his hands. "Spread your pussy open," he begs. "Let me see all of you."

My legs shake as I run my hands down my stomach, and slowly spread my pussy open for him.

"Christ, Gabi," he moans, his eyes darkening as he zones in on me. "Come here," he begs. "I'm dying to taste you."

I shuffle on his chest, getting closer to him until his tongue reaches out and licks the length of me in one slow, long lick.

"Oh god," I moan, closing my eyes.

"Teach me how to make it good for you," he says, flicking his tongue over my clit. "Let me know if I'm doing it right."

I grip his hair in my hand, and move my hips. "My clit," I say, moving my pussy over his tongue. "Suck it into your mouth."

He breathes hard against me, and presses soft kisses against my clit, before he wraps his mouth around it and sucks. "Like this?"

"God, yes," I moan, my hips moving frantically over his face. "More," I beg. "Lick me, Chris."

"Fuck, Gabi," he grunts, licking my pussy like an ice cream cone. His tongue flicks over my clit, teasing it with the tip of his tongue. "You taste so fucking good."

He groans, gripping my ass to push my cunt lower onto his tongue, alternating between french kissing my clit, and flicking it with the tip of his tongue. Pleasure racks through me until I've abandoned any rational thought, and start grinding against his tongue, moving my pussy over him.

"Your mouth feels so… *God*." I lean over him, gripping the headboard with one hand as I buck my hips, fucking his tongue.

"Fuck yes," Chris grunts, pulling me down on him. "Ride my tongue, pretty girl. Cover my face with your cum."

"Chris," I moan, bucking into him. I reach up and grab my tit in my hand, squeezing it in my palm as his tongue dips down, stuffing it into my cunt. "Yes. That's it. I'm gonna—"

"You're drenched," he grunts against me, flicking his tongue over my entrance before he makes his way back to my swollen, sensitive clit. "I could live between your legs for the rest of my life."

"Ughh," I moan, gripping the headboard as I ride his face, until the orgasm crashes against me, making my legs shake as I keep grinding against his face.

"God yes," Chris moans, and as my orgasm settles, I look behind my shoulder, noticing his fist curled around his cock. "That was so fucking hot." I turn back around, looking down at his beautiful face, drenched and sporting a grin. "God, Gabi, you taste…" He trails off, shaking his head.

"How do I taste Chris?" I ask with a smirk, raking a hand through his curly hair.

He groans and sits up, bringing our chests together until they press against each other. "See for yourself," he says, before he leans in and our lips meet in a hot and messy kiss. He cups my jaw, opening his mouth to tangle his tongue with mine, and I taste myself on him. I groan into his mouth, slowly moving my hips over his bare cock. I'm never going to get enough of him, and I was an idiot to ever think I could just be his friend.

Chris pulls back, with a pained expression, and a low whimper escapes his lips. "If you keep doing that, I'm going to come."

"Eating me out turned you on that much?" I ask, tilting my head with a smirk on my face.

He groans, running his hand through his hair and brushing it back. "You have no fucking idea."

I wrap my arms around his neck and lean closer until our lips meet in a kiss. "Then do something about it," I tell him, making my statement clear when I grind my bare pussy over his hard cock.

He grunts, holding my hips in place. "You want me to fuck you again?"

I shake my head slightly, and Chris furrows his brow. But a smile spreads across my face as I lean in and say, "I want you to make love to me."

30

First dates and photobooths

Gabriella

"Are you ready?" Chris asks, his hands covering my eyes.

I exhale nervously, staring into darkness. "Is this the part where you kill me?" I joke.

He laughs, removing his hands, and my eyes open, widening when I see the carnival we used to love hanging out at—the same carnival we went to on prom night. The night I kissed him. The night he left.

Turning around, my eyes widen even more. "You're kidding," I say, unable to speak as the familiar noise and music rushes back.

He returns my smile, shaking his head. "Did you really think we'd spend your birthday back in South Carolina and I wouldn't bring you here?"

I squeal in excitement and jump into his arms. Chris catches me effortlessly, laughing as I pepper kisses all over his face. "I love you. I love you. I love you," I repeat, making every inch of his face feels my kisses.

"I love you too," he says with a chuckle. "Happy birthday, pretty girl."

"Best birthday ever," I say with a sigh. "Without a doubt. This beats all of the other ones."

"Yeah?"

I nod, a grin on my face as I wrap my arms around his neck. This past week has been incredible, and this morning was just a continuation of that when Chris woke me up with a huge stack of pancakes, and twenty-two candles placed on top. And now, we're going on our first ever date. The thought makes my brows shoot up. This is our first date. *My* first date.

"You know... I've never been on a date," I confess.

Chris's brows furrow in surprise. "Never?"

"No."

"What about..." He starts to ask, but the muscle in his jaw tenses, and he stops himself. Now that I understand how much it pained him to see me with others, I don't like to bring up the topic. The mere thought of him with someone else makes me feel sick to my stomach, so I can't imagine what Chris felt all those years.

"Never," I tell him with a shrug. "The closest I came to a real date in high school was prom night. With you." He smiles warmly at the memory. "I didn't really go on dates with anyone else, I just—"

"I know," he finishes with a sad smile.

"I just wanted to feel good, have some company, and... It wasn't like it is with you," I admit, shaking my head. "It's not even close."

Chris smiles, his lips curving at the side as he leans closer, brushing our lips together. "I know I don't have the same experiences," he murmurs, pulling back slightly to meet my eyes. "But the kiss I shared with that girl doesn't compare to you either," he says. "Not even close."

My breath hitches, and I narrow my eyes at him. "Don't talk about her."

273

Chris chuckles, his hands resting at my waist. "Jealous, pretty girl?" he teases. "I've got to say, I really like seeing you like this." He leans in, placing a soft kiss on my jaw.

My hands instinctively clutch his hair. "You're mine," I murmur as he continues kissing down my neck.

"I'm yours," he confirms with a subtle nod. "I always have been." He pulls back with a smirk, running his thumb over my bottom lip. "You know, I guess I have one of your firsts now," he says playfully. "Your first date."

I breathe out a laugh, running my hand over his soft hair. "You can have all of them," I tell him. "I never want to do this with anyone else."

His smile sends a flutter through my heart as he lowers me to the ground, intertwining his fingers with mine as we make our way toward the Ferris wheel.

"Are you up for it?" Chris asks.

I nod, looking up at him with a smile. "I'm not drunk this time."

He chuckles warmly, and we step inside the pod, closing the door behind us.

"I'm actually glad you're not drunk," he admits as the Ferris wheel starts to move.

"Yeah? Why?"

The corner of his lips lift in a smile. "Because," he murmurs, leaning closer until his hand grazes my jaw, cupping my face. "I can do this, and you'll remember it this time." He leans in, brushing his lips against mine. Slow. Soft. Patient.

When we pull away, he wears the prettiest smile on his face, and it makes me want to kiss him again.

"I still think about the last time we were here," I tell him.

"I'm surprised," Chris replies with a chuckle. "You were so drunk, you couldn't even walk."

I playfully push at his shoulders, but my laughter fades into a sigh. "I wish I remembered earlier," I admit. He turns to me with a frown. "I wish I hadn't forgotten," I continue. Our eyes lock, and Chris lets out a sigh.

"Honestly, me too," he says. "So much happened that night, and a part of me thought you'd wake up and regret it, or tell me it meant nothing," he says, swallowing hard. "And after I left, I almost didn't want to reach out to you." A crease forms between his brows. "I didn't want to hear you say those words," he adds with a sigh. "When I called you that day..." He shakes his head, running a hand through his hair. "I was waiting. Waiting for you to bring it up. Waiting for you to say it was a mistake, but..."

"I didn't remember," I finish for him, guilt settling in my stomach as he nods.

When Chris called a week later, I was so stunned by hearing his voice for the first time that I didn't even have a chance to remember what happened that night. I just wanted to know he was okay. I was confused as hell, and sad that he had left me without so much as a word, but I was also just glad to know he was safe.

I held onto hope that he would come back. I imagined us going to college together. But as weeks turned into months and Chris told me about his visa and plans to study abroad, I lost all hope.

"You never brought it up. And I was so damn confused as to why, until it clicked," Chris says, his voice soft. He swallows, brushing his fingers against mine. "Part of me wanted to tell you," he admits. "I wanted you to know it had

275

happened. It killed me to keep this all to myself every time we texted or talked. But I figured telling you would only mess things up further, and I had already screwed up by leaving. I didn't want to make it worse."

I wonder what would have happened if he did tell me. How would I have reacted? What would I have said?

"Is that why you never visited?" I ask him tentatively. "You were worried you wouldn't be able to keep it a secret?"

He shrugs, pressing his lips together. "Part of it, I guess. I was scared our friendship would change. I was out of my mind in love with you for years, and I didn't know how to handle it," he admits with a sigh. "But it wasn't just that keeping me away."

My brows furrow with concern. "Then what?" The Ferris wheel resumes its slow rotation, but I keep my gaze fixed on him.

"My dad," he says, his jaw tightening. "The longer I was away, the more I hoped he wouldn't have control over me anymore," he explains. "I was so scared of having to face him again that..." He shakes his head. "I hate that he still affects me," he admits bitterly. "He's in prison, and he still has a grip on me."

I scoot closer to Chris, holding his face in my hands. "He doesn't," I assure him. "He's locked up miles away, and you're free, Chris. You and your mom are free from him."

He exhales heavily, closing his eyes briefly. "Yeah," he murmurs, his shoulders visibly relaxing. "I'm free." I nod reassuringly, brushing his hair back. His Adam's apple bobs as he swallows. "My mom's free."

"Have you... gone to see her yet?"

He shakes his head, eyes locking on mine. "Will you... Will you come with me?" he pleads, begs. God, he's so nervous, and I can't even imagine what he's feeling.

"Of course I will," I assure him without hesitation. "I'll go anywhere with you."

His eyes light up at my response. "You will?"

I nod, leaning in to press my lips against his. "You know, our star signs are compatible," I say with a smile.

He lets out a laugh. "They are?"

I nod again. "I looked it up," I admit.

He chuckles, lifting my hand to his lips and plants a light kiss on my knuckles. "You needed proof to know we're meant to be?" he teases. "Because I knew way before yesterday."

"It wasn't recently," I explain. "I looked them up a long time ago."

His brows furrow slightly, an amused expression crossing his face. "When?"

I swallow nervously before answering, "Senior year."

His face drops. "As in high school?"

I nod. "I started falling for you back then," I admit. "Or maybe even before that, I'm not sure. But I knew I loved you by then."

He shakes his head, a mixture of frustration and regret evident on his face. "Fuck," he curses under his breath, running a hand through his hair. "We wasted so much damn time, Gabi. If only I had told you or—"

I cut him off with a kiss. There's no point in wondering what might have been when we have each other now. "It's okay," I reassure him. "We have plenty of time to make up for it," I say with a smile. "The stars say we're meant to be."

Chris returns my smile, his touch gentle as he brushes my cheek with the soft pad of his thumb. "Hell yeah, we are. But even if we weren't, I'd fight the stars to be with you." His words make my heart thump against my chest as his eyes locks onto mine. "You're my best friend, Gabi," he continues. "But you're also the love of my life."

Tears well up in my eyes, and I shake my head, trying to compose myself. "Don't make me cry. I worked hard on my makeup."

He chuckles. "And you look beautiful," he says. "You always do."

Our lips brush together, and we got lost in each other, showing the other how much we love each other.

"Ride's over," the guy interrupts, making us break apart to see him chewing some gum as he waits for us to get off.

Chris takes my hand in his as we step off the ride, and I glance behind him. "Look, the photobooth is open."

He smiles as we make our way toward it, climbing inside and closing the curtain.

"Remember the last time we were here?" he asks, inserting coins into the machine, but then he chuckles. "Probably not. You were already wasted by then."

"I remember," I reply, meeting his warm, chocolate eyes. "I remember wanting to kiss you."

Chris holds my gaze for a second and then blows out a breath. "I was so close to kissing you," he admits.

My stomach flutters. "I wish you had."

A smirk spreads across his face as he cups my cheeks, pulling me closer until his lips meet mine in a soft kiss. The camera flashes but we're lost in the moment, burning this moment into my memory, comparing it to when we sat here five years ago, and how everything has changed since then.

Pulling back slightly, I run my fingers through his hair. "You may not have been my first kiss or my first time, but you'll be my last," I tell him with conviction. His smile widens, and I continue. "I love you, Chris. And I've never said those words to anyone but you."

He rests his forehead against mine, his thumb slowly rubbing against my cheek. "I love you too, pretty girl. And I'll never say those words to anyone but you."

31

Home visits

Christopher

I think I've forgotten how to breathe.

Either that, or I'm having a panic attack.

Gabi squeezes my hand, pulling me out of my thoughts. I turn to face her, taking in her beautiful features. Her eyebrows knit together as she searches my eyes. "Are you okay?" she asks, so attentive, so patient, so kind, and fuck. I love her so fucking much.

I nod, feeling the shake in my body fade away when I meet her eyes, The corner of my lips lifts into a smile. "I'm always okay when you're with me," I tell her, because it's the truth. Somehow, she always manages to calm something deep inside me whenever I look into her soft blue eyes.

"I'll always be here with you," she says, giving my hand a gentle squeeze. It's crazy how a simple touch from her makes my heart race. You'd think I'd be used to it by now. I've been in love with her for most of my life, and I slept in her bed almost every night for years. But now that we're together, every touch feels different... more intense. I don't think I'll ever get used to it.

I let out a breath, running a hand through my hair. "I couldn't do this without you, Gabi." I tried. So many times.

I've lost count of how often I searched for flights, scrolled through my contacts to get to hers, stared at the phone wondering how she was, what she was doing… if she hated me.

God, I hope she doesn't hate me.

The love of my life steps in front of me, holding my face in her hands, cupping it in the soft, warm embrace of her hands. "You won't have to do anything without me ever again."

I like the sound of that.

Fuck, I *really* like the sound of that.

I nod, taking a deep breath as I raise my fist to the door. My hand trembles, and with another shaky breath, I finally knock.

Nerves wrack through my body as I wait for her to open the door. My heart pounds with each second I wait.

But when the door finally swings open, it's not her on the other side.

I blink, taken aback by the middle-aged man standing in my childhood home.

"Hello?" he says with a polite smile. "Can I help you?"

I turn to Gabi, blinking in confusion. "I uh…" I shake my head. Did she move somewhere else? Did she… I swallow, hard. I can't even think about that being a possibility. I turn back to the man standing in front of me. "I was looking for Eleanor?"

"Honey, who's at the door?" Her soft, familiar voice catches my attention, and I widen my eyes as my mom appears behind the man, looking up at me. "Chris?"

Her voice sends a shiver through me, and I swallow hard, struggling to contain my emotions. "Hi, Mom."

"Chris?" The man beside her glances back at me.

"Yes," my mom answers, stepping in front of him to wrap her arms around me. I feel my jaw tighten as she hugs me. "This is my son."

My eyes begin to well up. She doesn't hate me.

My mom pulls back, studying my face. "You're so grown up," she says, pinching my cheek.

I swallow hard. "It's been a long time."

She nods, and I notice a sad smile on her face, but it leaves just as quickly when she waves us in. "Come inside." She turns around, heading into the house with the man, whom I still know nothing about.

I squeeze Gabi's hand tightly, taking a deep breath before stepping inside.

My eyes widen as I take in the sight.

The old, worn-out brown couch has been replaced by a long white one, with colorful pillows and cozy blankets. The staircase, which was chipped from my father's fists, is now painted white. Paintings hang on the walls, there's fresh flowers in vases, and the sun streams in through the open windows.

I blink, feeling like I've stepped into a different world. This doesn't look like the same house at all.

It's lighter, brighter, and the usual smell of whiskey that rotted my nostrils for years is no longer lingering.

"Would you like anything to drink?" my mom asks, drawing my attention. "Michael made some lemonade this morning."

I blink. "Michael?"

"Yes. My, um…" She smiles. "My boyfriend."

"Boyfriend?" I repeat, furrowing my brows. My mother has a boyfriend?

"A little more than that," my mother's boyfriend—apparently—says, kissing her on the side of her head. My eyes widen involuntarily at the sight. What the hell is going on?

"Well, he uh, he proposed."

My eyes widen even more. "You're engaged?"

She nods, a smile spreading across her face. My shoulders relax as my heart quickens at the sight of her happiness. It's been so long since I've seen her smile like this. Even when I lived here, she rarely ever smiled.

But now she looks genuinely happy.

She has Michael.

She's engaged.

And I knew nothing about it.

"So... about that drink?" Michael asks.

"Sure," I say, blinking as I take it all in. "Thanks."

He nods. "And you?" he asks, turning his head to Gabi.

I turn my head, seeing Gabi smile at him. "Sure. I love lemonade."

Michael plants one more kiss on my mom's head before he turns around and head out of the living room.

My mom turns to Gabi, flashing her a warm smile. "Gabi, right?"

Gabi tilts her head. "You remember me?"

My mom laughs, shaking her head. "My son never stopped talking about you. It's hard to forget."

Gabi turns to face me, and I meet her eyes with a sheepish smile. "You did?"

It still surprises her how much I talked about her, thought about her, *still* think about her. I chuckle, nodding. "Yeah, I did." I used to mention hanging out at Gabi's so often that my mom eventually asked if we were together, even trying to have the safe sex talk with me.

I quickly shut down that conversation, assuring her we were just friends and would always be.

Little did I know I'd be standing here with Gabi by my side a few years later, as my girlfriend.

"I also met you once," my mom says, catching me off guard.

I raise an eyebrow. "You did?"

As far as I was aware, Gabi had never met my mom. She had met my dad once, but I had begged her never to come back here. Unfortunately, it was too late. Once my dad saw her, he latched onto that. The bastard knew I was in love with her and used it against me to hurt me every chance he got.

"Yeah." Gabi swallows when I look to her for confirmation. "I came here the morning after…" She doesn't finish her words, but she doesn't need to. "I was wondering where you had gone, and your mom opened the door. She told me you had left."

"I didn't know where you had gone," my mom adds. "I didn't even know if you were in the country." A laugh escapes her, but it's strained.

My lips drop into a frown. "I'm sorry."

"For what, honey?"

Where do I even start. "For going so far away. For not reaching out the past couple of years." I swallow the gravel in my throat. "For leaving you that day."

"Honey…" She shakes her head. "I don't blame you for that. You needed to leave this place. I understand."

"I should have visited, though," I say, my voice quivering. "I should have come back and seen you."

She lets out a sigh. "This place had bad memories for you. I understand why you wouldn't want to come back."

"Not anymore," I say, glancing around the house that feels like my old home and a strange place all at once. "You really made a change here," I tell her.

"I did," she replies with a smile playing on her lips. "I made it my home."

Michael returns with the lemonade, handing us each a glass before stepping away, giving us a moment alone.

My eyes shift toward my mom once Michael leaves. "You're happy?" I ask her. I don't care that she moved on, or that she's engaged. I just want her to be happy for once.

The smile on her face tells me the answer, but she answers anyway. "I am."

I nod, relieved. "And he treats you well?"

She lets out a laugh. "Yes," she affirms, removing the boulder sitting on my chest. "Very well."

"Good," I say with a nod. "I'm happy for you." I glance down, seeing the ring on her finger. "When's the wedding?"

"Oh not for a while," she says, waving a hand. "We're actually thinking of moving first."

"Moving?" I ask her.

"I might have changed some things, but the memories still linger sometimes," she says, her slender throat swallowing. "We wanted a new place. With new memories."

My brows dip at the thought of no longer having my childhood home. It's... weird. But I know that she's right. This place holds too many bad memories to outweigh the good ones, no matter how much has changed.

"So, are you staying around here?" my mom asks, with a hopeful smile on her face.

But my face drops.

Fuck.

I was so happy.

These past few days I have thought of nothing else but being with Gabi. Finally being able to kiss her, and touch her, and tell her I love her.

I was so happy that I completely forgot I'm leaving.

In two weeks.

I turn my head and lock eyes with Gabi. Her smile doesn't reach her eyes, and it breaks my heart.

I swallow harshly. "No. I'm uh…" I shake my head, glancing back at my mom. "I actually live in London."

She blinks. "Oh."

"Yeah. I uh…" I rake a hand through my hair. "I'm going back in a few weeks. I have one more year left until I graduate."

Her eyes soften. "Well, I'm very proud of you Chris. For making something out of yourself even after everything that happened."

I nod, swallowing when the emotions climb up my throat. "Thank you, mom. And uh… thank you for saving me that day," I tell her, my eyes getting glassy and blurred as I lock eyes with her.

She shakes her head, her own eyes growing teary. "I should have done more," she says. "I shouldn't have let him hurt you. I should have left him. I should have…" She sighs. "I should have done *more.*"

"It's okay, mom," I promise her. "We're both free of him now," I say, repeating the same words Gabi said to me.

Beside me, my best friend tightens her hold on mine, showing me she's here for me.

"Yeah," my mom agrees, her shoulders relaxing. "We are." Her eyes flick to mine, and uncertainty swims in them. "Have you heard from him?"

I nod, my jaw clenching. "He calls sometimes," I say, not wanting to tell her he calls way too often for my liking. "I never answer."

"Good," she says with a nod. "You don't need him in your life, Chris."

"I know, mom. But I do need *you*."

My mom's eyes tear up and she stands up, embracing me in a hug. "Promise you'll visit me," she begs.

"Of course I will." When we pull away, I smile down at Gabi. "Besides. I have someone else I'll need to visit too."

My mom brings her hand over her mouth. "You two are…" She gestures between us.

"Yeah," I nod, sliding my hand into Gabi's. "She's my girlfriend."

Girlfriend.

My chest jumps at the words. How long have I seen her be someone else's girlfriend? How long have I wished her to be *mine*? And now she finally is.

"That's amazing," my mom says with a huge grin on her face. "I always thought something was going on, but he told me you guys were just friends."

"We were," I say with a shrug. "But I was always in love with her." Gabi smiles up at me, and my heart starts to beat again.

"I thought so," my mom continues. "You wouldn't believe how much he talked about you," she tells Gabi.

I narrow my eyes. "Okay, mom. She gets it."

"No, please, carry on," my girlfriend says, grinning at my mother. "I love hearing about how much you love me."

"I'll be sure to tell you every single day for the rest of our lives," I tell her. "Let's leave before she pulls out the baby pictures."

Gabi gasps. "Oh my god. Baby Chris? I have to see it."

"Perfect," my mom says, indulging her. "I have a stack of photo albums."

"Yay." Gabi pulls away from me, following my mom toward the cabinet where she stores the photo albums.

I let out a laugh, watching the two women I love.

Maybe not all memories in this house have to be terrible.

32

Pay up

Gabriella

"Gabi, you have to let me drive." His tone is a warning, but a grin plays on his lips as I lean over and press another kiss to his cheek.

"But you're so pretty," I murmur, trailing kisses down his jaw.

A groan escapes his lips, urgent and needy. "Gabi," he says, his voice thick and husky, and so hot it drives me crazy. "We're going to crash if you keep that up."

I hum against his skin, trailing my tongue along his neck. "You're the only person I'd want to die with."

He chuckles, shaking his head. "As much as I love hearing that, I kind of want to live a few years with you first."

My smile widens, and I pull back to meet his gaze. "Yeah?"

He nods, his eyes softening. "I want to make up for all the time we've lost."

My lips curve into a smirk, and I tug my bottom lip with my teeth. "What are you going to do to make up for all this lost time?" I ask, running my hands down his arm.

Chris groans again, tearing his eyes away from me. "We're nearly home," he says, his voice strained. "You can do whatever the fuck you want to me when we get there."

My stomach flutters at the sound of him calling the apartment 'home' and I let out a sigh, leaning back into the seat. "Fine." I reach over to the console and turn up the music while he drives. He insisted on driving the whole way back, claiming I was a danger to everyone on the road or something. I have no idea where he got that from, but I wasn't complaining.

I just don't understand how I lasted living with him for so long without kissing him, because these past two days were hell. I want to kiss Chris all the time. Every second of the day.

Ten minutes, and a few more stolen kisses later, he pulls up outside our apartment, and turns the car off.

Our eyes lock for a second, a charged silence passing between us. I don't know who moves first, but we lean in and our lips crash together. There's too much room between us, and I need to be closer. I lean in further, dragging my hands over his chest, around his neck, and tug on his hair.

Chris moans into my mouth, making me even more needy for him. I shiver against him, swallowing his moans as he kisses me. "God, Gabi," he groans, lifting his hand to cup my cheek. "You're killing me."

I chuckle against his lips, leaving a few lingering kisses before I pull back. "We can't have that," I joke, opening the car door and stepping outside.

Chris follows, locking the car as we make our way inside. As soon as we make it into the elevator we're back on each other; his hands roaming over my body like he's mapping it, exploring it, memorizing it with his touch. I cling to him, kissing his lips with a desperate need.

Kissing Chris is unlike anything I've ever experienced. I've kissed many people—many. Most of them, I can't even remember their names or faces, and others were pretty good. But this…

All of those kisses combined couldn't compete with Chris.

The elevator dings, and Chris pulls back with a hazy look in his eyes.

"Why'd you stop?" I ask him.

He grins, brushing his thumb over my bottom lip. "We're almost at our door, baby."

A shiver runs down my spine at the nickname, and I smirk, tugging my bottom lip between my teeth. "You called me baby."

Chris chuckles, running a hand through his messy curls. "I did."

I lean into him, wrapping my arms around his neck. "I like that."

"Yeah?"

I nod, pressing my lips to the corner of his mouth. "It makes me feel like I'm really yours."

His eyes soften as he caresses my cheek, looking deeply into my eyes. "You've always been mine, Gabi. Even if you didn't feel the same. There's only ever been you for me."

His words make me suck in a breath as our eyes lock together. I could stare into them forever. "I wish I had realized my feelings for you sooner," I admit.

He shakes his head, his brows dipping. "Don't do that," he says. "I don't want you to regret any of your decisions or experiences because of my feelings. Besides…" He smirks. "We got there in the end. I got you in the end."

I smile and dive back in, kissing him. He opens up for me, and my tongue traces over his, tasting and savoring him, showing him how much I love him. There's not a single word in the English language that could express how deeply my heart aches for him, how much he's meant to me all these years, and how empty my soul felt without him here.

And how empty it's going to feel when he eventually moves back.

I shake the thought away, kissing him deeply, and slowly walk backwards until my back hits the door.

"Gabi," Chris murmurs, leaving my lips so he can trail kisses down my jaw and neck.

"Hmm?" My breath comes out heavy and husky, and I keep my eyes closed, feeling his touch everywhere.

"We're here," Chris whispers against my ear, before reclaiming my lips.

God, I want him so badly. We're just a second away from being inside our apartment, but I can't bring myself to move, not wanting to miss a single second of his lips on mine.

"Open the door," I whimper, pleading him as I grind myself against his leg. "I need you, Chris."

"Fuck." His groan makes my clit throb, and I feel his hand reach around me to unlock the door.

We stumble inside the apartment, immediately grasping at each other, desperate to get rid of the clothes between us.

"Surprise!"

My eyes widen as I pull away from Chris and spin around, only to see my friends standing behind me. Their eyes mirror mine, wide with surprise, and I swallow, wondering what the fuck is happening.

"I fucking knew it," Aiden says with a grin, holding out his hand. "Pay up."

Groans echo as Grayson and Lucas reluctantly pull out cash and hand it over to Aiden.

"I'm so happy I'm too broke to make any bets," James says with a chuckle.

My brows furrow as I shake my head. "Can someone tell me what's going on?"

"I bet you guys would get together," Aiden says with a grin as he pockets the cash.

I narrow my gaze at him. "Yeah, I got that. The question is why the hell did you guys bet on us, and what are you doing here?"

"We wanted to celebrate with you, since we technically missed your birthday," Madi says. "But I see you guys are busy," she adds with a smirk.

"And the bet?" I ask, raising an eyebrow at the guys.

Grayson lets out a sigh. "This guy was so cocky, claiming you two would be together by the time you got back," he says, gesturing toward Aiden, who still wears a smug grin. "And I really wanted to shut him up and prove him wrong."

I raise my brows. "So you bet against me?"

He shrugs. "It was so obvious how you two felt about each other, but I figured you'd hold off for at least a week." He rolls his eyes. "But obviously that didn't happen."

Rosie chuckles at Grayson's reaction to losing and turns her attention to Chris and me. "So, are you two finally together now?" she asks eagerly.

I glance at Chris, and he smiles as he reaches for my hand, our fingers intertwining. "Yeah," he says, his chocolate eyes never leaving mine. "We're finally together."

"Thanks to me," Aiden chimes in with a grin.

I raise an eyebrow skeptically. "You literally did nothing."

He lets out a scoff, crossing his arms. "I take offense to that," he says. "I think I did a lot to help you guys realize your feelings for each other."

My eyes soften and I let out a laugh. He might not have been the reason we got together—though he clearly thinks he is—but he helped me a lot during a time when I didn't have anyone to confide in. What I had told Chris was the truth. I talked to Aiden about him. But what he didn't know was that I told him about how I felt about Chris. About the first time I ever felt my feelings change for him, and how I missed him so much.

"I feel like I've missed out on a lot," James says with a frown. "I hate living so far away."

I let out a laugh. "Me too," I say with a sigh. "You're the only funny one around."

"Excuse me?" Aiden pipes in, and Leila narrows her eyes at me.

"Yeah, what was that?" Chris says with an arched brow, amusement written on his face.

Before I can clarify that I'm joking—because clearly, *I'm* the funniest one around—James walks toward us, staring up at Chris and tilts his head. "You must be Chris," James says, narrowing his eyes. "Heard all about you. These assholes can't stop talking about you. Kinda feel like you've replaced me."

"Trust me, no one can replace you," Lucas assures him with a laugh. "You're still the center of attention, don't worry."

"Alright, I feel better then. Hi, I'm James," he says, offering him a smile.

"I gathered," Chris says with a laugh. "I'm Chris," he replies, returning the smile.

James lets out a low hum, a smirk lifting his lips. "The boy toy."

"Boyfriend," I correct with a grin as I look up at Chris. I've never loved that word more than I do right now. When Chris called me his girlfriend at his mom's house, my heart was pounding so loud I genuinely thought I'd pass out.

He's been just my *best friend* for so long, that adding another title to our relationship makes it so much more exciting.

"Boyfriend?" James asks, eyes widening in surprise. "Wow, you move fast."

"Way too slow, actually," I chuckle. "This has been a long time coming."

"Well, I'm happy for you," James nods, a genuine smile spreading across his face. "I wish everyone could be as happy as I feel when I'm with Carter. Kinda wish he was here right now." He sighs. "Why does he have to *work* anyway?"

"Rent? Food? To be able to afford your expensive lifestyle?" Lucas says with a tilt of his head.

James groans, turning his attention to his childhood friend. "I hate when you're right."

I flinch as a furry creature rubs against my leg, meowing. "Ahhh. Get it off me!" I shout, clinging to Chris in an attempt to escape it. But the asshole cat follows me, meowing and pawing at my leg.

"What the hell is that thing doing here?" Chris asks, stepping away from it.

"It's a cat," Aiden explains with a raised eyebrow, scooping up his pet. "And Tiger just wanted to say hi. But I guess cats aren't your thing either." He sighs, stroking the black and white fur. "You two really are made for each other."

I flick my eyes to Chris, and he smiles back at me. "Yeah," he says, his eyes locked on mine. "We are."

"So does this mean you're sticking around now?" Leila asks Chris, gesturing to our hands intertwined.

The mood sours as we glance at each other, and I see his throat moving as he swallows. "No," he says, meeting my eyes, a frown forming on his lips. "I still need to go back to London."

I know this. I know he has to go back. He told his mom the same, and we've talked about it. But it doesn't hurt any less to hear it all over again.

"Well, the mood just soured," James interjects with a nervous laugh. "Let's put some music on and get the alcohol out, because I'm starting to get bored."

The guys chuckle, and Rosie leans over to grab the speaker, connecting it until upbeat music fills the apartment, and James comes back with two full cups in his hands.

"Are you okay?" Chris asks, lifting my chin with his hand to meet his eyes.

I force a smile, and simply nod, pressing my lips together. But his frown just deepens. Chris knows everything about me, and I know he can tell when I force a smile, but what does he expect? I just got him back after all this time. And I have to lose him all over again.

Chris is leaving.

In just two weeks.

And there's nothing I can do to stop it from happening.

33
Matchmaking skills

Christopher

Ten years.

Ten years I've been in love with my best friend, never imagining we'd actually end up together.

Now here I am, grinning like an idiot, watching her laugh with her friends, throwing her head back with a beautiful smile that makes my heart squeeze. I love seeing her happy. I love being the reason for her happiness.

It took us forever to get here, but I wouldn't change a thing.

"You're welcome, by the way," Aiden says, draping his arm around Leila's shoulders as she joins us, sliding beside him.

"For what?" I ask.

He lifts his head, gesturing toward Gabi. "For that."

"What are you talking about?" Grayson interrupts, his brows furrowing in confusion.

"I'm the reason they got together," Aiden says with a shrug.

"You did absolutely nothing," Grayson scoffs, shaking his head.

Aiden's brows pull together. "That's not true," he argues. "If it wasn't for me—"

"They still would have ended up together," Leila interrupts, rolling her eyes. "They were always meant to be. You didn't change that."

I chuckle at Aiden's frown. Gabi and I have been a long time coming. It was a game of truth or dare and years of tension between us that finally brought us together. But seeing Aiden's expression, I feel a twinge of guilt, so I nod anyway. "Thanks," I tell him.

His lips quirk. "Thank god someone appreciates me like I deserve."

"And I don't?" Leila chimes in, teasing her boyfriend.

He smiles instantly. "No, you do," he confirms. "It would just be nice to hear someone appreciates me for my matchmaking skills."

"Matchmaking skills?" Grayson asks with a snort.

"Want me to remind you how you got Rosie again?" Aiden says, arching his brow.

Grayson's smile slips, and he lifts his hand, flipping Aiden off.

I chuckle, watching their interactions. I'll have to ask Gabi what happened between Grayson and Rosie.

I remember feeling nervous when I first met Gabi's friends. Meeting new people has never been my strong suit. I've always preferred to sit back and just listen.

But these guys… They've become more than just Gabi's friends. They're my friends now, too.

"I do so much for this group," Aiden sighs dramatically. "And no one recognizes it."

"Your head's too big anyway," Leila teases back.

Aiden's hand curls around Leila's waist as he grins up at her. But Leila looks past him, making Aiden turn his head, and his smile fades when he sees a girl standing nearby.

"Hey," she says with a flirty smile, biting her bottom lip.

Aiden swallows, his brow furrowing. "Um, hi?"

She moves closer, trailing a hand along his arm. "You're Aiden Pierce, right?"

Leila's eyebrows shoot up, and she glances at us in disbelief. "Is she… Is she serious?" she asks, her jaw dropping.

"Yeah," Aiden replies, tightening his hold on Leila's waist.

"Hmm…" The girl smiles, running her hand along his arm. "You know, I've watched your games, and—"

"Excuse me," Leila interrupts sharply, narrowing her eyes at the girl. The girl finally shifts her gaze to Leila standing beside Aiden. "Do you not see me right here, with his hand on my waist?" Leila asks, arching a brow.

Aiden's lips curve into a smile as he looks down at his girlfriend.

"That girl is dead," Grayson murmurs, chuckling as he shakes his head.

"Oh…" The girl looks down at Leila, furrowing her brows. "I didn't know."

"Well, now you do," Leila says sharply.

The girl frowns, glancing back up at Aiden. "Sorry."

"Yeah," Leila replies, narrowing her eyes. "You are."

The girl turns around and disappears into the crowd.

"Did that really just happen?" Lucas asks, shaking his head.

Leila lets out a sigh. "It happens too much for my liking," she murmurs. "I hate it."

"Me too," Aiden replies, adjusting his cap as he grins down at Leila. "But I've got to say, I find it hot as hell whenever you chase them away. It's exhausting having to deal with them."

Leila rolls her eyes. "I bet it's so exhausting having hundreds of beautiful girls wanting to sleep with you."

Aiden curls his hand under Leila's chin, lifting her head. "It is when you're the only one I want," he says with his eyes locked on hers.

Leila's lips part, and she smiles briefly before narrowing her eyes at him. "Stop trying to flirt with me."

Aiden laughs, shaking his head. "I'll never stop flirting with you."

"If Gabi was here, she'd barf," Grayson says, taking a sip of his drink.

"Nah." Aiden slides his hand around Leila's waist. "She's in love now," he says, glancing at me. "She doesn't mind seeing other people in love anymore."

I chuckle, shaking my head. "Trust me. She still hates it."

Gabi's never been into PDA. Even with her boyfriends in high school, she didn't really touch them, hardly ever kissed them. But she was never like that with me. She always touched me, held me, cuddled with me.

My lips quirk at the thought. I like that she wasn't as touchy with anyone else, like she is with me.

"Hey. It's you again."

I lift my head, recognizing the girl with short hair who had hit on me at the first party Gabi brought me to. My brows furrow as she smiles at me. What was her name again? Fuck, I forgot. I remain silent as she moves closer to me.

"Are you here with anyone?"

I swallow, glancing around. Aiden's lost in conversation with Leila. I scan the crowd, spotting Lucas and Madi together on the couch, and Grayson catching up with Rosie, leaning in to kiss her. But I don't see Gabi anywhere.

"I guess not," she continues, sliding her hand up my arm.

My throat tightens as I instinctively try to step back. "Actually, I—"

"What the fuck are you doing?"

My heart leaps in my chest.

Gabi.

I'd recognize her voice anywhere.

I turn around, seeing my best friend Gabi's eyes narrow, focusing on Tiffany's hand resting on my arm. "Why the fuck are you touching my boyfriend, Tiffany?"

God, that word coming from her lips makes me smile. And I want to hear it again. Actually, I never want to stop hearing her say it.

"Boyfriend?" Tiffany asks, glancing up at me with furrowed brows. "He told me he wasn't here with anyone."

I frown. "I didn't say that."

Gabi's eyes soften briefly when they meet mine before she shoots a glare at Tiffany. "Leave him alone," my girlfriend says sharply. "He doesn't want you."

Tiffany arches a brow, moving her hand higher up on my arm. "Are you sure? He seemed interested," she says, clearly trying to provoke a reaction from Gabi.

I take a step away from her, and reach for Gabi, intertwining our fingers. "I'm definitely not," I tell Tiffany. "My girlfriend is ten times hotter than you'll ever be."

Tiffany glares, her mouth dropping open, and I feel Gabi's hand tightening around mine, as Tiffany lets out a grunt and turns around, walking away.

I glance down at Gabi, her eyes fired up with a jealousy I've never seen before. Fuck, she looks so hot right now.

"Are you ready to go?" she asks.

"Hell yeah."

34

Use me, Gabi

Gabriella

As soon as I shut the door closed behind me, I reach for Chris, sliding my hands around his neck to slam my lips into his. Chris lets out a low groan as soon as our lips touch and his hands fly to my face, tilting my head back while the other grips my hair as the kiss deepens between us.

I tug at his bottom lip with my teeth, softly nipping him, earning a soft noise that escapes from his throat. Chris groans as our lips collide once again, in a hungry, passionate kiss that has my body growing hot with each passing second. His hands grip my waist, pulling me closer as our tongues brush together, each touch so intense and urgent and so overwhelming I can't breathe.

"God, I hated her hands on you." I tug at his black t-shirt, wanting it off. He helps me out, lifting his arms until it's off his body, and I throw it across the room.

Chris moans into my mouth when I run my fingers through his hair, tugging the strands. "Me too."

I quickly work the buttons on his jeans, eagerly tugging them down. Chris kicks them off until he's left in nothing but his black Calvin Klein boxers. His hands wrap around my waist, pulling me close as he captures my lips in another passionate kiss.

"I don't like the thought of anyone else touching you," I admit, breathing heavily between kisses.

Chris lets out a grunt, his hands cupping my face as the kiss deepens. "Me either," he murmurs, his voice thick with lust. "Only you're allowed to touch me." I moan into his mouth, loving the sound of that. He pulls back slightly, smirking down at me, and runs his tongue over his bottom lip. "But I'm kinda loving the attention you're giving me right now."

I arch a brow and give his chest a light shove, making him fall back on the couch, grinning up at me. I straddle his left leg, leaning down to press my lips against his jaw. "You like making me jealous, baby?" I ask, my breath hot against his skin.

A rough groan escapes his throat as he thrusts his hips up, his hands gripping my waist tightly, grinding his cock against my leg. "You have nothing to be jealous about, but *fuck*. I really like seeing you like this. You look so hot right now."

I know there's no reason for me to be jealous. Chris didn't want Tiffany. I could see it from a mile away. I know he only wants me. But the thought of her fingers trailing up his arm, leaning into him, thinking she could take him from me, still makes my blood boil.

He's mine.

He always has been.

A soft moan leaves my lips as I move my hips, grinding against his leg, my body burning with need for him. My hands slide across the nape of his neck, fingers threading through his hair as I cup his face, making him look at me. "Do you trust me?" I ask, my breath mingling with his.

His eyes sober, and he nods. "With my life."

A smile spreads across my face as I dip down to brush our lips together. "I want to try something," I murmur, tugging at his bottom lip with my teeth.

The noises he makes drive me insane. My head feels dizzy when he parts his lips and a pained whimper escapes his throat. "You can do whatever you want to me," he says, desperation dripping in his tone. "Use me, Gabi."

Fuck.

A shiver runs up my body at his words, and I climb off his lap, staring down at him. My body heats at the sight of him sitting on the couch, looking up at me, waiting for me, *wanting me.*

I turn around, and make my way into my room, scanning around until my eyes land on what I'm looking for. With a grin, I grab it, and run my hands over it, before I head back into the living room.

As soon as I enter, I find Chris waiting for me in the same position he was before, his eyes immediately drawn to what I have in my hand, and his eyes widen.

"Fuck," he grunts, and my eyes fall to his hands, seeing him rub his cock over his boxers.

I lick my lips. "Take it off."

His fingers curl around the hem, and he tugs his boxers off, throws them away, his cock bobbing free, long and hard, and glistening at the tip.

Chris drops his hands to his lap, his fingers an inch away from curling around his cock, but I reach out and cover his hand with mine, arching a brow at him. "Don't touch yourself."

A deep groan escapes his throat and he reluctantly lets his hands fall away. My lips curl into a smile as I push the button, the roaring sound of the vibrator filling the silence between us.

A strained exhale escapes him. "If I have to watch you play with your pussy and can't touch myself I'll die," he says, his chest heaving with each breath.

I grin wider as I close the distance between us, chuckling. And people say *I'm* the dramatic one. "Don't worry, you won't have to watch *me* use it."

His eyebrows knit together in confusion. "What do you— Ohhhh fuck." He groans when I place the vibrator against his cock, letting the ripples of pleasure run through him. Another moan leaves his lips as I run the vibrator along his cock. "God, Gabi."

"Mmmm." I smile, loving how needy he looks right now. "That's it, baby. Let me hear you."

"Fuck," he moans again, tipping his head back when I circle it around the tip of his cock. His hips buck up, chasing the friction, and the pleasure. "Let me touch you," he says, sounding so deliciously desperate as he moves his hips faster. "Please."

"Uh uh," I murmur, shaking my head slowly. A teasing smile plays on my lips as I pull the toy away. "Hands on your knees."

An aggravated groan leaves him, but he does as I say, placing both hands flat on his knees, just like I instructed him to. Heat fills my core, and I can feel my pussy dripping at the sight of Chris naked, and desperate to come. Soft, beautiful noises escaping his lips.

I straighten up, slowly sliding off my jeans and underwear, letting them pool around my ankles before stepping out of them. Chris's eyes zone in on my pussy, his eyes growing darker as he watches my every move. I love his eyes on me. I love how he looks at me like he wants to devour me. Like he needs me to survive.

I tug my tank top off over my head, standing completely naked in front of him.

His eyes slide up my body until he locks in on my tits, and he lets out a deep groan. "Fuck. This is torture."

My lips curl into a smile and I shake my head. "You don't even know the half of it," I tease.

He breathes hard, looking confused. "What do you mean?"

I climb on top of him, positioning myself on his lap, my legs on either side of his. His cock is so close to my pussy, I can almost feel him. Chris's breaths quicken, his hands moving to make room for me on the couch, but he doesn't touch me. Placing them beside his legs, he looks up at me, waiting for my next move.

I turn on the vibrator, and his eyes widen, his lips parting on a shaky breath. They follow the vibrator as I bring it down between us, and place it just right so it hits my clit, and rubs against his cock.

"Oh fuck," he groans, sliding his cock against the vibrator.

"Yes," I moan, grinding against the toy, feeling the heat of his cock brush against me.

Chris squeezes his eyes closed, his fists curled up on the couch. "Gabi… mmfuck." His whimpers make me wetter, and I grasp the back of his head, my fingers tangling in his hair.

"Look at me," I tell him, breathing hard as my clit vibrates and pleasure rolls through me.

His eyes snap open, and he looks at me as I grind on his lap, moving my hips so my clit makes contact with the vibrator.

"Oh fuck," he grunts, tipping his head back. "I'm gonna come."

"No you're not." My tongue darts out, tracing along his throat, feeling his Adam's apple ripple beneath it. "Be a good boy and wait for me."

He lets out a soft whimper, shaking his head. "I can't."

My fingers tangle in his hair as I give him a slight tug. "Yes you can. I want you to come inside me." He moans at my words, moving his hips even faster. "Don't come yet."

Chris shakes his head, soft groans escaping his throat with every breath he takes. "Then you need to get on my cock right now, or else I'm blowing my load."

I move against the toy, feeling the pleasure build inside me. "If you come when I told you not to, I won't make it nice," I warn him.

A moan rips from his throat, and he starts to lift his hands, almost reaching for my hips. His fingers curl into fists, and then he lowers them back to the couch. "Gabi," he pleads, his voice desperate and needy. "I can't. Fuck. Please let me come."

"Not yet." I move the vibrator to rub against him harder than before, a shiver running through my body when his moans get louder. "Hold on."

He moves his hips faster, and I can tell he's right there. "Gabi," he pants, his moans coming out harsher, louder. "Fuck. Fuck. Fuck."

His hips jerk uncontrollably, and before he can stop me, I quickly pull the vibrator away, watching as his cock explodes, cum spurting all over his stomach, and my legs. He groans as he keeps coming, thrusting his hips up to try and get some friction.

"Fuck," he cries out, unsatisfied as his hips still moving as cum ripples out of him

I trace a finger along the cum dripping on his stomach and bring it to my lips, sucking lightly on it. "A ruined orgasm," I tut, shaking my head. "How sad."

His breathing steadies when his orgasm settles, and he narrows his beautiful eyes at me. "You're evil."

"I told you to wait," I say with a playful smile. "I warned you it wouldn't be nice if you disobeyed me."

He sighs heavily, running a hand down his face. "I couldn't. You were naked in my lap, grinding on the vibrator and… Ughh." I glance down, seeing his cock start to harden between us.

My lips pull into a smirk as I slide my fist over his hard cock. A soft whimper leaves his lips as I move my fist over him. "You're hard already," I muse, stroking him so slowly he groans. "You still want to fuck me?"

"Yes. Fuck yes," he says with a nod.

I let out a sigh, moving my hand away from his dick. "I don't know if I should let you," I say. "You're a bad listener."

Chris shakes his head, letting out a heavy breath. "*Please. I'll be good.*"

I arch a brow, smirking down at him. "Promise?"

"I promise," he says, licking his lips. His hands find their way to my waist, and despite my earlier instructions, I can't resist the feeling of his touch. His soft hands glide over my back and settle on my hips, gripping them. "I'll be so fucking good," he says. "Please, Gabi. Please get that soaking tight pussy over here, and sit on my cock."

"Fuck. I love when you talk dirty," I tell him.

His lips curl into a smile and he breathes out a laugh. "I have about a million dirty thoughts in my head right now."

"Like what?" I ask, intrigued, scooting closer until the tip of his cock brushes against my clit.

A heavy breath leaves him. "Like, I want you to lick my cum and kiss me so I can taste it."

A shiver runs through me, and I almost buck into him, desperate to get him inside me. But I smile and lean down, running my tongue lightly over his stomach, cleaning up all the cum he spilled. Chris lets out a grunt when I lean down further, taking the tip of his dick into my mouth.

His chest rises as he breathes hard, and I lift my head, and brush our lips together. He moans when our tongues tangle together, tasting himself, and his hands reach up, cupping my breast.

His thumb runs over my nipples, tugging on the metal bar, and he groans, ripping his mouth away from mine. "Fuck," he says, his eyes darkening at the sight of my tits in his hands. "And these," he says, swiping his thumb over my hard nipple. "God, I want to bite them, tug them between my teeth until you come with nothing but my mouth on your tits."

Jesus. My pussy clenches, and I look down at him with furrowed brows, wanting him to do just that and any other thought roaming through his head. "I thought you were shy."

He chuckles, shaking his head. "Not with you," he says, meeting my eyes. His other hand cradles the back of my head as he pulls me closer, meeting my lips in a soft kiss. "Please come here," he murmurs, looking down where we're just inches apart. "I need to feel you." His hand falls from my breast, and he fists his cock, giving it a slow, hard stroke.

"Hands off," I say firmly. His brow furrows briefly, but withdraws his hand obediently. "That's mine," I affirm, replacing his hand with mine.

Chris nods, his lips parting on a gasp. "It's yours."

"Only I get to touch it," I say, stroking him as he gets harder and harder in my fist.

"Only you get to touch it."

I smile, loving how he gives himself to me so willingly. I lean down and press my lips against his. "You'll be good?"

"Yes," he says with a nod as he brushes his lips against mine. "Just… fuck." He pumps his hips up, fucking my fist. "*Please*, Gabi."

I moan into his mouth, wrapping my fist tighter around his cock. "You're so pretty when you beg."

I withdraw my hand from him and lean back slightly. Chris breathes heavily, his eyes fixed on me. My fingers glide down my stomach, trailing lower until they dip down. Chris sucks in a breath when I rub slow circles on my swollen, sensitive clit. A moan tipples out of me as I start to move my hips.

"Gabi," Chris pleads, his eyes hazing over.

I scoot closer, lift on my knees, and grab his cock, stroking him a few times before placing it at my entrance. Chris's hands fly to my hips when his tip enters me, and he groans as I sink down, slowly until I'm full.

"Fuck," he grunts once I'm seated down all the way. "You feel so good." He pumps his hips up, fucking into me. "You feel better than anything I could ever imagine."

I lift off him, slamming back down, his cock filling me up with every thrust. "And all those fantasies you had of me?" I ask him.

Chris shakes his head. "They didn't live up to this," he says. "Not even fucking close."

I smile, slamming back down on him. "Good."

One hand grips my hip, helping me to lift off his cock, while he slides his other hand to my front. He brushes his thumb over my clit, applying just the right amount of pressure, and I moan at the feeling.

I grind against his hand, lifting off his cock. "Chris," I gasp, wrapping my arms around his neck.

"I love hearing you," he murmurs, his voice coming out as choppy breaths. "I love every noise you make."

"You make me feel so good," I say, unable to think about anything but the pleasure rolling through me.

Chris pumps into me, his thumb moving faster, and harder, making the pleasure build inside me. He leans down, swirling his tongue around my nipple, before he wraps his mouth around it, and lightly tugs at the bars with his teeth.

"Oh fuck. I'm gonna come."

He pulls off my nipples with a pop and groans. "Fuck yes. Fuck yourself on my cock, Gabi."

"Chris," I moan, feeling his thumb speed up on my clit. "Don't stop. Don't… fuck." My orgasm crashes through me, spilling onto his cock as my lips part on a moan.

My body grows hot with pleasure as Chris keeps tunneling his cock into me, lifting my hips so he can pump inside.

"God, Gabi," he grunts, clutching my ass in both of his hands. "Your pussy squeezing my cock is the best fucking feeling in the world."

313

My lips part on a silent gasp, unable to speak as Chris fucks me from below. I don't speak when his hands spread my ass open. And I don't say a word when his fingers dip between, and the pad of his thumb slowly grazes my tight hole.

He breathes heavily, and our eyes lock together. "Has anyone been here?" he asks, pressing his thumb deeper the slightest bit.

Nerve endings I didn't know I had light up, and a moan rips from my throat when I shake my head. Chris's breaths come out harder, his eyes hazing over.

"You want to be my first?" I ask him, pressing my ass against his finger until it slips deeper inside me.

Chris's eyes flutter closed and he keeps moving his cock inside me, slowly, leisurely. "I want to be your everything."

My stomach flutters. "You already are," I tell him. "You always have been."

His throat bobs as he swallows, and his thumb presses deeper into me. "You want to?"

I nod, moaning as I sink onto his thumb. "I want everything with you."

Chris groans. "Fuck, Gabi. You're so fucking tight here."

I smirk, leaning down to flick my tongue over his lips. "Then stretch me out."

"Pass me the lube," he says, slowly pumping his cock into me.

I quickly lift off his cock, smiling as he groans when it slaps his stomach, and turn around, grabbing the bottle of lube before I hand it to him, climbing back on his lap.

Chris breathes heavily, the only sound between us the soft click of the cap. He looks down at it briefly, then lifts his gaze to meet mine again. "Are you sure about this?"

I reply by kissing him, moving my hips over him, showing him how much I want this. When I pull back, his eyes are hesitant, but filled with lust as he pumps out some lube onto his fingers, spreading it around.

He grabs my hips with one hand, while the other makes its way to my ass again, this time, using his finger to breach me until he slips in.

"Oh fuck," I groan, clutching onto him when he slides deep inside me.

"You want me to stop?" he asks, breathing hard.

I moan, shaking my head. "Fuck no," I tell him, slowly sinking down on his finger. "I want more."

"Yeah?" His middle finger joins the other, pumping into me, slowly stretching me out.

"Fuck," I groan, moving my ass back and down over his fingers. "God, that feels so good."

He groans. "I want inside of you so bad."

"Do it."

"Already?" he asks, furrowing his brows. "I need to stretch you out some more."

I let out a whine, unable to take this feeling any longer. I want to come so bad, and I want to do it when his cock is inside me. "Please, Chris," I plead. "I need you. It feels too good."

A heavy breath leaves his lips and he presses his lips against my forehead. "Baby," he murmurs. "My cock is thicker than this. It'll hurt."

"I don't care," I moan, needing him so bad. My vision has gone blurry, and I feel nothing but the immense pressure of his fingers inside me. "Please," I whimper, moving my hips to take him deeper. "Please, Chris."

"Fuck." He slowly removes his fingers, and I let out a cross between a gasp and a moan at the feel, but then I feel his cock tapping against my tight hole, and my body shivers. "I don't want to hurt you," he says, his chest rising with every breath.

I shake my head slightly and wrap my arms around his neck. "You won't," I assure him, knowing he's incapable of hurting anyone. Leaning down, I kiss him. "Just go slow."

He nods, and presses his cock at my entrance, pushing into me. My ass tightens, and he lets out a breath. "You need to relax, baby," he murmurs, rubbing his cock against my hole. "This won't work if you tighten up on me."

I let out a breath, and try to relax, opening up for him until the tip of his cock can push inside me. "God," I breathe out, my eyes squeezing closed.

"Fuck, Gabi," Chris grunts. "You're so tight." He pushes his cock into me, slowly, groaning as he fills me up. "Oh fuck. You're strangling my cock. Jesus. This feels so amazing."

"Chris," I gasp, my body growing hot as his cock fills me. "You feel so deep."

He groans, slowly lifting my hips and dropping them again. A moan spills from him, and he shakes his head. "Fuck. My head's going to explode."

"No," I whimper. "Fuck me first."

Chris chuckles, and he leans in, tugging at my nipples, playing with the piercings with the tip of his tongue. "These drive me crazy," he says as he keeps fucking my ass. "They're so fucking hot."

I've never loved having nipple piercings more than I do whenever he looks at me. The way his eyes narrow and heat makes me lose my mind.

"I don't know if I can keep going much longer," he says, his brows dipping as he fucks me.

Soft moans leaves his lips that make my pussy drip and I feel an orgasm cresting. It's nothing like it's ever been, though. It's strong, and different and… "Fuck."

My pussy clenches, and I throw my head back, moving on him faster as the orgasm rolls through me.

"Oh fuck," Chris grunts. "You're so fucking tight. I'm gonna… Fuuuck." Chris pumps into me, and my ass fills with his warm cum spilling into me. He keeps moving his hips until he's completely empty.

I rest my head on his chest, the sound of our heavy breaths the only noise between us as we come down from the high.

"Fuck," Chris says, out of breath. "That was…"

"We definitely need to do that again," I say, lifting my head to meet his eyes.

Chris laughs, running his hands up and down my naked back, and his cock twitches inside me. He smiles, his chocolate eyes softening when they meet mine. "I'll give you anything you want, pretty girl."

35

You're already a part of me

Christopher

I've never been one to wake up early.

I love my sleep.

But I'd gladly stay awake forever just to watch *her*.

She's so damn beautiful.

A smile spreads across my face as I admire Gabi sleeping peacefully on her side, her arms propped up under her head, and her lips parted.

My eyes drift down to her naked body, the thin white sheet covering only her lower half. I can't help but smile, my hand instinctively covering my mouth.

We've been officially together for a few weeks now, but sometimes I still can't believe she's here with me. After all those years, I can't believe she's finally mine.

I still remember the feeling of sleeping in the same bed as her, with her head on my chest, my arms around her, wishing I could kiss her. I loved cuddling her, but it was hard to act like my feelings towards her were purely friendly.

I felt so guilty for being attracted to my best friend when she didn't feel the same way. I'm not sure when her feelings changed, but I know she didn't feel that way in the first few years of our friendship.

Still, I waited. I waited patiently, even though there was a good chance she might never feel the same. And I was okay with that, honestly. I wanted Gabi in my life however I could have her, even if it meant just being friends.

She's always been my best friend, and that will never change. But now... I get to kiss her whenever I want.

Moving closer to her, I lean down and press my lips against her cheek. Gabi lets out a cute little sound that makes me chuckle. I plant another kiss, this time on the corner of her mouth, and then one more on her lips.

Gabi groans, opening one eye to peer at me. "I want to sleep," she whines, her words slurred as she slowly wakes up.

I press my lips together to stifle a smile, brushing her hair out of her face. "Sorry, baby," I whisper, leaning down to plant one final kiss on her forehead. "Go back to sleep."

She lets out a sigh, rolling onto her back. "It's too late now. I want more kisses."

I chuckle and wrap my arm around her waist, pulling her closer to me. Leaning down, I brush our lips together once more.

"Morning breath," she murmurs against my lips, attempting to pull back, but I hold her face, continuing to kiss her.

"I don't care," I say, diving back in to kiss her again. "I'll always kiss you."

A soft moan escapes her, and I savor the sound. "Really?" she asks, teasingly tugging at my lip with her teeth before soothing it with a lick of her tongue.

It drives me wild when she does that. "Yeah, pretty girl."

She smirks, her hand tangling in my hair. "What if I was covered in chocolate?"

I chuckle and play along, dragging my tongue over her cheek. "You'd taste so sweet." I move my lips back to hers, and she responds by pushing me onto the mattress, straddling me.

God, yes.

I love when she takes control.

Her lips leave mine when she starts kissing my jaw, dragging it down my stomach. She presses her lips against the lower part of my stomach, and my cock twitches, knowing it's going to have Gabi's soft, warm mouth around it soon.

But before she can do just that, my phone rings.

I groan in frustration, squeezing my eyes closed. "Just keep going," I plead, wanting her mouth more than anything in the fucking world.

"Are you sure?" she asks, glancing up at me. My head goes dizzy at the sight of Gabi kneeled between my legs, and her mouth an inch away from my cock.

"Yes." I swallow, hard. "I literally couldn't give a fuck about anything else right now."

Gabi chuckles, and when the phone *finally* stops ringing, she flips her hair over one shoulder, gripping my cock in her hand.

"Mmffuck yes," I grunt, thrusting into her fist.

"You're so needy this morning," Gabi muses, dragging her soft, wet tongue over the length of my cock.

A moan builds in my throat. "I'm always needy when it comes to you."

She glances up at me with a smile on her face, but it fades when my phone rings again.

"God damn it," I groan, irritated. I run a hand down my face as the loud ringing fills the room. With a sigh, I reach for the nightstand and grab my phone, wondering who's calling. My expression falls when I see the name on the screen.

Gabi climbs up my body, resting her arms on my chest and propping her head on them. "Who is it?" she asks.

I swallow hard, glancing at Gabi as the phone keeps ringing. With a heavy sigh, I turn my phone to show her the screen. Her eyebrows furrow in concern, but then her eyes widen when she reads 'South Carolina County Jail'.

"Your dad?" she guesses.

I nod, running a hand down my face. The air between us turns cold, and every good, happy feeling I had evaporates into thin air.

"How long has it been since you talked to him?" Gabi asks.

I shake my head, staring at the screen again. "Not since the day I left."

She nods, her lips pursed. "Is there a part of you that wants to go see him?" she asks. "I could go with you and—"

"Fuck no," I cut in sharply, shivering at the mere thought. I cup her face in my hands, letting out a heavy sigh. "I tried so hard to shield that part of my life from you, Gabi." Her brow furrows, but I continue. "Remember when you asked why we never went to my house?" I remind her. "It's because I didn't want you anywhere near him. I didn't want him to see how much you meant to me, how much I loved you." I shake my head in frustration. "And I'm definitely not bringing you around him now. I don't... I don't want you to see the person I become when he's near," I admit, my voice catching. "Weak and fucking broken."

Gabi lifts herself up, cradling my face in her hands. "You are not weak or broken, Chris," she says firmly with a frown.

"I hate that he made you feel that way when to me, you were the beacon of light I was always searching for." Her words bring tears to my eyes. "You were the one person I could always count on."

I manage a small, sad smile because... fuck. That's all I ever wanted to be for her. "You were the only thing that made me want to get up in the mornings," I admit, my throat tightening as my nose starts to tingle. "You were the reason I survived in that house for as long as I did."

Her eyes begin to well up, and she shakes her head. "I just wish you told me," she says, her voice cracking. "I wish you didn't have to go through it alone."

"I know," I sigh, brushing my thumb over her soft cheek. "But I didn't want you to see me differently," I tell her. "I didn't want your pity or sympathy, especially when you had your own issues with your dad." Her eyes soften. "I just wanted to be a safe place for you, Gabi."

I glance down at her arm, running my thumb over the old, faded white scars on her wrist. My throat tightens, and I try to swallow past the lump forming there. I vividly remember the day they were bright red, blood dripping all over the floor. It's a memory that will forever haunt me.

"And I failed at that," I whisper, tracing her scars with my fingers.

She takes my hand, wrapping it around her wrist, and I lift my head, meeting her eyes, as she shakes her head. "Don't you dare blame yourself for that. You didn't fail me. You saved me," she says, her voice breaking into a sob. "I was a mess, my head was a mess, and I felt like I was drowning." She pauses, shaking her head again. "But you... You were my lifeboat. You were the reason I made it through. You were the reason I wanted to keep going."

"Gabi..."

"You didn't fail me, Chris," she repeats, kissing my lips. "You've never failed me."

I breathe out a sigh against her lips and return her kiss, pulling her closer by wrapping my arms around her waist. I always want her near me, close to me. Fucking attached to me.

Pulling back slightly, I brush her brown hair behind her ear. "I love you."

Her pink lips curve into a smile that takes my breath away. "I love you too," she says, her blue eyes sparkling.

I glance down at my phone, which is no longer ringing, and swallow hard. "I don't want to see him ever again," I admit, to myself and to Gabi. Part of me held onto that call, thinking I still wanted him in my life. Part of me still wants to be his son, to be loved by him.

But he had eighteen years to love me, and he never showed any sign of it. I don't want him in my life. I don't need him in my life. All I need is my mom and this girl right here in my arms.

Gabi nods, running her hand through my hair. "That's completely understandable," she says. "Dads suck."

I chuckle, knowing both our dads are assholes. "So fucking much."

She smirks and locks eyes with me. "Hey, Chris?"

I sigh at the feel of her hands running through my hair. "Yeah, pretty girl?"

"Truth or dare?"

"You're insane," I breathe out a laugh when I finally see what my dare is.

My girl smiles brightly up at me. "I'm fun," she corrects.

I shake my head, letting out a laugh. "I'm pretty sure those words are synonymous when it comes to you."

"Is that a no?" she challenges, arching a brow. "Because if I remember correctly, you don't back down from a dare."

I take a deep breath, running a hand through my hair as I glance back at the tattoo shop. "You really want to do this?" I ask her.

She nods, squeezing my hand. "You're part of me already. So why not prove it?"

Turning towards her, I hold her face in my hands. "I don't need a tattoo to prove that," I tell her. I swear every breath I take is proof of the way I love her. I live and breathe to *love her*.

"I know," she replies, sighing as she leans into my touch. "But I want to look at it when you—" She pauses, pursing her lips and glancing up at me warily.

My brows bunch when I figure out what she's saying. "When I leave," I finish for her, the reality sinking in. Because whether I like it or not, I'm going back in less than a week.

Just one week left with the love of my life.

My best friend.

I just fucking got her. I don't want to leave her again. I don't want to be miles apart from her again, only hearing her voice through a phone. I want to see her every day, touch her, kiss her, wake up with her.

I squeeze my eyes closed, dropping my hand from her face.

Gabi's soft palm traces my face, making me look back at her. "It's not just that," she says with a hint of sadness. "I thought it would be nice to cover my scars with something pretty." My heart starts to beat again. "So every time I look down, I won't see the worst moments of my life," she continues, her eyes locking onto mine. "I'll just see you."

Fuck.

How can I say no to that? I can't. That's the most beautiful thing I've ever heard, and if I can help her move on from the darkest time in her life, then I'll do it.

I'll do anything for her.

"Let's go," I say, tugging on her hand.

"Wait, really?" she asks, her face lighting up as I guide her across the street towards the tattoo parlor.

"Yeah, Gabi," I reply with a grin. We stop right outside the tattoo parlor, and I look down at her. "You know I'd do anything for you. Even if it means sticking a thousand needles in my skin."

Her gorgeous blue eyes roll playfully. "You make it sound so dramatic."

I furrow my brows at her. "That's literally what a tattoo is, Gabi."

She lifts her shoulder in a shrug. "My piercings didn't hurt."

I groan at the thought of them, then playfully tug on her hand, pulling her closer so she stumbles into me. I wrap my arm around her waist. "They're the sexiest things I've ever seen," I murmur against her lips.

She smiles and blinks, pulling back slightly. "See? Sometimes a little pain is worth it. Besides, imagine having me on your body."

I tilt my head back, laughter escaping my lips. "Are you planning to put your face on my arm, pretty girl?"

"No," she replies with a smirk. "Something better."

"What?" I ask, feeling a little nervous.

She shakes her head, pursing her lips. "You'll have to wait and see."

"I thought we were getting matching tattoos."

"We are," she confirms.

My frown deepens. "Then what is it?"

She leans up on her tiptoes, planting a quick kiss on my lips. "Do you trust me?"

I breathe out against her lips, tightening my hold on her waist. "You're the only person on this whole damn planet that I trust with my life."

Her smile falters slightly. "That's scary," she says. "You trust me that much?"

"So much," I affirm with a nod.

"What if I mess up in the future?" she asks, her brows furrowing.

"You won't," I say with a shake of my head. "You couldn't." I lift my hand, cupping her face, and brush my lips against hers. "I've been in love with you before I even knew what love was. There's nothing in this world you could do that would make me stop loving you," I reassure her, locking eyes with her beautiful blue ones.

"Even if I make you get a tattoo?" she teases, raising an eyebrow.

An amused smirk crosses my lips, but I nod. "Yes."

She tilts her head, considering. "Would you lie on a train track for me?"

I chuckle at her question. She really doesn't know the lengths I'd go for her. "Name the time and place."

Her eyes widen. "Kill someone for me?"

I hesitate, then shrug. "I've never been the best at fighting, but for you, I'd try."

Her lips part, brows knitting together. "Rob a bank?"

I laugh, running my thumb over her cheek. "We'd be filthy rich," I say, my heart pounding as I look at her. "There's nothing, Gabi," I repeat. "Nothing that would make me stop loving you. Nothing I wouldn't do for you."

She lets out a shaky breath and shakes her head. "You don't have to do this," she insists. "They say couple tattoos are bad luck. You can back out—"

"No fucking way," I interrupt. "I'm not scared of bad luck. You want this tattoo, so we're getting this tattoo," I tell her, tucking her hair behind her ear. "Are you ready to go in?"

She nods, a smile spreading across her lips, and we enter the shop together.

Twenty minutes later, and I'm dying.

This shit hurts like hell.

"Oh fuck," Gabi grunts, squeezing my hand tightly. "This hurts way more than the piercings did." She glances at me, biting down on her bottom lip to stifle a scream, her eyes squeezed shut in pain.

Yeah, my girl talked a big talk outside, but now she's clinging onto me while we both endure this pain.

"You still don't hate me?" she asks, her eyes searching mine.

I let out a laugh through the pain, focusing on my beautiful girlfriend. "I love you."

She winces, a pained whimper escaping her. "How the hell can you laugh at a time like this?" she says, gripping my hand tightly as the tattoo artist works on her arm.

I shrug, unable to tear my eyes away from her. Partly because I can't get enough of looking at her, and partly because if I glance down and see the needle in my own arm, I might pass out. "Because I'm with you," I reply.

The buzzing of the needle stops, and I raise my head to see my tattoo artist step back. "All done."

"You too," the girl tattooing Gabi says, wiping a towel on her arm.

I glance at Gabi, and she lets out a deep breath. "You ready to see it?"

I tighten my grip on her hand and bring it towards me, pressing my lips against her knuckles. "I'll love whatever you chose," I reassure her.

She sighs and smiles, looking down at her tattoo on the inside of her arm. I follow her gaze and look down at mine, in the same spot.

My brows furrow as I take in the thin strokes of black ink. There's a small clef surrounded by delicate lines resembling stars. I gulp at the sight, feeling my eyes start to tear up.

"Music has always been a huge part of us," Gabi says, prompting me to lift my head to look at her. "And... the stars say we're meant to be."

Fuck.

I rise from the chair, my heart racing as I reach for her face, cradling it in my hands before I lean in, and press my lips against hers, because I'll die if I don't. Her lips part on a gasp and I groan, savoring her taste. Savoring the softness of her mouth against mine as our tongues brush together in a kiss that shows her how much I love her.

"Does that mean you like it?" she manages to ask between breaths.

I shake my head slightly, pulling back just enough to meet her eyes, then grasp her arm, pressing my lips against her new tattoo, just above her scars. "I love it."

Her eyes widen with hope, a beautiful smile spreading across her face. "Really?"

"So fucking much."

Her face brightens with another smile, and she lets out a sigh. "It was the best goodbye present I could think of."

My smile fades into a frown. "This isn't goodbye, Gabi," I insist. It just can't be. I won't allow it.

She sighs again, nodding. "I know."

I'm not buying it. Not at all. I cradle her face in my hands, locking eyes with her deep blue gaze. "I mean it, Gabi. I'll be back," I promise. "We can visit each other. This isn't goodbye," I say firmly, feeling my heart ache at the thought.

She nods, tears pooling in her eyes, which breaks my heart all over again. "It's just one year," she says, her voice quivering.

"Exactly." I wipe the tears from her cheeks. "I waited ten years for you," I remind her with a soft smile. "I can handle one more. I'd wait forever if I needed to."

She lets out a deep breath, her tears drying up. "I just don't want to let you go after I finally got you."

Jesus. Her words break me. I shake my head, pressing my forehead against hers. "Please don't let me go," I whisper, planting a kiss on her forehead. "I don't want you to ever let me go."

"I can't," she murmurs, wrapping her arms around my waist. "I couldn't even if I tried. You're a part of me, Chris. Always have been."

I wipe under her eyes with the pads of my thumbs, and smile at her. "Now more than ever," I say, holding up my arm with our matching tattoo.

She breathes out a laugh. "I love you."

I'll never get tired of hearing her say that. I waited so long to hear her say those words. Every time she says them, it feels like a dream come true.

"I love you too, pretty girl."

36

Three more days

Gabriella

I slide into the booth beside Madeline and let out a sigh. "Alright, fine," I say, raising my hands. "I'll show you guys."

Grayson turns, his brows knitting together. Does he ever smile? Probably only when he's alone with Rosie. "What are you talking about?"

Everyone's eyes are on me now, and I roll mine in response. "My tattoo," I clarify. "Since you're all so desperate to see it," I add with a shrug.

Chris chuckles, sitting beside me, but Grayson's frown deepens. "Literally no one here knows what you're talking about."

"You have a tattoo? Damn, that's hot," James says with a grin.

"You haven't even seen it," his boyfriend, Carter, points out.

James shrugs. "Tattoos are hot."

Carter, who has zero tattoos, narrows his eyes. "You think so?"

James's eyes widen, realizing his mistake, and he shakes his head vigorously. "No, of course not. Ew, I hate tattoos," he says, trying to sound convincing but failing miserably, and I can't help but laugh.

"You got a tattoo?" Madi asks, her eyes wide with surprise.

"Matching ones," I say with a grin, glancing at Chris.

Chris shrugs, running a hand through his hair. "She asked."

"Of course," Aiden says with a laugh, shaking his head. "I doubt there's anything you wouldn't do if she asked."

I nod, resting my head on my boyfriend's shoulder. "He even said he'd lie on a train track for me."

"That's not surprising," Aiden says with a smirk.

"What's the tattoo?" Rosie asks.

I lift my sleeve, and Chris does the same, revealing our new ink. As they look down, I notice their smiles falter, their brows furrowing as they see the faded scars, piecing it all together.

I can see why it would be surprising, since I never even told the girls before. I didn't want them to know there was a time when I was broken. The only person who knew what happened was Chris. Until now.

"I wanted a new memory," I explain, seeing the sadness in their eyes, but I keep smiling. "Get rid of the bad, and cover it up with a memory that means something."

"It's beautiful," Grayson says, his brows knitting together.

"Yeah." Madi swallows hard, staring at my arm. "What made you want to get a tattoo?"

I shrug, pulling down my sleeve as I look up at Chris. "I wanted to feel connected to Chris," I explain to them.

Aiden lets out a soft laugh, shaking his head. "I don't think you needed a tattoo to do that."

Chris wraps his arm around my shoulder, pulling me to his side. "I told her the exact same thing."

Turning to Madi, I continue, "But I also wanted to settle something between us." Her eyebrows furrow. "Remember the bet we made two years ago?"

Her brow arches. "Vividly," she says, flicking her dark red hair behind her shoulder.

We made a bet that whoever fell in love first had to do a forfeit. Hers was dying her hair red, and mine was getting a tattoo.

I chuckle. "Well, I didn't think it was fair that you dyed your hair since I'd always been in love with Chris," I tell her with a shrug.

Her mouth gapes open. "So, you're telling me I dyed my hair for nothing?"

I chuckle. "Well..." My lips twitch. "Not for nothing. It was entertaining for sure."

"Glad to be of service," she says dryly. "Can I dye it back now?"

"Sure."

Her boyfriend, Lucas lets out a groan and plants a kiss on the top of her head. "I'm gonna miss the red."

Madi smiles up at him, and I can't help but smile too. I remember when she was adamant about avoiding love because of her shitty ex-boyfriend. And when Lucas came into her life, she didn't even entertain the idea. But I'm so happy they're together. I'm so happy that they get to stay together.

In the same city.

The same country.

I glance at Chris, my smile fading. We only have three days left.

Three days until he has to leave.

Three days until I have to say goodbye.

His eyes meet mine, and he smiles, cupping my face in his hands. "I'm so proud of you," he says. "I know it must have been hard to show them the scars."

My heart swells with love for him, and I lean into his palm. "I can do anything when you're with me."

His eyes soften, but a hint of concern creeps in, his smile fading into a frown. He won't be with me, though. Not for a whole year.

"Gabi—"

"Aiden Pierce."

Our heads turn as two girls approach our booth, their eyes fixed on Aiden, who has his arm around his girlfriend, Leila.

"I heard you're joining the Chicago Bulls," the blonde says, twirling her hair.

Leila lets out a sigh, turning her head away.

Aiden presses his lips together in a tight smile. "Yeah, I am."

Aiden was a big deal when he attended Redfield, but now that he's been drafted into the NBA and is headed to a professional team, he's going to be even bigger.

"I love Chicago," the brunette beside her friend says. "And basketball. I could come visit you sometime," she suggests, leaning on the booth.

Aiden's smile fades slightly, and he arches a brow, tightening his hold on Leila. "I'm good. My girlfriend will come visit me."

Leila turns her attention to the girls and gives them a fake smile, narrowing her eyes as she waves at them.

The girls frown and then turn around, heading toward the table where the football team is hanging out.

Leila narrows her eyes at Aiden. "This is what it's going to be like, isn't it?"

Aiden's brows furrow. "What do you mean?"

Leila sighs, rolling her eyes. "Girls flirting with you all the time," she says, her voice tinged with hurt. "And it's only going to get worse once you're gone. You won't be here anymore"

Aiden arches a brow. "Well… no, since I graduated."

Leila swallows, looking up at him. "I know. You're leaving me."

Aiden's face falls into a frown, and he gently cups Leila's face in his hands. "I'm leaving Redfield," he assures her. "I'm not leaving *you*. I'll never leave you."

"It's the same thing," she replies with a shrug. "Girls will be flirting with you all the damn time, and it's going to be ten times worse than it is here."

Aiden shakes his head, brushing her brown hair out of her face. "How many times do I have to tell you that I only want you?" he says. "Doesn't matter who flirts with me. My only thought is, 'my girlfriend is so much hotter'."

Leila rolls her eyes. "Don't patronize me. I just wish you'd call them out and tell them to get lost," she admits, swallowing hard.

Aiden purses his lips thoughtfully. "Do you want me to wear your face on a t-shirt?" he asks with a hint of humor. "Because I will if that's what it takes. I'll do anything to earn your trust."

335

She sighs, shaking her head. "I do trust you," she says. "It's just… hard."

"I know," Aiden murmurs, pressing his lips to her forehead. "But it's only one year, and then you'll come with me."

Leila raises an eyebrow, a playful smirk on her face. "How are you so certain I'll want to come with you?" she teases.

Aiden smirks back, knowing full well his girlfriend loves to tease him. "Because I *need* you to survive, gorgeous," he says with a smile. "My heart beats for you. Are you going to stop my heart?"

Leila lets out a sigh, a small smile tugging at her lips. "I guess not."

Aiden leans in and presses his lips against hers.

Chris grazes my chin with his hand, turning my head to smile down at me. "How are you feeling after that love confession?" he says teasingly. "Any nausea?"

My stomach churns, but not because of Leila and Aiden. It used to bother me seeing all my friends in love when I thought my feelings were unrequited, but not anymore.

I love seeing them happy.

They deserve it.

But the churning in my stomach is the realization that I'm going to be alone all over again.

Aiden will only be an hour flight away in Chicago, and will come to visit Leila often. Grayson will be nearby, working at the garage until Rosie graduates, and Lucas will still be here at Redfield.

But Chris...

I swallow down my emotions. "I need a drink."

Chris frowns, searching my eyes. "Are you okay?" he asks warily, knowing our history with using alcohol and drugs as a coping mechanism. It's been a while since we've leaned on those crutches.

"Yeah, I'm fine," I assure him. "I just need a drink."

His frown deepens, but he stands up and lets me pass. My body feels hot, my face feels puffy, but I squeeze my fists, determined not to cry.

I reach the bar and flag down the bartender, ordering a vodka.

Chris appears by my side, lifting my face to meet his eyes. "Gabi, I know you," he says, his eyes searching mine.

I close my eyes briefly. He knows me better than anyone. Always has. Of course, he'd know when I'm on the verge of a meltdown.

"I know you do," I admit with a sigh.

He furrows his brow. "Which means I know when something's wrong."

I shake my head, tears threatening to spill over. "There's nothing wrong," I lie. "I just want to go home."

His frown deepens. "You want to go home?" he repeats. "Now?"

I nod, stepping away from the bar.

I don't want a drink.

I don't want to numb myself.

I just want to be with him.

"We only have three more days until you have to leave," I tell him, swallowing hard against the lump in my throat. "I just want to be with you until then."

His eyes soften, and he nods slowly. "Okay," he says, taking my hand in his. "Let's go home."

37

The first time I ever saw you

Gabriella

Eighteen hours, thirty-two minutes, and twenty-five seconds.

That's how long is left until Chris boards a plane and leaves—for an entire year.

I'm trying really hard to be happy for him, knowing he has a job he loves, friends who treat him well, and a whole other life there. But I can't help but feel sad that he won't be here with me.

Almost as if he senses my thoughts, his eyes crack open, and he blinks up at me, stretching his arms over his head. "Hey, baby," he murmurs, his husky voice sending a shiver down my spine. "You're up already?"

"Yeah," I reply, my lips curving into a smile when he turns on his side, and wraps his arm around my naked waist, pulling me closer to him. "I've been up for hours."

His brows dip as an amused smirk crosses his face. "That's new."

"I wanted to look at you," I admit, staring into his kind, brown eyes I love so much.

Chris smiles, cupping my face before pressing his lips to mine. "I always want to look at you."

I try to smile, but it slips as a sigh escapes my lips. "It might be the last time I'll look at you."

His face falls, and his brows furrow. "Gabi—"

"Just let me memorize every part of you while I still can," I say, swinging my leg over his hips to straddle him, and place my hands flat on his chest.

"Mmm hell yes," he grunts, his hands flying to my hips.

"Shhh." I narrow my eyes at him. "I'm memorizing."

He chuckles, pressing his lips together. "Memorize away, baby."

My hands cradle his face, and I trail my fingers up his cheeks, running them over his eyebrows, staring into the chocolate pool swimming in his eyes. "Your eyes are so pretty."

"Right back at you," Chris says, swiping his thumb over my hip. "They're like the ocean. Strong and beautiful, sucking me right in."

"And your hair," I say, running my fingers through the curls on the top of his head. "I love your hair."

"I love yours," he murmurs, tucking a strand behind my ear.

I melt into his touch, my fingers trailing down to trace over his bottom lip. "And your lips." I sigh. "You have the best lips," I say, leaning down to press a kiss to them. "So soft, and pretty, and—"

Before I can say anything, Chris curls his hand over the back of my head and presses my head down, before kissing me. His big hands hold my waist, and he flips us over, his body covering mine.

He pulls back, and looks down at my naked body pinned under him, his eyes zoning in on my tits before groaning, diving in to capture my lips once again.

I moan into his mouth, my lips parting on a gasp when he moves to my neck. "I love your kisses," I tell him, tangling my fingers in his hair.

He lifts his head, his lips quirking. "I love *you*."

His words make my heart pound against my chest, and I smile, tilting my head at him. "You want to memorize me now?"

"No."

My brows furrow. "No?"

He shakes his head. "I don't need to."

"Oh?" I ask, intrigued.

He shifts on his elbow, running his hand over my hips. "I've thought about nothing but you for the last ten years," he clarifies. "I've memorized every inch of you, Gabi."

"Every inch?"

He nods, leaning down to press his lips to mine. "Every." Kiss. "Single." Kiss. "One."

I cradle his head in my hands, staring into his eyes, feeling my heart ache and beat all at the same time for him. I love him so much. And he's *leaving*.

His smile slips seeing my expression sadden, and he drops onto the bed with a sigh. "I'll be back," he says. It's all he's been saying for the past three days.

"I know," I say with a nod.

"I hate seeing you upset," he says, running a thumb over my cheek. "This is supposed to be a happy day. We can put on a Channing Tatum movie?" he suggests.

I let out a chuckle, loving that he's embracing my movie crush, but I shake my head. "You know what would make this a happy day?"

He doesn't even let me finish my sentence. My best friend grins, pulling me out of bed and throws his t-shirt over me, then slips on his sweatpants before guiding me towards the kitchen.

"I didn't even say anything."

"Your eyes did," he says with a smirk, wrapping his arms around my hips and lifting me into his arms before setting me on top of the counter. Standing between my legs, he looks up at me as I wrap my hands around his neck. "You want pancakes, don't you, pretty girl?"

"Yeah," I reply, feeling my throat tighten. *I want you more.*

He leans in, and presses his lips against mine. "Then I'm making you pancakes." He steps out from between my legs, and grabs a bowl and a bunch of ingredients I didn't even know I had, and starts mixing them together.

"I'm going to miss having pancakes," I tell him with a sigh. "I've gotten so used to them while you've been here."

He chuckles, meeting my eyes. "I'll miss making them for you."

"Then that means you should stay," I say, tilting my head with a sweet smile that he smirks at.

"I wish I could," he says, his smile slipping.

"But you have to go." I nod, pressing my lips together, swallowing my emotions. "I know."

To distract myself from welling tears, I straighten my posture and force a smile as I reach over, dipping my finger into the pancake mix.

"Hey, hands off," Chris says with a laugh, moving the bowl away from me. "It's raw."

"Still delicious," I say with a shrug.

His lips twist into a smile as he starts scooping the mixture onto the pan, and I sneak another lick of the batter.

"There'll be no pancakes if you keep doing that," he says with a chuckle. "Besides, you might get sick."

"Then you'll just have to stay here and take care of me," I tease, trying to lighten the mood. But Chris's smile fades, and he places the cooked pancake on a plate before turning off the stove. He then walks over to me, his expression soft as he takes my face in his hands.

"Are you sure you're okay with this, Gabi?" he asks, his eyes searching mine. "I wish I could stay, you don't know how much." He shakes his head, exhaling heavily. "Fuck, I hate this."

"I know," I reply, my bottom lip quivering. "I know you can't stay. You have a job, and school… I *know*. I just… We'll be so far away, in different time zones, and I guess I don't want you to be so busy that you forget me."

His eyebrows shoot up in surprise. "Are you… Are you kidding? I…" He closes his eyes for a second. "Gabi, I haven't *stopped* thinking about you for ten years," he says, his eyes locking with mine. "There's no way I could ever forget you. You're always at the forefront of my mind." His lips press together, and he blows out a sigh. "I still remember every detail of the very first time I ever saw you."

"You do?" I ask, my brows furrowing as I try to remember it.

He lets out a laugh. "Yeah, pretty girl," he says, dropping his hands to my hips as he steps between my legs once again.

342

"You were wearing a flannel shirt around your waist, and your hair was in two braids."

My face scrunches up. "Ew."

He lets out a laugh. "I thought you were so fucking pretty," he says, making my heart skip a beat. "I just kept looking at you, watching as you did your tricks on your skateboard. And then I fell over." He laughs. "I was so distracted by you, that I fell on my ass." He looks up at me, swallowing. "But then you noticed me, and you rushed over toward me, and helped me up. I was so blindsided by you, that I didn't know what to say," he admits with a nervous laugh. "I just kept staring at you while you asked if I was okay over and over again."

"I remember that," I say, tilting my head. "I thought you'd hit your head or something."

He shakes his head. "Nah. just scratched my knee," he says. "But you still helped me up, and grabbed hold of my skateboard. That's when you noticed my Spiderman stickers, and you said 'I love Spiderman'," he mimics in a girly voice that makes me narrow my eyes.

"I definitely did not sound like that."

"And then I finally found the courage to talk to you, and we ended up talking about spiderman, and then—" He pauses, pressing his lips together.

"What?" I say, my brows dipping.

He sighs. "Don't hate me."

My frown deepens. "Why? What did you do?"

His lips curl in a sheepish smile. "I told you I was new to skateboarding."

I blink. "You weren't?"

343

"No. I'd been skateboarding for a little over a year by then," he admits, pulling me closer to him. "I just… I really wanted to see you again."

"You did?" I ask, my breath catching in my throat.

He nods, his hand cupping my face. "I asked you if you could teach me some tricks," he reminds me.

The memory comes rushing back to me. "We spent two whole weeks meeting up every day so I can teach you."

The corner of his lips lift. "Yeah."

My heart races in my chest. "You liked me then?" I ask, unable to believe what he's telling me. We were just twelve at the time. And he's telling me he liked me since the moment he met me?

He nods again, brushing his thumb over my bottom lip. "Always," he affirms. "I've loved you for so long I wouldn't know what it feels like to not love you."

My eyes start to tear up, and I try to blink them away, but they keep coming. We lost so much time. So much time we could have been together if I had just realized he was everything I wanted.

"Chris," I say, my voice breaking.

He covers my lips with his, kissing me until I can't breathe, until all I can focus on is him. His taste, his touch, his warmth. When he pulls back, tears glisten in his eyes as he looks into mine.

"It's just one year, Gabi," he reassures me.

"I know," I say, though my heart still aches.

"We'll get through this," he promises. "And then when we graduate, you'll get into your dream dance school, and we'll go to New York together. We'll live in a small, shitty

344

apartment, maybe get a dog, and I'll make you pancakes every morning."

"Every morning?" I ask, loving the sound of that.

"Every. Single. Day."

I let out a breath, my shoulders relaxing, and my lips curl into a real smile as I picture our future together. "I can't wait."

38

Flights and goodbyes

Christopher

Today fucking sucks.

For the past three days, all we've done is spend time together. Cooking, playing video games, kissing, making love. Each day has been amazing, but there's always been this pang of hurt in my chest because we both knew it had an expiration date.

We knew this was coming. We tried to prepare for it, but it doesn't hurt any less.

My heart feels like it's been carved open every time I look at Gabi and see the look on her face.

It was supposed to be one summer.

Just one summer where I'd visit her, and then go back.

But so much fucking happened in that time.

The thought of getting on a plane and moving to the other side of the world breaks me apart.

Her eyes meet mine as we walk into the airport, and the pain in them crushes me. My stomach drops, and I force myself to swallow hard.

Dropping my suitcase, I cup her face in my hands. "I'll be back," I promise, wanting her to believe it. The moment I graduate, I'm booking a plane and coming straight to her.

"I know," she says, forcing a smile that doesn't quite reach her eyes, which are glassy and wet, breaking my heart.

Fuck.

I can't.

I can't handle seeing her cry.

I can't bear to see her so upset because of me.

I wrap my arms around her, pulling her close against my chest. Pressing my lips to the top of her head, my heart thumps out of control.

"This isn't me leaving you, Gabi," I reassure her. "It's not like last time."

She lets out a heavy breath, but remains silent, and that *hurts*. She doesn't believe it. She's afraid I'll leave and never return, like I did four years ago.

Reaching into her back pocket, she pulls out something old, and blue and my heart goes haywire. My eyes lock on my old navy baseball cap. "You should probably have this back," she says, heavy breaths leaving her lips.

I take the cap from her, feeling my heart break. I'm not letting her give this to me like it's a goodbye. Like she'll never see me again. I open it up, and place it on her head. "You can give it to me when I come back," I tell her. "Because I *am* coming back for you, Gabi."

Pulling back slightly, I lift her arm and place a kiss on her wrist, where her tattoo rests, her scars faint beneath them. A sob catches in her throat, but she swallows it down.

"I love you, Gabriella Miller," I say, keeping my eyes locked on hers. "So much. You have no idea how much." Tears stream down her face, and my throat tightens.

She nods, lifting her hand to cup my face. "I love you too," she says. "So much I can't fucking breathe." Her voice cracks, and I lose it.

I grab her face in my hands and kiss her. Her lips part, and I glide my tongue over hers, wanting to savor every moment of this kiss, wanting it to last forever.

"Chris," Gabi mumbles against my lips. "People are staring."

"I don't care," I mutter, shaking my head, pulling her close to me for another deep kiss. "I don't see anyone but you."

She wraps her arms around my neck and returns my kiss, gasping into my mouth. But then, she cries out, sobs racking through her.

I pull away, looking down at the love of my life, tears streaming down her face.

"Don't cry," I plead, my voice cracking as I lift her chin to meet my eyes. Her blue eyes are filled with tears, and it tears at my heart. "Please. It breaks my fucking heart."

She shakes her head, wiping away her tears. "I'm fine. I promise."

"Make a joke," I say. "Laugh. Anything. Please." I need to see her smile, to hear her laugh. The thought of leaving her breaks me inside, but I can't bear for her to be in pain.

I want Gabi to laugh. I want her to smile. I just want her to be okay.

Gabi lets out a shaky breath and shakes her head. "I don't feel like laughing right now," she says, her lip wobbling.

I wrap my arms around her, and just fucking hold her. I *need* to hold her. I don't want to let her go.

But then the loudspeaker crackles to life. "Attention, passengers. This is the first boarding announcement for Flight 247 to London."

We reluctantly pull apart, and my eyes lock onto hers. "I have to go," I say, my throat tight with emotion.

She nods slowly. "I know."

Fuck. My eyes burn and I look at my best friend, the love of my life, the only reason I want to breathe in this world. I grab her wrist, lifting up, and trace my fingers over her tattoo, keeping my eyes on hers as I spell out:

I love you.

Her chin wobbles as tears fill her eyes, but then she lifts her lips into a smile. "I love you, too."

Her glassy blue eyes I love so much, completely shatter my heart. My trembling hand reaches for her face, my heart pounding furiously as tears stream down her cheeks.

Swallowing the painful rock in my throat, I shake my head, unable to tear my eyes away from her. "Tell me not to go, Gabi," I manage to choke out, feeling my world collapse in my arms. "Tell me not to get on that plane."

But she shakes her head, like I knew she would. Because she's fucking amazing, and doesn't care whether me getting on that plane completely breaks her heart. "I can't do that," she says, her eyes closing as she leans into my palm. "You need to go."

A heavy breath leaves my lips. "I don't want to."

"I know," she says, lifting her head to look up at me. "But you need to do this." She reaches her hand out, brushing my hair back. "It's only for one year. We'll be okay."

I take a step towards her, cupping her face between my hands, and lean down for one last kiss.

She responds with a soft moan against my lips, but then she pulls away. "You need to go, Chris," she says, her voice thick with emotion as she subtly wipes under her eye.

"Not yet," I murmur, looking into her blue eyes. "I don't want to let go just yet." I dive in for another kiss, feeling her body melt into mine as she opens up for me.

"You're going to be late," she mumbles against my lips.

Swallowing hard against the lump in my throat, I reluctantly release her and take a step back.

"Go," she mouths silently, and I tear my eyes away from her, forcing myself to move towards security.

I can't resist looking back, though. Every few steps, I glance over my shoulder at her, my heart aching as I see how small and distant she looks now.

"Sir, please place your bags inside the bins."

I keep my eyes on Gabi, hardly able to see her face from this distance.

"Sir."

"Hmm?" I ask, tearing my eyes away from Gabi, shifting my focus to the security guard gesturing towards the belt.

"Your bags, sir," the guard repeats.

I look back again, staring down at her from over the railing. My stomach drops, and my heart aches, a hollow ache spreading through my chest.

I can't fucking breathe. My throat closes up, and I struggle to breathe. I try so hard to get air into my lungs, but I can't. Not without her. I've tried being without her before, and it was torture. I just can't. I fucking can't.

Turning around, I race down the stairs, my hand sliding down the railing as I leap two steps at a time. My shoulder bumps into people along the way, but I don't care. All that matters right now is seeing her. Being with her.

I turn the corner and spot her, her small frame huddled as she sobs quietly. Her head is bowed, and she doesn't notice me as I sprint towards her.

Then, she lifts her head, and our eyes lock. The tears pause, and her lips part in surprise. She shakes her head slightly as I exhale heavily, and approach her, my heart pounding in my chest.

I grin, probably inappropriate given her tears, but I can't help it as I take those final strides toward her. She looks up at me, confusion knitting her brows.

"What are you doing here?" she asks. "Shouldn't you be at security?"

"I'm not going," I say, still a little breathless.

"What?" Her brows furrow deeper. "What do you mean? Did your flight get cancelled?"

"No," I say with a smirk.

"Then why—"

I cut her off with a kiss.

Without waiting for her to finish her sentence, I cup her face in my hands and press my lips against hers. A soft sound escapes her, and I savor it, smiling into the kiss.

"I'm not leaving," I murmur against her lips between kisses. "I'm not leaving you ever again."

My hands settle on her waist, and I lift her effortlessly into my arms, her legs wrapping around me. She gasps in surprise, her eyes widening as she pulls back slightly. "What?"

My smile widens as I tuck a stray strand of her hair behind her ear, cupping her face gently. "I left once before, and it was the hardest time of my life being away from you, Gabi," I confess. "Back then, we were just friends, and it nearly drove me insane. But now... Now that I finally have you in my arms, now that I can kiss you like this?" I shake my head, letting out a small laugh. "I don't think I can ever be without you ever again."

Her lips part in shock. "You're joking."

"Not about this," I assure her, brushing my thumb over her bottom lip. "I don't joke when it comes to you, pretty girl."

Her brows furrow with concern, tears glistening in her eyes. "But what about school, and your job?" she asks. "You've worked so hard for this. It's just one more year."

"One year without you," I say, narrowing my eyes. "I can't do it, Gabi. My heart was breaking with every step I took towards that plane."

"Chris," she says with a sigh, her touch soothing against my cheek. "You were so close to graduating."

I shrug. "I'll figure it out," I assure her. "I'll transfer schools, get a new job. I'll do whatever it takes if it means I can stay with you."

Her eyes shimmer with tears, but a hopeful smile flickers across her face. "You mean it? You're really going to stay?"

"Yeah," I reply, a chuckle escaping me as I stroke her cheek. "I'm staying."

"For good?" she asks, searching my eyes.

I nod, pulling her closer and pressing my lips against hers. "For the rest of our lives."

39

What happens now?

Gabriella

One Year Later

I never thought this day would come.

These past four years have been filled with so many fun and unforgettable moments, but I've also faced some hard times, and seriously considered quitting more than once.

But, here I am, graduating from Redfield University, surrounded by my best friends.

I glance at them as we line up, ready to walk onto the stage. Madi's fidgeting with her gown, and breathes out a sigh. "Are you guys nervous?" she asks.

"Nah," I reply with a smirk. "I'm so excited to get out of here."

They let out a soft laugh, but Rosie purses her lips. "I really loved the past four years," she admits. "I love who I've become here." Her brows furrow as she looks between us. "I'm really going to miss you guys."

My eyes burn, but I blink it away, my lips curling into a smile. "I'm going to miss you guys too," I tell them. "You've become more than just friends," I admit, swallowing hard as their eyes turn to me. "You're my sisters."

Rosie's eyes well with tears. "I'm going to cry," she says, her voice cracking.

"Rosie, don't… Fuck," Leila groans. "Now I think I'm going to cry."

I chuckle. "If Aiden heard that, he'd race over here."

"Funny," Leila says, narrowing her teary eyes at me.

"You think I'm kidding?" I ask, arching an eyebrow. "That guy is totally whipped for you."

She rolls her eyes, knowing it's true. "Like you can talk. Chris would die before he ever let you cry."

I purse my lips together. He's seen me cry more times than I can count. He's seen every part of me—the ugly, broken mess—and he always managed to pull me out of the darkness. But I could see how much it hurt him, how it killed him to see me like that and how powerless he felt.

The truth is, Chris didn't have to do anything. Just being there was enough. All I ever needed was him beside me, holding me, playing me his new favorite song, *loving me.*

When he left all those years ago, I thought my world would end. Without my lifeboat, I felt like I was sinking.

But here we are. Five years later.

Together.

Finally.

I look up, spotting him standing in line, running a hand through his hair nervously. I wish I could have been there beside him, holding his hand. After all, he transferred schools just to be closer to me.

"Christopher Hudson," the announcer calls.

He lifts his head, and a smile spreads across my face as I watch him step confidently onto the stage to receive his diploma. The girls and I stand, clapping as he walks across the stage, and I whoop, shouting his name.

He turns towards me, his face lighting up with a grin. He reaches down and touches the tattoo on his wrist. I mirror the gesture, our eyes locking. I silently mouth 'I love you.'

His smile sends my heart somersaulting, and he mouths back, 'I love you too,' before walking off the stage.

"Someone fix my cap," Leila grumbles. "It keeps getting in my eye."

Rosie chuckles and reaches over to adjust Leila's cap, tucking the string behind her ear.

"Rosalie Whitton."

Her eyes widen, and she freezes. "Oh crap. That's me."

"Go," we all encourage her, and she finally remembers how to move her feet, walking onto the stage, her white heels clanking on the ground.

I turn my head at the sound of a whistle, spotting Grayson clapping and grinning up at his girlfriend. I wasn't the biggest fan of him initially, especially after what happened between him and Rosie. But seeing how much he adores her—and all the candy he's bribed me with—I can't help but smile. It's clear how much he worships my best friend.

She deserves that.

Rosie deserves to be happy, loved, and treated like his angel.

"Leila Perez," they call out.

Leila flicks her hair behind her shoulder and strides onto the stage, her long, golden legs visible beneath her gown as she collects her diploma. She turns her head towards the crowd just as Aiden starts clapping, cupping his mouth to whoop.

"That's my girl!" he shouts proudly. "That's my fucking girl up there!"

People glance back at him with a mix of surprise and amusement, but Aiden doesn't give a shit. He'd proudly proclaim Leila as his from the highest mountaintop.

Leila beams, unable to contain her smile as she locks eyes with Aiden. He shakes his head in awe of her, a wide grin spreading across his face.

"I'm nervous," Madeline says, chewing on her bottom lip.

"Why?" I raise an eyebrow. "You just walk up there, grab your diploma, and walk off."

Madi shoots me a glare. "What if I trip? Or my dress flies up? Or—"

"None of that will happen," I assure her with a laugh. "You're overthinking it. Just focus on Lucas when you get up there, and everything else will go smoothly."

She scans the crowd for Lucas, and visibly relaxes when she spots him, a soft smile spreading across her face.

I sigh, giving her a reassuring pat on the back. "What will you do without me?"

She meets my gaze, laughter twinkling in her eyes. "I honestly don't know." She swallows hard. "I'm going to miss you like crazy."

My throat tightens, and I manage a smile, trying to push down the emotions threatening to surface. "I thought you were going to say you'd finally have peace and quiet."

Madi shakes her head, smiling. "Quiet is overrated."

I blink in surprise. "It is?"

She nods, her smile widening. "I miss your loud music, your funny jokes, and even your late-night drunken rambles."

I chuckle, remembering our time together over the last few years. Sure, we might have gotten on each other's nerves a little sometimes, but I'm really going to miss her.

I open my arms and pull her into a hug, which makes Madi gasp playfully. We're not really huggers, and Madeline hates physical affection unless it's from Lucas. So I give her a quick pat on the back before we awkwardly part.

"Well, that was weird," she says.

"I agree. Let's never do that again."

She nods, letting out a chuckle. "Deal."

"Madeline Davis."

She turns to me, eyes wide with nerves. I give her a reassuring smile. "Go. You've got this," I whisper, trying to calm her nerves.

She nods, takes a deep breath, and turns towards the stage. Madeline reaches the center, accepts her diploma with a smile, and then scans across the crowd. Her eyes light up when she spots Lucas quietly clapping and smiling up at her.

He doesn't make noise like the other guys, but his expression says it all. Their love is quiet and pure, and so amazing to witness.

A smile spreads across Madeline's face as she locks eyes with Lucas, the tension melting away, and walks off the stage, gracefully.

"Gabriella Miller."

I put on a smile and step onto the stage. Honestly, I thought Madeline was being silly worrying about tripping, but now it's all I can think about.

Please, for the love of all that is holy in the world, don't let me fall.

"Yeah!"

I turn my head to see James standing, clapping and whooping. I laugh and shoot him a wink, before accepting my diploma before I walk off the stage to join the girls and Chris, who immediately intertwines his fingers with mine.

I turn my head, and Chris presses his lips to mine in a soft kiss.

Four years ago, I was miserable. Lost in alcohol and partying, desperately trying to forget how alone I felt.

And now here I am, happier than ever with the love of my life standing beside me.

He pulls back, holding my face and smiling down at me. "We did it," he says.

I let out a laugh. "Yeah. We're finally out of here."

"Hey," Rosie interjects, narrowing her eyes. "We all had amazing memories here."

My shoulders drop, knowing she's right. Even if I had some tough times, and felt a little lost in the beginning, I loved my time here. I loved meeting these girls and spending the last four years with them.

"I agree," Madeline says with a sigh, glancing up at Lucas. "It's where I met the love of my life."

He smiles and leans down to kiss her.

I blink. "Oh hey. I just witnessed that without gagging," I joke, grinning at Madi. "I think I deserve a medal."

She laughs, shaking her head. "I'm going to miss you."

"Me too," I admit, the air growing quiet as we all glance at each other. "What do we do now?"

"We live our lives," Aiden says with a shrug, wrapping his arm around Leila's shoulder. "I'll play some ball, marry this girl, put a baby in her…"

"Excuse me?" Leila interrupts, raising an eyebrow at him.

Aiden grins down at her. "Yes, gorgeous?"

"When did we discuss this?" she asks.

Aiden shrugs, adjusting his cap. "I've been thinking about it a lot," he confesses.

Leila's eyes widen in surprise, and I bite my lip, finding the situation amusing. "And you didn't think to clue me in on these plans?"

Aiden chuckles, shaking his head. "Of course I did. But I can't tell you *everything*," he teases. "I have to keep your proposal a surprise."

Leila's eyes widen even more. "Proposal?"

"Someday," he murmurs, leaning down to kiss her cheek. "When you least expect it."

Her eyes flutter closed at his kiss, and they pull back, a smile spreading across her face. "What if I say no?"

We all exchange glances, smirks forming on our faces. There's no doubt in anyone's mind that she won't say no. Those two are meant to be together.

I should know.

After all, I'm with my soulmate.

Aiden grins, and I swear their teasing is their own kind of foreplay. "Then I'll keep asking until I turn it into a yes," he tells her.

"And you think that will work?"

Aiden nods confidently, kissing her again. "It did before."

Leila's smile brightens, and I know she'll say yes whenever he asks, even if that day happens to be tomorrow.

"Anyone else making any life-changing decisions?" Grayson asks.

I bite my lip, glancing at Chris, who meets my eyes and nods. "I'm moving to New York," I announce.

"You are?" Madi asks, raising her eyebrows in surprise, joined by Rosie and Leila. Only Chris knows, as I found out just a week ago.

I nod, unable to suppress the smile spreading across my face. "I received the acceptance letter from my dream dance school last week."

"Wow," Rosie says, her eyes lighting up. "That's amazing. So, I guess we'll be close by, then."

Grayson shakes his head, running a hand through his hair. "Just when I thought we'd finally got rid of you," he teases with a smirk.

"Don't worry," I reply, pressing my lips together in amusement. "I'll be right there to annoy you."

Grayson sighs dramatically, turning to Rosie. "Are you sure about New York, angel?" he asks, his tone teasing. "We could go anywhere else. Paris is far."

Rosie laughs, knowing he's joking, and leans back into him. His arms wrap around her waist, and he drops a kiss onto her blonde hair, closing his eyes with a smile.

"Are you going to New York with her?" Madi asks, glancing at Chris.

Aiden scoffs and shakes his head. "Dumb question. That guy will go anywhere with her."

Chris doesn't hesitate to confirm. He lifts our intertwined hands and wraps his arm around my shoulder, smiling down at me. "I made the mistake of leaving her once, and it was the worst decision of my life. I'm never leaving her again," he says, his eyes locked with mine. "Wherever she wants to go, I'll be there."

I love him.

I love him so much I can't even put it into words.

All I want to do is jump into his arms and kiss the hell out of him because the emotions inside me are so overwhelming.

But since we're surrounded by our friends, I won't.

"I can't believe this is the end," Rosie says, her face falling into a frown as she swallows.

"It's school. It had to end sometime, angel," Grayson says, pressing a kiss to the top of her head.

She sighs. "I know. But… I've had so much fun with you guys," she says.

We all nod, understanding exactly how Rosie feels.

Leila rolls her eyes, and opens her arms wide. "C'mon. Let's hug it out."

We gather around her, wrapping our arms around each other in a tight embrace.

"Wait for me!" James slides in beside me, and we make space, welcoming him into our group hug.

I close my eyes, feeling a wave of emotion welling up inside me. I blink back tears, trying to keep my composure.

Grayson clears his throat. "Can we join, or—"

"No," I reply, cutting him off.

He sighs, and I can't help but laugh as I pull back from the hug.

"Do you guys want to go to Murphy's?" I ask them. "One last time?"

They nod, returning to their boyfriends as we head toward the bar we loved to hang out at.

Chris squeezes my hand tighter, and I glance up at him. "We're finally here, pretty girl," he says with a smile.

"We are," I reply, thinking of all we've been through to get here. "So, what happens now?"

Chris stops, his hands cupping my face as he looks at me with his beautiful brown eyes. "I've loved you for half of my life, Gabi. And now I'm ready to love you for the rest of it."

EPILOGUE

It's the little things

Christopher

Four years later

My girlfriend is the most beautiful girl I've ever laid eyes on.

Seriously, the first time I saw her, she changed my life. I was twelve, obsessed with Spiderman and video games, and then there she was, and everything changed. I loved how carefree she was, never a worry in the world. She made me laugh, smile, and she turned my world upside down. It didn't take long before I found myself stumbling over my own feet just to be near her.

I fell in love with her long before I even understood what love meant. I was just... hers. Always hers. From the moment I met her, it was always Gabi for me, even if she never saw me the same way.

And sometimes I still pinch myself, unable to believe that the girl of my dreams is here, naked, in my bed.

I playfully poke her cheek, a smile spreading across my face when she groans.

"One more minute," she mumbles, grabbing her pillow and covering her face with it.

One more minute, my ass. Gabi would sleep all day if she could. I pull the pillow away from her face, and press my lips to her cheek. "Baby, you need to wake up."

She groans again, burying deeper into the covers, and then I feel a sharp pain in my leg.

"Ow. What the—" I narrow my eyes at Gabi. "Did you just kick me?"

"You were disturbing my sleep," she mumbles, her eyes still closed.

I chuckle, shaking my head. "You need to wake up."

She lets out a mixture between a groan and a whimper, her face contorting. "Why?"

"They'll be here soon," I remind her.

She groans louder and shakes her head. "Send them away."

I sigh, my hand smoothing up and down her back. She snuggles closer, and it might even be making her sleepier, but I can't resist.

"I don't think they'd appreciate that," I say with a chuckle.

"They'll understand," she murmurs, shifting slightly so I can continue rubbing her back. "I really need to sleep. You kept me awake all night."

I scoff out a laugh. "Me?" Unbelievable. Says the woman who rode my cock for hours to the point where we needed multiple water breaks, before she hopped back on.

She doesn't say anything, realizing she's wrong, and I let out a sigh. "Fine. Just so you know, they'll probably end up eating all the pancakes."

Her head shoots up, eyes widening. "You made pancakes?"

I smirk, knowing exactly how this will go. "Maybe."

"With chocolate chips?"

"Of course. What else?"

"And syrup?"

"Mhmm," I nod, watching as the sleep leaves her body when she sits up. My eyes follow her ass jiggling when she jumps out of bed, and I can't help but rub a hand over my mouth, pinching my skin slightly. So fucking lucky.

"Fine," she says with a sigh, pulling on my t-shirt. My body tingles as I watch it hang loosely on her. Fuck, I love seeing her in my clothes.

"I knew that would get you up," I tease with a smirk as I join her.

Gabi shakes her head. "I'm not even mad," she says, opening our bedroom door. "Because I know I'm about to devour those…" Her brow furrows as she spots the empty kitchen table. "Where are the pancakes?"

I press my lips together. "I sort of haven't made them yet."

"What?" Her eyes widen as she whirls to face me. "But you said—"

"I said maybe," I reply with a smirk. "You just assumed."

She glares at me, arms crossed. "I want a divorce."

I blink, chuckling. "We're not even married."

Yet.

Gabi shrugs. "Might as well be."

I smile. God, I love this girl.

I chuckle, pulling her close and planting a kiss on her lips. "Get dressed, baby. They'll be here soon, and I don't want them seeing you like this," I say, glancing down at her wearing only my oversized t-shirt.

"You'll make pancakes?" she asks, her eyes hopeful as she gazes up at me.

I nod. "I promise."

Her shoulders slump in relief, and she heads back into our bedroom. As she closes the door, I catch a fleeting glimpse of her stripping my t-shirt off her gorgeous body.

I groan, tempted to join her and recreate last night. But I promised her pancakes, and if I don't start making them soon, she'll get grumpy.

Grabbing a bowl and the ingredients, I begin mixing the batter just as the doorbell rings.

"What? Already?" Gabi groans. "I'm not dressed yet."

I chuckle. "Take your time, baby. I'll open the door."

Quickly washing my hands, I head to the door. Before I can even reach it, Nova bursts into the apartment, her little arms wrapping around my legs. She's so tiny, not even reaching my knees, and I laugh as I kneel down to her level.

"Uncle Chris!" Nova says, her words a bit broken and excited. "Daddy said Aunt Gabi play with me."

I glance up at Aiden, catching his smirk as he swings an arm around Leila and lets out a laugh. "What?" he says with a shrug. "Nova loves her."

I shake my head, letting out a laugh. Yeah, Nova goes crazy for Gabi.

"Aunt Gabi is getting dressed," I tell Nova, gently lowering her to the ground. "But you can go play with Milo while you wait."

"Really?" Nova asks eagerly, looking up at me with those big green eyes and flushed pink cheeks that make her look like a carbon copy of her mother.

"Really," I confirm with a smile, setting her down.

"Milo!" she squeals and runs towards our dog, wrapping her arms around him.

"God, she's getting so big," I say, watching Nova play with Milo, a smile tugging at my lips.

"Don't say that," Leila playfully scolds. "You'll make Aiden cry."

Aiden lets out a groan, his eyes fixed on his daughter as she plays with Milo, filling the room with her giggles. "I just wish she could stay little forever."

Grayson interjects with a grin, "That's wishful thinking. Kids grow up, man."

"I know," Aiden sighs. "I guess I'm looking forward to seeing the person she'll become," he admits with a smile, looking down at his wife. "I hope she turns out like you."

Leila's expression softens. "You don't want her to be like me."

Aiden shakes his head with a smile. "I want her to be exactly like you. Kind, caring, and beautiful—"

"And stubborn," Leila adds. "Don't forget the stubborn part. If she's anything like me, she'll give you attitude."

Aiden chuckles. "I can handle that. I know how to deal with strong women."

Leila's lips curve into a smile as she steals a glance at their daughter, then turns back to Aiden. "I kind of hoped she'd take after you," she admits with a subtle smile.

"Yeah?" Aiden grins, leaning in to press his lips to hers. "Maybe the next one will."

Leila freezes, her eyes widening. "The next one?"

Aiden smiles, brushing his thumb against her cheek. "You're an amazing mom."

"I know."

"And Nova adores you."

"I know that too," Leila replies with an arched brow.

367

I suppress a smile, quietly observing them.

"Don't you want another baby?" Aiden asks.

Leila lets out a sigh. "A boy this time."

Aiden's brows furrow. "Nova needs a friend."

"She can't be friends with her brother?"

Aiden's eyes light up at the word, a grin spreading across his face. "Is that a yes?"

Grayson clears his throat. "Are you two planning a baby right here?"

"Are you going to conceive it here too?" Madi adds with a laugh.

A groan, one I've grown accustomed to, echoes from the other side of the room, and I turn to see Gabi walking out of our bedroom. Her hair is less messy now, a touch of makeup on her beautiful face, and she's wearing a short white lace top, and a short denim skirt that makes me swallow a groan. She's so fucking beautiful.

"Please don't," she says, arching a brow at them.

"Aunt Gabi!" Nova leaves Milo's side and sprints toward Gabi, arms wide before she wraps them around her legs.

"Ew. A child."

"Gabi," Leila chides, narrowing her eyes at her.

Gabi chuckles. "I'm kidding. Calm down." She shakes her head, a faint smile playing on her lips as she gazes down at Nova. "Come here." Gabi bends down and scoops Nova up. "My god, you've grown so much. Last time I saw you, you were this big," she says, pinching her fingers together.

"This big?" Nova mimics Gabi, pinching her fingers too.

"Mhmm," Gabi confirms, gently booping Nova on the nose. "So tiny."

"Nice to finally see you," Madi says. "Late as always."

"I'm not late," Gabi replies with a frown. "You guys are just early. Seriously, did you have to come so early?" She groans dramatically.

Madi narrows her eyes. "It's one in the afternoon."

"Exactly," Gabi retorts, shaking her head. "So early."

Grayson scoffs, shaking his head. "You really haven't changed a bit."

It's been a while since we were all together. Leila and Aiden live in Chicago, Madeline and Lucas in LA, and Rosie and Grayson travel all over the place. But we've always made it a tradition to spend all the big holidays together. Easter, Christmas, birthdays, and even the Fourth of July, which is why we're all here.

"Neither have you," Gabi says with a teasing smile. "Still ugly I see."

Grayson sighs, turning to his girlfriend. "Angel, remind me why we're here," he says.

Rosie lets out a laugh, clutching Grayson's face in her hands. "Because we always spend the holidays together, and this year it's Gabi's turn to host," she tells him. "And we love Gabi."

"We do?" Grayson asks, arching a brow.

"I do," Nova chimes in, smiling up at Gabi. "I love Aunt Gabi."

Gabi's lips widen into a grin as she leans down, pinching Nova's chubby cheeks. "I know. Everyone does." Nova giggles, and Gabi starts walking over to join us. "How old is she now?" Gabi asks, settling onto my lap. I lean back, making space for both Gabi and little Nova.

"She's almost three," Leila replies with a sigh. "I can't believe how fast the time has gone."

"I know." Gabi scoffs, brushing Nova's hair back. "I still remember when you were screaming during her birth. Everyone in the hospital could hear you."

"She was so amazing," Aiden says, shaking his head as he looks at his wife. "I was in awe."

"And I was dying," Leila replies, narrowing her eyes at him. "Maybe we can trade places next time."

Aiden laughs, wrapping his arms around her. "I love hearing you say *next time*."

Leila sighs, smiling up at him. We all know she loves Nova deeply, and it was only a matter of time before they had another baby.

I glance at Gabi, seeing her smile and play with Nova. My mind starts to wander, imagining what it would be like to have a child with her. I envision a baby with Gabi's blue eyes and my curly hair, seeing our features intertwined in a little baby.

Fuck.

I need to calm down.

There's something else I need to do first before I can start thinking about that.

"Can I have my baby back?" Aiden asks, raising an eyebrow at Gabi.

Gabi shakes her head, hugging Nova close. "I've grown attached."

Aiden chuckles. "I don't know if that concerns me or not." He turns to me with a teasing grin. "Chris, you ready for a baby yet?"

I shrug, unable to suppress a smile. "Maybe."

Gabi glances at me, her eyes widening slightly. "You are?"

I shrug again. "If you want."

She seems taken aback, blinking and licking her lips nervously. "Really?"

I laugh at her reaction and nod. "Look at her," I say, glancing at Nova with her wavy brown hair and big green eyes. "She's adorable."

"Thanks," Aiden says with a grin as he wraps an arm around Leila, looking down at her affectionately. "It's all her momma," he says, planting a kiss on Leila's cheek. "And a little bit of me."

Leila rolls her eyes playfully. "She's literally your twin."

"Are you kidding?" Aiden scoffs, shaking his head. "Those gorgeous green eyes and those pink chubby cheeks? She's drop-dead gorgeous. That's all you, baby."

Leila parts her lips, her eyes glistening as she looks at her husband, and Aiden leans down to kiss her, his hands cupping her face until she gasps into his mouth.

I chuckle, knowing exactly how he feels. There are times when I can't stand looking at Gabi without wanting to hold her, kiss her, touch her. Anything, just to feel her close against me.

"Alright," Grayson interjects with a sigh. "There's a kid in the room."

Aiden and Leila break apart, still smiling at each other. Aiden laughs, glancing over at Grayson and nodding toward Rosie. "What about you guys?" he asks. "You want kids?"

Rosie glances at Grayson and shifts on the couch beside him. "Maybe one day," she says. "We haven't really talked about it."

"Really?" Aiden raises an eyebrow.

Grayson shrugs. "She's one of the most sought-after fashion designers right now," he says. "You really think we have time to think about a baby with everything else going on?" He shakes his head but then glances at Rosie. "Besides, I'm happy with it being just us for a little while longer."

Rosie smiles up at him, and he leans in, pressing his lips to hers.

"I don't know," Gabi muses, her gaze fixed on Nova. "They seem pretty easy to me."

Leila and Aiden burst into laughter. "Oh god," Leila says, shaking her head. "I can't wait to make you eat your words once you have a baby."

I glance over at Madi, noticing the subtle smile on her face as she watches Nova. Madeline and Lucas have been married for a little over a year now, and seeing how she's looking at Aiden and Leila's baby, it's clear she might be considering having a child of her own.

"What about you guys?" I ask Lucas and Madeline. They turn their attention to me, their eyes widening a bit. "Are you planning on having kids anytime soon?"

Madeline gulps nervously and glances at Lucas. "Um… I don't know. We want them, but—"

"We're trying," Lucas says, wrapping his arm around Madeline's shoulders and pulling her close to him. Madi visibly relaxes, tilting her head to look up at her husband.

"We're not in a rush," Lucas adds, smiling down at Madi.

"Ew." Gabi lifts her hands and covers her ears. "I don't want to hear about you guys raw dogging."

"Gabi," Leila chastises. "Can you please not say that in front of my daughter?"

Gabi glances at Nova who's completely blissfully unaware, playing with Gabi's hair. "She doesn't know what it means," Gabi says as she glances at Nova with a smile.

I watch the woman I love so enamored with the baby on her lap, and I smile, imagining our future.

Can't wait to spend the rest of my life with her.

And I can't wait for tonight.

"Did you bring it?"

Grayson slides beside me, nudging me on the arm, and I quickly glance at Gabi and the girls walking together in front of me. Aiden's holding baby Nova on his shoulders, and Lucas walks behind the girls.

"Yeah," I tell him, reaching for my jacket pocket where I feel the box.

"Are you ready?"

I nod, then blow out a breath. "Nervous."

"I can imagine," he says, breathing out a laugh. "But there's no reason to be. You guys were made for each other."

I love hearing other people say that. I've always known she was the one for me, but hearing other people see the way she's my soulmate makes it that much better.

"She's my best friend," I tell him, keeping my eyes on the back of her head as she laughs with her friends.

"Yeah."

"She's everything to me," I say, feeling my heart ache for her. "I can't wait to make her my wife."

We walk in silence for a few seconds, the only sound the gravel crunching under our feet, and then he blows out a breath. "I know exactly how you feel."

I turn to look at him, seeing his face twisted as he looks at Rosie ahead of him. "Then why aren't you guys married by now?" I ask him. "You know Rosie is head over heels in love with you."

"I know," he admits with a sigh, running his hand through his hair. "I love that girl more than anything in the world, man. But I don't want to mess up her dreams. She's wanted this—her own designer firm—for so long, and she's finally got it. She works so hard, and I'm so proud of her, and I don't want all of that to be pushed aside because of a wedding or a baby," he says. "I can wait a little longer if that means she'll be all in when the time comes."

My eyebrows lift, knowing he's right. A wedding, and babies on top of a full time career is a lot, especially since they travel a lot. But I have no doubts Rosie would willingly put all her attention toward Grayson and their baby, if they decide to have one.

I feel a hand cup my shoulder, and turn to see James, grinning as he swings his arms around me and Grayson. "So, what are we talking about?"

Grayson arches a brow at him. "Where the hell have you been all day?"

James' eyes spark with mischief. "I thought you didn't want to hear my sex stories anymore."

Grayson groans. "Enough said."

"Are you sure?" James asks. "I could tell you what position—"

"I'm good."

I press my lips in amusement, and James shrugs. "Hey, you asked."

"And I regret it," he replies with a sigh. "Where is Carter, anyway?"

James grins. "You mean my husband?"

"Yeah," Grayson says with a laugh. James hasn't stopped saying the word 'husband' since he and Carter got married a few months ago. Their wedding was great. Small, and intimate, and a hell of a lot of drunk dancing.

"He went to buy me a hot dog," James says, letting out a content sigh. "Best husband in the world."

Grayson furrows his brows, looking back at James. "It's just a hot dog."

James shrugs in response. "It's the fact that he didn't even make me ask. He just knew what I wanted, and did it." His lips curve into a smirk. "It's the little things, Grayson. Keep up." He taps us on our shoulders, and runs back toward the hot dog stand where his husband is.

I glance back at Grayson with a smirk. "It's the little things," I repeat, which he scoffs out a laugh at. "I'm serious, though. If you really want to marry Rosie, then do it," I tell him. "She loves you, man. She's all the way in right now."

Grayson turns his head, locking eyes with the girls, or more specifically one girl, as they're pointing up at the night sky. "Yeah," he says. "Maybe."

I tap his shoulder. "I need to go get something."

His brows dip. "What?"

"I'm getting Gabi some cotton candy," I tell him, gesturing to the cotton candy stand as I shoot him a wink. "It's the little things."

He lets out a laugh, and flips me off as he heads toward the girl, wrapping his arms around Rosie the moment he gets to her. She turns her head and they kiss.

I shake my head. I don't know how that guy can't see how much she loves him.

Reaching into my jacket, I feel the box sitting in there, and my heart starts to race as I grab my wallet, and buy Gabi's favorite. Blue cotton candy.

I head toward her, and press my lips to her cheek, holding out the cotton candy for her to grab. "Hey, pretty girl."

Her eyes widen at the stick in my hand. "I love you."

I let out a laugh. "Are you talking to me, or the food?"

She takes a big bite out of the cotton candy and blinks up at me. "Both?"

I scoff out a laugh, wrapping my arms around her. I can't wait to make her my fiancée.

The sky roars as the fireworks start to go off, and our heads snap to the sky watching as they burst and fill the dark sky with color.

Gabi leans her head against me, and my heart soars. "I can't believe eight years ago, we were pretty much in the same position, but worlds apart," she says, turning her head to face me.

My jaw tightens when I think back to prom night. How so much happened that night.

"Not for me," I tell her, clutching her pretty face in my hand.

"No?" she asks, tilting her head.

I shake my head. "Loved you then," I admit. "Love you now."

Her lips part, and I swallow.

This is it.

"Actually, I lied."

Her brows furrow, and she presses her lips together. "You did?"

I nod, swallowing the rock lodged in my throat. Fuck. This is harder than I thought. "I loved you then. I really fucking did. But I can't say my love for you is the same as it was eight, hell even ten years ago." I breathe out a sigh, lifting her chin with my thumb. "Every year, my love for you grows, Gabi. It grows so fast I can't even keep up." Her lips part in surprise, and I force myself to continue. "You make my head dizzy," I admit. "You're my best friend, my girlfriend, and my favorite person in the world all at once."

"Chris," she murmurs, her voice hoarse.

The fireworks are still bursting around us, but I keep my eyes on her.

"I love you more than I can even explain. I love you more than there are grains of sand under our toes." My eyes start to burn. "I loved you when you were just my best friend, and I love you right now as my girlfriend." I swallow, locking eyes with her bright, blue ones. "And I want to love you even more as my wife."

Her eyes widen, and her jaw drops. "What?"

I smooth my thumb over her cheek, before I drop down to one knee, and she covers her mouth, tears building in her eyes.

"Yes!"

I furrow my brows. "I haven't even asked you, yet."

"I don't care," she says, shaking her head. "It's yes."

I tilt my head in amusement. "Will you at least let me ask?"

She nods, tears falling down her face, and I reach for my jacket, and pull out the box, opening it to reveal the ring. "Gabriella Miller. Will you marry me?"

"Yes!" she yells, falling onto her knees to kiss me. I hum a laugh as she continues to press her lips against mine. "Yes. Yes. Yes."

I let out a laugh, pulling back. "Do you want to see the ring?" I ask, knowing she didn't even glance before dropping to her knees.

She wipes her eyes, and glances down at the box, taking in the silver ring, engraved with little stars on it. Her eyes widen. "Chris."

I clutch her face in my hands, and press my lips to hers. "The stars say we're meant to be, right?"

She bursts out crying again, and wraps her arms around me.

"Don't cry, baby."

"I can't help it," she says, her voice shaky as she tightens her arms around me. "I'm marrying you," she says, pulling back to look at me. "You're marrying me."

"Yeah," I affirm, smiling like an idiot.

She shakes her head, a smile on her face, and tears running down her cheeks. "I love you, Chris."

"I love you too, pretty girl."

And I can't wait to love her for the rest of my life.

THE END

Acknowledgements

Wow. I can't believe we've made it to the end of the Campus Games series! It feels surreal to reach this milestone. This series is like a piece of my heart and soul, with every character reflecting a part of me. Writing this final book was especially personal and helped heal a part of me, and I hope Gabi's story resonates with you as much as it did with me.

A massive shoutout to my incredible Patreon members— thank you for being my personal cheerleaders and keeping my spirits high. You all are the best hype team anyone could ask for!

To my amazing beta readers. You took my chaotic manuscript and turned it into something resembling a book. Your feedback and support were invaluable. And a big thank you to the editor who helped polish this book into being the best it can be.

A special thanks to my cousin, Tatiana, who not only cheered me on during the early, messy drafts but endured my endless rants about these fictional characters. I owe you a lifetime of chocolate.

And last but not least, a heartfelt thank you to you, the reader. You picked up my book, gave it a chance. Thank you for your support, likes, shares, comments. You are the reason I get to continue doing what I love, and I hope this story brings a smile to your face.

Thanks for sticking with the Campus Games Series, and I can't wait to share more stories with you guys.

About the Author

Stephanie Alves is an avid reader and writer of smutty, contemporary romance books. She was born in England, but was raised by her loud Portuguese parents. She can speak both languages fluently, though she tends to mix both languages when speaking. She loves to write romantic comedies with happy endings, witty banter and sizzling chemistry that will make you blush. When she's not writing, she can be found either reading, or watching rom coms with her two adorable dogs cuddled up beside her.

You can find her here:
Instagram.com/Stephanie.alves_author
Stephaniealvesauthor.com

Printed in Great Britain
by Amazon

46042686R10219